WHAT I Should HAVE SAID

What I Should Have Said

A Small Town Military Romance

R.L. Atkinson

Copyright © 2024 by Rianna Atkinson

All rights reserved.

No part of this publication may be reproduced, distributed, or transmitted in any form or by any means, including photocopying, recording, or other electronic or mechanical methods, without the prior written permission of the publisher, except as permitted by U.S. copyright law. For permission requests, contact [include publisher/author contact info].

The story, all names, characters, and incidents portrayed in this production are fictitious. No identification with actual persons (living or deceased), places, buildings, and products is intended or should be inferred.

ISBN: 9798875742613

Book Cover by: Miles of Oats Studio Design

Editing by: MH Editorial

To all the girls who want romance with spice that will make your emotions race, but also keep your mama happy

Contents

Content Warning	XIII
1. Chapter 1	1
2. Chapter 2	9
3. Chapter 3	17
4. Chapter 4	27
5. Chapter 5	38
6. Chapter 6	50
7. Chapter 7	62
8. Chapter 8	72
9. Chapter 9	81
10. Chapter 10	91
11. Chapter 11	105
12. Chapter 12	111

13. Chapter 13 125
14. Chapter 14 131
15. Chapter 15 139
16. Chapter 16 146
17. Chapter 17 156
18. Chapter 18 168
19. Chapter 19 175
20. Chapter 20 184
21. Chapter 21 194
22. Chapter 22 201
23. Chapter 23 209
24. Chapter 24 223
25. Chapter 25 231
26. Chapter 26 241
27. Chapter 27 251
28. Chapter 28 264
29. Chapter 29 271
30. Chapter 30 278
31. Chapter 31 285
32. Chapter 32 292
33. Chapter 33 305
34. Chapter 34 313

35.	Chapter 35	323
36.	Chapter 36	333
37.	Chapter 37	344
38.	Chapter 38	353
39.	Chapter 39	361
40.	Chapter 40	369
41.	Chapter 41	377
42.	Chapter 42	390
43.	Chapter 43	402
44.	Chapter 44	416
45.	Chapter 45	424
46.	Chapter 46	430
47.	Chapter 47	437
48.	Chapter 48	448
49.	Chapter 49	455
50.	Chapter 50	463
51.	Chapter 51	473
52.	Chapter 52	483
53.	Chapter 53	492
54.	Chapter 54	503
55.	Epilogue	514
	Acknowledgements	523

About the Author

Content Warning

My romance novels span a spectrum, featuring clean language with only kissing to mature language with non-explicit sex scenes—diet spice. Regardless of spice level, all of them are written to evoke tension and a desire to swoon for the characters and their relationships.

Please see my TikTok video about spice levels for more information.

This novel has mature language, mature sexual themes, consensual and descriptive touching along with descriptive foreplay, and emotionally driven non-descriptive sex scenes. This is a rather spicy, <u>diet</u> spice novel.

Trigger Warnings: conversations about past abuse, stalking, heavy violence, descriptive gore, death, kidnapping, on-screen torture

Chapter 1

A small bell jingled as I pushed open the heavy oak door to the quaint antique shop. Stepping inside, my nose was assaulted by the musty smell of wood and history, suspended like the dust motes that swirled around me in the dim lighting. French-polished vintage furniture and thrifted goods littered the inside. Like a hound dog with its nose to a scent, an alert shiver of anticipation ran down my spine. This was my favorite kind of place, holding memories long forgotten by each item's previous owners.

Drifting between scattered stacks of goods, among ornate purples, deep browns, faded pinks, and scratched grays, a grandfather clock ticked in the background—a dusty sentinel abandoned in a corner. I rounded another collection of haphazardly stacked furniture and almost collided with the smiling storekeeper.

"Hello, Miss," he said, his voice squeaking. He adjusted owlish spectacles that perched on the tip of his birdlike nose. "Anything I can help you with today?"

I smiled kindly. "Just browsing, but thank you." He nodded sagely and blinked unusually rapid.

"Do let me know if you need anything," he replied and ran his wiry fingers over his thinning hair. He tugged at the hem of his plaid button-up shirt and scurried off toward the back of the shop, disappearing behind the counter display that sparkled with beautiful jewelry. With eagerness nipping at my heels, I turned my attention to the row of books before me.

The comforting smell of aged paper that had been thumbed through for centuries laced the air and soothed my soul. Everything was so peaceful. As I browsed, a little of the heaviness left my heart. Maybe moving here wasn't as foreboding as I had once thought it to be.

I ran my hand across the spines of the hardcover books as I heard the jingle of the doorbell once again. Ducking behind another row of dark cabinets, I melted into a world that had always held tranquility for me.

There wasn't anything in particular I was looking for, but I would know it when I saw it. Last time I visited an antique shop like this one, I'd found the most beautiful set of lamps that now adorned each side of my bed. Maybe I'd find a new pair of nightstands to match.

Muffled voices reached my ears as I continued to wander around, tucking a wavy strand of ash-brown hair behind my ear. Sliding the claw clip from my coarse tresses, I adjusted the bun and slowly wrapped it back behind my head.

WHAT I SHOULD HAVE SAID

Breaking the stillness of the moment, a strange ruckus sounded outside. Screams suddenly shot through the air, and every nerve of mine stood on end. Adrenaline seeped through my veins, pricking needles beneath my skin as I inched carefully around the haphazard display of furnishings toward the front door.

Something was not right, and I needed to get out of here.

The screams ebbed nearer to the little shop I was in, increasing my desperation to leave. Shouting male voices filled the gaps between the screams, and several pairs of heavy boots pounded past along the sidewalk. I stopped behind a mahogany bookcase, my nose pressed to musty book spines straining to hear as everything fell still.

The silence was deafening. Not a shout rose from the world outside, not another wail filled with terror echoed through the sky. Whatever it had been, it seemed to have passed, but curiosity clung to my fingertips, urging me forward. Creeping along the aisle, staying close to the bookshelves, every intake of oxygen grated like sandpaper, and somehow, I just knew that this pause was only temporary.

A pair of shadows almost as wide and tall as the doorframe rippled past the entrance at the same instant I found myself back at the front of the store. They brutally shoved themselves inside, nearly ripping the bell right off of the hook.

My breath hitched, and I turned rigid.

Two large, unshaven men with sweat dripping down their faces, darkening the collars of their black T-shirts, immediately saw me. Staring at my frozen statue, their beady eyes darkened to a glare and scanned my figure. Fear tore through me, numbing my senses to everything else.

There was no escape.

"Don't look so scared," one hissed, sickly sweet, as his partner snapped the lock on the door behind them.

There was no hope.

Then he pointed his gun at my forehead. Shock ripped through my veins as my eyes narrowed in on the hollow tunnel that held death just a finger twitch away.

"Time to move, bitch!" He waved the barrel toward the back of the shop.

My heart spasmed and nausea cramped my stomach.

I stumbled back a couple of steps, dropping the claw clip that never made it back into my hair.

"MOVE!" he snarled, stomping toward me and bracing the muzzle against my temple. Nodding, I ducked my head and let the pressure from the gun guide me.

Police sirens wailed outside the antique shop, as I shuffled forward, head down. Every tiny breath filling my chest was painful, soaked with panic. *After everything, this was how I was going to die!* I barely registered a thin, kittenish mewl that escaped my lips.

The two men followed closely at my heels. Rounding a few shelves, they herded me away from the windows and door as I caught one last glimpse at what they must have already known—police vehicles and officers crowding the streets.

"Move your ass faster!" the man shouted once more, clicking the safety off. Ice cleaved through my veins, a thousand tiny needles pricked my skin as we crashed together toward the far side of the store. And then a hand jerked around my hair, knocking my glasses askew. Sweat dripped from every pore as my body trembled, fear turning every rational response in my head upside down.

"Shit! Shit! Shit!" the assailant behind me screeched.

And he kicked the back of my knees, shoving me to the floor. I collapsed and slammed hard against the scuffed timber. The wood bit into the skin of my legs through my jeans upon contact.

"Ow," I involuntarily cried out. And the side of my head rammed into the glass jewelry case.

"SHUT UP, BITCH!" he shouted.

Blinking through the dizzying haze, I hesitantly adjusted my glasses and lifted my eyes to the man closest to me.

"What are we going to do?" he whined to his companion. He rocked in place, panicking.

The larger man moved so they were face-to-face and said, quietly but menacingly, "Don't you bug out on me. You promised me you weren't going to be a problem. Get your shit together, NOW!" He shook his head, clearly annoyed with his partner, and bumped the large, black duffel he was carrying against his leg. A few stacks of money plopped out of the unzipped top, drawing my attention as it scattered on the floor, and then it clicked.

It wasn't *me* they wanted. The bank was directly across the street.

The scuffed toes of a pair of military-style boots were suddenly hidden by denim-clad knees appearing at my eye level. Cold metal rammed against my forehead, jerking my attention away from the duffel. "Is there another way out?" the smaller robber barked, rubbing the muzzle into my skull, his eyes crazed like a cornered fox.

"I-I-I don't know," I stuttered, ignoring the dull thumping of a headache with my heart rate that pumped in the red zone.

I was trapped. They were trapped, and the only leverage they had was me.

"Get her phone," the other man, who was more solidly built than the one pointing the gun at me, finally said.

The barrel of the gun dug harder into my temple and I whimpered.

"Give it to me," he hissed. I dug through my purse, whipped it out, and tossed it his way. None of this was worth my life, even if I already doubted I was getting out of this alive anyway.

I inhaled a shaky breath as the metal left my skin and the man next to me stood up. He threw my cell at what I assumed was the ringleader of this duo and shook his head in agitation. "And you know what else I want to know? How did the police get here so quickly? I staked this place out—"

"Shut up! I'm tryin' to think," his boss growled and plonked the duffel down. "Go pick up the stacks of money that fell out," he commanded, the black holes that passed for his eyes locking onto mine.

The one beside me rocked his head sideways, his neck cracking like a dry branch, and I took the opportunity of the momentary distraction to scramble into the corner, desperately trying to put space between them and me. The two men swapped places. My first captor crouched down beside the duffel as his boss squatted down in front of me.

Dark, merciless eyes stabbed into my soul, and then his hand shot up and clamped around my throat. Jerking me forward, he asked in a low growl, "Is there...another way...out?"

I shook my head, partly because I didn't know, but mostly in desperation to break free from his hold. Digging his fingers in, he tightened the pressure around my windpipe, and I winced, seeing popping stars. Wheezing, through the straw-like opening that was left, my chest ached for air. Alcohol and pungent sweat raked my nostrils with every strained pull for oxygen.

A sinister chuckle left his chest. "Well, I hope—"

A thud behind him cut him off.

"What the fuck?" His hand left my throat as he spun around.

And a hulking figure barreled out of the shadows, crashing into my captor.

I collapsed onto the floor, rasping as crisp, clear air filled my lungs. I painfully gulped in the oxygen my cells needed, finally feeling some sort of orientation as the stars cleared from my vision. As my senses returned, shattering glass and clanging books snapped my attention to the robber struggling in vain against a stranger. The two huge men railing on each other in the gloom was like a scene from a dystopian movie.

Backpedaling, I tried to distance myself from the nasty fists raining hell onto the robber's face, it was fast becoming clear who had the upper hand.

I pushed myself off the floor and then held back a shriek at the sight of the other bank robber lying crumpled and motionless behind me, unconscious. His body had been strewn beside the duffel, and his arms were limply splayed beside him. Laying neatly on top of the unzipped bag full of money, was the black handgun that had been pressed against my head.

Was he...?

I urged myself to not think about that.

My heart pounded, my eyes darting around the antique shop, sifting through the shadows as hope filled my figure. I should run. This was my escape. Someone was here to rescue me, and I was free.

But no matter how much I urged my body to do something, it wouldn't move. Screaming at myself did nothing. Mentally pounding at the barriers within my mind did nothing. I remained physically immobilized, locked as effectively as if jailed within its hold. Despite all of the self-defense training from my father, I couldn't muster up any sort of action. He would have been very disappointed in me.

And then, with the sound of snapping bones, everything became stock-still.

Nothing but heavy breathing sounded in front of me, a direction I dared not look for fear of what I might see—what I might find, because no matter how much I denied it, I knew what the lack of any movement probably meant. What that *sound* had most likely meant.

Run, Jane. Run! I urged myself. But my body remained rigid as the scent of bloody death mixed with the musty, dank air around me and a shroud of black panic began to steal coherent thought. This was it, this was the last moment that I drew my last breath on this earth.

Out of the gloom, a man appeared and stalked slowly toward me like an apparition. A looming, silent hulk who moved with such stealth I was certain that fear itself would be terrified.

My heart skipped a beat, and time resumed, snapping me out of whatever terror stupor I'd been locked into. My feet thundered across the floorboards and around several packed mantels. Freedom awaited me, beyond that front door.

Ahead, just around this last pile of goods, toward the sirens wailing in the streets, was my escape and safety.

Chapter 2

I finished giving my statement and sat on a stone bench watching as the coroner's vehicle drove away, carrying the bodies of the two dead criminals. Two men who had been subdued by a lone man. A man that I'd seen only briefly but owed my life to. A police car hauling the duffels full of money taken into evidence followed soon after. A few feet away, my rescuer was calmly recounting how the events unfolded to a few straggling officers—although they said we would still need to come by the police station to make everything official.

My gaze drifted back to the strange man who, from the little I'd seen of him, seemed far too composed during the entire ordeal. I, on the other hand, still gripped my purse against my chest tightly, my palms sticky and wet. It had been a couple hours and still my heart hammered in my chest.

My mind raced. I was feeling equally embarrassed and grateful, yet my mind swarmed with thoughts of disbelief that I'd been involved in such a situation, where someone had stepped in to save me. I was also annoyed that someone else *had* to rescue me, knowing full well that I had the capability to defend myself, and yet I'd frozen like a rabbit in front of a diamondback.

I tried to smooth out my simple cropped sweater, only managing to make the baby-blue wrinkles worse, as an imposing shadow fell across me. I glanced up, shading my eyes from the sun. As though I had conjured him, there he stood, his head tilted, watching me with...sympathy?

I blinked in surprise, shocked by how soft his eyes looked. I had expected condescension but instead saw compassion in his fiercely direct gaze. A small smile danced lightly across a full mouth that complemented hazel, almond-shaped eyes. Shadows defined his precisely-carved, primal bone structure, the dusting of a dark beard barely disguising the hard angle of his jaw. My eyes drifted to his broad shoulders and the expanse of a well-muscled chest beneath his shirt, my heart pattering like a fairy sprinkling dust before I realized I was ogling, and I hurriedly looked back up, feeling a guilty blush spread swiftly across my cheeks. I'd never seen anyone up close who was so confident and majestic. So bone-tinglingly alpha.

"Here," he said, handing me my phone and the claw clip I dropped earlier. His deep voice was gruff, sounding unfazed by the situation that we had just experienced, or my obvious ogling.

"Thank you," I whispered in embarrassment, my fingers grazing his palm. Startled by the electric shivers that zapped me upon contact, I quickly retracted my hand and shoved the phone into my purse. Unable to look directly at him, I wound my hair back into the clip, adding, "For all of it. I should've done something, but I just couldn't seem to move." My voice sounded octaves higher than normal, showing my nerves at being around such an imposing presence. I dropped my gaze to the sidewalk, feeling as useless as the dead leaves that fluttered around my white sneakers.

His soft chuckle made me turn as he sat down beside me, hitching his pant legs to accommodate his thighs. I had to force myself to focus on his face as he said calmly, "Totally understandable. You're a civilian after all. Two armed men held you with a gun to your head, so why would you expect yourself to not be afraid?" He lifted one large hand, fingers lacking any rings, and brushed at some debris from the sleeve of his gray jacket. My eyes traced the fine crimson specks that had dried. It would need dry cleaning to get the blood out.

I turned to face him, annoyed by his reasonable tone. "You didn't seem afraid. Besides, I've practiced basic self-defense for most of my short, twenty-seven years on this Earth."

His thick brows lifted in amusement and understanding. "Real life situations are entirely different. Most people don't walk around prepared for situations like this, and you can practice all you want but until you experience it..." His voice drifted off.

The defensive annoyance curdling within my stomach dissipated, and my shoulders sagged. *If only he knew.*

"And you've experienced it?" I quietly whispered. Though, for whatever reason, I knew the answer without needing a reply. Lost in contemplation, his hazel eyes drifted from me, and he stared forward at the shop window in front of us. Not moving and barely blinking even when the door was flung open.

"Here!" the shopkeeper shouted, grinning wildly as he rushed out. "I was packaging it in the back when everything went down. The police finally let me get it for you." His eyes focused on me. "My wife ought to be grateful that, for once, I didn't turn up my danged hearing aid. I'm so happy you're alright my dear."

Clasped in his extended hand was what looked like a necklace case. He clicked it open, displaying a simple chain hung with two jewels entwined within an elegant, handcrafted infinity design. Small, gold, and classy.

"That's stunning," I said in awe, while comprehending that it was not through a miracle that the man beside me had come into the store.

"She's right," the shopkeeper said, closing the box and handing it over to the stranger who'd rescued me.

"Not too cheesy for a birthday present?" he asked with an uncertain frown.

"Not at all. Your wife is one lucky lady," I cheerily replied, and he smiled broadly, carving deep dimples in his cheeks and making the corners of his eyes crinkle. I still felt like a rabbit, but this time I was caught by the spotlights of his eyes.

"Actually, it's for my mom." He shut the velvet case, the snap breaking my trance.

"Oh. Well, then your mom is one lucky woman."

He lifted a thick, dark brow questioningly as he glanced toward me. The waves in his short hair reflected the gold of the setting sun, and I tipped my head, intrigued and unashamedly relieved to hear that he wasn't married.

My gaze slipped again to his hands that lay clasped against thighs that were severely testing the stretch of his pants.

There was something about him...

A sharp ringing pierced the air.

Wait. No. What was I thinking? Snapped from my inappropriate thoughts about a complete stranger, I stuffed my hand into my purse and dug through the mess, ripping my phone out and glancing at the caller.

"Look, I really should get going to finish giving my statement or whatever." I quickly stood and started to walk away, pressing the phone to my ear.

"Hey!" my rescuer shouted after me. "HEY!"

"Thank you again!" I called out over my shoulder. "Hi Mom!"

"WHY DIDN'T YOU CALL ME THE MOMENT YOU WERE SAFE?" my mother cried out, and I closed my eyes, gathering some patience. She'd heard.

I rushed through the front door of our small white home. My mom restlessly paced in the living room, while my brother lounged unperturbed upon the gray couch. As I bit my bottom lip, she finally stopped, her arms crossed over her chest.

"Jane Eileen Barlow," she stated coldly; her gray eyes, that were the same as mine, bored directly into my soul.

"Mom, I'm fine. I promise. The police needed my statement, and it took—"

"I DON'T CARE! My daughter was held hostage by some bank robbers, and I found out through a news channel. Not you." She tapped her toe against the soft blue rug stretching beneath the coffee table.

"The police had my phone because—"

"Because?! It doesn't matter!" she snapped, her face taut with anger.

"Mom," my brother finally said, pushing himself off the sofa. Reaching around from behind her, he wrapped an arm around her shoulders, offering her a smidge of comfort. Though not overly tall, he swamped her petite frame that I'd inherited. My brother resembled my dad, although he'd gotten my mom's wispy, light brown hair, and I'd gotten my dad's dark, wavy mane.

"Noah, you better sit your butt back down on that couch—"

"Mom. She's fine." He cut her off and gestured toward me. "See? Here in one piece. You know, since Dad was an FBI agent, and he spent so much time training us, you shouldn't worry so much."

"It's *because* of your father that I do worry that much," she whispered defeatedly, her shoulders sagging. She released a sigh and plopped down on one of the gray recliners, her eyes fluttering closed. The low light did nothing to disguise the deepening lines around her mouth and cheeks. "I know that you two can handle yourselves if you need, but we've been here for a week. That's all, and somehow danger has already found you."

I padded softly toward the other recliner as Noah sat on the edge of the coffee table. "We already lost him. I can't lose either of you two." Gently, I rested my hand on top of my mom's and entwined my fingers with hers. "Your father was a great agent and was still killed. I know that the agency tells us we are safe, and that his death does not mean there is a threat to our family, but I still worry. Which is why I moved us. So, how safe are we really?"

Sharing a meaningful glance with my twenty-year-old brother, I sighed. "Mom, we're resuming our regular lives, just in a different place. I get the opportunity to start fresh, teach a new grade and different subject, and Noah is headed back to college."

She took a resolute breath.

"Things are all good. We are *all* okay," I quickly added with a smile, while replaying the memory—and shame—of a muzzle jammed hard between my eyes.

Noah grinned, his thin lips pulling wide, his usual cheerful demeanor, full of humor, returning to his blue eyes. "Besides, transferring to a new college made changing my major easier than I expected. You know I was wanting to do that anyway."

My mom sighed and closed her eyes. Her long lashes lay still for a moment before she opened them again. Patting my hand, she leaned back against the chair and stared morosely at the blank television.

"You're right," she muttered after a long minute, and I raised my brows at Noah. He nodded, acknowledging that we'd only managed to halfway convince our mom. "You should get some dinner before turning in," she said tiredly. "It is your first day teaching tomorrow, and I can only imagine how nervous you are jumping into it in November."

She was right. I'd been so preoccupied with what had happened at the store, I'd totally forgotten why I'd gone shopping in the first place. Nervous was an understatement. I was an emotional wreck. High school was very different from elementary school, let alone starting fresh this far into the school year. That antique shop visit was supposed to have soothed my anxiety.

It had definitely helped me forget, that's for sure. But now, with mom's words, all those nerves came bubbling back up. Hoisting myself out of the depths of the gray leather chair, I walked around my mom and headed toward the kitchen behind her.

The beautiful, marble countertop sparkled, and the pungent smell of ammonia hung in the air. Dishes dripped on the drying rack beside the sink on the island. Sliding the plate of food my mom had left for me out of the fridge, I fed it into the microwave and leaned against the island counter. Tilting my head back, I waited for the food to finish heating.

The gray and white interior of this home was too new and unfamiliar despite the family pictures that already hung throughout the house. The microwave beeped, and I pulled my plate out, turning around to see my father's picture staring back at me from its mounted place on the wall beside the dining room nook. He had been so proud to serve his country, and that was evident by the look on his face in that picture. I still remembered each promotion he'd received. Each time he was recognized and honored by a case he'd solved.

I also remembered long nights of him sitting at that very table we brought from our old home. He'd poured over whatever case he was working on, barely aware of anything that was going on around him. But he'd never forgotten to take the time to hear about what new, stupid drama I was experiencing. Or what boy had just broken my heart.

A tear slid down my cheek. I miss him. So much.

Chapter 3

I stood in front of the full-body mirror in my bedroom, running a hand over my dress. It was black and flared at the waist, reaching to my shins, and paired with a white turtleneck beneath the thick tank straps. I tugged on a pair of white booties and pushed my oversized glasses onto my face. Looking over myself critically, I sighed.

This was as good as it was going to get today. I'd spent the time styling my hair in gentle waves but chose to lessen the amount of makeup I typically wore. With my hair styled properly, I was confident I looked capable and professional.

I thought all of that would've helped me find myself this morning.

Another drawn-out sigh escaped my lips.

"Here I go, Daddy," I whispered sadly to the picture tucked into the frame of the antique mirror. The vintage theme matched the entirety of what I'd been turning my room into. I'd managed to thrift the pair of beautiful vintage lace curtains that were draped over my window. My bed frame, the dresser, the table lamps, almost everything in my room I'd snagged at some antique store or another. Even the sea-green quilt I smoothed out on my bed was a thrift shop find.

One more deep breath filled my lungs as I grabbed my thick school bag and walked out the bedroom door. In spite of the early hour, I needed the extra time to get things ready despite already visiting the school during off hours to set up my classroom.

The small town didn't have much, if any, traffic during the peak hours. Leaving before the light broke the horizon meant there would likely be none whatsoever. Turning my gray Civic into the school grounds, I found that I had my choice of spots at this early hour. Slipping my teaching badge over my head, I nodded to myself in the rearview mirror. There was no going back.

The large brick building loomed above me, casting a long shadow across the parking lot, as the sky was illuminated behind it. Soft pinks painted the serrated mountain line that spread in the background. Standing guard for millions of years and probably millions more, their solid granite heart gave me hope for stability and that this new life in Redwater, Idaho would turn out okay. Picking up and moving to the middle of nowhere had been hard enough, let alone without my own rock, my father.

Giving up my independent lifestyle to move back in with my mom and my brother had been a hard decision, yet at the same time, I hadn't hesitated. My mom had lost so much that we couldn't allow her to be shunted across the country by herself, away from everyone and everything she knew because her soulmate had been violently wrenched from her. The vow they'd made to be partners for life shattered murderously. But in spite of the grief, I still dreamed of one day having a love like theirs, though up to this point, romance seems to have eluded me.

My shoes sounded like a metronome as they clicked to the top of the concrete stairs, where I pushed open the door and walked inside. Sauntering onward through the second set of doors, I took a moment to look around. The brightly lit common room in front of me was completely empty. Large pillars encircled the gathering area, alternating between onyx and crimson, the school colors. Painted vividly upon the pale brown floor roared a massive Wolverine.

The Redwater Wolverines. It really did sound intimidating, and from what I'd heard, the school excelled in nearly every sport that they competed in. Though best known for its wrestling and weightlifting teams, none of the others lagged far behind.

When it came to academics, however, I'd been forewarned that most students didn't push themselves, and I'd found the school's academic ranking to be mediocre at best.

Turning left, I began walking past the office when a smiling blonde lady with kind eyes caught my gaze with a vigorous wave. "Hi!" she called out, pausing me in mid-step.

I recognized her from the few meetings I'd attended while sitting silently and observing in the back. Her face had soft features like mine but was weathered by time. Her bright blue eyeshadow was matted in the wrinkled lines at the corners of her almond-shaped, hazel eyes.

"Good morning," I politely answered, returning a small smile.

"You must be Miss Barlow, our new history teacher. I've seen you at a few meetings, and of course the principal told all of us about you. We are so excited to have you be a part of our team." She grinned widely, and stood up from her chair. I watched as she quickly maneuvered to the door to my right and exited the brightly lit office. Bouquets of beautiful—but obviously fake—flowers were littered amongst stacks of paper and the two computer monitors at her desk.

"I'm Nancy Pitts, the front office manager. If you need anything, *anything* at all, you just call. I know more about the ins and outs of this school than I'm probably supposed to," she twittered and punctuated this statement with a limp-wristed wave and a dramatic look around the empty hall. "Oh, and just a reminder, the elementary kids are all on the second floor; which makes that off-limits to any student in seventh grade and up. Gosh, I never asked... Have you had a tour yet?" She sidled up beside me and pushed some shoulder-length hair behind her ear.

"I know how to get to my classroom, the cafeteria, and the teacher's workroom downstairs. That's about it," I answered, and she clicked her tongue.

"That's no good. I know you need to get prepared for your first day, so I'll give you a tour sometime later this week. Oh!" She lifted a finger and quickly hustled back to her office. I quietly followed, stopping at the office window as she rifled through a stack of paper.

"One more thing. These are for you," she said and handed me some of them. "You'll need to pass these out to your sixth-period class. It's for the Veteran's Day assembly that's coming up. And..." Her voice trailed off once more as she searched through a few other papers. Ripping one from the middle of the stack, she extended it forward.

"Here it is! A school map. Shows you where everything is located until we have a moment for that tour." She looked up and winked, pushing the paper across the counter.

"Thank you so much," I replied and placed it on top of the stack she'd already given.

"Hmmm. There is one more thing. My youngest, Dayton, is in your sixth period. He and his friends do nothing but chat all the time, so you absolutely have my permission to call me anytime he's acting up." She grinned again, her lipstick bleeding into the fine lines fanning her mouth, and I chuckled in agreement.

"Okay, that will be really helpful," I answered and nodded her way. "Thank you again, Mrs. Pitts."

"That's Nancy to you. Have a wonderful first day!" She waved me on my way as energetically as if I was departing on a cruise, and I began to wander back through the hallway. Reaching the stairs, I gripped the red railing and descended carefully to the next level where my classroom was located. It was echoey, dark and not yet bustling with students down here. In hopes of having my first day run smoothly, I'd arrived extra early to give myself more time to prepare.

My first hour was way too quiet, the class was half asleep for most of the time. No matter how cheerful or engaging I tried to be, I saw more drool and heard more snores than I'd ever experienced in a classroom in my life. The second hour wasn't quite as bad. They were still reasonably quiet, but at least they weren't sleeping. I utilized the projector at the front of the class more with these older students than with the younger kids, feeling excited to be teaching history, the subject I am most passionate about.

During my lunch break, I decorated my classroom a little more. Propping up fun trinkets I'd collected over the years and adding a few indoor plants, as well as a small mushroom fairy fountain upon the edge of my desk.

The final period arrived faster than I expected, and I was at my desk, entering some grades while waiting for students to filter in.

The bell rang, and a flood of kids swung open the door. It bumped against the wall and rattled a few of the books stacked to my right.

I jumped, startled by the abrupt sound.

They were back. Those robbers were about to...

I exhaled slowly as my mind refocused on each group of kids filtering inside. No, we are okay. The criminals were gone. Dead. I was in class, teaching at my new school and new job.

I studied the cliques of teens who were just beginning to navigate their way through life. My heart leaped out to the girls who were just as self-conscious as I'd once been. The ones whose bodies were growing faster than most others, burying them in a heavy worry that, just because they didn't look like the skinny, popular cheerleader, they weren't as deserving as everyone else.

I was once that girl.

I wished I could plant myself inside every teenager's mind and tell them it gets better.

A second before the final bell rang, a group of four boys came blundering through the door. They were laughing as loudly as they could about something, half of them sitting on top of the desks in the very back. One boy up front rolled his eyes and then buried his nose back in his book. A couple girls giggled flirtatiously and wiggled their fingers at the boys.

WHAT I SHOULD HAVE SAID

I shook my head, knowing exactly what was going on.

Finally, the bell rang, but the kids did not settle down. Standing up from my desk, I walked to the front of the class and stopped, waiting. A few students noticed and sat patiently, slowly causing a rippling effect through the classroom until the four boys in the back paused talking and finally faced me.

"Dayton Pitts, I assume?" I said, staring blandly at the boy in the middle of it all. He had blond hair like his mom, with almond-shaped eyes as well, his chiseled features beyond the young age of fourteen or fifteen.

He raised a defiant eyebrow. "Who wants to know?"

"What year was the Declaration of Independence signed?" I asked, clasping my hands behind my back.

He snickered. "Who cares?"

"How many Bill of Rights are there?" I ignored his attitude. Two of the boys around him slid into their seats, chuckling.

Dayton shrugged his shoulders and flashed a sly grin at a cute redheaded girl a few rows ahead of him.

"Alright, how about something more modern. When was the internet invented?" I asked, and he furrowed his brows, snickering again.

"Why does it matter if I know this stuff or not?" he replied, and I shrugged my shoulders.

"I guess it really doesn't."

"So, why do you care if I know the answers or not?"

"I guess I don't."

His mouth fell open. "Wh-wh-what?" he stammered. Light streamed through the windows to my left, illuminating the beautiful painting that hung in the back of my classroom. "I thought teachers cared."

"That's true," I replied and watched him. "What I don't care about is whether or not you can spout off some random facts you've memorized. History is important. We can learn so much by examining it and hopefully not fall prey to the ever redundant saying that if you refuse to learn from history, you're destined to repeat it. For example, we all know the famous story of Al Capone, yes?"

I paused, watching Dayton as he studied me, intrigued, and then continued. "My father had a case once. There was this nasty drug cartel that was tearing up the streets. Nothing that the FBI had done up to that point made any sort of difference. Until, one of my dad's CI's managed to get his hands on a single document. One man, the boss of this gang, had made one fatal mistake that my dad now knew."

The red headed girl shot her hand in the air, "What's a 'CI'?"

"Good question," I remarked. "CI stands for Confidential Informant. They're someone who works for the police to provide inside information about criminal activities."

"What'd they find?" she continued.

I smiled. "Money reports. Documents that recorded he'd been lying about his income for years."

Dayton snorted. "Al Capone is all over the internet; you can Google what he did and how he got caught."

"Exactly my point." I tucked my hands behind my back. "In the end, they were able to charge the gangster with the truly heinous crimes they wanted him for in the first place, but it was the tax fraud that allowed the FBI to serve an arrest warrant, and subsequently raid his house."

"Okay? So, what does that have to do with this class?"

A few chuckles from his friends egged him on.

WHAT I SHOULD HAVE SAID

"You answered that question yourself. A little lesson in history and maybe he wouldn't have tried to lie to the government about his taxes, which led to his arrest."

Dayton pulled his bottom lip between his teeth, chewing on his words. But instead of saying anything, he slid off of his desk and plopped into the chair, the mischievousness glinting in his eyes seemingly quelled—at least for the day.

I inhaled deeply and paced to the whiteboard. "There will be no seating charts in my class, unless warranted. You are old enough to police yourselves when it comes to that. I expect you to pay attention, to raise your hand if you have questions, and please, at least let me know when you need to go to the restroom. Don't just stand up and leave. If you give me respect, I will return it, understand? But, if you lose it, this is your only warning."

Everyone nodded, and I smiled inwardly.

Class went smoothly after that, though Dayton still gave me a little attitude. He appeared to be a good kid, simply reveling in the attention his peers gave him—much like a certain brother of mine.

I handed out the papers from the office right before the bell rang and signified the end of my first day. Kids scooped up their backpacks and hustled noisily out as I returned to my desk with the pile of quizzes that would help me assess what they'd learned so far.

"Miss B?"

I glanced up to see Dayton paused beside the door.

"What's up?" I asked, and his lips lifted with a vexatious grin.

"Until tomorrow."

I watched him for a moment as he stared at me.

Then I tipped my head in a single nod. "Until tomorrow."

He scurried out of class, and I couldn't help but chuckle. My earlier reservations concerning teaching a new grade, a new subject, had vanished. Now it felt rather exciting, adventurous, like the beginning of something unexpected.

Chapter 4

"**N**oah!" I shouted, bounding up the stairs with my gym bag shrugged over my shoulder. "Let's go! I want to be back in time for dinner!"

Stopping in the mudroom, I tugged at my dark blue leggings and glanced at my watch. If we left now, we'd most likely beat the evening gym crowd, and with it being my first time at this specific location, I was already nervous as is.

"Coming! I've barely had a minute since getting home from school!" my brother grumbled in response. I tugged my high ponytail tighter and tapped my foot. I'd had enough time to remove my makeup and change outfits, even eat a snack before now. What could he possibly need more time for?

Loud pounding rattled the walls as he emerged at the top of the stairs, huffing and puffing.

We marched out the door, and I slid into the passenger side of his blue Ford F-150. He turned over the engine, and we cruised down the road listening to some music. I shook the pre-workout in my bottle and stared out the window.

Peace. That's all I wanted. A moment of rest, but inside me was a cauldron of worry. Each of my bones ached, wondering if when we rounded the next corner, those two men with guns would be standing there, waiting for me. *But they're dead, Jane.* I rationalized. Then, like a rat chasing its own tail, I changed the narrative, continuing to berate myself. *And that, too, was all because of me.*

Deep inside, I knew these thoughts were irrational, but it was as if a constant pounding knocked at the back of my head, warning me to look out because someone, somewhere, was going to jump out from the shadows. Not for the man who had held me hostage, but to take *me* down. Because it was *my* fault that two men were killed.

That beautiful, mysterious stranger was coming for me next. I had forced death at his hands, and now my dues were up. I was certain that soon enough he was going to come knocking.

Though, a small glimmer of light pierced through the heavy sludge in my brain. The glow was urging me to let him find me. To make it easy for him. As if I subconsciously wanted to see those deep-set, intense eyes. I wanted to get another chance to study the golden flecks that surrounded his pupils, and the ocean that swirled around the darkened hue.

"You look nervous." Noah's voice startled me, and I jumped, a squeak escaping my mouth.

He chuckled, and I shook my head in annoyance.

"Yeah, 'cause there's people," I answered. He rolled his eyes and scratched at his side.

"You teach people all day, so how is this scary and that isn't?"

"They aren't adults. Plus, I never said it wasn't scary." I stuck my tongue out at my brother. It was his turn to shake his head but in exasperation. He wasn't overly muscular or lean, but I had to admit he was a decent-looking guy, plus he was really comfortable to be around, and made friends everywhere he went. Which I did not.

"And how are adults different from kids?"

"They just are." I huffed, wanting this conversation to end.

"You and your stupid social anxiety," he muttered under his breath, and I slugged him in his bicep.

"Ouch!" He winced and rubbed at the quickly forming red spot. "Careful, how am I supposed to work out if I'm already injured?"

"Stop being such a jerk."

"Don't hit so hard."

"Then don't be so rude."

"I was just speaking the truth."

"Then I'll hit you as hard as I want."

He pursed his lips and turned off of the road, pulling into the gym's parking lot. It was fairly packed despite the small population of the town.

"Jane, look at me," he said as he turned the truck off. "This isn't about the gym, is it?"

I sighed. He was right, it wasn't. This had way more to do with what happened at the antique store yesterday. Every little thing set off my anxiety, so yes, okay? There was definitely some stress concerning a new gym, new people, and new crowds. But it was the intense fear that, at this new place, someone might pull out a gun again. That was what held me crippled.

"No, it's about the gym..."

Lie.

Noah's eyes softened, knowing. But I was so grateful that he didn't utter a word about that, instead changing tack. "You've been lifting for a few years now. There's no need to be worried about anyone staring because your form looks really nice. You even have visible muscle and strength to show off." He paused and winked at me, throwing a final dig my way. "Despite still being short."

I rolled my eyes and looked away. Smiling out the window.

"You'll be just fine. You're safe, and I'm with you this time," he finished, and I pursed my lips, counted to three, then exhaled slowly.

There it was. A tear welled up in my eye. He knew like he somehow always did, and in his own, frustratingly annoying way, he reminded me that I was not alone.

Noah clambered out, so I quickly did the same, not wanting to be left alone. It was a short walk, too short of a walk, into the gym where we stopped at the front desk and scanned the passes Noah got for us a few days ago.

I could see the massive weights set up behind the desk as we passed through the entryway. It was packed; nearly every squat rack was already full. The deadlift platforms were crowded, but luckily, a few racks for bench press were still available, and I hustled over to one.

Slipping my headphones on, I set up the barbell and began working. Things went smoothly despite the crowded room. The familiar musty scent of rubber mats and sweat mixed with chalk helped ease my nerves as I moved from the bench to the dumbbells.

Grabbing my duffel, I moved to the free weights section. Behind the rack of dumbbells, a row of mirrors lined the wall. I hated facing the mirrors, especially with all of the other people watching, so I dropped my duffel to the side of the row of weights, out of the way, and quickly grabbed some heavier dumbbells.

Scanning the free benches, my heart thumped wildly in my chest as I heaved the dumbbells against my sides. Only one was unoccupied. As quickly as I could, I waddled over to it and turned around, putting the mirrors behind me as I backed up to the bench.

And sat down.

Planting on something that was definitely *not* the bench.

I shot upright with a shriek, dropped the dumbbells, and spun around.

My hands slapped over my mouth as I stared at the face I'd just sat on.

"Oh my gosh. I-I-I—" I stuttered.

The man blinked in shock. His brows twitched, flashing from confusion to something unreadable as he slowly sat up.

And it dawned on me. This was the very man who had rescued me from the bank robbers, only yesterday, looking at me with a stunned expression somewhere between amusement and annoyance.

"You?" I gasped in horror.

His black hoodie was pulled over his head which hid his hair and cast dark shadows across his chiseled features. It hid his intense eyes that I'd been yearning to see, coating them in a gray hue. He balanced his dumbbells on his knees with deliberation, a pair of perfectly fitting black sweatpants straining against his thick quads. Everything felt extra warm as sweat pooled in the middle of my lower back. I wanted to pinch myself. Surely that had not just happened.

Especially to someone who looked so incredibly...well, gorgeous.

"I didn't see you. I thought...this bench was...my music was loud, and I couldn't hear anything else. I'm *so* sorry," I squeaked out as my cheeks flushed red, and I slapped my hands to my mouth. Amusement twitched across his face.

"Hi again," he said, tipping his head as he draped his headphones around his thick neck and pushed his hoodie back from his hair. There they were, those bright hazel eyes I hadn't stopped thinking about, their softness offsetting mature features that were hardened from a life I somehow knew I never wanted to experience.

I stopped talking, transfixed, every ounce of embarrassment floating away. He watched me, his facial features expressing nothing, but his eyes widening ever so subtly as his body relaxed forward. All I could see was him, this yearning for something that I couldn't quite decipher. Freedom? Relief?

...Me?

My hands slid away from my mouth to dangle by my sides. If eyes were the windows to the soul, his appeared haunted, as if desperately seeking some sort of release from a world I didn't understand. Perhaps because of my empathy, I'm certain I saw anguish dancing behind his darkened pupils that flickered between my gray eyes and down to my lips.

I exhaled slowly and tipped my head, mirroring him, unaware of the smile that slowly crept upon my face.

Then his brows knitted together, the softness ripping away from his gaze. Lines etched into his forehead as he snapped his eyes away from mine.

Heat rushed back into my cheeks. I had not just been caught ogling. Not again. Especially over a man whose face I'd...

No. No. Oh my gosh. I was the reason he killed two people yesterday, and now...

My eyes widened in horror, and I quickly bent down and gripped the ribbed metal handles of the dumbbells I'd dropped.

"Sorry, I am so sorry." I apologized again and shuffled away as quickly as I could. Of course, on my first day, I had to go and embarrass myself. In front of someone who I'd already made myself out to be a fool.

"Hey!" I heard him call out as I snatched my duffel and sprinted toward my brother, who was finishing a set of squats.

I stared at my brother, ignoring the urge to look back while impatiently waiting for him to finish his set. Noah slowly turned his head and furrowed his brows, seeing my expression. He quickly racked the barbell as I lost my restraint and glanced back at the stranger.

He was stalking my way. All powerful, and hunky-like. Ugh... Of all people, why did it have to be *his* face I sat on? Why was it someone so imposing and hot?

"We have to go," I quickly said as Noah pushed his noise-canceling headphones off one ear.

"What? Why? I'm just finishing squats and still—"

"Noah! We are leaving, *now*!" I demanded through gritted teeth as the man wove around a group of teens. Grabbing Noah's bag, I shoved it against his chest and seized his wrist.

"Jane, what the hell is going on?" he asked as I began to drag him toward the exit. I didn't bother to give him time to remove his knee sleeves or re-rack his weights. It didn't matter. We weren't coming back. Ever.

"Shut up and follow me," I snapped, shoving through the glass door beside the entrance and turning back to see that, just as the door snapped shut behind us, the man halted. He pulled his lips tight, clenching his jaw and furrowing his brows as he watched me drag Noah across the lot toward his truck.

"JANE EILEEN BARLOW!" Noah shouted as I repeatedly yanked at the door handle, desperately begging for him to unlock his truck. He clicked the key fob, and I nearly knocked myself over as it shot open.

"Get in!" I seethed, my cheeks hot and prickling, as he jumped into the driver's seat and tossed his gym bag to the back. Then he simply sat still, staring at me like I'd grown two heads out of my ass. He did not make a single move to drive us away from the gym.

"What are you doing? Why aren't you turning the truck on?" I desperately whined.

"I will, once you tell me what the hell is going on. Why did we have to leave?" He crossed his arms and glared at me stubbornly.

"Just because," I muttered and glanced back at the gym, making sure we hadn't been followed.

"Because why?"

"Because *something* happened."

"Obviously, dummy. Now, what was this *something*?"

I ducked my head in embarrassment. "I may, or may not... have sat on someone's face," I muttered low and quick.

"What? Say that again," he said, raising a brow.

"I sat on someone's face," I repeated louder, watching his mouth fall open.

"You did what?" He looked at me in disbelief, a grin breaking over his face before finally sticking the key in and turning the engine over.

"I SAT ON A GUY'S FACE!" I shouted in defeat, and he roared with laughter. Slowly, he began driving the truck out of the parking lot and onto the main road.

"You sat on some dude's face." He laughed harder, his eyes watering, grinning at me as I closed my eyes and covered my burning cheeks with my hands.

"Not just some dude. It was the guy that saved me at the antique store."

With that said, he nearly drove us off the road.

"Oh, this is too beautiful!" He gasped, between fits of unrestrained howling.

"Will you stop? Now we can never go back!" I cried out in horror, which only made him snort harder.

"How did you even manage to do that?" he asked, once his laughter had faded to a simple chuckle.

"You know I don't like lifting facing the mirrors, and I thought the bench was empty..." I muttered and leaned my head against the window.

"And with your headphones, you probably didn't hear him lay down on the bench."

I shook my head. "He had headphones on, too, so he probably didn't hear or see me either. So now we need to find a new gym."

"Why? If some chick sat on my face at the gym, I certainly wouldn't be complaining," he teased, red-faced and snorting, for which I slugged him in his arm again.

"NOAH!" I cried out as he laughed. "I didn't mean to, okay?"

"Was he at least hot?"

"Seriously!?" I responded, bewildered.

He threw his head back and laughed. "We can't go to a new gym," he immediately stated.

"Why not?" I gasped.

"This is the only gym in town. And my college is a forty-five-minute drive one way, so that can't happen either. For you, anyway. I could stay after class and—"

"You wouldn't dare," I snapped as he pulled the truck into our driveway.

"Well, I'm not missing out on lifting simply because you're embarrassed," he argued as we hopped out of the truck and plodded toward the front door. Twisting the handle, we stepped inside, and I kicked off my shoes.

"I'm not going back and risking being seen. Plus, I can guarantee that others probably saw it too!" At those words, my stomach twisted into tight knots. This couldn't be happening.

Noah inhaled sharply and stopped walking. "Fine. Then how about we go at a different time."

"Thank you!" I gasped in relief. "We could go—"

"What are you two doing home so early?" my mother interrupted, turning around from the oven and wrinkling her brow at our expressions.

"Jane sat on a dude's face," Noah announced, throwing a thumb nonchalantly toward me.

"NOAH!" I cried out in horror as my mom's mouth fell open.

She held the hot dish between her two oven mitts, staring at me. "You did what?"

"It's not like I did it on purpose!" I whined and threw my head backward in embarrassment.

"Was he attractive?" she asked.

"What?" I gaped in disbelief.

Noah shrugged his shoulders. "I don't know. I didn't see it happen."

"Damn it," my mother cursed and placed the glass pan onto a hot pad.

"Seriously? You hear I sat on a guy's face and all you want to know is if he was hot?" My eyes flashed between my brother and mom.

"Well, it might be my only chance for grandkids since neither of you seems too interested in getting married any time soon," she casually replied.

"I'm only twenty, mom. Give it some time!" Noah quickly replied.

I rolled my eyes and shook my head in disgust. "Well, we aren't going back to the gym at the same time tomorrow, so I won't have to see him again."

"Bummer," my mom muttered. "Now, go clean up and come eat." She pulled some plates out of the cupboard.

"We can go after dinner tomorrow. That should be enough time for a new crowd to be at the gym," I said to my brother's wide back as I trailed behind.

"Whatever you say. I still think he'd be excited to see you after what happened. But that's just me." He shrugged, tensing his shoulders expectantly, and I obliged, punching him square in the back once more.

Chapter 5

After another day of fairly smooth sailing at school, I was waiting once again dressed for the gym. Dinner had been leftover lasagna, and I was ready to use the energy that came from a delicious meal to pump out some intense lifting. Noah bounded up the stairs, ready to roll.

The drive to the gym was silent as I stared out the window trying hard not to but still remembering the last time and hoping it would go better today. But it wasn't the only thing on my mind; in fact I was desperately trying to think of anything else. I told each class yesterday that on Veteran's Day, I'd love to have a few military members, whether active or retired, come in and share some of their experiences. If any student had a family member or friend that they knew in the military, they could invite them to come and sign up on a sheet I'd hung by the door.

Only one person had signed up. So I'd expanded the offer to the students themselves, sharing stories they'd heard from anyone close to them. Still, that didn't add anyone else to the list. Maybe this idea would go horribly wrong. Maybe they didn't know many military members. However, from doing local research—figuring that, as a history teacher, I should at least make an effort to know a little history about the town I was teaching in—I'd learned that this town had a history of kids enlisting right out of high school.

"Worried about the gym?" Noah's voice pierced my thoughts.

"Huh?" I pulled away from the window.

"We've been sitting in the parking lot for ten minutes, with the truck off, and you haven't moved."

"Oh." I shifted in my seat. "School stuff, too, I guess."

"Not what happened at the antique shop the other day?" His eyes softened, my baby brother gently prodding like he always did.

"I mean, that's still on my mind, but today went a bit smoother. Except, Noah, it's my fault two people were killed that day, and then I—"

"No," Noah sharply said. "You aren't going to do that. They died because they did something wrong. They held a gun to your head, Janey. That man who rescued you, saved you, he did that to make sure you and *he* didn't die. It's not your fault."

I didn't say a word, not sure how to tell him that I was grateful for his reassurance and comfort, but that didn't lessen the feeling of foolishness that consumed me.

"Janey," he prompted once more, and I glanced his way.

Putting an empty smile on my face, I nodded once. "All good."

He narrowed his gaze suspiciously and stared. I knew he saw through the bullshit, but instead he exhaled slowly. "Mmmk," he replied, jumping out knowing I wouldn't say much else.

I quickly climbed down and followed him into the gym, which looked as packed as it had been yesterday. We swiped our key fobs and walked around the corner, where I halted in my tracks. A shiver ran up my spine, igniting something warm in the pit of my stomach that mixed with panic.

"You've got to be kidding me." I groaned and turned to my right, ready to immediately slip out the exit door.

"Where do you think you're going?" Noah wrapped his hand around my forearm.

"He's here. Why does he have to be here? What kind of 'thank you for saving my life' was sitting on his face?" I cried out, scared, and Noah scanned the gym, looking for someone he'd never seen before. I stared at the man in the squat rack as he repped out an impressive 405 pounds on the bar with extreme ease.

The black hoodie was once again pulled over his head, but this time he had on a pair of regular onyx shorts that clung tightly to his burly, tanned thighs. Veins twisted down his legs, a hint of tattoo flashed at the hem of his shorts, as he racked the bar and grabbed another pair of forty-five-pound plates. So, that set was a warm-up?

He hadn't noticed me yet, still focused on his work out, but his presence swallowed me in. Why couldn't we have a normal interaction? Something like a simple "hello, I'm so and so"? My heart raced heavily in my chest as I watched him position himself like a ghost built to dance with death underneath the bar.

"Look. Just ignore him, I doubt he feels any sort of guilt over what he did at the antique place. I missed my workout from yesterday and won't miss it again today," Noah grumbled, then quickly shot off.

"Noah!" I hissed, trying to grab him but to no avail.

Tearing my gaze away from the stranger, I slipped into the gym and circled away from where the man was squatting, heading for an empty deadlift platform. Maybe luck was on my side today and he wouldn't see me.

So, I began working, ignoring everyone around me. Finishing my top set, I re-racked the weights and put the barbell away, then moved toward the dumbbells once more. I grabbed some heavy free weights and scanned my surroundings thoroughly. He wasn't in this secluded portion of the gym, though my heart twinged with a faint sense of disappointment as I stepped toward the farthest corner I could.

Yeah, I'd embarrassed myself and looked like a complete wimp in front of him, but he did something to me. Stirred feelings in my stomach that I hadn't felt since long before my father died. While there was no room for any sort of feelings like that right now in my life, I couldn't deny that it felt strangely exhilarating to be teased by them. Almost freeing from the heaviness that seemed to have befallen me like I was simply waiting. Waiting for life to return or resume on its normal course. This stint in Idaho felt like a pause in living, full of nervous apprehension of a danger that wasn't supposed to be looming just around the corner.

I hugged the dumbbells against my quads and slowly began doing some Romanian deadlifts, trying to distract myself from my own thoughts.

Sweat trickled down my face and trailed along my spine by the time I finished my last set. Ducking my head into my shoulder, I wiped my eyes against my shirt and took a step forward. My body bounced hard against a wall of thick muscle, knocking me off balance, and my butt plummeted toward the ground. An arm wrapped around my waist, stopping my fall right above the rubber mats.

The dumbbells banged against the ground with a dull thud as my eyes looked to those of the person I'd ran into.

The same person whose face I'd sat on.

"Oh my gosh," I mumbled, mortified, as I locked onto the intense hazel eyes that I was becoming all too familiar with. My eyes widened, acutely aware of his musky sweat and the strength of his arm easily supporting me. My heart jumped to my throat as my stomach flipped. He studied me, curiosity etched upon his face. His tongue flicked out, wetting his lips as his gaze danced down my figure.

Everything roared within me, he didn't seem annoyed or—

Then, like a bolt of lightning snapping across a blackened sky, his features tensed up, and a mask of cold stoicism plastered over his once alive features.

Shoving myself from his embrace, I snatched the dumbbells from the ground and did an awkward slow shuffle toward the weight rack, the hairs on my neck standing up knowing he was watching me.

I faced him and gritted my teeth. "Sorry. Again. For it all," I stammered and then ran toward Noah who was doing some lat pulldowns.

"HEY!" I heard the stranger shout, and, as if it was déjà vu, I began pacing beside Noah who pursed his lips while finishing his set.

This time however, the stranger didn't leisurely follow me. Instead, he put a missile lock in on me, and stalked quickly around the gym to shut off my escape route. Slinging his headphones around his neck, he pushed the hood back from his head and ran a large, veiny hand through his wavy hair.

A hand that I wanted to be against my body and not just catch me from my fall.

Scratch that thought. No. No. Absolutely not. What was I thinking? I needed to get out of here.

"Get up and let's go." I tugged at Noah's collar once he finished his set. Impatiently shoving his headphones off his ears, he glared up at me, and this time, there was no amusement in those blue eyes.

"What is it this time?" he snarled, actually baring his teeth and taking me aback.

"Well, he's here. Again. And—"

"Let me guess, you sat on his face again."

"No! But I did run into him. Literally. Please," I begged, tugging him off of the machine. But it was futile. Just as I'd managed to take a step toward the exit, calloused fingers wrapped around my wrist and pulled. Noah's eyes widened in awe, and he mouthed at me, "That's him?"

I nodded and pinched my fingers together, sliding them across my mouth, silently telling him to shut it.

I spun to the man whose eyes narrowed when they connected with mine, a glint of pain hidden behind the cold, stoic mask. His jaw clenched, the glare hiding everything else on his face, and I started apologizing. "I'm really sorry. Seriously, I didn't see you and—"

"I know," he stated, cutting me off. "Here." He turned my palm up with one hand while the other slapped something against it. I glanced at the small picture he'd placed against my fingers. "This fell out of your purse that day."

His eyes slid to my brother, delivering a numbing stare.

"Thank you. I really didn't mean to bump into you. Or...you know, what happened yesterday." I sheepishly sucked my bottom lip between my teeth. His jaw knotted, but nothing changed on his face.

"Anyway, I'm sorry, again." I turned away to rid myself of the anger rolling from his shoulders, shoving my hand against Noah's arm. "Let's go," I hissed through my teeth. Noah's gaze snapped over my shoulder, and his eyes widened as the stranger finally stomped off. I refused to look at him and add insult to my embarrassed horror.

This entire time, he'd merely been trying to get my attention so he could return this picture of Noah and me. The last picture taken before our dad was killed.

My shoulders sagged.

Noah's head dipped toward me. "I'm straight and even I think he's hot."

"Shut up, asshole," I muttered, sneaking a look back at the man as he returned to his lifting routine. Watching him flex, every part of my entire body heated up, a mixture of hormones betraying me and embarrassment from acting so childlike. Maybe, I should simply go tell him thank you and at least introduce myself.

Wait, no. I'd done enough already.

Shoving the picture into my gym bag, I turned to Noah. "C'mon. Let's go."

"Seriously?"

"Yes, seriously. And tomorrow we go back to our original lifting time. That way we won't risk running into him again."

"Wasn't that the point of going at a different time today?"

"Yes. But obviously that didn't work and that dude is being creepy or something."

Noah rolled his eyes. "Would it really be that bad if he was interested in you?"

I tipped my head, looking back at the stranger. Butterflies tumbled in my stomach, brushing dainty wisps against the walls. No, it probably wouldn't. Even with his broody and rather odd, standoffish behavior, he was something else. Something that had me constantly torn between being super upset that he was showing up every—

The man's eyes suddenly snapped away from the mirror he was working in front of, and his gaze rested on mine, tearing me from my thoughts. Shrouded by his stone-like features, I slunk away within my mind, the intensity of his gaze loud yet unreadable despite knowing he was reading me like an open book. His hands tightened around the ribbed handles of the dumbbells he was holding, the pump of his body threatening to burst all the seams of his hoodie.

Then his brows twitched, he shook his head as though annoyed by a fly, and turned away, looking down at the floor.

I took a deep breath. "Yes, it would be that bad," I finally replied, my voice breaking.

Noah rolled his eyes. "Are you still in the 'avoid all men because of that one bad dude who was a creep and hit you, so every guy is like that' mode?"

I sneered at my brother, shoving him away. "This has nothing to do with that or him."

"He wouldn't leave you alone. Are you sure you're not subconsciously projecting this fear that every dude who even pays you a smidge of attention is going to stalk you like Sam did?"

"Noah, will you shut your face hole?"

He groaned. "Look, this very hot, very sweaty man probably changed his time to try and avoid you, like we'd done to try and avoid him."

My shoulders fell. Part of me was disappointed that my brother was possibly right.

"Fine. Let's go back to our original time tomorrow and we'll have an answer," I mumbled, not really convinced.

"Unless he's thinking the same thing, idiot."

It was my turn to groan. "Hurry and finish your workout and let's go."

"Think you can manage without running into sweaty hottie again?" He grinned and winked at me. I slugged Noah as hard as I could, and this time, he winced in real pain.

My heart steadily pounded in my chest as the truck rattled closer and closer to the gym the next day. My thoughts distracted by work. At least two more kids had added their names to the list by the end of the school day, which made me a little more hopeful of success. But since we were nearing the end of the week, that only left four days to sign up before Veteran's Day came upon us next Wednesday.

School stressed me out. All of this with the assembly had me anxious, but as Noah pulled us into the gym's parking lot, that added even more anxiety. Stupid anxiety. Though I was determined to be a little less of a baby today.

Even if he was at the gym, I wouldn't force us to leave. Noah was being extra patient with me, which seemed a little odd. Though, he was probably giving me more grace than normal because of everything that happened at the antique store. All the more reason why he deserved to finally have a decent lifting session.

The moment we entered the gym, Noah escaped as quickly as he could. I scanned my surroundings, my heart in my throat as I prayed that he wouldn't be here.

I tugged at my gray tank top and adjusted the waistband of my black leggings in nervous anticipation.

Then my heart fell to my stomach. There he was, doing some curls in the free weights section. Again, with that stupid hoodie hiding every delicious muscle that I really wanted to see.

Why? Just why was he here? What cruel monster was cooking up my fate, and what dumb, embarrassing thing was I going to do today?

Maybe I should just muster up the courage and go say hi instead of letting this awkwardness float between us. The least I could do is introduce myself, seeing as I'd already made a fool of myself three times now. Besides, what if Noah was right?

Ugh, I didn't even know why I cared so much. I should just let it go, let him go. But there were these strange sensations that constantly rippled beneath my thoughts and my skin. My stomach did this thing every time he grunted, igniting a heat low in my core. I unintentionally lingered, hating how much he was consuming my thoughts.

One normal interaction with an introduction should get him off of my mind. Not giving myself time to reconsider, I shrugged my duffel higher up my shoulder and marched confidently toward him.

He placed the dumbbells on the mats beside a bench and sat down, taking a swig of his drink. My feet stopped moving the moment I was beside him.

And so did my brain. I said nothing. I did nothing. And for a moment, clear irrational calm stole through me—something unexpected and so desperately desired.

His brows slowly raised, and he tilted his head so his eyes could meet mine. And we stared right into each other. So deeply, I almost forgot to breathe. It was like diving headfirst into another universe, and I was drowning in the pit of night rimmed in gold dust.

Not a single expression danced across his features, he looked like a Greek statue displayed in a museum. The only thing lacking, or technically not lacking, were clothes. Slowly, the tension in his jaw slackened, and he lifted his chin slightly.

My heart nearly burst through my ribs, pounding like a thousand horse hooves thundering across a meadow. Those eyes held the burden of the world.

Then the spell was broken. He raised his brows after another second and looked to either side of me. Pulling his lips into a thin line, he clenched his jaw, sighing heavily. Sliding the hood off of his head, he pushed one side of his headphones off of his ear and waited.

I sucked in my bottom lip, realizing I hadn't actually thought about what I was going to say when I'd gotten his attention. We remained still, and even with the distance between us, I could feel the heat radiating from him as we silently studied each other. Studying every shadow that etched the hollows of his eyes and cheeks beneath the strong ridge of his brows, my mind slid into unknown territory. I very much liked how defined his features were. I liked the razor sharpness of his intense, hazel eyes, the hard angle of his jaw. He was as mesmerizing as a siren.

Finally, he shook his head, a quick frown creasing his brows before he moved to put his headphones back on.

"Wait," I blurted out, and he paused, widening his eyes and pursing his lips. "I'm Jane." Then I inwardly kicked myself in the shin. That was so stupid. Stupid. Stupid. Stupid.

"And?" he bluntly stated, the singular word slicing through me like ice.

"And I thought I should introduce myself seeing as we seem to continually run into each other," I quietly muttered, scratching my scalp.

He moved his head up and down, very leisurely. "Alright." He shoved his headphones back on and picked up the dumbbells. Standing up from the bench, he took a step forward and immediately went back to work.

"Alright?" I mumbled under my breath, frustrated. "That's it?" Rolling my eyes, I turned to walk away. "What a jerk."

"Griffin." His voice stopped me in my tracks. I froze as still as a statue. A second later, he said, "My name's Griffin."

Dutifully noted. Without turning back, I sighed once more and continued walking away. There was no need to linger or look, no matter how strong the desire was to glance back over my shoulder. I was nothing but a pesky fly interrupting any sort of peace.

Today was shoulder day, so I walked to a squat rack to set up for some overhead press. Heavier than usual because I needed to burn off some steam. At least this time I wasn't leaving the gym embarrassed. All of that embarrassment washed away the moment he'd acted that way toward me. I'd apologized enough already, hadn't I? Why couldn't he at least be semi-cordial to me?

Chapter 6

T he closer it got to Veteran's Day, my list for guest speakers was beginning to fill up, which was exciting. Now that it was the week of the assembly, all the stress that came from preparing for it was finally fizzling out. Even better was the fact that I hadn't had any more run-ins with that jerk-face at the gym for the remainder of last week or over the weekend. Though there was a curiosity that was constantly sparked when I caught sight of him, despite his rather confusing attitude toward me.

He never lifted without his black hoodie. I wanted to know why.

The big sweatshirt did nothing to hide his absolutely exquisite steel frame or muscles built of solid concrete, so that couldn't be the reason he never lifted in a simple T-shirt. Okay, so I selfishly wanted to see what he looked like without it, which was a carnal thought—one I shouldn't even be having—but all the same.

You know what? It didn't matter. He wasn't worth the time I'd already spared thinking about him.

Noah's lab was running late, so he told me to hit the gym without him. Luckily, for whatever reason, Griffin was nowhere to be found, and I was able to have yet another peaceful and successful lifting session. Afterwards, I headed to the market in search of protein powder and a few other things. Hating new supermarkets, I was wandering back and forth between aisles, trying to get my bearings.

The speckled, white tile squeaked beneath my gym shoes as I rounded yet another corner from which came a strong smell of spices.

Ughhh! Another wrong aisle.

I meandered through shelves of flour and sugar, the fluorescent light above me flickering as I continued past the baking nuts and oil. Another shopper turned down the row I was on, one wheel squeaking rhythmically on her blue shopping cart.

Feeling frustration mounting, I decided that if I couldn't find the protein powder here, I'd shoot for another local store before resorting to ordering it online.

Executing a spin on my heel, I stepped out from the aisle and slammed directly into someone's large, very hard body.

"I'm so sorry!" I exclaimed, rubbing my forehead, my breath almost knocked out of me.

"My bad," a deep male voice replied.

My heart jumped, instantly. I knew that voice and raised my widening eyes to meet Griffin's. His features twitched, threatening a smile, but then he forced a frown, any warmth on his face turning cold. But there was definitely a hint of something else glinting behind his icy mask. Something indecipherable straining to be released, something that looked heavy.

I compressed my lips in annoyance—not at him, but at myself. Why was it that almost every time I saw him, it was in a circumstance like this? And why did he have to be so attractive? I hated that I consistently felt this way around him.

"Hi," I said, averting my gaze from his oddly captivating hazel eyes.

"Why is it always you?" he muttered. "I swear, everywhere I go, you're somehow there."

"I feel the same exact way!" I threw my hands on my hips.

"Are you following me?"

"No. I'm actually trying to avoid you."

"Well, try harder." His gaze remained cold and indifferent.

I glared at him in return. "And what about you? You could try harder to avoid me! Why is it on *me* to avoid *you*?"

"Because!" He towered over me, his gaze darkening as he closed some of the gap that had formed between us. Stumbling back, I glanced around in hopes of assessing my escape and caught sight of something. My gaze narrowed.

No, some*one*.

Someone who made my stomach turn, acidic bile scraped away at my insides.

"Shit," I hissed under my breath. Griffin's mouth was moving, I could see that as he ranted about something, but his words became background noise and then altogether ceased as my attention zeroed in on a person who shouldn't be here. Who had no *right* to be here.

A person who had also stopped moving and was looking straight at me, his lips stretched into a blood-curdling, sickening grin of recognition. Our eyes locked, and he let out a dramatic sigh, his hand sliding briefly between his legs to adjust himself.

I gagged, my body fighting between disgust and panic. Each breath of mine shallowed, the air around me thinning. "Why now?" I exclaimed, turning my eyes back to Griffin. Better yet, how was he even here?

"What the hell does that mean?" Griffin's voice filtered into my strained thoughts.

"Shush for a second would you," I insisted, ignoring him.

"Don't tell me to shush when I know something is wrong." His voice was sharp as color bloomed in his typically stoic cheeks. Barely registering his words, I strained to keep my eyes locked on Griffin but used my peripheral vision to track the man taking assured, threatening steps toward me as his tongue rolled around his lips in a clear message.

This could not be happening. Nobody, not even my one and only friend knew where we moved to. And now he was here? Had he not done enough? The hairs on my arms stood up with each microsecond drawing his threatening figure closer.

"Turn around. I'm not here," I muttered as the man continued marching toward me. My heart raced, my breath sharpening. I was his target. Tears filmed my vision, turning each person around me into a blurry outline. "No. Nope. How is this even possible? How did he find me?"

"Okay, what are you going on about?" Griffin demanded, his voice becoming commanding, and it tunneled my vision solely to his towering frame in front of me, locking it away from the blond-haired man that was deliberately walking my way. I sucked in sharply, blinking back the water in my eyes.

"Hide me. Pretend to be my boyfriend. Hold my hand. Do something. Please! I'm begging you!" I pleaded.

Griffin crossed his arms in front of his chest, his pecs bunching beneath the gray, long-sleeve knit shirt. Under any other circumstance, I would have been ogling over his fashionable jeans that sculpted out his legs or the way his shirt formed upon every muscle on his body. But not now, not while Sam was stalking me hungrily like a lion to prey.

I gripped a handful of his shirt. "What the hell?" Griffin muttered, his eyes widening as I rose to my toes.

"Please. Do something. Anything, I am begging you," I blurted out again, searching Griffin's face for the compassion I'd seen once before. There was no time to explain, and honestly, no way I would tell this stranger about what Sam did to me.

"Please," I whispered in final desperation.

His gaze flicked around the store and landed on Sam, who was close enough that I could see the green of his eyes. Darting his attention back to me briefly, he took in my bottom lip trembling in desperation. Sam was less than half an aisle away. It was now or never. I inhaled sharply, seeing Sam's sickening lustful gaze locked onto me, and his hand slid down himself—again.

"You owe me," Griffin warned, and I nodded.

"Anything." I was desperate, and I didn't care what the cost was.

"Jane!" I heard Sam call in a wheedling voice full of ownership, the way he might call a lost, timid dog, and I flinched, feeling the ghost of his fist.

"Griffin..." I begged.

Griffin's jaw tensed up for a moment, the final moment of debate flashing between his eyes. As if part of him knew he shouldn't do whatever he was about to do, but he lost that fight. He gripped my chin, jerked my head upward, and pressed his frame against mine. The warmth of his body heat blanketed my figure, my racing heart pounding against his solid chest.

Instinctively, I took a step backward, bumping into the shelves as his eyes bore into mine.

Hungry.

They darkened as he placed his other hand above my head, bracing himself. My breath hitched for a split-second, and then his lips pressed hotly against mine.

In shock, my eyes flew wide open as his closed.

He was kissing me.

Properly. Like a lover.

The way I had always imagined one would.

Inhaling sharply, I became putty in his embrace. Closing my eyes, my fingers tightened their grip on his shirt as he slid his hand from my chin to the nape of my neck and his lips explored every inch of my mouth.

Lips as soft as velvet ignited the slow burning fire in my core. Every moment denying my feelings drained away. I forgot we were standing in public. Forgot Sam. I became aware of nothing but the sensation he was eliciting as he teased a response with his teeth, lips, and tongue. Sliding my swollen mouth over his, he pressed his hips deep against my body and snaked his calloused hand around my waist with a low groan. The heat of his skin branded my exposed torso as his other fingers tangled in the base of my hair, tugging at the greasy ponytail I hadn't bothered to fix.

He was kissing me like I'd never been kissed before. When his lips parted slightly, I quickly followed suit, unable to resist any of his demands, and his tongue slipped between my teeth.

He tasted sweet with a hint of peppermint. My body melted, my skin electrified, that low pulse back between my legs. But I absolutely invited it this time. I breathed his breath and he breathed mine. I'd never been so intimate with someone. Never felt so alive. I didn't know how I was still standing when all I wanted was to hook my legs over his hips and feel every part of him pressed deeply against my throbbing center.

Pulling back for some air, I didn't let him take a break for long as I dove right back in. I wanted more, begged him for more, and he tightened his hold on my hair around the base of my neck keeping me where he wanted. I shoved my tongue shamelessly into his mouth this time, and he fisted the back of my white cropped top.

And he didn't fight it. Instead, he seemed to be welcoming it, losing self-control over his own actions. To hell with how public this all was. He tugged at my hair, tilting my head up a little higher, and stole back control. I gladly relinquished as he ran his tongue over my lips tasting me and then slipped it into my mouth once more.

Raising higher onto my toes to try and sever some of the height difference between this six-foot-three-inch man and me, I boldly pressed myself harder against him. Tighter... more... I wanted it all.

Eventually, he pulled his mouth away and let his lips hover just above mine. Hot breath washed over my face, fanning my own flush. I wanted him close to me. To not lose his touch or his hold on my body.

But as we stood there, I slowly came to my senses, dazed by what had just happened. And a little upset that it had ended so abruptly, while also confused and shocked by how good it felt. I forgot that we didn't particularly like each other.

My eyes shyly met his. Watching me, his expression was indecipherable. Still on fire, I had no urge to look away from the most intense gaze of his I'd witnessed yet.

An invisible string tugged me toward him, luring me with the desire to trace my fingers along his jawline. I shouldn't. That was crossing a line that was very clearly drawn in the sand.

But I had no control as my hand raised to his face.

He didn't balk at my touch, didn't flinch as I gently brushed my fingertips across his skin. I wanted to memorize the outline of his strong neck and pronounced features, as if he was crafted from stone and expertly polished.

As my fingers neared his mouth, however, he sharply stepped away. Immediately, the searing heat in my soul dissipated, and a cold shiver trickled down my spine.

Wanting to look anywhere but at him, I searched the aisle for signs of Sam in time to see a blond man fade around the corner, but not before he shot a glare at Griffin who hovered in front of me. I knew that look, too; our charade had not deterred him. For now, he would leave me alone, but he would be back. The thought made me nauseous.

"He's gone now. Thank you." I cringed inwardly, as Griffin raised his chin and stared above my head.

"Right." He looked down his nose at me for a silent second before bluntly dropping his bombshell. "Since I had to pretend to be your boyfriend, you get to return the favor this weekend by being my girlfriend at my mom's family reunion."

"What?" I swung my gaze back to meet his eyes, incredulous.

He cocked a single brow. "You agreed to anything. This is "anything" and how you can repay me."

"But your entire family? You want to lie to them?" I rebutted, trying to find a way out of this den of wolves he was about to throw me in.

"I want some fucking peace." He closed his eyes briefly and shook his head.

That, I could understand. I wanted that too. I wanted to never see Sam again, to not have someone put a gun to my head. I wanted to be left alone to live a mundane, uneventful life. One where I no longer thought about all the traumatizing events that had occurred within such a short period of time. But he wanted peace from what? A meddling family? Attention that was unwarranted?

His brows twitched; something in his gaze softened as I looked up at him through my lashes. There was a tenderness and yearning in his eyes, a desperation for something I also sought, while everything else on his face pulled tight.

"Surely it can't be that bad," I quietly muttered, not as steady in my conviction to get out of this. I owed him, didn't I? For more than just this.

He scoffed. "Every family has their issues; mine is just a little more overbearing than usual."

"And a girlfriend will fix that?"

"I just need you to cast enough doubt with my family so they think we are madly in love. Then it'll all be over after this weekend, and we can both go back to boring, calm lives."

I opened my mouth, ready to snap at him, but paused. Fighting this, denying him was a very selfish thing to do. With very little information, he helped me in a time of need. Despite everything weird between us, despite the heavy internal mess he seemed to be dealing with, he stepped up when I needed him most. If all he wanted in life was a small amount of peace, what right did I have to deny him of that? At least one of us could receive that.

He shook his head, filling in the silence I'd left. "Whatever. I'm not fighting you on this. I should've known better because of how you've been acting," he said, annoyed. Mystified, I watched as the walls slammed back up around him and he turned away.

Quickly, I pinched his sleeve. "No, stop. I'll do it. I told you I would, so I'll do it."

His gaze narrowed, and he studied me for a moment. Swallowing stiffly, his Adam's apple bobbed and then his shoulders sagged, screaming relief.

"Here." He shoved a hand in his jean's pocket and pulled out his phone. He offered it to me. "Put your number in, and I'll text you with more details whenever they give me some."

Slowly, I slid the phone from his fingers, avoiding his eyes and making sure to not brush his skin. How on earth had I managed to end up in this situation? Why and how was Sam here?

Plugging in my information, I handed his cell back to him.

"Thank you again," I said, finally looking at him. Whatever softness I'd once seen in him had well and truly fled. The man was a walking, talking steel pole, who I imagined had a molten core.

"Mmmhmmm," he muttered, walking away before I could stop him with anything else. One week. I'd known him for a little more than a week, and it looked like I'd done nothing but frustrate him. Why I cared so much, I wasn't sure, but it only made me more annoyed.

He treated me like I was some idiot, even someone he greatly disliked at times. Yet, when he kissed me, that hadn't seemed so spiteful. He hadn't gagged at the thought, and technically, I hadn't even asked him to kiss me. That had been his action on his own. I'd merely asked him to hide me.

Shaking my head in confusion, I exited the store in a dreamlike state after managing to find some of the usual protein powder I'd been looking for. Nobody kissed someone like the way he kissed me if they hated that person. Would they? I wouldn't voluntarily kiss someone that I was indifferent toward like *that*. Someone I barely knew.

Yet, I had. I kissed him back. Savagely, with no restraint. And why did I have to have liked that kiss so much? I was more than annoyed with him. He constantly showed up at the worst times, but I still kissed him, and I really liked it. A lot. Even let it go on probably longer than was necessary. For a moment during it all, I'd completely forgotten why he'd kissed me in the first place.

I slid into the driver's seat of my car and locked the door. My fingers mindlessly traced my swollen and throbbing lips, desperately wanting to feel his again. It wasn't like I'd never been kissed before. I'd had plenty of boyfriends growing up. This was different, though, in a way I couldn't explain it. Maybe all of this animosity that I had towards him was my own fault.

Drawing a deep breath, I placed my hands on the steering wheel and clenched my teeth, giving it a shake "No. You're not going to do this, Jane. Once this weekend's favor is up, you will ignore him no matter how often you see him. He is not worth the frustration or time."

But damn was he hot.

And he made me feel things I hadn't wanted to feel in such a long time.

Turning the car's engine over, I put it into drive and headed onto the road. Luckily, Noah hadn't been there when that had all gone down. Nobody else had to know that Griffin kissed me or that Sam was somehow here. Nobody needed to know that I was spending the weekend at a family reunion playing "pretend happy couple" for Griffin.

A small twinge of sympathy drifted into my heart. If this afforded him a small amount of peace for a day, then I could do this. He'd done the same for me, if not more.

Chapter 7

"Miss B!" Dayton called out as the rest of the class hustled out into the hallway at the end of the day.

"Don't forget about the assembly tomorrow and shortened class periods!" I shouted over him, hoping that at least one student was listening.

"Miss B!" Dayton called again. I pushed my extremely large, bug-eyed glasses up my nose as he hustled up to my desk.

"What's up, Dayton?" I asked, gathering the last stack of papers from the front, and plopped myself down in my chair with a sigh of relief.

"I did it," he said giddily.

"Did what?" I asked, brushing some paper lint from my white blouse and blush-colored straight-leg trousers.

"I convinced my older brother to come tomorrow. To the assembly, at least. I know you needed to know by today if we are having someone come share a bit of their experience in class, but I was hoping you might give me an extension?" Dayton tucked his hands around his backpack straps and widened his hopeful eyes.

"You were telling me about how stubborn he can be. Sounds like someone else I know," I teased, and Dayton rolled his eyes.

"Anyway, he's home on leave for a bit or whatever it's called when you're waiting for the next deployment, which Mom is hoping will be his last and he'll finally retire. I'm going to work on getting him to come; he's really cool and has some sick stories. If I can get him to share any..." Dayton's eyes glazed over, falling somber.

"Let me know as soon as you can tomorrow if your brother will be sharing any of his stories. I'll make sure there is time if he is," I softly answered, and Dayton's eyes lit up.

"He's the coolest guy, even if he is a bit bullheaded."

I smiled gently as Dayton pushed himself off of the lip of my desk. "You're the best, Miss B! See you tomorrow!" He waved and jogged toward the door.

"Dayton!"

"Yes, Miss B?"

"Even if he doesn't stay tomorrow for my class, it doesn't mean he doesn't care about you."

Dayton shuffled his feet and stared at the wall for a moment, his eyes glazing over. "I know," he finally replied and then disappeared out into the hallway. I really hoped that Dayton believed that and truly knew that. Though I didn't know his brother, I knew that any time in the military would change a person. The FBI had changed my dad, and he didn't see nearly as much violence as someone in the military probably did. I just hoped Dayton truly understood that.

Once I'd managed to sort through all of my papers, I headed home, my thoughts now on my planned evening workout.

Noah swiped his card first at the gym and disappeared as quickly as he could. I rolled my eyes but couldn't blame him; I'd ruined several of his lifting sessions already. But not today. I put my head down, turned the music up on my headphones, and got to work—determined to not get distracted by anything else.

Sweat beaded on my forehead and dripped down my nose as I finished my last set of squats and racked the barbell. I was quite proud of myself today; they'd felt good, and I hadn't run into Griffin at all. Dabbing my face with my towel, a shiver ran down my spine as if someone was watching me. Lowering the rag, my eyes met Griffin's steady, unblinking gaze.

Of course.

He sat on a bench, forearms resting on bulging thighs, with his usual hoodie pulled low over his forehead, as magnetic and darkly brooding as usual.

I stared, unable to peel my eyes away from his.

He seemed hot and bothered.

I imagined to him I must look the same. I'd gone from zero to wild in a matter of heartbeats. Everything in my body roared with burning flames, and that familiar slick, wet feeling erupted between my legs. I wanted his lips back against mine. I wanted to feel his calloused hand tug me forward like he had. I liked his aggressive passion. I wanted him to kiss me like that again, annoyed that it awakened something primal in me, a chained and starving beast that was demanding to be fed.

He could take his frustrations out on me anytime. Especially if it left me feeling exactly like I had in that store. Or maybe more. I feared that my own self-control was flying out of the window, no matter how desperately I was avoiding any sort of man drama.

Once again, he broke the spell by pressing his fingers to his eyes and shaking his head. He ran a hand over his mouth and looked around the gym in all directions—at anything but me. *What the hell was his problem?*

That was definitely it.

Annoyed, frustrated, and entirely fed up, I stomped over to him as he casually stepped away from the bench. Without thinking, I grabbed the back of his damp sweatshirt.

"What the hell?" I snarled.

He glared down at me. "I should ask you the same thing."

"I didn't give you a dirty look like you did me."

His jaw tensed, knotting a couple of times. "I don't get you. How could you?"

I threw my hands in the air in frustration. "How could I what? I have no idea what I did to piss you off, but you seem to hate me or something! I've apologized for everything that happened! And it was all an accident anyway! Besides, I was the one that looked like a fool, not you."

"An accident? I mean, yeah, most of it was, but you asking me to pretend to be your boyfriend, was that an accident? You agreed to be my girlfriend this weekend, was that an accident? You asking me to kiss you, was that an accident?" He was calm, too calm. He hadn't yet raised his voice despite knowing he was pissed at me.

Which was only frustrating me further. *What was up with this guy?*

"I didn't ask you to kiss me," I seethed between my teeth, not wanting to draw attention despite the rage that was slowly filling me up.

"Oh, right. You simply what? Wanted me to hold your hand? Like that would've stopped whoever that jackass was from coming over." He tugged his sweatshirt from my fingers, and I stumbled a step backward.

"Well, I mean, I guess it wouldn't have," I muttered.

"Good. So you agree you asked me to blatantly cross a line."

"What line? What are you talking about?"

"The fact that you have an actual boyfriend, and in front of him, you've had the nerve to come over to me!"

I furrowed my brows and bit my bottom lip trying to figure out what he meant. He glared at me as if it was obvious, while to me it was as clear as mud. "Please explain what you're talking about. I am so lost."

"I'm talking about the fact that you are clearly cheating on your boyfriend, and he's simply watching it all go down!" I followed his hand as he gestured toward the back of a person I knew all too well.

"Wait, you mean, Noah?" I tossed a thumb at my brother who pulled his last deadlift.

Griffin closed his eyes and shook his head. "You know what, this will be so much easier if I just go tell him myself." He placed his headphones around his neck and began to stalk toward Noah.

"Tell him what?" I jogged after him.

"You know what really pisses me off? I didn't peg the girl I met at the antique store to go for a guy who looks like he's barely out of high school, and I'm typically good at reading people," Griffin called out over his shoulder, refusing to look at me.

And I nearly tripped over my own feet as it hit me. His first introduction to Noah and I was with the picture that had fallen out of my purse. Add that to everything else he'd seen, and that we hardly look anything alike, no wonder he would think we were dating, not siblings.

I gave a highly unladylike snort.

"What's so funny?" Griffin asked, stopping in his tracks as I raced to catch up. He'd made it nearly two-thirds of the way over to Noah.

"You think I'm dating Noah? That big oaf right there with a baby face who still hasn't had his second nut drop yet?" I snickered as Griffin's brows drew together thunderously.

"And now you're talking about him like that?" Griffin stared wide-eyed at me in horror as I bent over and placed my hands against my knees, snorting again, trying to hold back the laughter that was consuming me. My messy ponytail fell in my face, some of the hair caught in the collar of the black halter top I was wearing.

"And now you're mocking me. Awesome. Some girlfriend you are," he muttered. "All the more reason I'm excited he's going to learn about all the shit that you've pulled."

I raised a hand wordlessly, begging him to stop, but that bus had already left. Griffin quickly approached Noah.

"No," I choked back the laughter. "Stop." But it was barely a whisper as they bumped fists after greeting each other. Now this was a conversation I had to hear, so I quickly jogged their way.

"Wait, what?" Noah said looking blank as Griffin gestured toward me once more.

"Again, I'm sorry to be the one to tell you man, but she's cheating on you," Griffin replied, and Noah doubled over, unable to contain the snort and laughter that erupted from his belly, and I realized we might not have looked alike but could sure sound like it.

"Griffin!" I called weakly, my stomach muscles cramping from laughter, and he looked between Noah and me, bewildered.

"What the hell is going on?" Griffin pushed the hood off of his head and threw his hands out to the sides in question.

I raised a finger and attempted to choke down the next fit of laughter that was working to burst through the seams. "Griffin, he's not my boyfriend," I said.

His hands fell slowly to his sides. "He's not?"

"I'm her little brother," Noah managed to snort out, and Griffin closed his eyes, his expression relaxing upon his face. Relief befell his stiff figure, and I bit the inside of my bottom lip, waiting for the rest of the humor to die off.

Noah coughed a couple of times and shared a look with me.

"Though I appreciate you being willing to inform me since you thought she was," Noah quickly added formally, his grin threatening more laughter. Griffin inhaled deeply before shaking his head sheepishly. A small smile formed on his lips as he opened his eyes.

"Well, shit makes waaay more sense now." He heaved a heavy sigh. He nodded politely toward Noah, who offered him another fist bump, and then Noah subtly wiggled his brows in my direction. My brother put his headphones back on, returning to his next set of deadlifts.

Griffin faced me, the anger completely eradicated from his chiseled features. He stiffly walked my way. "I should probably apologize for being a bit of a dickhead."

"Yeah, you should."

"You should've made it more clear that you weren't dating him."

"How obvious do I need to make it? Should I wear a sign that says 'he's my little brother' wherever I go?" I lifted my gaze to meet his burdened hazel eyes.

And he gave me a goofy grin.

"You really are a dickhead," I muttered, but man, it felt good to not be annoyed with him. Filling my lungs with a fresh breath of air, I continued. "Could we have a do-over introduction?"

A gentle smile caressed his lips. "Hi, I'm Griffin, and I'm not usually that much of a dick."

"Only half a dick," I teased, and he shook his head. "It's nice to meet you Griffin. I'm Jane, and I'm not usually that annoying."

"No, you're just a smart ass with anxiety." He winked, and I gasped, feigning shock.

"How'd you know?"

He chuckled and walked toward the bench as I followed behind, curious about something. "By the way, if you thought I was dating someone, why did you still kiss me and ask me to be your fake girlfriend?" I asked.

He sat on the edge of the black plastic and looked directly at me. "I wanted damning evidence before I blew someone's relationship up."

"Oh?"

"And, if I recall correctly, you kissed me back, smart ass," he added with a crooked grin. I liked his smile. This was the man I remembered from the antique store.

"*You* kissed *me*. That's all that happened."

"Alright, whatever you say." He winked and laid back on the bench. "Now, either spot me or go to your next exercise. I've rested too long."

I walked behind the bench as he set himself up beneath the barbell. "Do you even need a spot?" I asked, and he grinned wickedly as he unracked the weight and began to effortlessly rep it out. My eyes raked across his frame, his hoodie bunching around his muscles with each press. My skin tingled at the sight.

I forcibly snapped out of my shameful ogling. "Also, in case you were wondering, my brother is twenty, so he's not that young," I said, hopefully covering up the very blunt stare I'd been giving him.

Griffin paused halfway up a rep and then finished, racking the barbell with a clang before sitting up and facing me. "Still a baby. You robbed the cradle."

"We aren't dating, Griffin!" I cried out, and he boomed his sexy laugh, making the girl beside us look him over openly. Her eyes widened, and a blush crept upon her cheeks before she quickly hid her face again.

"I know, smart ass."

Man, this guy was infuriating and exciting—but I liked this 180-degree turn that we'd accomplished. This banter was much more fun, and well, it fed my ego a little. "Another question, why did you wait so long to find out if we were dating? Why didn't you ask me about it sooner?"

He closed his eyes, raised his brows, and then looked at me like it was obvious. "I tried to ask several times, even at the grocery store, but you have a nasty habit of always running away before I have a chance."

I sucked in a breath and grimaced. "Right. Soooo, have you learned anything about this weekend?" I quickly changed the subject as my cheeks heated up.

"Well, yeah. I learned I'm not taking a cheater," he chuckled, his eyes alight with humor.

I stuck my tongue out at him watching his fingers tousle through his hair, eliciting a very ill-timed feeling of arousal in my stomach. "My mom says they'll finalize plans hopefully by tomorrow night."

"Okay, keep me posted," I said, biting back the desire of needing his hands on me, and headed toward the dumbbells, feeling a thousand times lighter. At least he wasn't mad at me anymore.

Unable to resist a look over my shoulder at his hunched figure watching me walk away, I couldn't help but chuckle out loud. I couldn't believe he'd thought I was dating Noah and that had been the entire rift behind Griffin's confusing animosity.

But it also begged the question, why had it bothered him so much? Did he have certain feelings that annoyed him because he thought they were unrequited? A small spark flipped within my stomach, tickling hope at the edges of an idea I shouldn't even be chewing on.

Chapter 8

Alone in the classroom, the wall clock informed me with zero care that I was running a little behind, again. I entered the last grade update and logged out of my computer, feeling a little out of whack for not having to take responsibility for an entire class during an assembly. For the first time in my career, I had been asked to sit with other faculty members in the stands of the large gym instead. Standing, I smoothed out the wrinkles in my navy dress and ran a hand over the frizzy ends of my otherwise neatly-styled wavy hair, and checked for smudges on my glasses.

On the move, I used my phone camera as a mirror and dabbed some subtle lip gloss over my full lips. Our guests deserved the utmost respect I could give them, so I'd put in extra effort today with my clothes, even wearing a pair of low, closed-toed, chunky heels. They were white and matched well with my classy, but simple long-sleeved, ruffled dress.

It exuded a timeless appeal in my opinion, and several of my students commented that I looked extra nice today. How grateful I was, as well, for the effort that they'd all put in during the presentations in each class period. I had some hope after all that these kids understood or at least attempted to recognize the sacrifice that so many men and women make for the country that we live in.

My heels clicked up the stairs, echoing through the halls that were already bare as most of the students and staff had made their way to the recreation center. I slipped my phone in my pocket, and walked quickly, following the directions that Nancy had given me on my first day. As I neared the rec center, where a set of large, double red metal doors stood wide open, the hum of people chatting was underscored by a faint drum of music as it rolled into the hallway.

Stepping around the corner to my left, my phone buzzed in my pocket. As I pulled my cell out, a message flickered on the screen from an unknown number.

> *Got more details for this weekend. Chat after lifting?*

There wasn't even a name at the end, but I knew who'd just texted me. Griffin. Relief blanketed me. At least I wasn't going to be heading into this pretend relationship completely blind. Although, concerning personal details about him, I felt like I was.

Clicking to reply, I started to type out a message when I heard my name.

"Miss B!" Dayton shouted from behind me.

Turning, I saw him jog up. "Hey, Dayton. Why aren't you in the gym yet?" I responded with a smile, stopping beside a water fountain between massive trophy and picture cases.

"Because I owe you an answer," he said and then lowered his voice. "I was also thinking my brother would be less likely to say no to you if you asked him personally."

Backing away, I furrowed my brows. "What do you mean?"

"Miss B, I want you to meet my brother before the assembly begins," he said loudly, and tossed a thumb over his shoulder as two people rounded the corner, immersed in a conversation.

Nancy was wearing a nice pair of pearl earrings that matched her classy, black skirt and red blouse. She had her hand tucked in the elbow of her companion.

And my heart jumped in my throat as my eyes rested on the piercing gaze of none other than Griffin himself.

It took everything in me to not move a muscle, to not let my mouth fall open as Dayton ran up to his side and grinned. Nancy was beaming with pride as Griffin's face suddenly dropped the grin. Right before he turned into that all-too-familiar cold, expressionless statue, his eyes snapped wide with shock. He flexed his fingers next to his black uniform pants, sucking in air as Nancy pulled her grip from his elbow and brushed some lint off of the shoulder of his pristine Dress Blues.

A uniform that I recognized.

The peacoat-style navy jacket with those gold buttons fit him too perfectly, and the black necktie was expertly wrapped around his collar, but my eyes were drawn to the barrage of medals covering his left breast pocket. Above those, a golden insignia was pinned. An eagle, with its wings spread wide, held a trident and rifle in each claw, crossing in front of what looked like an anchor. I didn't know what it meant, seeing as I wasn't too versed in all the different specialties and whatnot of the military.

"Miss B, meet my brother Griffin Marsh. Or half-brother, technically." Dayton leaned closer to me and whispered, "Mom had him when she was sixteen." Then he grinned at his brother. "Griffin, this is the coolest history teacher I've ever had."

I forced a stiff smile to caress my cheeks, which were threatening to turn beet red at any moment. Pushing my glasses up my nose, I nodded formally. "Hello. Pleased to meet you."

Griffin stared at me, tight-lipped.

"It's her class that I want you to come to. After the assembly," Dayton added.

Nancy chuckled. "You're still on that? You really think that he will stand up in front of a class and speak?"

"Mom, you're not helping my case," Dayton hissed at Nancy.

I cleared my throat and approached the group, unable to break my gaze from Griffin. His eyes remained locked onto mine, but I couldn't read what he was feeling or thinking. I was simply doing everything in my power to maintain my composure. Things just got a hell of a lot more complicated. "Dayton says you have a few cool stories. Anything you've learned over the years would be insightful for my students." Swallowing stiffly, I lifted my chin slightly, trying to pretend like we'd never met before.

"Just a few? I'm pretty sure he has more than just a few cool stories with twenty years in the military," Nancy butted in, smiling proudly at her son as she straightened one of the other medals placed below the eagle insignia.

Griffin moved for the first time since seeing me. It was subtle, but I watched as he clenched his newly clean-shaven jaw and adjusted the white cover tucked beneath his arm, almost embarrassed by his mom's proud tone of voice and praise.

Griffin still hadn't said a word, and Dayton's hopeful expression faltered slightly as his eyes connected with the stoic expression of his brother.

"Twenty years?" I gasped, genuinely shocked. *How old was he?*

I glanced at my phone to hide my surprise.

"It's a long time, right? Now that he's served the full twenty years, his grandpa has really been pushing him to retire," Nancy continued.

An idea suddenly tumbled through my mind as his mom talked. My cell was still unlocked from the previous text I hadn't had time to respond to. His text. Quickly, I typed in three words and pressed send, hoping he'd be able to look at his phone.

"With that amount of time served, your knowledge will be invaluable." I lifted a taunting brow at Griffin. "Plus, it kind of sounds like you're being a chicken and are afraid of speaking in front of a few teenagers." I nodded toward my phone.

Dayton and his mother glanced at me, their jaws dropping open, and then back at Griffin.

"I wouldn't know what to say to them," he muttered, finally speaking.

"Yep, I was right. Sounds like you're scared of looking like a fool to me," I said again, and Dayton widened his eyes, a subtle horrified giggle escaping his throat.

"Not watching where you sit would be foolish." Griffin lifted a brow; his eyes glinted with a mischievousness that had that fire roaring low in my belly again. And I sucked in air through my teeth. How dare he bring that up. I saw him dig through his pocket and then drop his gaze to his phone. I hadn't heard anything; he must have kept it on vibrate.

Nancy's brows twitched, drawing closer in confusion as Dayton's eyes narrowed curiously, his teenage radar on full power.

"Well, good thing you won't be sitting when giving the speech," I bantered, and a smirk lifted on his lips as he stuffed the phone back in his pocket.

"Oh, so there would be someone to *hide me* while standing up front instead?"

That was low. I pursed my lips. "Chicken."

"Definitely not."

"*Bawk Bawk.*"

"I'm not scared of speaking in front of some teenagers." His eyes sparkled, competitiveness haunting his gaze. He was getting a kick out of this, and I couldn't lie, so was I.

"Oh, big tough guy, are we?" I taunted, and he raised a single brow but said nothing.

"*Bawk, bawk, bawk.*" I mimed a chicken again as Dayton began to laugh, and Nancy looked lost. Griffin shook his head and closed his eyes.

"Fine. I'll do it," he stated, and Dayton cheered.

"Knew you could do it. You're the best, Miss B! See you after the assembly." Dayton grinned, and Nancy shook her head, chuckling uncertainly. She mouthed 'thank you' to me as they passed by, leaving me standing in the now empty hallway, gobsmacked and wondering how on earth things could get so complicated so quickly.

The harsh reality of the complexity of everything settled over me. I'd done what had been necessary for my student, ignoring the information that I'd just been given that had changed everything.

Griffin was Dayton's half-brother. My student's sibling served in the military for twenty years, and that insignia had to hold some significance. I needed to google that to figure out what it meant, but that was for later. Right now, I was more concerned about the fact that he'd been in the military for twenty years. I wasn't even twenty years into adulthood. Assuming that, by strange happenstance, Griffin enlisted at seventeen, that would make him at least thirty-seven years old.

Ten years my senior. And he knew that. He knew how old I was, even when he kissed me. Yet he'd said *I* was robbing the cradle.

Slowly, I trekked toward the small, side entrance of the gym to the right of the large, crimson double doors that were wide open. Cracking it quietly as a hush fell over the gym, I snuck inside.

On the main floor of the gym, rows and rows of aluminum seats faced the stage and were filled by a sea of service men and women, who were all in full dress uniform. Family members were mixed in, standing out heavily amongst the pristine collection of veterans and active duty alike. Students sat on the opposite side of the gym, swamping the bleachers that rose two levels high and speckled the track that circled the gym on the second floor.

I quietly made my way around the railing and up the side of the bleachers on the right. Sifting through a few people, I found an open spot next to another teacher I'd made acquaintance with on my second day of school. Amy grinned and patted the space beside her as I parked my bum.

WHAT I SHOULD HAVE SAID

While my body was physically present at the assembly, my mind was somewhere else. The man that I was pretending to be dating this weekend also happened to be a colleague's son and a student's brother.

Would this not be awkward for Dayton, and also Nancy? Didn't I have a moral obligation to disclose? Though, technically this was fake and would only last for a weekend.

Also, how could Griffin be comfortable lying to them? Now he was expecting *me* to lie to people I knew as well. Plus, my head could not move past his age, assuming it was correct. I kept plugging in the math over and over on my phone's calculator.

Again and again, using addition, subtraction, multiplication, and division. Every sort of math tool I remembered from my college days, I used to try and get a different answer. Every time it was the same. That was assuming he was seventeen twenty years ago. He could very well have been eighteen, which made it even more dizzying.

"Jane," a whisper pierced my ear.

"Hmmm?" I mumbled, staring at the thirty-seven that was blaring up from my phone.

"No matter how you put those numbers in, the answer is always the same," Amy quietly said beside me, which only made my stomach sink deeper.

She was right. Besides, Griffin and I were both very much consenting adults.

My phone buzzed, an alert popping up at the top of my phone.

> *I'll stay after so we can talk.*

From Griffin again. He hadn't acknowledged my message about being in his debt, but it also wasn't him ignoring it. If I played it right, maybe I could get out of owing him a second favor, and then after this weekend, everything would go back to normal. Except there was a part of me that knew it never could. I quickly typed a response.

> *You've spent a long time in the military, so what's so bad about retiring?*

My finger hovered over the send button. Was this even appropriate to ask? At some point we would need to exchange life details, but were we there yet? I hadn't even known his last name until today, or that he had served for twenty years, or that Dayton was his brother. I still didn't know his favorite color, or something as simple as his age.

Shaking my head, I erased the message and locked my phone. That was entirely too personal to ask, even if I was curious why he wasn't. Though, now that I knew all of this, the events at the antique store made a whole lot more sense.

Somehow, I found myself flowing with the sea of people as the assembly let out. My feet dragged me back to my classroom while I continued to chew on my thoughts. This wasn't happening. Not on top of everything else. Life wasn't supposed to be this convoluted. Not since I'd already lost my father. Everything was supposed to feel numb and empty, wasn't it?

Chapter 9

About half of the students had returned from the assembly by the time I made it back to my classroom. I smiled brightly, trying to shovel the thoughts that were consuming me to the side. They weren't important right now. Three other veterans in full military dress uniforms sat beside their kids, each beaming with pride.

The fact that Dayton and Griffin weren't here yet gave me a smidgeon of time to regain my composure. So, I approached Becca's father who was an Army Lieutenant Colonel and engaged in small talk while we waited as students continued to filter inside.

My peripheral vision caught a towering shadow cross the door frame about ten minutes later, and I wasn't the only one who noticed it. Almost every head turned as Dayton walked in with Griffin tagging silently behind. He had a naturally commanding presence, which I could see the other veterans pick up on as the Lieutenant Colonel beside me even raised his brows at his entrance. His gaze slipped across Griffin's medals and insignia, and the Lieutenant Colonel's eyes widened.

Griffin, however, simply scanned his surroundings, met my gaze for half a second, slid a chair beside Dayton's desk, and stretched out his legs.

The room fell quiet; those who continued speaking did so in hushed tones. I couldn't stop staring. His aura had always carried confidence, but this was different. A silent dominance that I'd only heard of but never experienced until now.

Or maybe I only felt it was different because I knew more now.

With a deep breath, I quietly excused myself and walked to the front of the class. It was completely silent by the time I was facing everyone, and the few students who weren't in their seats immediately returned. Girls consistently glanced between each other and then back at Griffin, who was leaning back in his seat, legs crossed at the ankles, arms loosely folded. He looked like a bored movie star. I swallowed dryly and agreed with the girls. I kept looking too.

"I'm quite surprised most of you didn't just play hooky after the assembly," I began, and it earned a few chuckles. "Though I am excited that you didn't. This has probably been my favorite day of the year so far."

"You've been here for a week and a half, Miss B," Dayton teased, and all of the girls giggled.

"Very true. So, you guys better step it up if the guests are more entertaining than you are," I responded quickly, and Dayton rolled his eyes as all of his friends taunted him and slugged his arm. Griffin even managed to crack a small smile before tucking his chin toward his chest.

"So, who wants to go first?" I continued, and Dayton's arm shot in the air.

"My brother will." He grinned, and Griffin actually paled a little. He shook his head subtly, but Dayton seemed oblivious.

A couple of girls blushed and giggled, glancing between each other and Griffin. Sitting beside his little brother, I could see the similarities now. Same eye shape, even a similar facial structure.

"Come on up." I waved at Griffin and quietly walked toward my desk. This was going to be so entertaining, and I was glad I was here for it. He lifted awkwardly out of the small chair and trudged to the front. Despite his large frame, each footstep barely made a sound. That was how he seemed to have appeared out of nowhere back at the store. His trained silence, stalking up the aisle, flashed an image of him barreling at my captor.

My heart raced wildly in my chest and my skin flushed. Was a man supposed to be this…intimidating?

Once he was at the front, he shot me a glance that told me I was in trouble for this, and then he faced the group. He didn't say anything for a moment as stray giggles echoed throughout the room.

"Uh, I don't really know what I'm supposed to say. Dayton and your lovely Miss B roped me into this last minute," he began uncomfortably and ran a hand over the back of his neck. "I'm Griffin and have been in the military for the past twenty years. I'm currently a Navy SEAL waiting for my next set of orders."

My mouth fell open. Navy fucking SEAL? The insignia. The Trident. No wonder even the Lieutenant Colonel noticed his dominance. Or maybe it had to do with all of the medals and whatnot pinned beneath that.

Griffin stopped and lifted his shoulders slightly, glancing at me in question.

"Go on," I urged, covering up my shock with the prompting.

"Yeah! Tell us more," one girl called, and then she clamped a hand over her mouth as her face flushed. It was the cute redhead that Dayton constantly flirted with.

"Like what?" he muttered, and it took everything in me to stop myself from making a smart ass comment. He was nervous. Griffin hadn't broken a sweat when he killed those robbers. Or when his own life had been threatened. But in this moment, the back of his neck was beginning to glisten.

"How about why you enlisted in the first place?" I prompted instead with a soft smile.

"I was seventeen. At the time, it felt like I only had two choices. They were either enlist in the military or enlist in the military." His brows furrowed. "I grew up here like most of you. There isn't too much to do, and while it's a good town and relatively safe, it also doesn't lead to many prospects after high school. My mom was a single mom at the time, and we were dirt poor. I hadn't given two shits about—" he winced as giggles erupted. "Sorry." Griffin glanced at me, and I nodded for him to continue. "I hadn't cared about grades because I worked after-school and weekend jobs through most of high school, just trying to make sure we had food on the table the next day."

He paused. "So, my options were the military or the military. I'm happy. It didn't turn out too bad for me. But my advice to all of you is to give yourselves more of a choice than I did. Pay attention in school. Study hard. Then, if you still want to join, do it."

Griffin stopped talking and clenched his cover in his fingers, guardedly. The cute redhead, Marcy, raised her hand. He looked at me again, confused.

"Yes, Marcy?" I said, and she grinned.

"Tell us an actual story. You're a Navy SEAL and have all those medals and stuff on your uniform, so like that's the coolest thing ever. I've seen you guys on TV and in movies. You must have done some awesome things. You know, like going after a bad guy or whatever. Your motivating speech was nice, but I'm pretty sure Miss B wants something history-related," she sweetly said, and I bit back the smile.

"Uh," he paused, clenching his jaw, and muttered under his breath. "I'd rather be blowing up a terrorist's house right now."

I snorted, unable to contain my reaction as the students' mouths fell open in tandem.

"Everyone heard that, didn't they?" he grumbled, and I sucked in my lips, nodding.

Clearing his throat, he took a deep breath. "Obviously, this is not my forte. Speaking in front of students is entirely different from commanding a mission. Most of what I've done is classified, and the other stuff isn't appropriate for teenagers."

Glancing at Dayton, I watched his shoulders sag. And Griffin noticed it too.

The Lieutenant Colonel cleared his throat, and every pair of eyes snapped to him. "Just leave out some gory details, Commander. Maybe talk about whatever mission gave you one of those medals hanging on your chest."

Dayton's eyes brightened as his Navy SEAL brother gave a curt, respectful nod. I highly doubted what was about to come out of Griffin's mouth related to history at all, but I wasn't going to stop him.

"I'd been a SEAL for just a year when I got this one. It's the Global War on Terrorism Expeditionary Medal." He tapped one of his medals on the second row. "So, I wasn't a commander, but rather at the bottom of the pecking order. We were at a classified location in Afghanistan going after a…a classified guy who did some seriously fu—" He stopped himself and grunted. "He did some really gross things that had landed him the title of a terrorist and the United States' next high-value target. We learned of our mission and executed it in under two hours."

Silence spread across the room as everyone glanced at each other.

"That's it?" Marcy called out, and a mischievous grin spread across Griffin's face.

"That's all I can tell you. Let's just say that the bad guy is dead, and the good guys made it home in time for dinner."

The ominous, very vague story must have done it because a relieved grin crept onto Dayton's face. Everyone except Marcy, who opened her mouth to speak, seemed satisfied as well. Until a figure flitted across the doorway. A small, brief shadow filled the frame, and it didn't grab anyone else's attention except mine.

And Griffin's.

"Come on!" Marcy urged as I stared at the blond-haired man peeking around the corner displaying a stomach-curdling grin. Sam had somehow found me.

A quick glance at Griffin showed his mischievous smile had disappeared beneath a calculating mask, his eyes now drilling Sam with the laser focus of a Belgian Malinois. My skin prickled, fear bubbling through my veins. He'd found me. Again. How did he know I was here? And why was he here of all places? What was he intending to do?

The sickening smile slid from Sam's face as he belatedly noted Griffin's presence and his predatory stance beside me at the front of the class, eyes raking over his towering frame encased in Navy Dress Blues. Whatever stage fright had been holding onto Griffin immediately dissipated as he watched the figure that was now gaining more than just our attention.

The timbre of his voice lowered as he addressed the room but kept his warning glare on Sam.

"We went in, covered by the dark of a moonless night. Orders were to leave no survivors, not one. Six of us against an entire camp full of an unknown number of assailants." Griffin's voice fell deeper still, the threatening tone growling a warning through the classroom. Their enthralled silence blanketed Sam who hadn't moved a muscle, captured by Griffin's darkened gaze. It felt surreal, like watching an apex predator about to pounce.

"The house was built on the shore of a black lake that was ice cold even in the middle of summer. We dove under, the water numbing every sense in our bodies despite the wetsuits. As swiftly and silently as the death we were there to deliver, we stroked forward, breaking through the surface with not a ripple to be seen. We reached a massive stone wall that rose toward the starless night sky. Silent as shadows, we scaled the barrier that surrounded the house. My knife slit through the throats of two enemies before they even knew I was there," Griffin continued, his voice flat, his stare full of icy intensity.

He had morphed into death itself.

"My team and I breached the entrance, and, within two minutes, found our target. He was neutralized without a scream. The entire undisclosed compound was painted red by the time we were done. Most details of this mission are classified, but just note that the operation was such a success that remaining enemy combatants thought it was an inside job and they ended up turning on each other. Gutting each other like pigs at slaughter."

Griffin paused. Nobody moved, including Sam who remained frozen like stone in the doorframe. And then he slunk back, picking up the undercurrent directed at him.

As if some new magical exoskeleton appeared, a hardened exterior of someone who faced death and laughed in its face cloaked Griffin. Almost taking pleasure in the look on Sam's face while recounting this story.

Griffin spoke again, emotionless, unmistakable venom directed at the man who was stalking me. "I can make death look like an accident. Like it was a cheating spouse. Like it was the side piece, a jealous kid, or leave so little that there are no suspects and not a body part left to put in a fucking wooden box to send home to your mommy."

I followed the line of his cold stare. Sam couldn't seem to look away despite his trembling. Griffin had unpacked him completely. Had a captivating, obliterating, hold on him, and I knew. This story wasn't for the kids in the room, but a chilling warning. He was threatening the very man who had clearly passed the realm of creeper. He had exposed the coward.

"Be very careful what you do next," Griffin hissed, and Sam flinched. A split-second later, he turned tail and fled. The world around me resumed, time whirring to its original speed as I watched him flee, left with another reason to be grateful Griffin had been around. Instead of it feeling inconvenient, I was happy he was here. It was oddly relieving.

And a little terrifying. Owing Griffin felt more weighted now. More... bound.

"That. Was. Sick," Marcy exclaimed, snapping me out of the intense mental battle I'd been locked in.

"Okay, class," I butted in, noticing the wide-eyed looks of a few of the parents. My heart was racing like a horse in my chest, though I wasn't sure if it was still racing from being afraid of Sam's presence, from Griffin protecting me again, or the possibility of a rebuke from the principal if any parent reported this.

"Don't glorify it," Griffin quickly grunted. "It's still killing people. Even if it is bad people."

I pushed my glasses back up the bridge of my nose. "Exactly. Any more questions?"

"Yeah! Do you have a girlfriend?" Marcy cheekily called out, earning a glare from Dayton.

"He's old, Marcy. That's gross," Jackson said. Dayton glanced at the thin but tall boy who was his sidekick and nodded aggressively.

"When I turn eighteen it won't be," she sassed in response and batted her eyes at Griffin.

"Any *other* questions?" I stepped in again.

"Really, though. Do you have a girlfriend?" one of Marcy's friends asked.

"Guys. That's not—"

"I do." Griffin quickly cut me off. Whispers danced around the room, and he refused to glance my way. A shiver stole down my spine. How could he just announce that in front of everyone? Our as yet undeclared fake relationship, for the purpose of one weekend, was becoming more complicated by the moment. We had enough to deal with concerning his brother and mom, how could he add this?

I thought he wanted peace, just like I did.

"Alright, thank you for sharing your story," I said, unintentional iciness slipping in my words.

But he either didn't notice or chose not to respond as he stalked to his seat at the back of the class and sat next to his brother. I was grateful the Lieutenant Colonel stood up volunteering to go next. The rest of the visitors were vastly more prepared than Griffin's off-the-cuff delivery, and their stories were more rehearsed, though I struggled to pay attention. My mind was absolutely swimming with everything that was muddying the supposed calm life I moved to.

Chapter 10

"I need to...apologize to your teacher. I'll meet you later," Griffin said to Dayton as everyone was leaving. Quick thank-yous and praises were given to me as my students slowly exited.

"Why didn't you tell me you had a girlfriend? Or Mom? Or at least your dad?" Dayton asked, shocked, and Griffin tightened his jaw.

"It's all new, so I—"

"No. You weren't afraid to tell the entire class but couldn't tell your brother in private first?" Dayton crossed his arms, in mimicry of how Griffin looked when he got scary, but it only lasted for a second before he grinned.

"What?" Griffin questioned, confused.

"You should bring her to the reunion this weekend. Mom will be so excited! Plus, nobody would try to marry you off again." Dayton jigged in place as Griffin chuckled.

Marry him off? Again? As in more than once?

"Go." He put a hand on his brother's head and tried to guide him out of the room.

"Oh come on. Even if you two break up afterward, it'd be a good test to see if she's worth it anyway," Dayton pressed, fighting against his brother's grip.

"Go. Your crush is getting away." Griffin wiggled his brows and subtly nodded toward Marcy. Dayton shot his brother a dirty look but turned around and scurried out after Marcy.

I sat at my desk and pretended to busy myself with work as the classroom became silent and empty, leaving me alone with Griffin, who hung back in the shadows. It wasn't until even the hallway was completely quiet that he straightened from leaning against the wall and emerged from the darkness, arms folded.

Glancing over the top of my glasses, I watched and waited. He cocked his head curiously, evidently expecting a dressing down as I said as emotionlessly as possible, "We have a *lot* to talk about." Yes, I was very grateful for what he did concerning Sam, but I was more swallowed up in apprehension for this weekend.

He nodded and walked toward me, sitting on top of the desk directly beside me. I continued to type on my computer, trying to buy myself more time and ignoring the warm, hulky body near me.

"Something of an understatement, considering the circumstances," he agreed. Griffin leaned back and casually studied the classroom. He knew I was stalling but didn't push it.

"So, start," I said shortly.

"Huh?" he asked, furrowing his brows, and I spun in my chair, pushing some hair behind one ear.

Going all "Miss B" on him, I gave him an earful. "You accused me of robbing the cradle when you thought I was dating someone seven years younger than me. You're thirty-seven. No matter how you do the math, that's ten years older than me. TEN YEARS!" I shouted as he folded his arms defensively.

"I know," he drawled

"And you still kissed me?"

"*We* kissed."

"Shut it. I'm talking," I snapped, and he leaned back once more. "You kissed me knowing how old I was and asked for me to pretend to be your girlfriend." I raked my hair. "Also, there is no way that's happening now that I know that Dayton is your brother and Nancy is your mom."

"Why not?"

"What would everyone think? He's my student, and your mom is my colleague. It might even get me in trouble, and I can't have that sort of attention." I stood up from my desk and marched around to him. He lifted a single brow as I fumed in anger and hissed low through my teeth. "Do you know how awkward and complicated that's going to make things? I already have enough to deal with, and it's not like we can just up and move again if I fuck shit up here!"

Griffin's surprised expression would have amused me in any other circumstances as the wheels turned in his head. But he quickly became intrigued. "And why exactly *did* your family move here?"

"That's not the point, Griffin," I argued, which he found amusing as he chuckled. "Don't laugh. How can you continue to lie to your family? Especially now, because you're also forcing me to lie to people I know as well."

"Sometimes lies are necessary," he firmly stated.

"Griffin, this is not one of your missions!"

"Obviously." Griffin sighed and uncrossed his arms. "Have you never experienced a time where a lie protected someone you loved?"

"You can tell yourself that, but the only person you're lying to is yourself. The truth always finds a way out," I snapped. Everything was coming to a head, and I was exhausted by all the lies and secrets. I'd experienced enough of them growing up because of my father's occupation, ones that had protected my family. And now, lies and secrets seemed to gather around me like a rolling stone collected moss.

He shook his head, looking down at the tile. "As a kid, there is no gray area when it comes to telling the truth or not, but as an adult, you know it's not really that straightforward," he continued. "Look, I don't like the idea of dragging you into this, but please."

"How does this lie protect your family?" I asked pointedly. His eyes glazed over for a moment, lost somewhere in a world I probably didn't want to experience.

He didn't answer, and silence lingered uncomfortably, wordlessly informing me that it hadn't been my place to ask.

"Thank you, by the way," I quietly added, splitting the stillness. His eyes returned to mine. He furrowed his brows. "For what you did when Sam appeared."

"What's his deal anyway?" Griffin asked, and I shrugged.

"It's a long story," I muttered.

"I've got plenty of time."

Filling my lungs with a breath of confidence, I decided to just tell him. "He hit me because I refused to kiss him."

"He did what?" Griffin snarled.

"How about this: a story for a story?"

He nodded.

"Sam constantly asked me out on dates, but I always said no. Eventually, word spread around, and people began telling me *I* was the ass for refusing him because he was a 'nice guy.' So, I caved. Despite my gut instinct, I agreed to a date. During dinner, he ordered *for* me, never let me speak, and then afterwards told me, since he did such a nice thing for me by paying for the food, I had to kiss him. I told him in no uncertain terms, no. So, he slapped me across my cheek. My dad didn't raise a wimp, so I slugged him in the nose and shut my apartment door in his face."

"Nice." Griffin grinned, and I couldn't help a laugh.

"Anyway, he wouldn't leave me alone after that. Constantly apologizing for slapping me and then turning it back on me, telling me I needed to apologize for hitting him. He touched himself in front of me at one point and followed me everywhere I went."

Griffin's eyes widened, and he tipped his chin toward me. "Again, he did what? That's fucking gross. Please tell me you called the cops or something."

I slunk back and leaned my bum against the lip of my desk. "I had no proof that he stuck his hands in his pants by the time I dialed 9-1-1. Probably the only nice thing about moving was the fact that I would leave him behind and he'd have no idea where I was going," I finished. "Which leaves me concerned, seeing as he followed me. Showing up so quickly after moving here, there's no way he found out by happenstance. There couldn't be."

"Are you in witness protection or something? You said your dad was in the FBI and what not," he asked, and I shook my head no.

"Your turn."

"Oh, come on. Just answer that one question and then I'll tell you something," he prodded, and I rolled my eyes.

"My dad was killed in the line of duty, and because of the case he'd been working on, the FBI recommended we move just for an extra precaution. They don't have any indication that we are in danger, but it was high profile enough my mom also thought it was best."

"Makes sense." His face softened. "Alright, ask something."

I looked away. Where to start? What to ask? What was worth knowing? "Okay, why won't you retire? It's been twenty years."

He shook his head. Slowly at first and then more vigorously. "Ask anything else," he said. "Please." The element of vulnerability in his voice caused me to widen my eyes in surprise. He was always in control, always fully in charge. Even when he'd been nervous in front of the class, he was a picture of stoicism. Now he was practically begging me to not dig at that wound.

"Why are you single?" I asked and winked.

He plopped his cover on his lap and leaned back against the palm of his hands. "My last girlfriend cheated."

I waited.

"Four words? That's it?"

Griffin pursed his lips and narrowed his hunter eyes.

I wiggled my brows, and he shook his head slowly, chuckling to himself. "Fine. It's not exactly easy being with someone who's gone for months if not years at a time and comes back unable to share what they've been doing. Five years ago, my girlfriend at the time cheated. I had another one before her that was nice enough to at least break up with me instead of cheating. After that, other than some casual relationships between orders, I've had nothing serious. I simply find it far easier being on my own," he countered and waited for my reaction.

"Not every woman is like your exes were. There were a couple times that the case my dad was working on took him away from our home for a few months at a time. My dad was my mom's everything, and she patiently waited for him to come home and loved him enough to trust him while he was gone," I quietly replied. He gently smiled, a small recognition of his pain, and then his eyes became soft.

But not quite as soft as they'd been after he saved me at the store.

"Is it just your mom and brother now?" he asked, and I nodded. "I'm sorry about your dad."

"Me too," I whispered. My pulse was racing, yet I felt calm at the same time. It was confusing and exhilarating all at once.

We sat in comfortable silence, communicating a thousand things without saying a word.

Eventually, I sighed and spoke. "So, how is this weekend going to work?"

"Right," he muttered. "I figured we could say we met at the gym, so it's a new relationship, and it'll make it easier to keep the facts straight."

"That's not what I meant, but that works." I chuckled, and he glared teasingly at me. "Though you better not bring up what happened at the gym. No one needs to know."

"Why not?" He grinned like a giddy teenager, and I shook my head.

"That's not part of the deal."

"You made me stand up in front of your class."

"I do that everyday; it's not that scary."

"Teenagers are terrifying."

"*Bawk, bawk, bawk.*" I clucked at him.

"Well, I guess I'll just tell everyone that we met when you sat on my face in the gym then."

"You wouldn't dare." I pushed off of the desk and stepped closer to him.

"Try me." He stood, towering over me. "It would make our relationship believable, considering it's been a long time since I've let a girl sit on my face."

"So, *that's* your thing." Refusing to act shocked, I gave him a crooked grin instead.

"You'd like it," he said, his voice lowering.

"Except, apparently it's been so long, I bet you've forgotten how to eat out properly," I responded without hesitation.

"Want to find out? Because all that time without has left me with quite the appetite," he answered in kind, and, with coal rolling hot and warm deep within my core, my eyes flickered to his lips. The same lips that had kissed me only two days ago. Passionately and with perfection. They were soft, and I could smell the hint of sweetness that I'd once tasted on his mouth that was oh so close once more.

I merely had to tip onto my toes and lean forward to claim him, and they would be pressed against mine. I could already taste his tongue, feel his hands against my skin and—

My cheeks flushed red as he cleared his throat.

Griffin perched back on the desk.

What was that? Spinning around, I blinked and slapped my cheeks a couple times. That was obvious flirting, was it not? No, it was just practice for selling the story this weekend. Yes, that was it. Weak-kneed, I found my chair and sat staring at my computer screen, unable to look him in the face.

"We should, um, go over basics. You know, like, uh…favorite colors," I stammered, struggling to speak coherently as I tried to calm my heart and quench the fire that had begun to brew in my core.

"Yeah. Definitely," Griffin muttered, and I glanced his way. His jaw was clenched tightly, and he stared at the painting at the back of my class. "I like blue. Really any shade of blue, but I prefer dark blue most of the time."

I nodded, still in a daze over everything that was happening. "Plum. Like a medium plum color is mine," I managed to say, and finally Griffin brought his eyes toward me.

"You look different today," he said, tilting his head and studying me.

"Well, I do shower once in a while. So that's probably it," I teased, lightening the mood, and was glad when he chuckled, breaking whatever strange yet not entirely uncomfortable tension had slowly filled the room.

"That's always good."

"Why do you always wear a hoodie at the gym?" I blurted out, and he blinked, taken aback by my question.

"What?"

"You always have a black hoodie on. The one with the gym logo on it. You're clearly a strong and muscley guy, so why would you always hide it? Especially when you have a pump?" I explained, gesturing toward him.

"Have you been checking me out?" he teased with a little nod.

"No. Of course not"

Yes!

"You've totally been checking me out."

"And you're totally giving me a headache." I pulled my lips into a thin line, and he grinned wider.

"How so?" he asked, his brows wiggling.

"Since I've known you, I've been riding the world's worst roller-coaster. After the robbery, you were nice to me. You saved my life. The next you're all cold and pissed. Then you kissed me and then were upset again, accusing me of cheating. Now you're being nice again. So, how long do I have to wait until next time you're mad?"

"Well, if you were better at communicating, we wouldn't have had all of those mix-ups."

"And if you didn't assume things, it wouldn't have gone like that."

"I didn't assume for very long but, had I not, I might not have kissed you."

"Which you'd obviously be bummed about."

"And you wouldn't."

"Exactly."

He shook his head, a light smile upon his handsome face. His beautiful eyes twinkled. "If that's what you have to tell yourself."

I rolled my eyes for the hundredth time and began whirling in circles on my chair. "So, back to the original reason that you're here. What'd you learn?"

He watched me as I spun. "They've rented an Airbnb in Bear Lake. The Utah side, actually. We'll leave Friday, I guess once you're done with work, and come back Sunday."

I planted both feet on the ground and stared at my messy whiteboard. "What?! I thought this was like a couple-of-hours-on-Saturday type thing."

"Me too," he murmured, and I slapped my palms violently on my desk.

"Nope. Not happening. I am NOT staying overnight with someone I just met."

"Oh come on. Again, have you forgotten that you've already sat on my face?"

Enough was enough, and I shot out of my chair, fists ready to slam against his chest. I knew it was an overreaction, but I couldn't help it. As I swung toward him with all of my might, he caught my wrist. So, I threw my left, and he clamped around that one, too, letting me wriggle like a worm on a hook.

"Stop."

"No." I gritted my teeth and rolled my wrists, trying to slide them from his hands that swamped mine. I was strong, but he was stronger.

"Jane. Stop," he said again, his voice light as he chuckled.

"Let. Me. Go." I grunted, shoving as hard as I could against his grip, and this time he twisted me around and pulled me hard against his torso. I crashed against him and no longer was I the only one breathing heavily.

I could feel the tension in his body vibrating through the both of us. Holding me tightly, he swamped my entire figure.

I squirmed in his grip, a girlish giggle full of frustration and humor rising in my throat.

"Stop, smart ass," he teased, his gravelly voice tickling me close above my ear as I pushed uselessly against his hands that were cradling my arms upon my body.

"This is a very unfair fight." I tried one more time, but was barely able to move a muscle. So I stopped fighting him and listened.

His breath rhythmically brushed across my left ear, and his heart beat fast but steady against my back as my chest rose and fell rapidly. Despite knowing that I had no chance of standing my ground against him, I wasn't afraid. If I had been serious and wanted him to let go, I somehow just knew he would.

Slowly, his grip relaxed around my wrists, but his arms remained around me, swallowing me in his once again exhilarating scent of citrus. Savoring the heady sensation of him still and unmoving against me, I didn't try to shuffle away. I didn't want to. The muffled ticks from the clock mounted on the wall cascaded around us, but it was his breath, his heart that I was listening to. The sound of it ignited every suppressed sense of desire, arousal creeping through my core like a hot coal on a summer bonfire night. Maybe this weekend wasn't going to be so terrible. Plus, getting away meant even more distance between Sam and me.

"If it makes you that uncomfortable, I'll get you a hotel or something," he whispered, but I slowly shook my head. No. I wanted him close, no matter how rocky of a start we were off to.

"We aren't sharing a bed, though," I quietly answered, and feeling his chuckle in response.

"A floor is not the worst thing I've slept on."

"I bet there is a couch you can take," I answered and stepped half an inch forward, creating just enough room to turn around and face him.

"Sometimes, even a couch is too comfortable," he muttered laconically, as I lifted my eyes to meet his. They were heavy, his sculpted features etched with a burden that he had long been carrying on his own.

Without thinking, I reached up and traced his jawline with my fingers. Just as I had when we kissed. Drifting gently along his skin, I brushed my touch across his brows, the tension in his face slowly melting away. He closed his eyes as I let my hand fall back to my side. This man carried the weight of the world. And even though it seemed to be burning around him in a way I didn't understand, he kept the flames to himself. In a way I also couldn't make sense of.

"You should probably go before Dayton or your mom gets suspicious," I whispered, breaking the silence. He blinked lazily and ran his tongue across his lips.

"Yeah, I probably should. Still gotta hit the gym," he winked and gave me a pained smile.

"Watch where you lay down next time, I can't have another girl sitting on my fake boyfriend's face until after we fake break up," I teased, and he shook his head, smiling.

"And you watch where you sit down. I don't want to beat up another guy because my fake girlfriend wasn't watching whose face she decided to sit on." He shoved his hands in his pockets and gave me a final smile before turning toward the door.

"I didn't decide to sit on your face, Griffin! It was an accident!" I cried out as he exited the classroom.

"Whatever you say, smart ass," I heard him say as he disappeared into the hallway.

Chapter 11

Noah pulled into the parking lot at the gym, my heart thrilling in nervous anticipation of seeing Griffin.

Jumping down from the truck along with my brother, I followed quietly behind him. Noah had glared at me in suspicion several times on the drive here. As soon as he shoved the door open, he faced me and squinted his eyes.

"What's up with you today?" he demanded, blocking my path to enter the gym.

"Nothing?" I responded. But that wasn't entirely truthful. There was more on my mind than even this intimidating weekend that was quickly approaching. Griffin had consumed all my thoughts, and in such a way that left me utterly confused. Part of me was waiting for the rollercoaster ride of him becoming annoyed again, while another part of me was craving something entirely different. Something more personal, an intimate secret that I would carry to my grave at all costs.

He'd upset the balance of things enough already.

"You're not a very good liar, you know that?" Noah replied, raising a brow and turned around. He scanned his pass and entered the busy gym.

"How so?" I snapped defensively, trotting after him.

"Your voice becomes really high-pitched," he nonchalantly answered. "Now shoo, I'm finishing my workout today." Noah disappeared as quickly as he could, leaving me alone before something else ruined his lifting session.

I scanned the gym, hopeful that I would see Griffin but also praying that I wouldn't.

My eyes landed on his hooded figure in the corner of the gym, doing some pull ups. I watched for a moment, impressed by how easy he was making those pull ups look, and once again wondering why he hadn't answered my question about his hoodie. Despite how strong I was, that specific exercise was the death of me.

I hated to admit it, but I could stand here all day and watch him do that.

Shoving my purple headphones on, I turned the music up loud and got to work. During the entire lifting session, Griffin and I made eye contact several times. We stared at each other for a bit but never once approached the other. I wasn't really sure why, but there didn't seem to be this intense need to converse with him.

Just catching him watching me was enough.

Me looking at him was enough.

On the drive back home, Noah wouldn't stop talking. Poking and prodding at why I hadn't talked to Griffin. "Every time we've been to the gym, you and sweaty hottie have had at least one conversation. But not today," he accusingly said.

"Well, wasn't that a delightful change then?" I murmured in response.

He pursed his lips and shook his head. "How disappointing."

"If you like him so much, then why didn't you go talk to him?" I shot back and turned away, becoming lost in intrusive thoughts that invaded the sweet ones of Griffin. A blond-haired man with a disgusting smile poking his head around the corner of my classroom kept sweeping aside Griffin's intriguing smile and the whisper of his touch.

My stomach twisted in knots over this upcoming weekend, wondering how Dayton and Nancy would react when we showed up as a couple. Especially when we inevitably "broke up." I worried that it wouldn't be Griffin's heart that would break, but his mom's and brother's hearts. Not because they liked me, but because it would mean that he was alone again.

Part of me was saddened by the knowledge that Griffin wasn't exactly a strong believer in love, to the point where he felt more comfortable being alone. To him, that was easiest. He held everyone at arm's length, including his family. And he seemed hell-bent on believing that no matter how true and pure love was, it wasn't forever.

Nothing lasts forever, I knew that too well. But I also believed that the pain that came from a great love was worth it. It had been worth it for my parents. I had felt that from my father in the way he treated my mom. How blissful and sweet was a love that also brought such immense pain.

My shoulders collapsed with the weight of all the worry, and sighing, I waited for Noah to turn the engine off before climbing out and meandering into the house. Our mom was quietly humming to herself as she finished cooking dinner. Leaving her to it, I trotted down the stairs and tossed my gym bag into the corner of my room.

In my mirror, a disheveled apparition stared back. My hair stuck out at strange angles from the messy bun I'd wrapped it in. My face was red from exertion, and a few of my old acne scars were glaringly evident upon my cheeks. My light-colored lashes looked nonexistent without mascara, with the added effect of making my pale-gray eyes look even larger and rounder.

This was a face that desired love, yet I wasn't sure I was deserving of what my parents had. Of what I craved. All the horrible names I'd once been called in high school came flooding back. Strange. Pizza face. Bug eyes. How odd that I could go from feeling so confident and sure of myself to feeling like absolute dog shit in minutes.

My eyes drifted to the picture of my dad. I needed him now more than ever, and he wasn't here. Unexpectedly, the weight sitting on my shoulders crumpled me to the floor, and self-pity overwhelmed me. It wasn't supposed to be my responsibility to take care of my mom. I wasn't supposed to eventually walk down the aisle at my wedding alone.

But this was the life that I was living, and I had to accept it. Sitting up, I rammed positive thoughts into my head. This life here in Idaho was my new reality. All of these strange things that had happened over the past couple weeks were my new life. I can and must be strong for my mom and Noah.

Getting to my feet and peering at my reflection, I made myself reconsider that those features I'd once been teased about weren't that ugly after all. I bared my teeth in a smile. Out loud, I told the girl with the soft cheeks and pretty smile that she was a badass—strong as an ox, smarter than many, and muscular in all the right places—and she should never forget that. The confidence that my dad had constantly drilled into me flooded back in full-force. He was gone, but what he taught me didn't have to be.

Bounding out of my room, I took the stairs two at a time and waltzed into the kitchen. After sliding across the floor in my socks, I skidded to a stop between my mom and Noah as they were sitting at the dining table, which halted their conversation.

"What *is* going on with you today?" Noah asked, raising a brow.

"I was overwhelmed with all sorts of things and also sad about Dad. But I'm good now. And I'm going away this weekend." I grinned and spun around in a circle. "Okay, that's all!"

The stunned look on both my mom's and Noah's faces was quite satisfying.

"Going away?" my mom stammered.

"Since when?" Noah asked, bewildered, mashed potatoes slopping from his fork.

"Hmmm. Since I was invited two days ago. Anyway, I'll be leaving straight after work on Friday and be back home on Sunday."

"Where to?" my mom asked carefully, setting her fork down and crossing her arms.

"Bear Lake. Utah side," I answered with a smile.

"With who?" Noah poked his fork in my direction.

"Are you sure it's safe?" my mom butted in before I was able to answer Noah's question.

"Of course. Mom, I'm not going very far, and again, the FBI hasn't heard a whisper that we are targets of the cartel from Dad's case. You said I should be going out on the weekend, so now I am." I clapped my hands together and skipped away.

"COME BACK HERE!" Noah shouted.

"Jane, I'm not finished asking questions!" My mom called after me, but I rushed down the stairs as quickly as I could. Avoiding having to come up with a story about who I was going with had been my top priority, and I had been successful. Now to just continue to evade that question until I left on Friday.

Chapter 12

It was extra cold this morning, and a light dusting of snow was finally falling. I ducked into my car, leaving extra early to avoid any questions from my mom or Noah concerning this weekend. And, because of everything that happened yesterday at school, I'd forgotten some papers that I was supposed to grade, so I needed extra time to get those done this morning.

Pulling the door closed, I turned over the engine to warm it. Brushing a few snowflakes from my hair, I checked my reflection in the mirror. The brightness was back in my eyes, and my mascara was expertly applied. My imperfections did not make me ugly; no, they were unique. Imperfections, I told myself, make us human.

I brushed a hand over my patchwork jumpsuit and tugged at the collar of my white turtleneck that I'd paired with it. Strange was also okay with me because I felt pretty in this outfit. Backing out of my drive, I found temporary peace in the darkness as I maneuvered my car through the quiet streets.

Until I came to the first stop sign and something felt off. It took me longer to slow down, like my brakes didn't catch for a moment.

Shaking the bad feeling that started to creep over me, I told myself I must have simply hit some black ice.

Except it happened again. Lugging forward, the brakes didn't respond as quickly as normal. My heart rate accelerated as I stomped hard on the pedal at my third stop sign. The wheels didn't screech or lock up—nothing responded, and I completely missed my left-hand turn.

This wasn't something I was imagining. There was something really wrong with my vehicle. Pumping the brakes, praying that it was some black ice, or that the cold was affecting my car, I completely missed the next turn I needed to take to head to school.

My car blew through the empty intersection, and it didn't matter how hard I slammed the pedal to the floor, I wasn't stopping.

This wasn't ice.

This wasn't the cold, or frosty roads that had a light dusting of snow covering them.

My brakes were not working at all.

Missing another left-hand turn, I wildly whipped my head around, realizing that I'd been on this road maybe only once before, that was it. Not a single brick office building rising toward the gray canvas above seemed familiar. There wasn't an apartment I recognized. Not a single streetlamp flickering off as the morning sun rose was one that I'd seen before.

I had to pull over somehow before I got moving too fast. Before the emergency brake would become as ineffective as my regular brakes were proving to be.

My heart thumped heavily, warning me a little too late as I scanned the unfamiliar road I coasted along. A construction crew, not yet arrived for the morning, had left equipment lining the right side of the road, and the left side was bordered by cars parked overnight. There wasn't a vacant spot for me to pull over along either side of the road or an intersection that I could see that might open up the crowded yet unmoving street.

Now is not the time to panic.

There was no worry about being late to school; I'd left with plenty of time to spare. What I needed to do was call someone to come help.

Yes, that's it.

Not daring to take my eyes from the road, I fumbled blindly with one hand through my purse and snatched out my phone. I quickly asked Siri to call Noah and waited for the line to connect on my car's Bluetooth speakers.

The line connected and it rang.

And rang.

And rang.

Until his voicemail answered. Awesome. My stomach churned over. *It's okay, we are alone on this road, going a rather slow twenty miles an hour.* Tapping the "end call" button, I had Siri dial my mom's number next.

It rang.

And rang.

And rang.

Ramming my thumb against the "end" button, I hung up and bumped my head against the headrest. Of course neither of them was answering right now, they were still asleep. Inching forward, my eyes caught sight of a sign illuminated in my high beams, creeping closer and closer.

A universal sign with the picture of a wedge and car that meant that there was a hill with a steep descent up ahead.

A hill with a downward slide that was going to increase my speed, and, in all likelihood, launch my car out of control.

I inhaled a frightened breath, fighting the panic that was seeping bile into my throat. "Daddy," I whispered as a tear slipped down my cheek. He would've come. He would've known what to do. I banged the heel of my palm against the steering wheel as the scenery began to shift. Less buildings, more high concrete barriers rising along the sides of the road.

I wracked my mind on who to call that would—

And then it hit me.

There was one other option. Someone else who, even when he thought I was being an awful cheater, had protected me.

Giving myself a blast of oxygen for encouragement, I tapped the button on my steering wheel and paused before telling Siri to call Griffin. I didn't want to overstep my boundaries, but I did need help. There was no way I knew how to get out of this myself.

"Hey, Siri, call Griffin Marsh."

It rang twice before the line connected.

"Jane?" Griffin's voice slipped through the speakers, low and husky.

"I'm so sorry to be calling you this early."

"I've been up for a while, it's no big deal. What's up?" He sounded unperturbed that I'd contacted him. Man, it felt so nice to not have him upset at me.

"I need help, actually," I said with urgency in my voice as I curled my fingers tighter around the steering wheel.

"What's wrong, Jane?"

A fleeting moment of hope crept in as a gap appeared between some construction vehicles. But it vanished within a second as a forklift appeared, already taking up the spot.

"Jane? What's going on?" he prompted louder when I didn't immediately answer.

"I-I-I can't stop," I answered.

"What do you mean you can't stop?"

"I mean my brakes aren't working," I whimpered, pumping them hard again, desperately wishing that they would magically kick into gear.

"Where are you?" his voice remained steady as I heard shuffling in the background.

"I-I-I-I think I'm driving down that old historic road, where they're doing construction." I glanced around desperately for a street sign.

"There's lots of construction going on, Jane. I need something more concrete," he answered, a faint whine reverberating behind his voice. My eyes tore frantically around me, catching a sign to the apartments upcoming on my right, along with a turn. *Yes! Thank you! Safety away from the upcoming hill.*

"Jane, tell me where you are," Griffin prompted again as I signaled and guided my car too fast to the right, down the first intersection I'd seen in a while.

"There's an apartment complex called 'The Hills'. I just turned right away from the little hill that was coming up," I quickly answered proudly.

"No, don't turn right! Go straight!"

"Don't go right?" I gasped, glancing around me as the apartment complex jumped into my rearview mirror. My speedometer bumped up in speed—twenty-one miles per hour. "What's wrong with turning right?"

"You turned right, didn't you?"

"Yes, before you told me not to."

"Fuck," Griffin muttered.

"FUCK? GRIFFIN, WHY THE HELL DID YOU JUST SAY FUCK?" I shouted, panic shooting through me as my car dipped over the edge of a hill. Turning right hadn't helped me evade the impending descent. I had no idea what was ahead, the bottom of the downward spiral I just entered was not in sight as the speedometer ticked up—twenty-three miles per hour.

Twenty-four.

Twenty-five.

Twenty-nine.

Too fast. There was no ending in sight as I careened around a corner, the gradient of the hill becoming steeper.

"Jane, I need you to take a deep breath for me." Griffin's voice, sharp but even, came through the speakers.

I inhaled a shaky breath.

"Good girl, you're doing good," he answered my poor attempt to calm myself.

Suddenly, my car dropped into a one-lane road, everything around me coming in a blur as I barreled beneath a bridge. Bright yellow and green signs snapped past me, and everything continued to rip by faster and faster.

"The hill—a bridge," I choked out. "I can't...I'm going too fast—"

"I'm coming, Jane," Griffin said, but everything was a blur. My knuckles whitened around the steering wheel as cars came into view, moving along the highway that this unknown road spit out onto.

My heart raced, my blood snapping through my veins, and nothing but the sound of my pulse pumping heavily in my ears as terror crashed through me. Tears boiled down my cheeks as I laid on my horn and thundered into the traffic.

Downward, faster and faster I raced, zooming past cars that seemed to understand, dodging out of the way in the nick of time. I slammed my wheel to the side, weaving around a semi-truck, blaring on my horn as the hill continued to descend.

"I'm close, just hold steady for me," Griffin calmly instructed.

Despite that knowledge, the adrenaline continued to pump heavily through my veins, desperately seeking an out from the rapidly increasing strain of anxiety. I was lost with no end in sight.

And my car was now tipping over sixty miles an hour. A flash of green rose up on my right, a sign.

"There's an exit, Griffin! I see an exit!" I gasped in delight as the road finally started to even out.

"Don't take it," he commanded.

"O-O-Okay," I stammered, twisting my sweaty palms around the steering wheel. But my heart lurched as my eyes locked onto the steep ledge this road rolled over. "No, I'm taking the exit. There's a hill ahead, worse than the one I already went down!"

Glancing out my passenger side window, I blared my horn again, ready to jam the wheel to my right. Sweat dripped down my back, my skin baking hot with fear.

"Stay straight," he instructed, and there was a faint squeal of burning rubber over pavement in the background.

My mouth opened and closed as I eyed the nearing exit. There were wide margins off to the sides, dirt and grassy patches waiting without a single building. I wouldn't endanger anyone if I simply drove off of the road there.

"There's a-a-a hill." I gasped for air, laying on my horn again, hoping that the cars around me continued to part.

"I know, but turning too sharply at this speed could make the car roll," Griffin said.

Headlights flashed in my mirrors, snapping my gaze away from the exit, and a truck I recognized from the gym parking lot roared into view.

I blew out some air, the pulse in my wrists skipped a beat. "Griffin?"

"Hey, smart ass." Griffin's voice was calm and reassuring.

My bottom lip trembled, but for whatever reason, the sight of him behind me cleared the befuddlement from my mind.

"Griffin," I whispered and pointed the nose of my car toward the ledge.

"There's my good girl," Griffin said, sharp and clear.

As we tipped over the top, I laid on my horn. The blood drained from my veins, pumping only in my ears.

Faster and faster.

My car whistled toward the houses at the bottom of the hill. Houses that weren't that close together.

The traffic thinned the farther down the hill I roared, and I pulled my palm away from the horn, wrapping my hands tightly around the wheel. *Stay straight.* That was what Griffin had instructed.

"You're doing really good." His voice entered my car, wading through the thick sludge of terror in my mind. My eyes flickered down to the speedometer.

Bad decision.

Ninety-three miles per hour.

Everything roared past me in a blur. The trees, the one house, the single car. Everything was a mesh of colors, whirring past me. I stared straight forward, unable to look at anything else for fear that if I did, what little rational thought was left, would immediately flee.

My car lurched, bumping my frozen body around as if I was locked into a rollercoaster.

I blinked rapidly, and my brows twitched.

The bumping, the jostling, it was a county road. There were almost no houses around, and only my little car and Griffin's truck right behind me were on the road.

"Big breath, Jane," Griffin commanded.

I gulped in a thick wad of air.

"Good girl," he said. "Now, you're going to see the road turn to dirt about four hundred yards ahead. Stay on it."

I nodded my head to no one, unable to say a word. The muscles in my forearms were locked under the strain of the pressure I was applying to the steering wheel.

"Hold steady, Jane," Griffin said the moment my tires hit the frozen tundra of dirt dusted with muddied snow.

My eyes widened as a gradient *rose* in front of me. "A HILL!" I exclaimed. I don't think I'd ever been more excited to see a hill in my life. One that finally ascended in front of me.

A soft chuckle danced through the speakers of my car, and I watched as my vehicle began to inch toward the sky, and my speedometer reading gradually declined.

"Put your car into neutral the moment you can. Force it into neutral with all of that badass strength I know you have."

Sixty-miles per hour.

Fifty-five.

Forty-seven.

Thirty-nine.

Thirty.

My tires hit into compacted dirt, jolting along as each breath in my body became a little easier to take. More and more oxygen filled the cells that had so long been depleted as I simply waited. And I slammed the gear stick into neutral.

I waited for gravity to put the final kink into my car's runaway plan.

And just as the speedometer ticked to zero, I eased the car to the edge of the road.

"Now, pull the emergency brake the moment your car stops, and then put it in park," Griffin finished.

My car rolled another couple feet and then lugged, and I grabbed the brake, ripping upward. I lurched a little forward, but not much, and I pushed the lever, moving the gear stick into park.

"That's it," Griffin said, the rumble of his truck drowning out the excruciating needles pulsing beneath my skin. I sat entirely still in the driver's seat, staring out the front windshield. My fingers were numb from gripping the wheel and emergency brake so tightly.

A few tears slipped over my cheeks as the door beside me groaned open.

"You did really good," a soft voice whispered beside me. I shook my head, not able to speak but only taking shaky breaths and remaining frozen in place. A hand reached across me, attached to an arm covered in a black sleeve from the hoodie he was once again wearing. My neck felt as stiff as a board as I turned to look at him. This one had a different logo on the front.

Griffin turned the engine off, then gently unbuckled me from my seat. "You did really well," he calmly said again, softly prying my hands from the wheel and brake. My feet shakily swung from the car and he lifted me out. I couldn't seem to stop staring at absolutely nothing, my mind filled instead with flashes of oncoming traffic and the terrifying realization of having no brakes.

"Hey, smart ass. Look at me," Griffin instructed, his teasing insult snapping my eyes toward him. Those intense hazel orbs studying me were distracting and working their usual magic. I noticed the amber rings around his pupils—bright and focused, and quite pretty—contrasting with the greenish hue of the rest of his iris.

I blinked, feeling his hands stay gently around my upper arms, holding me steady. Slowly, my fingers inched their way to his forearms, and I dug them in, desperately searching for safety.

He didn't move, didn't push me away nor flinch from the pressure of my nails.

Once I'd managed to calm my breathing, I took another deep inhale and closed my eyes.

"Let's see what's going on," Griffin mumbled, his chest vibrating against my forehead even though I don't remember putting it there. I nodded, prying my eyelids open to find him gazing down, soft and encouraging.

I slowly pulled my hands from his arms and watched as he quietly walked toward my car. Faded jeans hugged his sculpted legs, and he tugged his hoodie tighter around his broad shoulders, drawing my attention away from the nerves still boiling in my veins to the fact that Griffin was here and looking like that. Popping my trunk, he used the jack to prop up the front of the car. It barely gave him enough room, but he managed to wriggle himself beneath my Civic to inspect the undercarriage.

"Well, shit," he muttered within half a minute and then slithered back out.

"What'd you see? Is there something really wrong? Did I ruin it?" I asked as he brushed the snow off of his back and his very nice ass that I didn't mind looking at. *Hold up, not now, Jane.*

"You should probably call the cops." He shook snow off of his leg, and his face morphed. That stone cold mask was back and plastered upon his chiseled features, the safety that I was just beginning to feel again whisked away in an instance.

"What?" I gasped. "Why?"

"'Cause some motherfucker cut your hydraulic line, and I'm pretty sure you and I both know who it is."

I crossed my arms. "No. I can't call the police."

"Why not?" he stated, glancing over my shoulder. "We know it was Sam."

"And do you have any proof other than whatever this hydraulic line is being cut?" I replied, and he clenched his jaw.

"It's your brake line, smart ass. Isn't that proof enough?"

"Proof that someone is after me, but guess what, he's not the only one that it could be. There's a reason that there are agents that check in with us every week. And a reason my mom uprooted us from our home, or did you forget?" I replied snarkily, and he shook his head.

"Obviously I didn't forget, smart ass. But you need to make some sort of report. There needs to be a record of this. That could've turned really dangerous really fast."

"Pretty sure it already was," I mumbled, crossing my arms with a pout.

His lips twitched, a smile breaking through his mask. "I had it under control." He winked.

"But reporting still could set off a massive chain of events that forces my entire family to move again," I argued. I was once again putting them in danger. "First the antique shop, now this?"

"Jane," he firmly stated, crossing his arms

"Look, I'll have my mom and Noah check their cars, too, just in case"

He sighed, drilling holes into me with his eyes as a tractor slowly rumbled past.

I waved my arms at him petulantly. "I need to get to school."

"I'll drive you." He nodded toward his truck. "And I'll go make the report since you're being stubborn and won't yourself. I'll get your car towed and fix your hydraulic line too. If Sam shows up in the meantime, you better call me. Immediately." I trailed behind him as he opened the passenger door to his truck. Fresh leather and warm air washed over me.

"Thank you," I said, and his lips twitched with a smile.

"Hurry on in, smart ass. Or you'll be late."

I bit back the giggle that was no doubt partly due to hysteria that bubbled within me. I think he enjoyed a little bit of this constant cat and mouse game we were playing.

Chapter 13

The lunch bell rang, and I sat back as the class dismissed, rubbing my temples. What a long morning it had been watching my class for any signs of rumors or a visit from Nancy or Dayton.

Taking a bite of my sandwich, I pushed aside the paper I was grading and started a new one. At least this was a mostly mindless task. Although my head constantly tried to wander as I dove deeper into the repetitive routine of marking student reports.

My phone buzzed against my desk, and I glanced at the screen. Two notifications waited from Griffin, and I paused, grateful for the excuse to take a break, and unlocked the cell.

> *Had to order the line since it was out of stock in town. Should get here tomorrow.*
>
> *And I'll come get you from school when you're done.*

I stared at the screen, surprised by the offer and the fact that he'd followed through. He was going to fix my car, but that also made me wonder if he contacted the police already as well.

Shoving another bite in my mouth, I typed a reply.

> *What'd the police say?*

Three bubbles appeared, and my stomach turned over, hoping that I wouldn't need to go in.

> *My buddy says there's not much we can do besides document it and wait to see if something else happens.*
>
> *Thank you. I'll let you know when I'm done with work.*

Setting my phone back down on the dark brown, wooden desktop, I returned to my work at hand. Relieved because no other vehicles were touched but also annoyed. And thoroughly confused.

"Miss B!" Dayton called out as the final bell rang, ending school for the day. I turned around from the whiteboard and smiled as he approached.

But my arms prickled with a surge of adrenaline. He knew, he had to, and that's what this was about.

"So, what'd you think of my brother?" he asked, stopping in front of me and hooking his thumbs around his backpack straps.

"What?" I furrowed my brows as he grinned.

"Isn't he so cool? Anyway, thank you for convincing him to stay, though Mom is pissed he swore and that he didn't tell anyone he has a girlfriend. I'm even a little upset that he just announced it to the entire class before saying anything to me first." His smile faltered.

I studied him, unsure of what to say as he pulled himself on top of a desk and I resumed writing instructions for tomorrow on the board.

"Anyway, we've got this family reunion over the weekend, and I think he's bringing her. Though Mom doesn't believe she exists, so she's in denial. The thing is, I've been trying to rack my brain and figure out who it could be. He's avoided every girl that's been practically handed to him on a platter for years now. Marcy thinks he's bluffing, too, which is so annoying because I thought bringing him would help give me an extra leg up with her. Now she's obsessed with my brother, so that backfired," he grumbled and folded his arms. I stopped writing and capped my marker.

"That's what this is all about, isn't it?"

He nodded. "If he is lying, then Marcy will continue being obsessed with him, even though I think it's kind of gross and Griffin's probably not thought twice about her."

I chuckled. I doubted Griffin even remembered her name or that he spoke to her yesterday.

"And if he's not lying?" I prompted.

"Then she'll be pissed at whoever is dating him but at least will be over him. Even though Griffin would never go near Marcy in the first place. That's illegal for one, and two, Griffin knows I like her."

"And what is it that you are wanting from me?" I questioned, tilting my head.

An embarrassed grin slipped across his face. "How'd you know that's where this is going?"

"'Cause it's you, Dayton," I taunted gently, clicking the marker cap off and on.

He nodded in affirmation. "Help. I would like help winning Marcy over before the upcoming dance."

"So, what, I should make a seating chart or something?" I wondered what I could do, and he shook his head.

"No. I need another opportunity to have Griffin show up to school with proof that he has a girlfriend. As long as it's soon enough before the dance, then I can swoop in and be the hero."

"You want me to find a way to get him to come speak again? That didn't exactly seem his forte if you know what I'm saying."

Dayton snickered. "No, it wasn't, was it? But no. I was thinking I'd accidentally somehow show a picture of him and his girlfriend. If she even exists, and if she doesn't, I need to find a pretend girl who will act like one." He slid down from the desk and approached me.

If I agreed to this plan, my face with Griffin would end up in the mind of not just Dayton and his mom, but Marcy and then others. Rumors would start all over school. I was already worried enough about what was going to happen this weekend when Nancy and Dayton found out it was me.

Even more so, I was stressed beyond my imagination concerning what would happen if they learned this was all fake, an act to get Griffin out of something. And if they learned that I had a crazy stalker, and as a result asked Griffin to practically sacrifice his reputation and dignity for me in exchange, that was also going to horribly explode.

"Please, Miss B. You're the only one who's even managed to get Griffin to speak. So it has to be in this class. Assign a project that we have to do on the computer or something, and I'll accidentally upload some pictures from my phone or something," he begged, staring at me with hopeful eyes.

I could end his misery right now and say that I was that girlfriend—fake girlfriend, but he didn't need to know that it was fake. Or I could skirt around an answer. Or I could lie.

There would be a lot of lying this weekend, so why not start now?

"Let me see what I can scrounge up," I answered with a smile, and he jumped up and down.

"YES! You're the best! Thank you Miss B!" he yelled, and then skipped out of my classroom. The moment his backpack was out of sight, the smile fell from my face. This was it. I would return from this weekend and probably get fired. Or everyone in the school was going to know, and people were going to say that I was playing favorites. Dayton would be the laughing stock of the school, or I would end up the butt of the jokes to keep him from being so.

Plus, what was his mom going to say? The staff would probably think I was hired simply because I was dating Nancy's son. No matter what, they wouldn't believe anything I argued to dispute that fact.

And there seemed nothing I could do. I owed Griffin. He'd saved me several times now, so if I had to put up with some embarrassment for the sake of his peace over two days, I would do so.

I quickly sent a text to Griffin that I would be ready to go home in thirty minutes and then finished prepping for tomorrow. Maybe I was overthinking things and this weekend wouldn't be so horrible. Maybe Dayton and Nancy would be okay with this and respect my wishes to keep things private from the school.

In the end, my actions and choices had landed me here, and I would accept whatever fate had in store.

Chapter 14

The parking lot was practically empty as I hoisted myself into Griffin's truck. He was dressed in a hoodie and some sweats, ready to hit the gym. I pulled the door closed and buckled myself in, lost in thought.

"Everything okay?" Griffin asked, and I pursed my lips.

"Obviously not," I grumbled, turning my attention out the window as he put his truck into drive and began guiding us toward the road.

"Jeez, that's some attitude," he muttered, and I whipped my head around, glaring.

"Are you seriously still okay with lying about us to your *entire* family this weekend? Do you not realize how much of a risk this puts me in? My career could be affected by this."

"And mine wasn't with what happened at the grocery store?" he snapped in return. He clutched the wheel with his right hand and leaned against the windowsill.

"Why would yours be?"

"Because there is still a code of conduct I'm expected to follow. My captain is...particular," he explained.

"Well, you chose to kiss me."

"And you liked it, so quit complaining."

"That's... That's beside... That doesn't matter," I stuttered, and a mischievous grin spread across his lips.

"No, I guess it doesn't," he snickered, and I sighed, biting back a smile.

"Jerk."

"Smart ass."

"Stop being so mean."

"Then accept that this weekend is happening. No one will figure out that it's fake."

I pushed my bottom lip out and scooted lower on my seat. "You better hope not."

He chuckled but didn't say anything else. I looked out the window, knowing that there was no out, and surprised that I didn't feel all that shocked by the insanity that had befallen me since my father's death. It had been one thing after another and honestly, it was a little fun. I was slowly getting high off of all of the adrenaline I'd been lapping up lately.

Griffin turned off of the main road and began to drive down the street to my house.

"Stop here. They don't need to know you brought me home. Especially Noah, seeing how I'll be leaving this weekend with you," I quickly said, and he drifted the truck toward the edge of the road.

"You're not dating Noah, so why does it matter?" he asked.

I rolled my eyes. "Just because. Plus, there's plenty of worry with everything that happened at the antique shop, and now this car situation. My mom's on edge enough."

"She knows about all of it?" He raised his brows, and I nodded. "My mom doesn't know about the antique store incident. And don't you dare tell her about it."

"Why not?"

"Because she doesn't need to think that I'm in as much danger here as I am when I'm deployed."

I studied his eyes. They were pained.

He seemed laden. Overwhelmed. Yet built like a brick house and sturdy as an ox. No matter the weight of the burden he was carrying, he would manage without folding. Without complaint.

"She definitely doesn't need to know about Sam then. Or what happened this morning. Or why my family moved here," I smiled, and he chuckled.

"That's all very true. Now go. I've got a gym session to get to, and you don't want to keep your family waiting," he answered and nodded toward my house.

"*I've* got a gym session to go to. You just show up and never actually work that hard," I teased, and he rolled his sparkling eyes.

"Out." He clicked the unlock button, and I giggled. My hand slapped over my mouth in shock as I stared at him. I actually giggled. Like a giddy little schoolgirl.

He kept his eyes on mine. Locked, enraptured by his stunning gaze, my hand slowly drifted from my mouth. His gaze darted to my lips before lifting lazily back up. My heart thumped erratically as his brows twitched and he leaned toward me.

My lashes fluttered, everything in me quickening, my heart, my breaths, *everything* as he inched closer and closer. To feel him kiss me again… I raised my brows, as he tipped his head just slightly to one side, and my lips parted a centimeter. A warm shiver ran down my spine in anticipation for the taste of his tongue against mine once more.

And a smile gently caressed his mouth before he winked, mischievousness sparkling in his eyes, and shot his arm across my body.

Snapping my lips closed, my cheeks burned, flaming hot in embarrassment as he shoved the door open for me.

"Get out of here, smart ass," he whispered with a knowing look, and I quickly slipped out of his truck. Mortified once again, I didn't dare turn around as I shuffled as quickly as I could along the side of the road.

What was that, you idiot?

Gravel and snow crunched beneath my brown clogs as I replayed what had happened. It was so easy to talk to him, to tease him. I wasn't afraid to speak my mind with him no matter how thick and high his walls seemed. Even when he was mad at me, I'd been able to stand up for myself. He looked at me in a way that sometimes sent chills through my spine.

Though he never really said much, he didn't seem to mind how much I spoke. I never walked on eggshells around him, even though I'd embarrassed myself plenty. It scared me a little, in a way that my father had never prepared me for. All of the self-defense in the world, and I was afraid of something that I held no tools for. Fortunately, no one was around when I walked into my house, giving me time to think before dinner.

Wrapping my hair into a claw clip, I grabbed my small suitcase off the bed and quietly slipped upstairs. Last night, it took every skill possible to keep the conversation from questions about this weekend or my car. Leaving before either of them were awake this morning was necessary to avoid the topic, so as I tiptoed into the kitchen, I left the light off and made coffee.

Carrying it outside, I was lucky nothing spilled on my green sweater or light-blue, high-waisted boyfriend jeans. Though I nearly dropped the carrying container that held the two cups onto my white sneakers as I pulled the front door shut with my toe.

Texting Griffin that I was ready, I began toting the suitcase behind me down the road. Shivering, I debated putting my coat on, the sound of my footsteps muffled by the fresh snowfall. I saw the headlights around the same time as I heard his truck's whistle turn onto my street. Jogging to meet him the last few steps, he pulled over to the side. As I attempted to open the door and not drop the coffee cups, he made his way around and took my suitcase out of my hands, tugged open the back door, and tossed it inside with extreme ease. Dressed nice but casual, his gray coat accentuated the width of his broad shoulders. A simple pair of jeans and a dark blue shirt beneath his coat made his eyes pop.

"I wasn't sure how you liked it. So I made one like mine," I said, extending a cup.

"Surprised you didn't make it black and then say some reference about it matching my soul," he teased, opening my door.

"I thought about it, but that seemed cliché. Besides, you can't make coffee dark enough to match your soul," I taunted while hoisting myself up.

"Ouch." He faked getting stabbed in the heart, then he shut my door, jogged around to his side, and got in. My heart did an odd flutter at the sight of him this morning. Something was different, as if he was somehow more comfortable around me. Pushing my glasses up higher on my nose, I couldn't help watching as he pulled himself into his truck. Every fiber of my body was consumed by flames at the sight of his hypermasculine profile against the early-morning sky. A silhouette that screamed physical strength and virility.

"Why do you wear those?" he asked, bringing me back to Earth as he turned the truck around and began to drive us toward the school.

"Wear what?"

"Those glasses. I've only ever seen you wear them at school and then once at the antique shop. I get not wearing glasses at the gym, but even at the grocery store you didn't have them on." He tapped the black rim and then returned his attention to the road.

"To see?" I questioned, and he pulled a mocking face.

"Obviously, smart ass. I'm asking why you choose to wear glasses when you clearly have contacts."

"Oh, I don't know," I muttered, looking out the dark window. I did know, I just wasn't sure if I wanted to say it out loud. It would sound so silly, like a schoolgirl's answer. Yet it was something that I would never stop doing.

"Well, they, um…look cute on you." His lips didn't twitch into a smile, and he didn't break a single emotion onto his face, so I couldn't tell what he meant by that.

"My dad gave them to me my very first day as a teacher," I admitted quietly, a tear slipping down my cheek. "It made me feel smart and confident, something I'd never believed I was."

Griffin clenched his jaw but didn't answer, and I drifted away in my thoughts. There was my dad's smiling face, that cheesy grin that always made me laugh. Despite his busy schedule, he'd never missed a major milestone of mine. He'd been there to send me off on my first date, for every school dance, and every time I'd needed a shoulder to cry on because some jerk broke my heart.

We pulled silently into a fairly empty parking lot once more. He put his truck into park, letting it idle, waiting for me to leave. But I needed to know something that had been itching beneath my skin.

"Do you live with your mom?" I blurted, and he swung to me, startled.

"I mean, sort of?" He tilted his head and looked at me.

"You're thirty-seven and living with your mom."

"And you're twenty-seven living with yours."

"My situation is a bit different."

"Have you not considered that mine might be too?" He ran his hand over his neatly groomed stubble that had grown rapidly over the past couple days.

"I wouldn't know. I hardly know anything about you. You are aware of what happened to my dad a couple of months ago as well as why we moved here. You know about Sam, and yet everything I've learned about you has come from someone else."

"We aren't actually dating. You remember that, right?"

"I'm not stupid, Griffin. But we also have to sell this, and what if someone asks me how I feel dating someone who's almost forty and still living with his mom?"

"Do you enjoy fighting with me?"

I pinched my lips and closed my eyes, frustrated. "Whatever," I muttered and opened the door. Obviously I didn't, but I was terrified this weekend was going to go pear-shaped in a hurry. He knew enough about me to make it believable because his family wouldn't know anything. Yet I barely knew anything about him, and his family would know everything. I didn't even know his biological dad's first name, or if his mom was still married to Dayton's biological father.

My head pounded with all of the questions I might be asked, wondering how I would be able to answer. He used his biological dad's last name, but I only knew that because Dayton had introduced him with that last name. I didn't even know if he called his stepdad 'Dad.' I was so sick of secrets yet, somehow, I was caught in a den full of them with Griffin.

Chapter 15

Going over the details in my mind, my foot bounced beneath my desk as I watched the clock. Sixth period would be over within five agonizingly long minutes. Then I would text Griffin that I was ready to leave, and he would follow me to my house so I wouldn't have to go inside before we took off to this weekend reunion that I was dreading. At one point, I'd been hopeful that it might be a sort of fun adventure, but after Griffin's strange defensive outburst earlier, I wasn't—despite the fact he fixed my car for me and brought it to the school parking lot.

Finally, the bell rang, and everyone jumped up from their seats. They dropped their papers in a stack at the end of my desk and bid me farewell for the weekend. Dayton grinned and quickly hurried out after Marcy, leaving my class empty within ten minutes of the bell ringing.

The hallways were deserted just as quickly. It was the weekend, and teenagers never wanted to stick around. I walked to the door, closed it, and flopped back in my chair. I debated letting Griffin know I would be done with my work in thirty minutes, but I badly needed some decompression time, deciding to give myself a few extra minutes to organize my classroom as well as be alone.

I was grateful that despite the crazy this morning, Griffin had fixed my brake line, but things felt weird. Double-checking that I'd closed my classroom door, I turned my speakers on and scrolled through my music. Once I found my early 2000s playlist, I clicked shuffle and waited.

Music bounced off the walls, giving me blissful nostalgia of songs that had definitely not been appropriate for my young, pre-teen self to have listened to. I spun around my classroom, putting things back where they were supposed to go and dusting off others.

Twirling back to the front of the room, I cleaned my whiteboard while singing along with the music. It was loud and made me happy.

This world wasn't real.

There was no death, no sorrow, as I got lost in lyrics that kept at bay all the pain that was in my soul.

Grabbing the eraser, I pretended to use it as a microphone. I wrapped one hand around the edge of the whiteboard tray, squeezed my eyelids shut, and belted out the words. Letting the music fill my soul and the notes that left my chest carry the weight I was burdened with.

Grinning to myself, I opened my eyes and froze. My entire body lit up with embarrassment, sweat pooling against my palms as each breath became shallow. My cheeks roared hot, burning torturously as I stared at none other than Griffin himself.

He was leaning against the edge of the doorframe, his arms and ankles crossed. "Don't stop on my account." His eyes creased, narrowing in delight.

"HOW LONG HAVE YOU BEEN STANDING THERE?" I screeched, dashing to my desk and pressing pause on the music.

Griffin chuckled and pushed himself away from the doorframe. He sauntered into the room, a pair of dark gray cargo pants clung nicely against his powerful legs. "You hadn't texted yet," he calmly answered and pulled himself onto a student's desk that was next to mine.

"And? I'm busy." I placed my hands on my hips defiantly.

"Clearly." He winked. "I didn't peg you for listening to that kind of music."

"I like a wide variety of music, I'll have you know," I snapped back.

"And the principal approves of you letting your students listen to that."

"Obviously I don't turn that playlist on during class."

Griffin gave an easy laugh. "Takes me back to high school hearing that stuff again."

"I was clearly too young to be listening to it at the ripe old age of seven."

He raised his dark brows, the stubble on his face a little longer today than usual. Even his wavy hair was starting to grow out. "That's right, you weren't even in double digits when that stuff came out."

"Yet, you were, once again, the one to tease me about robbing the cradle." I winked.

"Good thing this is all fake, now isn't it?"

"I'll agree with that."

He leaned against his elbows, wearing a simple, red, long-sleeve shirt. "How much longer will you be? I'd like to get there before it's dark."

"So you weren't worried about me at all. You only came to make sure that we left at a decent hour."

"Nailed it." He pointed a finger gun at me, and I sighed. Stalking back to the whiteboard, I finished erasing the last few words and placed the eraser down in the tray.

"I'm ready," I muttered, and he frowned. "Are you disappointed?"

"I was hoping for another show from you, but I guess only one will have to do."

"I will *not* be doing that again, ever," I promised and picked up my purse from beside my chair. Pushing it in, I swung my plaid coat around my shoulders and tugged it on.

"Bummer. It was cute," he mumbled, following me out into the hallway. I locked the door behind me and shoved the keys into my purse. Griffin stuffed his hands in his pockets, and we walked silently through the empty corridors.

"It was embarrassing, not cute," I finally said as we ascended the stairs.

"Everyone needs an outlet."

"Then next time, instead of being a creeper and standing in the doorway, join me," I blurted out without thinking. My cheeks still burning as I quickly jogged up the stairs, refusing to look at him.

What was coming over me? No matter the number of walls that I tried to put up around me, I seemed to be unable to keep them from crumbling down. My head stopped thinking, stopped working, and I was saying the dumbest things.

"Maybe next time I will," he said behind me, almost as if he wasn't sure he wanted me to hear it. So I didn't acknowledge him as we pushed open the school doors and stepped into the crisp winter air. More snow coated the ground, though upon the pavement it was mostly slush from all the tires driving over it.

"Thank you, by the way. For fixing my car," I mumbled as we approached my little vehicle that was parked next to his truck. I still could not bring my eyes to meet his.

"It was no problem. I'll follow you to your house," he responded as I opened my car door and slipped inside. I didn't wait to see if he made it to his truck before I peeled out of the parking lot.

Despite the upcoming events and my nerves being at an all-time high, I drove in silence. I felt like I was caught in a storm, being blown around without any control. My anchor had died months ago, and I was at the mercy of everything else around me. The fear that had taken hold in my soul the day that my mom had gotten that phone call was worming its way into every cavity left empty by my father's absence.

Griffin scared me.

But that fear didn't feel the same as the one I'd become so comfortable with, so accustomed to.

Pulling into the driveway, I pulled my car up to the garage and turned the ignition off. Taking a deep breath, I told myself that I would be okay. That despite my father's absence, I could still manage to be the girl he'd believed I was.

I quietly got out, locked the door, and paced to Griffin's truck that idled on the street.

"Last chance to change your mind," I muttered as I slid in, and Griffin's grip faltered as he reached to put the truck into drive. Giving him the opportunity to change his mind, I kept my face averted to the window while seeing nothing, praying for the strength to continue on this journey that I'd been thrown into if he chose. It seemed odd how much I'd fought this idea at first, but now, as I waited for his response, I realized there was a small part of me that hoped he wouldn't.

A couple more seconds passed and then he flipped the truck around and began driving us to the Airbnb cabin where his family was waiting, none the wiser of what we were about to throw at them.

That was his answer.

And I secretly liked it.

The drive wouldn't take too long, only an hour and fifteen minutes were ahead of us. He turned on music, early 2000s rock, and I relaxed. Despite my apprehension, it was an oddly comfortable sensation sitting beside him as he drove us closer to our destination.

I could hear him humming along with the music, so I swallowed my pride and began to sing. As loudly as I could. A slow grin widened across his face. His hazel eyes sparkled at me as they lit up, and I let loose.

Pulling my hair out of the claw clip, I tossed it around in a rock chick frenzy and faced him, pretending it was a microphone. He'd already seen it once before, a second time wouldn't hurt. He threw his head back, roaring, and then ripped the clip from my hands and belted out the next words. His voice wasn't professionally taught, but it had a nice tone. There was a certain grit to it that couldn't be learned.

Clicking my buckle off, I scooted over beside him. We continued to indulge in our personal mini concert as the road wound through trees and beautiful countryside that was coated in a bright, twinkling white.

His walls were still up tight, but it seemed like he had at least cracked a window and let me peer through. I could see a small side of him that wasn't visible before. It seemed he had all of these expectations from everyone else, but at that moment, the only thing he was obligated to do was to drive us safely to the reunion. The future would take care of itself

The stiffness that always encompassed his body was absent.

Even I felt free. Like a little kid once more who knew nothing about the cruelness of the world. I wasn't worried about my safety, or my mom's, or my brother's. I wasn't missing my dad, but I hadn't forgotten him either. The pain that normally weighed upon my heart seemed to have taken a break. Even if for half a moment. For the first time in a long time, I felt unfettered.

Chapter 16

Spinning the steering wheel, Griffin turned off of the main road that encircled the giant lake, and we rose upwards through more forest. I stared out the driver's side window, blissfully unaware that I was smashed against his side. The lake glistened. Water that had to be absolutely freezing but not yet frozen, lapped at snow-covered sand. The trees sparkled with icicles dripping from the tips of the branches.

"You know, you can see out your window, too," Griffin said lightheartedly as I pointed out the glass pane on his side.

"Yes, but the lake is on your side right now, and look at that." I sighed gleefully. Such an indescribable beauty. Awestruck, the primal purity of the mountain ranges that rose around it were a sight to behold. The wildlife that ran through the forest and slumbered away during the chilly winter were tucked back in caverns that remained a mystery to the world around it.

"Fair enough," he quietly said and lowered his right arm from the steering wheel. I scooted even closer, and he wrapped his hand around my waist to hold me steady. For whatever reason, it seemed entirely natural to let him touch me, and for a moment, I didn't quite realize the intimacy of what I was doing.

Not until he turned the truck to the right and the lake dipped out of view did I blink, and then my eyes widened. I had both of my hands braced on his thighs, and my face was practically pressed to his cheek.

My eyes slid to his in horrified recognition. Flying backwards out of his lap, he steered the truck to the right once more, and we pulled into a large driveway filled with at least ten vehicles. The cabin was wide and loomed over us as he put the truck into park. Large pine trees rose around it, but from the back, you could see the lake once more.

I sucked in my bottom lip as I stared at the slick garage. The siding was the typical bright orange with a green double front door waiting off to the side. We were here. The inevitable was about to come slamming into us.

"Thank you," Griffin suddenly said, ignoring what I'd just done, and I looked at him, confused.

"For what?"

"For doing this and keeping your word."

I watched him for a moment. It felt as though there was more to why he'd brought me than to simply acquire some peace from his family. But with his walls, I knew if I asked, he would simply skirt around the answer.

I nodded and gave him a soft smile.

"Oh, I need you to wear this while here." Griffin shifted and dug into his pocket. Pulling his hand out, a small, blue velvet box rested in his palm.

I slid away from him subtly and raised my brows in suspicion. "What is that?" Tucking my knees against my chest, I desperately wanted to believe that it wasn't what I thought it was.

"Look, it's just for the weekend. Please." Griffin flicked the lid open, and my jaw hit the truck floor. Not a sound or word left my lips as I stared at the massive ring. So extravagant, it could never be real; it was exquisite, antique-looking, and definitely something I would pick for an actual, real *engagement* ring. The sparkling diamond dupe rested in a rounded square-shaped setting with delicate flower petals along each long side. The rose-gold band and setting were littered with dainty jewels that glinted so piercingly I thought I would be blinded. It seemed too delicate for someone so hard-shelled and distant to have picked.

"It's utterly gorgeous, but that's a firm *no* from me," I stated, crossing my arms in front of my chest, while my betraying heart sang *Yes!*

He quickly looked away, his eyes flashing with a hint of guilt. "Please. I even got it at that little antique store because I knew you'd like it." My mind flashed to the case full of beautiful costume jewelry at the back of the store.

"I said no. We barely know each other, your family doesn't even believe I exist as a girlfriend, and you want to walk in there with me as your fiancée?"

He cleared his throat and inhaled sharply. "Celebrities get engaged after a couple weeks and—"

"We're not famous, Griffin! I'm a history teacher, for crying out loud. And all I know about you is that you're a twenty-year veteran Navy SEAL who refuses to retire and likes the color blue."

"*Exactly,* I'm a SEAL, and I'll....look, we're already here. Please." His teeth clacked together as he snapped his jaw shut. Hard.

I rammed my eyelids closed and bumped my head back against the window. *It was just for the weekend, right?*

I'd gone batshit crazy. That was the only explanation as to why I took a deep breath and, without another word, stretched my left hand toward him. Rough calluses scratched against my skin as cold metal slipped onto my ring finger. Pulling my face taut, I opened my eyes as he shoved his door ajar and jumped down from his truck without a word. The weight of the gorgeous ring felt like lead as I slowly climbed out while he snagged our luggage from the back.

The smell of clean leather was quickly replaced with fresh forest air—cold and crisp with a hint of wet snow mixed in with the pine that seemed to latch onto my clothes. I swiftly walked around the front of the truck and stopped beside Griffin.

I looked down at the glittering ring, feeling a strange sense of hollowness, then up at him as he stared blankly at the large wall beside the front door. He really was quite tall. His presence seemed larger than his already thick frame and louder than his words had ever been. The man seemed to have already lived a lifetime.

"Griffin?" I whispered urgently, ignoring how peeved I was with him over the ring, and placed a hand on his arm. He twitched and looked at me, blinking himself out of whatever state he'd fallen into.

He gave me a tight smile and then walked forward. Even he seemed to be dreading the moment that we were to enter this cabin. I followed him up the two steps to the large front door and waited as his hand faltered at the keypad.

His tawny eyes met mine, full of so much emotion that it surprised me. I couldn't decipher exactly what he was feeling, but he seemed totally overwhelmed. Overwhelmed with lying to people he loved yet desperate for the peace that this fake engagement would apparently bring. Overwhelmed with things I knew nothing about. Overwhelmed to the point he seemed to be drowning. He looked as if he were about to turn tail and flee, leaving me alone.

"Griffin, I'm here. Whatever you decide," I gently said. Not sure why I said those words, but the tension in his chiseled face seemed to ease for a moment. He nodded subtly and then typed in the four digit passcode.

The keylock turned, and he twisted the handle, pushing it ajar. The chatter that emanated died incrementally as we stepped further inside. Within the massive sitting room was a large group of women. Some were a little younger than me, others older than Nancy would be.

They spilled from a couple of armchairs and two large gray couches, surrounding a black coffee table with a marble top, warmed by a crackling fire behind them. Through massive windows streamed bright light with a clear view of the lake.

No one spoke, the only sounds were of children echoing somewhere else in the Airbnb. Every pair of eyes was looking at me, none of whom I recognized. Their gazes crawled over my skin like a horde of spiders searching for a meal, pincers poised to bite. I stepped closer to Griffin and tucked myself behind his right shoulder. He hadn't moved a muscle as they stared and he watched them in return.

Looking down at the shoes scattered on either side of us in the entrance, I wasn't sure if I should add mine to the pile or keep them on. Griffin's behavior rattled me, and I wanted to shake him out of whatever daze he was stuck in.

Or from the mental fight that he was engaging in with the oldest woman here.

I followed his narrowed gaze and was met with a nearly identical lion-like stare. Her eyes were a pale green but just as clear as his. She had bright gray hair that was permed and piled on top of her head. This woman's skin was weathered and leathery, yet she seemed quite classy.

A single pair of pearl earrings dangled from her stretched earlobes, and she touched a wrinkled hand to the edge of her hair. Adjusting a few of the curls, she pursed her pink-painted lips and then slid that icy stare to me. I understood immediately that this woman was the matriarch of the family, the way everyone paid homage in their quick glances at her and their seating surrounding her. She was the center of their universe and she commanded it.

I tucked tighter against his back, trying to disappear entirely. She slowly stood from her spot on the couch, swaying slightly as if an invisible breeze rocked her, and dramatically brushed a few nonexistent wrinkles from her floral blouse. She adjusted the waist of her blue slacks, and when she'd apparently decided enough time had passed, she walked toward us. She was tall and slender, old but regal; everyone's eyes tracked her and not a person spoke.

Griffin's stoic face tracked her as she approached. "Hi, Grandma," he said without inflection in his voice. I felt Griffin's fingers tighten his grip on my wrist.

"I didn't believe your mother when she said you were bringing someone. None of us did," she stated, her voice as dry and dead as cold ash, and deeper than I expected. She tilted her head to get a better view of me. "Shy one it seems."

Snooty voice, old money, I thought, feeling a chill race over my skin as her penetrating gaze slid dismissively over me. *We'll never fool her.*

"I would have the same reaction if every stranger in a room was gaping at me," Griffin said coolly, subtly pushing me farther behind him.

His grandma shook her head delicately as if in fear it might drop from her sunken neck. "Well, since we didn't think you'd *actually* bring someone, you are stuck in the grandkids' room with your brother."

Griffin remained still and stoic. "I haven't been in the grandkids' room for years," he muttered, and his grandma tutted, her eyes becoming crystal shards capable of drilling holes in steel.

"Griffin, we've asked you for years to bring a special someone and you never have, so we gave up hope of it happening and relegated you back to the young kids' room." His grandma spun around and elegantly glided back to the couch.

He watched her for a moment as one of the middle-aged women in the circle snickered. "I would've expected someone, well…different when he finally brought a girl." The lady batted her eyelashes as she shot her dig at me.

Griffin's gaze narrowed thinly, and the grip around my wrist tightened painfully. But he said nothing.

The woman clicked her tongue and waved a pale hand. "She is cute, I guess. Like a puppy that you can't wait to give back to their owner."

Griffin's jaw tensed, and his chest vibrated as he stepped forward. She had clearly crossed a line. "Watch it, Cara," he snarled.

"Oooh, someone's feeling touchy." His grandma shot her a cautioning glare. "What? I said she was cute." Cara sulked, and she smiled mischievously at me, but it didn't reach her eyes.

"Cute? I'll show you cute when I smack that snooty look off your face, bitch," I muttered under my breath. Griffin snorted, and I slapped a hand over my mouth.

"Did you hear that?" I whispered, and he nodded. "Did they?"

"I don't think so, seeing as she's still grinning," he whispered over his shoulder.

I stepped toward his back and curled a hand around his arm. Staying hidden but watching closely. His grandma became caught up in a quiet conversation with most of the other women, leaving an opening that I saw Cara snatch up. She turned to the lady sitting beside her and pointed at me. "Look at her glasses. They're huge. What does she think they do?" Her voice was just loud enough for me to hear.

"Obviously they help me see. Dumb dumb," I whispered, and Griffin tucked his chin slightly, biting back a laugh.

"What are you saying back there?" Cara called out, lifting a cup from the table and narrowing her eyes.

"Where's Mom?" Griffin asked, ignoring her question, and speaking loudly enough it drew everyone's attention back.

"Bathroom," his grandma said and nodded toward the hallway to our left. Her eyes raked down my figure once more, a sneer curling her nose upward, and then her eyes nearly bugged out of her head. "What is that?" A wrinkled finger adorned in a large ruby trembled, pointing directly at my left hand curled over Griffin's forearm.

His lips lifted in a sly grin. "Oh, yeah. Surprise! We wanted to announce it with everyone around, but I guess this works."

Silence.

Absolute, excruciating silence with every eye on my hand.

I wanted to fade into oblivion, be invisible for the rest of my life.

A thick sludge of shock blanketed the room. Apparently Griffin's plan did have the desired effect of shutting down every heart pumping blood around the group. I thought from her expression, his grandma might possibly have a heart attack, but then her face hardened, and I could see her mind calculating.

"Anyway, where's the room we are sleeping in?" he stated bluntly, breaking the state of frozen shock and setting time whirring once again. His grandma pointed to our right.

"Down that hallway; it's the large room on the right with the blue bunk beds. You'll probably be stuck with two top ones since the grandkids most likely took the queen beds on the bottom already."

"At least he won't have to share a bed with her," Cara said bitingly to the lady sitting beside her. Whispers floated around us, but it was Cara's nonchalant comment that had me curling my nose up. "She looks so uncomfortable to hold. All skin and bones."

"Cara," his grandma admonished half-heartedly as she leaned forward confidentially, whispering loudly enough for us to hear. "This will never do. But don't worry, they'll be lucky to see the weekend out."

I narrowed my eyes. "Just because my sweater drowns me, doesn't mean I'm not squishy," I muttered in annoyance, choosing to ignore his grandma, because unknowingly, though it made me feel sick to hear her, she was right on the money.

Griffin snorted once more. "Squishy?"

"Shush," I hissed at him, and the corners of his mouth lifted, a grin threatening at the edge. "Go suck on a lemon, you cocksucker."

"Damn, girl," Griffin said, grabbing the handle of my suitcase and tugging it forward. He glanced over at his aunt and nodded slowly. "She does kind of look like she's sucking on a lemonhead or something."

"Exactly!" I responded, leaving muddy shoe prints as I followed him down the hall.

Chapter 17

Beside a decorative table, he paused at a doorway set in the dark timber paneling and turned inside. I followed past a large closet already full of suitcases and clothes strewn over everything, including the floor. Rounding the corner to the left, I stared at the room. Three bunk beds pressed against the wall. Those on the bottom were queen-size and very much already occupied with sheets pulled down.

One twin-size on the top had been spoken for. A duffel sat on the middle bed which left either the one nearest to the entrance or closest to the bathroom available. Twisting my lips, I glanced at Griffin, who was studying the room with a frown. But then he turned his back to the beds, his attention caught by the view through the one window whose blinds had been left open.

This was my chance. I could either claim the one that would have most people walking past back and forth, or the one in the corner that was the most secluded. His eyes slipped to mine, feeling my gaze resting on him, and he knew.

I took off at the same time as he did, but I had already snuck closer to the one in the corner. Gripping the bottom rung, I climbed with Griffin at my heels.

"No fair," he whined as I swung myself up onto the top.

I grinned. "Ha! You snooze, you lose!"

He feigned a frown and hoisted his duffel over his shoulder, climbing up the opposite bunk. I looked down at my suitcase on the floor and back up at Griffin. He smirked, daring me, his long legs dangling over the edge, swinging in anticipation like a cat's tail before it pounced.

"Hey, Jane. Looks like you forgot your suitcase!" he sang, and I rolled my eyes, feeling a delicious tingle scoot through me at his teasing tone.

"Hey, Griffin. Looks like you got the suckiest bunk!"

"Aren't you just the kindest," he mocked, and I smiled, twisting over and flopping onto my elbows. Kicking my feet up behind me, I swung them back and forth.

"Exactly like your family."

"Did you really expect anything less?"

I sighed and crossed my arms, resting my chin on the back of them against the pillow, forgetting the expensive yet worthless symbol on my finger for a moment. "Not really. I figured they'd be judgy. I mean, apparently they've tried to arrange your marriage before?" I threw out the question that had been brewing on my mind.

He sat back against the wall and turned his eyes to me. "You heard Dayton's comment?"

I nodded. "I didn't want to sound rude and say something more."

"Rude isn't a word I'd use to describe you."

"No, just smart ass."

"Exactly." He kicked his shoes off the edge of the bed, and they thumped to the carpet below us, mingling with the rest of the mess. "You handled it better than I expected, if I'm being honest, though."

I shook my head and tugged the claw clip out of my hair. "Not really. I hid behind you most of the time."

"Eh, I appreciate that you didn't try to argue. That only makes things worse. Trust me."

"I don't understand how they are related to your mom. She's always been so kind to me." I spun some hair around my forefinger.

"Cara is my mom's sister-in-law. Let's just say that her marriage to my uncle hasn't always been smooth sailing."

I pushed myself upright and sat back, crisscrossing my legs. "By the way, how'd your mom like her gift?"

He furrowed his brows. "Her gift?"

"The necklace that—"

"Right! From the shop. She loved it. Though, again, please don't tell her what happened. She doesn't exactly know that there were some guys with guns in there and whatnot."

"Seriously, how does she not know?" I casually asked, tousling my fingers through my thick hair. "My mom knew before I even had a chance to call her."

His attention switched to my hands, combing through the wavy lengths. "Helps that I'm friends with a lot of the department and they know my mom. She'd worry herself sick thinking that it was part of something bigger. That someone may have followed me from overseas or whatever."

"Is that even possible?"

"Hmmm, yes, but highly unlikely."

"Well, *my* mom thinks that any hint of danger is the same cartel that killed my dad coming after us," I nonchalantly replied and then stopped moving. "Griffin?"

"Hmmm?" He looked into my eyes.

"What if it wasn't Sam who cut the line on my car? What if it *was* the cartel? Sam was able to figure out where I moved to, what's stopping them?" I whispered, fear blossoming as I put into words something I'd been holding to tightly. Griffin turned away and stared thoughtfully at the wall across from him, pinching his bottom lip.

"You said agents check in every week. If there was any sign of them—"

"They could miss those signs. My dad wouldn't tell us what the case was. I only found out that it was some massive cartel he was after because I overheard two agents discussing things after he'd been killed."

"Jane," Griffin said and turned to face me. "You're going to be just fine. Your family is safe."

"What if they're not? What if something I do gets them hurt too?" Tears welled up in my eyes.

"It's not your fault your dad is dead, Jane. What makes you think that you did something to get him hurt?" He watched me, his gaze full of genuine concern. I didn't know how to answer that. It didn't even make sense in my own head that I blamed myself. Before I knew it, I was blurting out my deepest worry that I'd never told anyone before, my words tumbling hysterically over each other. "But I made my dad late for work that day. I'd gotten a flat tire on the way to school, so my dad drove out to fix it for me before going into the office. If it wasn't for me and my stupid tire on my stupid car, he would have been on time, and he wouldn't have been killed that day."

"Jane," he whispered, his voice inches from my face. Somehow he'd made the distance from the other bunk without me noticing. But then footsteps pounding the hallway floorboards turned into our room. I glanced over the lip of the bunk, realizing Griffin's hands were clutched over mine, and over the ring at the same moment I met Nancy's shocked gaze. Her eyes slid from me to Griffin and back, her mouth opening in astonishment.

"Miss *Barlow*?" Her voice quivered. Griffin quickly jumped off the rung and rushed to her while I slowly pushed myself toward the ladder and began to descend.

"YOU ARE ENGAGED TO DAYTON'S TEACHER?" she screeched and grabbed Griffin's ear.

"Ow." He winced and gently pried her hand from his head. "Mom."

"No. This is not happening. Absolutely not. I do not believe it. Me getting pregnant as a teen isn't your fault, shouldn't be your burden to bear, so why are you doing this? You talk to her one time on Wednesday and then just happen to waltz in here with not a girlfriend, but a *fiancée*?

Is this some game? Did you pay her?" She shot her glare from him to me. "Is he paying you?"

I violently shook my head as Griffin spoke. "No, I'm not paying her, and—"

"Then you have something on her. This isn't real. This is obviously fake because I didn't see a ring on her at school earlier today." She smoothed out her ponytail and then threw her hands on her hips.

"Like I told Grandma, we wanted to announce it here at the reunion and have an official dinner celebration. Why don't you believe that we are engaged?" Griffin narrowed his gaze.

"Don't be naive, son. You met on Wednesday. It's Saturday. I know you well enough to know that you don't let anyone in that quickly, so there's no way this is real." She pointed between Griffin and me. "It has to be because of the deadl—"

"Mom, we—"

She interrupted him just as he had her. "Griffin, I don't need you to try and justify this any further."

"Mom, give me a second to—"

"Stop. Just stop."

"But Mom—"

"Griffin!" she shouted, and I stepped forward.

"We met before Wednesday," I quickly said, and her gaze narrowed toward me.

"Wh-what?" she stammered, and Griffin nodded.

"That's what I was trying to tell you. We met at the antique store where I bought that necklace." He pointed to Nancy's neck, and her hand flew to the small pendant dangling around her throat. Her gaze flicked between my face and back to Griffin's, still questioning.

"Prove it," she stated.

"Prove what?" Griffin asked, his eyes flashed to mine for a brief moment.

"That this isn't fake. Because if it is, so help me Griffin. I will call your superior officer. And Jane," she turned her attention to me. "I will make your life at work a living hell. To the point where you will not be welcome to return the following school year, and good luck getting another job ever again."

I clenched my teeth, surprised by her sudden shift toward me. She'd always been nice, so this intensity was unexpected, yet also so like Griffin had once been.

"It's real, Mom," Griffin said, lying.

"Like I said, prove it." She crossed her arms.

"How?" he asked.

"Kiss her," she bluntly stated, and my eyes widened.

"What?" Griffin responded.

"If you are actually engaged to her, this shouldn't be an issue."

"I'm not saying it's an issue."

"But you're not going to marry someone without already kissing them," she countered.

"Well, yes. But that doesn't mean—"

"If you don't stop arguing, I'm going to assume you haven't even kissed her yet."

Griffin sighed as I quietly walked up next to him. "We've kissed, but—"

I leaned forward and quickly pressed my lips against his mouth, cutting him off. If that's what it was going to take, then fine. I'll kiss him this time.

Griffin's eyes widened, and I quickly pulled away. He tilted his head, my heart raced in my chest as my cheeks flushed red.

That was dumb. I should not have done that, as he clearly hadn't wanted to kiss me again. His gaze locked onto mine.

Nancy lifted her brows and clicked her tongue. "I'm still not convinced. When did you know you loved her and wanted to marry her?"

"When she sat on my face," he answered bluntly, keeping his gaze steady on me.

Did he want to...kiss me, kiss me?

"What the hell! Since when?" Nancy shrieked, taken aback, but I was too mesmerized by his longing gaze to truly register what she was saying. I inhaled a deep, shaky breath as a smile twitched on his lips.

"At the gym, after we'd met, she wasn't paying attention to where she was sitting down, and I laid back on the bench right before she sat down on it...or rather my face," he explained. And his eyes stayed locked with mine, a yearning caressing his features. My heart raced, the world around me spun, everything turning fuzzy except for him.

"And what's her favorite song?" his mom asked.

"She likes the early two-thousands stuff." He took a step closer to me.

"And Jane, what is Griffin's favorite color?"

"Blue," I mindlessly replied, my lips parting slightly as his body heat overwhelmed me.

I think she asked something else, but neither of us answered, his chest pressed nearly flush with mine, my heart racing, each breath a shallow gasp as my eyes darted down to his lips.

More words, but they were muffled, and then gone with her footsteps as she finally left the room, leaving us alone.

Alone.

And he noticed, unleashing whatever animal he'd had on restraint. His hand wrapped around the back of my neck, and he jerked me toward him, crashing his lips against my mouth.

Aggressive and smooth, passionate and intense. Just as I remembered from the grocery store. He tasted as sweet and minty now as he had then, and his thumb slid from stroking the front of my throat to roughly cup one side of my face, his fingers digging into my hair. His other hand brushed against my bare cheek as his tongue shoved forcefully between my teeth, brooking no argument.

I gripped his sides and swallowed, twisting his shirt in my hands. Everything inside me burst into flames, roaring with desire to demand more from him. To give into the craving way his tongue tasted every part of my own tongue. I liked the gritty, wet feel of his tangled with my own as his chest rose faster and faster.

Panting breath escaped my lips as he broke away from my mouth for half a second, and I opened my drowsy eyes to meet his hazel gaze searing into mine. Then he slammed his lips with brutal passion against mine, demanding and giving at the same time.

The room disappeared as he pressed his body as tightly against mine as he could, his hips encasing mine undulating ever so slightly. I closed my eyes and fell. Fell into his kiss. Into his hands that were now gently running down my figure. Allowing my body to be pinned against his frame that was holding me tightly, my fingers slid up his chest, feeling his booming heart beneath the muscles.

He stepped us forward and gently pressed my back against the cold wall behind me. Caught between a hard, warm rock and the timber wall, I had nowhere to go, so I gave in to the sensations pummeling me. Completely. Knowing I was losing my mind, where my heart had already gone. His tongue slipped into my mouth again, and I welcomed him, sliding my hands around the back of his neck, pulling him in. One set of fingers weaved restlessly through his hair, vaguely feeling the ring catch.

A low pulsing danced in my core, aching for this man that I couldn't seem to get close enough to my own figure.

His hands slid further down my body, and then he lifted me from the ground. Guiding my legs around his waist, he pressed himself tighter against my frame. Arching his hips beneath me, his evident excitement fanning the flames between my thighs as his mouth left mine and trailed wet kisses down my neck, tingles erupting upon my skin in its wake.

My body felt achingly warm, my heart racing faster and faster as his tongue licked back up the path his lips had left. I gasped, unable to stop the rush that was spreading like a wildfire from my center. His breath quickened, brushing over my bare skin. I could feel his hardness pressing between my thighs, stunning me with his size. All I wanted was for him to get closer to me. I wanted this. I wanted him naked. I groaned at the thrill of these wild, uncontrolled thoughts, wrapping my legs even tighter around him and brazenly rolling my hips to accommodate the building pressure. Inviting him.

More.

I wanted more, and he accepted the invitation, not stopping.

His fingers dug into my thighs, sliding themselves underneath my ass. I moved my hand up the back of his head and tilted my head up further as he bit down on my neck, right below my ear, deepening the grinding of his hard cock against me, only denim separating us.

More. The pulse deep in my core roared, pounding faster as he pressed his hips harder against me. I dug my fingernails into the back of his neck, and he ran his seeking tongue across my ear curling inward urgently. My heart beat against his chest, his moving as frantic as mine, and somewhere deep inside, a tiny reasoning voice said, *you're losing control.*

I squeezed my eyes tightly, nipping Griffin's neck between my teeth and feeling him jump slightly, his groan vibrating against my lips as he exposed his throat to me further. Running my tongue wetly along it, I shut that bitch down.

"Oh! Shit!" a young voice exclaimed, bursting the sensual bubble that cocooned us.

My eyes snapped open, locking onto Griffin's panicked ones before he shot away from me, dumping my legs. My feet fell to the floor, but I wasn't steady, and I slammed against his chest. He caught me, wrapping his arms around me as we stumbled backward and crashed to the carpet.

I grunted as laughing started. Laughter that I recognized.

Burying my face against Griffin's chest, I groaned as he splayed his arms to the side, my hair covering his chest and my face.

"Mom told you what would happen the next time you used language like that," Griffin muttered, half-heartedly scolding his little brother. He flopped a hand against my lower back where my top had ridden up, brushing his fingers up and down. I was certain, sparks shot out beneath his touch on my bare skin.

"Yeah, but I don't think you're going to tell her," Dayton answered through his laughter.

"Why's that?" Griffin grumbled.

"'Cause I'll tell mom what I saw."

"Which wasn't anything."

"No. Not at all. I didn't see you with a girl's legs wrapped around your waist. Your face wasn't buried against her neck. You don't have a massive boner. None of that happened at all." He snickered again.

My cheeks flamed red-hot, and I pressed my face deeper into Griffin's chest.

"I was just doing what she told us. Mom told us to kiss," Griffin countered.

"That wasn't just kissing bro," Dayton taunted. "Now, who's your girlfriend?" I shoved tighter against Griffin's body, his fading excitement still very evident, knowing how the next seconds were about to ruin things.

Griffin kept a hand against my back and held me flush against him as he pushed himself into a sitting position, cradling me in his lap, my legs scissoring him. "Before you jump to conclusions, hear me out please," Griffin said to Dayton.

"What do you mean?" Dayton asked suspiciously, as Griffin gently pushed me away from his body. I swept my long hair to the side and turned to look at Dayton. He was standing by the door in a pair of still dripping navy blue swim trunks.

"Miss...Miss *B*?" he croaked, his face contorting with shock and then confusion. "What is? Nah, this isn't...you talked once...at school?" He shook his head, sending water flying, and then he dashed from the room. Griffin's head hung dejectedly.

"Go on," I said, lifting myself off Griffin's lap with my hands on his shoulders. "You should talk to him, especially before Cara tells him we're technically engaged." Stepping to the side, I watched Griffin stand before nodding, giving me a tight smile, and then quickly exiting the room.

Chapter 18

Griffin was gone for a while, giving me too much time alone with my thoughts. Long enough that I slid the ring off, showered, and changed into some pajamas. If you could call them pajamas. They were a pair of tiny shorts and a T-shirt I'd stolen from my brother. But I was cold and getting hungry. I hadn't expected to be in this type of sleeping situation. Or to have done what I did.

Never before had I felt so uninhibited, never dreamed I was capable of such rawness or power. Remembering his taste and the size of his desire pressing against me brought a smile to my bruised lips, and another rush of goosebumps.

Pushing the fake engagement ring back on my finger, the costume jewelry so good it could almost be real, I thought of Nancy who probably still didn't believe that we were engaged, but I had promised to sell it. So, wanting a bit more evidence to try and secure it in place, I climbed over to Griffin's bunk and dug through his duffel. I found his black hoodie he wore all the time and pulled it on top. If she saw this, maybe it would help convince her.

And, being honest with myself, I wanted to feel him against me, to smell his faint, citrus scent, and this hoodie would satisfy that. Ugh, I wasn't doing a good job at keeping things fake, because those feelings I'd experienced—that kiss—was anything but fake. From my perspective at least.

Finding my slippers, I padded out of the bedroom with my hair still damp, determined to try and make nice with his grandma at least.

I'd put in contacts in an effort to spare myself any discussion about my glasses again and, tensing with anticipation, rounded the corner finding myself in the sitting room. It was surprisingly empty. Even the kitchen was empty. So I plodded over and opened the door to the right of the fridge. Inside, the pantry was stocked with snacks of all kinds.

My stomach growled, reminding me that I hadn't eaten anything since lunch, and I grabbed a box of crackers. Shutting the door, I turned to find Cara, along with two others right behind me. Nancy, Griffin, nor his grandma were in sight.

"*Those* aren't yours," Cara snarled, and before I knew it, she reached forward and ripped the box from my hands.

"Sorry..." I muttered, and she snickered.

"Can't even stand up for herself." She dug her hand into the open Goldfish box and popped a few in her mouth. Chewing slowly she said, "Nancy told us that you're Dayton's history teacher."

"I am," I said, trying to regain some of the confidence I'd once sworn I had.

"And here you are, pretending to be his older brother's fiancée. What game are you playing?" Cara snarled.

"I'm not playing anything." My voice quivered, and I wrapped my arms around my body. I felt like I was back in junior high. Overweight and cornered by my bully all over again.

"How'd he convince you to fake it?" she pressured, stepping toward me. I shook my head violently, but still didn't say anything. "I don't understand how you can do this. To both of Nancy's sons. It's just so easy for you to lie, isn't it?"

I looked down at my feet, and Cara threw some Goldfish in my face. "Here. If you're a bit hungry, you can have those."

"Enough!" a commanding voice silenced the commotion, and I glanced up, hoping that maybe there was some kindness left in someone around me. But I was met with a hard stare from Griffin's grandma.

Cara leaned forward and hissed quietly. "If you hurt either of those boys, I will hurt you, and so will Nancy."

"I'm not doing any of this to hurt either of Nancy's boys. I care about them."

"That's Mrs. Pitts to you," Nancy snapped, appearing around the corner. "We're about to prepare dinner, so you should leave now." I watched as she approached, and Cara giggled childishly.

"You aren't part of this family, so don't expect food from us," she quietly added in triumph.

"Cara, I heard that. We don't speak to guests that way," Griffin's grandma pushed through the girls, but the look on her face was anything but inviting—opposite of the scolding words issued to her daughter-in-law. I was a lone coyote circled by a pack of hungry wolves.

That was it. I swung to my left and quickly dove out of the circle of girls, slipping back into the hallway and running past the bedroom.

I took the stairs two at a time and arrived in the middle of a family room. Brown, nylon carpet grated beneath my feet, and a pool table rested on the far side. A row of twin-sized bunk beds was set against the wall with a single bathroom door open kitty-corner from several bean bag chairs.

A gray couch and two brown leather chairs faced a television that a few kids were engrossed in. But I didn't stay there. I quickly grabbed a blanket from a basket beside the couch and dragged a chair out the sliding glass doors to my left. The porch had only a small dusting of snow upon it, but since the chair had come from inside, it was dry.

I tucked my legs up and draped the blanket across my body, dragging it to my chin.

Here I was, at last alone. Griffin must still be wherever the swimming pool was, but I couldn't stay down there any longer. I wasn't sure what I'd done to make them hate me so much. I'd barely spoken at all. Maybe that was what it was. Or maybe they were upset because I wasn't what they wanted for Griffin. Or they were trying to protect Dayton, knowing that if he got attached too soon, it would hurt him the moment we broke up from this fake relationship. Or maybe it was something else entirely. My head spun. This was worse than I had imagined it could be.

But really, why was I acting like such a coward? I was simply trying to do as Griffin asked. That was all. But since moving to this small town, I'd found myself in untenable situations over and over again where, unlike my usual self, I froze and acted like a baby. I couldn't seem to fight anymore. It was like something inside me had died the day my father had. It was as if whatever strength I had to stand up for myself withered away the moment it had sunk in that he was never coming home.

I curled up tighter on the chair and stared over the horizon. The sun was beginning to sink, brushing the landscape with a bright orange hue, shifting to golden-pink as it lowered. How incredibly beautiful it was. How misleading. I took a fistful of Griffin's hoodie and put it to my nose, breathing the calming citrus, closing my eyes.

The door squeaked to my left, and I glanced over my shoulder to see Griffin's towering figure. He shoved his hands in his pockets and sauntered my way, his shoes back on his feet.

"What are you doing out here?" he asked in a low voice. "In my hoodie."

"I needed some air," I mumbled, releasing the fabric, and pressed my chin against my knees, hoping he hadn't seen me literally sniffing it.

"Did someone say something?"

"I just wanted a snack," I whined, and he chuckled. "But they took it away, and then they told me that since I'm not a part of the family I don't get to have dinner. I'm hungry..."

Griffin's brows lowered. "Cara's husband and Brent should be here soon, which will help calm both of them down. Especially my mom. She'll look at things more logically, and with a bit of luck, all of this nonsense will end." Griffin offered a hand, but I narrowed my eyes, ignoring it and glaring at him suspiciously.

"And who's Brent?"

"My stepdad."

"Now, come on." He wiggled his fingers, and I shook my head. "I ordered food, smart ass."

"What?" I grinned cheerily, and he chuckled.

"I caught the ending of your confrontation with Cara."

I slapped his hand away and pouted. "Then what took you so long to come get me?"

"'Cause I chewed her out. Nobody treats my fake fiancée like that or takes away her food."

"Be careful, someone might hear you, and then your mom will be even more pissed. I seriously think she actually might try to kill me if she finds out this isn't real." I looked up at him, and he raised his brows.

"I'll protect you." He winked, and I rolled my eyes. "Oh come on. I've got Chinese food coming, and it should be here in…" he paused and flipped his phone screen toward his face. "In three minutes."

"Well, I do like Chinese food," I mumbled, and he stretched his hand out again. Placing my palm in it, he yanked and swung me up onto his back. Out of instinct, I locked my ankles around his waist, feeling the callouses as he tucked his hands beneath my bare thighs. Warmth filled my body as I pressed tighter against him. "How'd things go with Dayton?"

"I smoothed things over, except now he's grossed out by what he saw," Griffin said, ducking back into the house, while giving me a piggyback ride. I plopped the blanket down on the empty couch, wondering how long I was really out there for.

"Grossed out by what?" I asked as Griffin slowly began to descend the stairs.

"You kissing me."

"You kissed me back!" I cried out, and he chuckled.

"But you kissed me first this time."

"Blah blah." I mocked, and he smacked my leg. "Excuse me?"

"I'll put you down right here if you don't fix your attitude," Griffin teased, and I rolled my eyes. "And don't roll your eyes at me."

So, I stuck out my tongue instead, and he chuckled. We rounded the corner into the sitting room to find the kitchen now jam-packed. Most of the boys and men were still damp from the swimming pool, and within seconds, were already shuffling back down the hallway back toward the pool, carrying plates of food. Dayton glanced our way and wiggled his brows as Griffin plopped us down on the couch. Nancy wasn't scowling as intensely as before, but Cara was frowning.

"Wait, you talked to your mom, too, right?" I whispered, and Griffin nodded, tossing a sideways glance to the stiffly-uptight woman beside those two. She twisted a pearl between her fingers, ignoring her grandson and me. "How long was I up there?"

"An hour, I think," he replied, leaning back against the cushions.

"I'm sorry for overreacting," I mumbled, and he offered me a crooked smile, slinging an arm behind me.

"I get it. They've tried to arrange marriages for me before, I don't think you're overreacting."

"Now that I've met them, that doesn't seem as strange of a concept as it did at first."

He snorted as a ding echoed through the tension. "So, you're not upset that you came?"

"Not yet." I smiled as he stood up and walked to the door.

Chapter 19

I was happily munching on some Chow Mein, slowly feeling more and more content as the fire crackled beside us. Griffin was being extra sweet right now, which was surprising, and I was trying to figure out if it was all a show for his family that mingled in the dining room or if he was genuinely being nice.

"YOU LITTLE BITCH!" Cara suddenly shrieked, silencing the room, and Griffin and I both glanced up. She came running toward us, something clenched tightly between her fingers. "I knew it. Nancy knew it. We all knew it! How could you?"

I furrowed my brows, sliding my gaze over the few women left around us, and glanced at Griffin. "How could I what?" I asked.

"You're cheating on Griffin!" Cara shouted in revelation. Nancy stood from her chair in the dining room, and Dayton swiveled around with food in his hand he had yet to eat, which plunked on his plate. His grandma cocked a single brow, keeping everything else still upon her face. The other three women in the room, tucked their heads together and pretended to ignore the show.

"What are you talking about?" I asked confused. Griffin calmly set his chopsticks down and plastered a stoic mask on his face.

"I went through your purse while you were enjoying this time with Griffin." A wicked grin spread across her lips as she slid a finger along whatever she was holding. *Wait, hold on.* She'd gone through my things and wasn't even bothering to hide that fact.

"You aren't carrying a picture of your so-called fiancé that you're here with, but instead it's of some different guy!" She ran toward his grandma and wiggled what I suddenly knew to be the picture of Noah and me in her face. His grandma, however, merely raised her brows briefly at the photo before she swept her attention back to me.

"Cara. Give the photo back to Jane. *Now*," Griffin warned, his voice demanding as he rose from the couch. She swung her head toward me, her eyes rabid mad and crept our way.

"You're not even trying to hide it from him," Cara screamed, her hysteria as confusing as her hostility toward me, and then with a flick of her wrist she tossed the picture into the flames of the fire.

"NO!" I shrieked, leaping up from the couch as Griffin dove his arm into the blaze. He snatched the picture out of the roaring heat, waving it to douse the fire, the edges of the film singed black, but I could see the picture was otherwise fine. Griffin stomped out a persistent flame that was licking at the edges of the picture as I met him at the mantle. His brows stitched together, scanning the photo, and intrigue crossed his gaze, hesitating to return it.

Something seemed to have caught his eye, yet he'd seen the photo before.

My hands trembled as I snatched the burnt and slightly wrinkled image from his grasp, ignoring the hesitation. "How could you?" I muttered, trying to hold back the frustration and anger that was roaring in my head and threatening for me to undo our charade. Griffin had reacted so quickly, the fire hadn't even brushed against the sleeve of his shirt, but once again, he had to save me.

I turned to face Cara, tears of rage and sorrow streaming unheeded down my cheeks. "HOW COULD YOU?"

"How could I?" she asked. "How could you?"

"Did you even bother to keep looking through my purse after you found this picture? Or did you miss the picture of my father whom my *brother* looks exactly like?" I pointed at Noah in the picture. "Did it even occur to you that this might be my sibling? Someone that Griffin's actually met? Or are you seriously that deranged?" I snapped, my commonsense like the conversation around us, evaporating as I stalked toward her.

"This picture was taken two days before my father was killed. Taken by my dad at a banquet ceremony we attended. It's a picture of myself and my brother. My dad was receiving an award that day. This picture is one of the last things that I received from him, and you just tossed it into the fire like it was nothing," I cried out in pain, and she blinked in shock, her face blanching as she realized everyone in the room was now looking at her And not in a kind way.

"Griffin, how dare—" she began, but Griffin's eyes blazed with rage and he cut her off.

"How dare *you*," he growled. "Don't you ever fucking talk to her like that again. Or touch her fucking stuff."

"Cara, calm down, honey," his grandma added, but I didn't stick around for long. I needed out and somewhere alone.

Alone was familiar.

I raced through the hallway and turned into our temporary bedroom, tears once more threatening to crash down my cheeks. But there were a couple kids in there, so, I quickly stuffed the picture into my suitcase, turned on my heel, and ran further down the hallway. Dashing up the stairs, I looked around at the sitting room where a couple of older men were playing pool. Apart from a sideways look, they continued their game. *Young people drama,* I could almost hear their words in my mind as I paced. There was nowhere I could go to be alone.

Except for, I had a lightbulb moment, *maybe the bathroom.* I shot across the room, ignoring the confused stares I earned from talking to myself, and locked myself in. Collapsing to the gray, tiled floor, I leaned my head and back against the door and let everything out. Howling into a towel in complete silence, my throat ached, my eyes hurt, and my soul hollowed out. I felt like mania personified. Everything in my life was imploding in such a way that I had no words to describe.

I burned with anger. Seared with frustration. My father was dead, and that stranger had disrespected any lasting memory of him. I wasn't alone, yet somehow I felt lonelier than ever. The man that had taught me how to be courageous, how to fight, how to stand up for myself was killed. Gone.

Dead. Never coming home, and I couldn't accept that he, of all people, would never again walk through the front door of my house.

The strongest person I'd ever known was nothing more than a memory now.

My back shook as I pressed against the wooden door. The glass surrounding the walk in shower across from me was slowly fogging up. Even the mirror to the sink on the right had the beginning signs of steam from my tears. I couldn't handle this anymore. The whiplash from my emotions.

The loneliness.

The exhaustion.

The cowardice that I was exhibiting lately.

"You foolish coward, Jane," I whispered to myself.

"You're no coward," a deep voice quietly responded through the door.

I closed my eyes.

Griffin.

"You of all people know I am. I freeze anytime I'm stuck in a scary situation, or I run away. How is that not being cowardly?" I softly asked, choking through the tears that stained my cheeks.

There wasn't a response from him.

I closed my eyes and bumped my head against the door frame.

Repetitively, over and over again.

Exhaustion warped the last remaining flicker of hope within me. That insurmountable weight that came from loss plummeted heavily against my shoulders. Loss of a family member. Loss of my independence. Loss of true and absolute support. There was nothing, no one anymore. I stopped fighting the pressure to drown.

"He taught me everything. He knew more than me, and it still didn't keep him alive. How am I supposed to feel safe if it didn't protect him and he was stronger than me? What am I supposed to do without him?" I finally whispered, the truth that had been blackening my soul voiced into the world.

I heard a heavy sigh, but no answer. Not for a moment, and then a soft bump pressed against the frame. "Keep going. That's what you're supposed to do. Because he wouldn't want you to live in fear," Griffin gently said, and I felt silent, warm tears flood down my cheeks once more.

"But I don't know how to anymore," I confessed, quietly. So softly that I doubted he even heard me.

Except he muttered in response, "Me neither, Jane. Me neither."

I stayed there against the door for quite some time. Long enough that the muffled chatter I could hear outside slowly faded. Long enough that my bum turned completely numb from the ice cold floor.

Taking a deep, steadying breath, I stood up and cracked open the door. Glancing out, I saw Griffin sitting against the wall next to the frame that I was peering out from. His eyes were blank, lost in a world that would probably terrify anyone. His knees pulled up tightly against his chest and his eyes did not blink. Not a muscle twitched on his body. Fingers interlaced around his shins, I'd never seen someone look so lost.

There were two men lounging on the couch, both of them with their eyes closed and heads knocked back. A few snores escaped their mouths. They were asleep. Creeping into the fairly empty and now practically dark room, I crawled over to Griffin and tipped my head. He didn't even twitch, almost as if he wasn't aware I was in front of him, though he did finally, very slowly blink just once. Otherwise, not a thing in his glassy gaze changed.

Trapped in a world of anguish, written clearly upon his face that was held tight. His jaw was clenched shut, the moonlight cascading through the window casting deep shadows across each sharply angled line on his skin.

I reached forward and brushed my fingers across his lips. Lightly. He didn't move an inch.

"Griffin?" I whispered and placed my hand against his forearm. Suddenly, his head snapped in my direction, the glassy look in his eyes slipped away, and he blinked rapidly several times. His face contorted in a moment of panic before he inhaled and leaned his head back against the wall.

"Let's get out of here," he mumbled.

"That sounds nice," I quietly said, and he pushed himself off of the floor.

Griffin's hand wrapped around my wrist, and he guided me down the stairs and straight outside. My slippers soaked up some snow as he marched us toward his truck and ripped open the passenger side door, unexpected anger steaming from his frame. I quickly climbed inside, and he slammed it shut behind me. He was in the driver's seat and barreling down the road within half a minute.

He looked like he should be calm, but the way his fingers were gripping the steering wheel said otherwise. There wasn't a word spoken between us as he sped us toward an unknown destination. Someplace that was far away from the insanity that was his family. No wonder he was so desperate for some peace during a family reunion. I would do anything to get out of there too.

"I'm sorry that it's been horrible having me here," I quietly said as the truck slowed. The only sign he gave that he heard me was a clenching of his jaw. He turned off of the road, and the truck's high beams jolted across what was most likely a dirt path when it wasn't frozen over with snow.

Weaving through the deranged shadows laid down by ghostly, snow-laden trees, Griffin slammed on his brakes without warning. The nose of the truck lurched as we touched the edge of a cliff line. I stared out over the front of the vehicle at the beautiful lake, the path of moonlight glistening across the frosty water until scudding clouds stole it from view.

"You'd think having a stranger around would quench some of the crazy," he muttered, and I chuckled.

"Is it any better at all?"

"It's different, that's for sure." A strained laugh left his chest, and he suddenly swung open his door.

"Where are you going?" I cried out in shock.

"I need to clear my head," he muttered and shut the door behind him. I slumped backwards in my seat as he stepped in front of the headlights, took a fistful of his shirt and yanked it over his head. Surprised, I gawked, and then drew a long appreciative breath at the unexpected sight of his showcase. Elaborate monochrome, full-sleeve tattoos covered both arms and ran heavily across his mountainous pecs. Beneath, on his right side, a large rib piece had been worked, and as he turned away, I saw an intricate skull design was given pride of place between his shoulder blades. As he moved, flames etched across his back danced along his muscles.

But there was also a raised mark that wrapped like a snake around his right arm. It took a moment to realize that amongst the beauty of his ink was an interloper, a mangled scar that looked like a rope or chain had burnt through his skin.

Realization hit me as I studied the scar. That permanently disfigured skin was the reason he was *always* in the hoodie at the gym. My mind couldn't grasp who or what could have caused such an injury nor what it must be like to know it will never go away. As I mulled this over, I became aware that he'd unbuckled his pants and kicked off his shoes, leaving nothing but his white boxers on. Then he was nothing but a flash in the car lights as he darted forward and launched himself off the edge of the cliff.

Ripping open the door, I screamed into the night. "Griffin!" Shooting out of the truck, I slammed it shut behind me. Less than half a dozen steps and I stopped at the edge of the cliff, hearing nothing from below and afraid of what I might see.

Chapter 20

Kneeling down, I looked over and crumpled in relief as his head bobbed out of the ice cold water, the moon, having given up playing hide and seek with the clouds, surrounding him in a rippling halo.

"YOU SHITHEAD!" I shouted again as he wiped the water off his face and looked up at me, chuckling.

"You were worried about me." He grinned.

"You jumped off the edge of a *cliff*! Of course I was worried!" I responded, appalled.

"Well, are you going to join me?"

"Uh, no thanks. That water has got to be freezing." I swung my legs over the edge of the cliff as he laid onto his back to float.

"Oh come on. Quit being a chicken."

"I'm not a chicken, I just don't like cold water."

"Or you're afraid of jumping off that cliff into this refreshingly *brisk* water," he teased. "*Bawk, bawk.*"

"I am not afraid."

"I thought you liked adventure. I thought you were daring."

"I am!" I shouted, and he sighed heavily, laying back. My eyes floated across his body, like the water that he was bobbing on. I tried to not look, but it was so hard to avoid it. Massive and powerful. A body forged in the depths of a fire that no one should ever have to traverse through.

My gaze raked lower, briefly slipping down his legs where his right upper thigh showed more intricate tattoos. That's what I saw at the gym that day, peeking out beneath his shorts. But my eyes quickly rose, caught off guard by the glimpsed outline of his quite impressive package. His boxers had been tight to begin with, but I'd been too caught up in the shocking reveal of his scar to have noticed much before he jumped into the lake. But now, I couldn't *not* stare, especially since the water had made his boxers practically suctioned onto him.

I furrowed my brows, a little shocked by his size. Like I knew how it had felt beneath his pants when he'd shoved his hips against mine earlier, but still, the water was freezing, right?

Right?

"The water is cold, isn't it?" I shouted, watching as he moved his arms back and forth across the dark lake.

"Quite," he calmly replied.

"Really though? 'Cause you don't seem to be exhibiting any sort of signs that it's frigid. Like hypothermia or something?" I tucked my knees against my chest as a cold breeze whispered across the snowy ledge.

"Trust me, smart ass. My nuts are pretty much sucked up inside me at this moment."

"Doesn't look like it to me," I nonchalantly said, and he stiffened, his body suddenly crashing beneath the water as I slapped a hand over my mouth.

A wave washed back out from when he'd fallen beneath the surface and then his head broke through. He coughed, sputtering as water spewed from his mouth. I giggled as he wiped the moisture from his face and looked up at me, shocked.

"What?" he gasped, and I leaned my head back laughing.

"Oh, nothing." I waved my hand, and the shock slid from his face. A mischievous glint caught in his eyes.

"You were checking me out."

"No."

"Yes, you were. And you were impressed." He grinned as my cheeks flushed. I prayed he couldn't see it from there.

"No, I wasn't. It's just the angle from up here and the fact that your boxers are wet," I grumbled.

Splashing water in my direction, he smiled wider. "You can get a better look if you're closer."

"That doesn't make the water any less cold!" I bit my bottom lip, trying to change the subject.

"Chicken."

"I am not a chicken."

"*Bawk. Bawk.*" He clucked again and grinned, sinking back under the water after taunting me in the same way I'd done to him. That was it. I quickly pulled his hoodie and my shorts off then kicked my slippers off to the side.

His head popped back up and he shook the water from his hair. "*Bawk, bawk, bawk*, chicken!" he called out, as I ran toward the ledge and launched myself over it.

"Shit," I heard him gasp before he dove out of the way as I crashed through the icy surface. A million needles pricked at my skin, shocking me with the bitter cold of the water; though, in my head, I thought I'd been prepared. My body stiffened for a moment, trying to process the abrupt change in temperature, and then I managed to kick my way to the surface. Breaking the water, I pushed my hair behind my shoulders and looked around.

My teeth began to chatter as the wet T-shirt stuck to my body, hiding probably nothing, especially since I'd not bothered with a bra. Where was Griffin? I spun around one more time, trying to find him, when suddenly, heat enveloped my back.

Flipping around, I nearly smacked him across his face as he tried to sneak up on me. "See?" He brushed a strand of wet hair from my face. "It's not that bad."

Goosebumps spread across every inch of my skin. "N-n-n-not that-t-t-t bad?" I stuttered. He threw his head back and laughed.

"How are we supposed to get back up there?" I managed to breathe out.

"Climb, obviously," Griffin responded calmly.

"How are you n-n-not freezing?" My teeth chattered as I wrapped my arms around my body. He swam a little closer and pulled me into his embrace.

"I am, but I'm a SEAL, remember?"

"R-r-r-right." I pressed my cheek against his bare skin. Despite the surface of his body being cold, it did help to warm me up. My raised peaks upon my breasts poked through my shirt, hardened by the frost nipping at my skin. I knew he could feel them against his own body, but he didn't say anything about it.

"I didn't know your dad gave you that picture," he gently said, placing his chin against the top of my head. I shook within his embrace but managed to nod yes. Nothing else was said as he simply held me. Tightly, as if he, too was grasping for something unexplainable.

"It's strange carrying a picture of your brother, I know that. But I don't want to forget that day," I eventually whispered against Griffin's chest. "It was the last time I didn't feel so…"

Griffin remained silent, rhythmical warm breath washed over my head.

"So lost," I finally finished, feeling everything hardened within me burst open. All that was left inside me was shattered pieces of a heart that became broken all too long ago. My mind was a foreign land, filled with silence and nothing but dull pain that constantly pounded its heavy drums.

He continued to hold me upright in the water, and I quit doing my awkward kicking. Something changed in that hallowed silence. A thread stretched forward, wrapping tightly around the two of us, messily intertwining our fates.

Finally, he gently pulled away and smiled. "Should we go get warm now?"

I nodded, grateful that we were headed back, even if this was beautiful.

I dragged myself out of the lake, Griffin gently placing his hands against my waist, stabilizing me so I wouldn't sink back in. Shivering with goosebumps, I stood on the small bank below the cliff we'd jumped from. Snow hadn't touched the wet sand here, the outcrop covering it from the starry sky above us. I wrapped my arms around my navy blue T-shirt in a wasted effort to warm up.

He hoisted himself out with ease, water draining like rivers of tears over the muscles rippling across his body. His eyes scanned our surroundings, studying the best route for us to ascend back to the vehicle, and flickered briefly up to a ridge.

"This way," he urged and walked to the right. Stepping cautiously, he slowly talked me through where to place my hands and feet, guiding me up the side of the cliff after him.

I used dead shrubs and rocks, tree roots and piles of heavy, compacted snow to scale the side of the ledge. There was no pain from the cold because everything was numb as I focused on carefully doing exactly what Griffin told me to do.

Reaching up, my hand landed on the lip of the cliff, and I glanced to my right where Griffin hung beside me. He smiled and nodded encouragingly as I hoisted myself up over the edge and crouched down. My eyes met his as he let a crooked smile spread across his lips.

"Good girl." He winked, and I rolled my eyes.

"What'd you peg me for? Some wimp?"

He shook his head. "I've seen you squat before, wimp is not you."

"Oh, so *you* were checking me out?" I teased and stood up, turning around to move away from the ledge so he had room to swing up onto it.

He pulled himself easily up and over and I sighed at the exquisite sight. Each rolling tension-filled release of his muscle, each powerful contraction of his steel cut frame he used to push himself up.

The warmth igniting in my core did little, however, to quench the blistering cold that was now rumbling through my body. The droplets of water bound within the fabric of my shirt were slowly freezing, and I shook as I turned around.

My heart dropped, stopping my trembling in its tracks.

Just my luck.

Though I somehow wasn't as surprised as I should've been to see three sloppily-dressed men looming beside Griffin's truck. They took booming steps toward us, enclosing their small circle around me.

Heat blanketed my back, and a shadow oozed over my body, melding with mine. Griffin's outline tensed, turning into a statue of death, and they all stopped walking. The moon overhead darkened, silver streaks of light shot across the faces of the figures brewing into focus in front of me.

"Can't fight your own battles, kitten?" the sleazy one in the middle said, his nasally voice curdling my blood.

His fingers twitched, and the aluminum glint of his switchblade danced in his palm.

"Three on one ain't that fair of a fight. I'm just evening the playing field," Griffin snarled. His torso pressed against my back like a steel plate, vibrating deeply with each menacing word. Nausea filled the pit of my stomach with each second that ticked past.

Not a sound bounced around the little clearing we stood in.

Not a single dead leaf on a tree fluttered to the crisp, snowy footing.

Until one man on the left twitched, his shadow flickering across the forlorn space separating them and us, shattering the glass barrier that held everyone at bay.

The ring leader cocked his hand back and shot the knife through the air. Griffin's arm wrapped around my body and tackled me to the ground. Snow cradled me, softening our fall as the blade sliced into the frozen surface directly where we had been standing.

I stared at the crimson hilt standing beside my toes. That had been meant for me. To hurt me. That was supposed to have…

My own mind couldn't even finish that sentence. I knew what that meant. The purpose of it all.

Calloused hands slid up my arms, but I barely noticed the touch that only moments ago had sent such comforting warmth through me.

Gasping for air, my lungs pinched closed, burning with frozen terror.

"Run, Jane," Griffin commanded in my ear. My eyes bulged out of my head as I snapped my gaze to the man protectively cradling me beneath his body. His fingers slipped subtly across the ground and wrapped around a rock half hidden in snow.

"You need to run, and don't stop. For anyone. Okay?" he whispered, his hazel eyes disappearing beneath that trained, steely mask of death.

No. I wanted to fight, to be here with him.

Fear dug its spindly blades into my body, wrapping chains around any sort of preservation instinct that was supposed to kick in. I was back in that stupid antique store. Back with that gun pressed to my head.

"Jane," Griffin said, and pushed away from me very cautiously. "Please, run."

His eyes snapped to the three men, and he hurled the rock into the air, shoving me away as he flipped onto his knees. A dull thud echoed around me, and the man who'd thrown the knife groaned, slapping a hand over his forehead.

Our attackers darted forward, vengeance and rage on their minds. Eyes as black as night, trained on me.

"Get out of here, Jane!" Griffin yelled again, snatching the blade out of the snow.

"But—"

"NO! Run, and don't stop for anyone! Don't let anyone catch you! Not even me!" he shouted again, and launched himself forward.

Desperation jerked me upright, and I slipped, clawing up from the icy snow as his feet pounded across the ground. The knife left his fingers with precision, drilling into the thigh of the closest attacker. The man cried out and plummeted to the frozen earth.

I managed to get my legs under me and scrambled away from the group as a second man slammed into Griffin, dragging him to the ground.

"GRIFFIN!" I screamed, fear thickening my blood.

"GO!" he shouted as he rammed a fist into the side of the man's face. Black blood, which I knew would really be red, splattered across the pristine snow, teeth rocketing out of his attacker's mouth with a gurgle. Another fist connected with the other side, and Griffin thrust a knee into the man's gut, throwing him off like a ragdoll.

I darted away, clumsily sprinting toward the dense tree line ahead. Making the mistake of looking back, I saw an arm slip around Griffin's throat as my protector lashed a hand out and wrapped it around the ankle of a man pursuing me. I stopped, watching as that assailant slammed into the ground face first and the man with the knife still stuck in his leg made a feeble attempt to choke Griffin. A trail of darkness stained the snow behind him, and his hold loosened as he howled with pain.

"RUN LIKE HELL!" Griffin bellowed again, ripping the arm off of his throat.

I didn't want to leave him, it was three on one. "I can fight. I'm—"

"NO! GET THE FUCK OUT OF HERE!" he shouted, and jerked the man lying face-first in the snow toward him. "THEY WANT YOU!"

He was right. They were here for me, and I wasn't ready to die.

Chapter 21

My flight instincts finally kicked in.

I shot off, sprinting around a thick, pine trunk. My feet flew, numb to the piercing cold of frozen water beneath them. Hot breath puffed in front of my face as I pumped my arms faster, harder. Adrenaline fueled me, igniting the hot coal of fear roaring in my stomach and lungs.

My throat was numb, dry from the cold and breathing through my mouth, feeling blistered from sheer terror.

But I had to keep moving, had to keep going.

Every sharp exhale filled the eerily silent forest. Each shadow of a branch dove hauntingly in front of my path. Only the moon kept me company, and I prayed it wouldn't play games.

But I had to keep moving for Griffin. I had to keep going for me.

I crashed through the trees into a drift, falling to my knees and running a hand over the leafless bark around me. Up again. Weaving in and out, stumbling over patchy snow and rocks that dug into the soles of my feet, only barely feeling the pain, I pushed down the knowledge that this was a bad thing. A very bad thing. Self-preservation tried forcing a mental image of blackened frostbitten toes. I sucked in the boiling horror that had spoiled such an intimate evening.

But I had to keep moving, had to keep going.

Everything was going to be okay, if I kept running. If I kept dashing through the dense gray night. If I ignored the hollow echoes of the world around me collapsing.

Strained breaths burned, gasping for oxygen to fill my lungs. Everything around me was fuzzy, filled with static from the harrowing lack of air.

I needed to stop.

My legs were like Jell-O, limp and painful from running farther and longer, faster and harder than ever before.

I needed just a second or two.

Placing a hand against the scratchy bark of a tree, I paused. Bending forward and coughing, gasping for whatever oxygen I could choke down.

Silence. Absolute silence thickened the air around me. There was not a single creature of the night that broke the heavy sludge of desolate stillness amidst the forest. I dared not twitch, for fear that I would disturb the slumbering giant resting just an inch beneath the frozen blades piercing the numb pads of my feet.

Then the painted bubble of haunting depravity broke.

"Jane?" a husky voice echoed around me.

My eyes snapped up, darting around as my heart tore out of my chest, beating so fast that I should've died right then.

"Jane!" the voice shouted again, and my gaze whipped behind me.

Dark, hunter eyes appeared around a tree. Shadowy primitive markings scored across a chiseled face of stone and splattered carelessly over the body of the giant that stalked toward me. The stars whirled above me laughing, and the moon wanted to crush me flat; I could feel its weight pressing down. And I was so tired. Except he was coming for me. I had to keep going.

My legs moved, but I was going nowhere fast.

I knew him, but I also didn't. There was an unfamiliarity about the bare torso painted in speckled, deep crimson streaks. The tattoos that were etched across his pecs and swirled down his arms were a hazy memory, muddied by the terror that now ripped through me.

I shook my head, slapping frozen strands of hair against my skin.

Griffin said to run, to not stop for anyone. To not stop for even him. He was someone. Even if it was him, he was someone.

I was supposed to run.

So I did. Shoving off of the tree, my numb feet crashed across the snow, crunching heavily away from the hulking figure that edged nearer and nearer.

Every tree looked the same, every rock that I ran around, seemed to have the exact same edges as the last. There was not a distinguishing feature amongst the forest that gave me a sense of direction.

The snowy path below me sheltered footprints, indicating I was somewhere new, yet it all looked the same.

My lungs tightened, heavy with wet moisture that I was sucking in.

"Jane! Stop running," he called out again, and my footsteps faltered.

Cautiously, I peered over my shoulder. Waiting for my rescuer to find me. It was him. It had to be him, even if it hadn't looked quite like him, the man shouting for me was Griffin.

I should stop for him, right?

"Jane," his voice softened, his hulking frame appearing at a run out of the shadows.

I stumbled back a step. It was him, but I couldn't see past that steely mask the grim reaper had gifted him.

Spinning on my heels, I took off running again. Ignoring the painfully blistering sensation shooting up my legs. Each step sent shocks of needles ripping up my muscles, drowning out the blood pounding in my ears.

He said to run. I was running. Though, it dawned on me—if he was the only one hunting me down now, that had to mean the rest of the guys were gone... dead...? But either way, I was safe now, right? It wasn't like I'd tried to hide my tracks, I'd merely run like Griffin asked.

"Smart ass, stop!" Griffin bellowed, his gravelly voice bouncing around the forest.

And the tone of his voice shifted everything inside me. The cat and mouse game we'd been figuratively playing suddenly became very real.

And I didn't stop. But this time, not because of some foreign terror fueling the fire, but because I liked the idea of teasing him.

"Catch me if you can!" I taunted in response, ignoring the fear that had driven me so far into the forest before. My heart raced, finding a thrill in whatever primal game we were now playing. Blinding myself to the real reason I'd been running like he had asked.

With each tree I rounded, each breath I drew in, oxygen filled my lungs a little deeper.

Griffin was the one following me, chasing me. And only Griffin.

And I liked the thought of him trying to catch me, wishing now that he got some reward if he succeeded. And a reward that didn't just benefit him. One that had me sweating despite the cold, wanting for something that I certainly shouldn't be seeking out in this fake relationship. One that had my mind wandering back to every dirty feeling that caressed my body when he'd shoved me against the wall earlier.

My pace slowed half a second, and I jogged to the left around a group of pines.

And a shadow darted out in front of me. I skidded to a stop, bumping into the bare torso of the very man who had saved me.

"Gotcha," he growled.

I breathed heavily, letting my eyes slowly trace across his glistening body. "Such a shame you never stated what you won if you did," I mindlessly answered, voicing the thought I should've kept secret. Darkened specks of blood swirled with his trickling sweat, dripping down each abdominal muscle like a step ladder. His chest heaved deeply, the tattoos dancing like images come to life along his skin, and my hand lifted as if it had a mind of its own.

Hot breath washed over my head. "Such a shame," he replied, his chest vibrating as my fingers met his warm skin. Needles from delight and excitement pricked within my veins, trailing down deep within my core. A low pulsing began between my legs, aching for release from the man looming over me. It was unexpected and ill-timed, but my body was working in its own realm. I'd been cold, and now I was hot, like slow-moving lava flowed through my veins.

I tipped my head, goosebumps erupting over Griffin's body as my fingers drifted across his pecs and then over his shoulder. He shuddered as I tracked my caress with my eyes, down his bicep, tracing thick veins that ran like rivers down his forearms and along the back of his hands.

My touch lingered, his own fingers flexed as I paused. Staring, trying to deny every desire that was going through my mind and body.

Griffin slowly turned his hand over, exposing his palm to me, and I rested mine flat against his. So small and petite compared to his, so delicate and soft compared to the calloused rough skin that had brought so much violence and pain to others.

"We have to get you warm Jane. There's a real risk of hypothermia. You've been running out here too long." His voice sounded distant, strained knowing that this was the right thing to do, but it was as if he wasn't quite ready to leave. Maybe he liked this rather animalistic game we had briefly played.

"Are they dead?" I whispered, breaking the solace that had spanned between us.

Griffin didn't move. I brushed my fingers lightly down each digit of his, eating up the sparks that snapped between us.

"Do you want them to be?" he muttered.

"I just want to be safe."

"They won't hurt you. They won't come after you again."

I lifted my gaze to his eyes, leaving my touch against him. "That wasn't really an answer."

They could be dead or they could just be seriously injured, or they'd run off; but as I studied his piercing hazel eyes, I exhaled slowly. I didn't really need to know if they were or not. As long as they wouldn't be able to get me, I was fine.

A shiver jolted down my spine, reminding me that I was still standing barely dressed in the middle of a snowy forest at night.

"Let's get home," he gently urged, slipping his hard and bloodied fingers into mine. I hated that this signaled the end of whatever we'd just started. I hated the idea of leaving this rather strange solitude we'd darted off to.

But what I hated the most was the uncertainty that now swirled between us. My entire body ached for him. Begging to be touched by him, to have everything between us consummated in the most raw and feral way known to humankind. But I also knew how unrealistic that possibility was.

For all of this was fake.

Chapter 22

I trailed behind Griffin as he led us back to the truck, which wasn't far away. In my panic, I'd unknowingly run in a circle, and we easily followed my tracks. Distantly, my mind was aware that I was cold, but it was swimming with the shock of everything that had just happened.

Back where I had left Griffin with the three men, all I saw was dark, crimson-stained snow, but not a soul in sight. Letting go of his hand, I walked to the edge of the cliff and began to gather the clothes I'd left strewn beside his. He pulled his pants on as I tugged his sweatshirt over my head, the dry clothes helping warm me as I pulled my wet, and frozen feet into my slippers.

"What did they want with me?" I asked, as my sluggish brain changed tack. "Am I safe?"

His jaw knotted tightly. "I won't let Sam hurt you, okay?"

"*Sam?* Sam sent them? Why does he always show up when you're around?"

"I don't know why he chooses whenever I'm around. Maybe it's just lucky timing on our end. And yes, they told me Sam paid them a decent chunk of money to come collect you. Apparently, from what little they were told by Sam, you remind him of his ex-wife."

I did a double-take. "I had no idea he'd been married before."

"I'll do some digging, but I bet it was a really messy marriage and even worse divorce. Maybe she even tried to lock him up but didn't have enough evidence or something to get the charges to stick." Calloused fingers brushed some hair behind my ear, heat pluming instantly into my face, and I sighed. The fear that consumed me was slowly being released by a demon of a different kind, one less tortuous. One that promised purpose and freedom.

"Sam's kind of a fool, isn't he?" I chuckled nervously, getting in the passenger side door that he held open.

"Why do you say that?" he asked. His shirt was draped over his right arm, hiding the large scar that I wondered if he was self-conscious about.

"After you threatened him, he still sent guys after me with you around," I answered.

"Jane, he sent the guys instead of coming himself *because* of the threat," he stated evenly, then shut the door and walked around the front of the truck. So, did that mean Sam was done trying? My mind went blank as

I watched Griffin wrestle into his shirt as he approached the driver's side door.

Everything in me immediately roared with that dripping desire as each muscle on his body flexed, making his tattoos come to life. Whhhyyyy....? I groaned to myself, annoyed with how quickly my hormones and thoughts betrayed me. It took every ounce of strength in me to tear my gaze away from him and refocus.

Griffin hopped up into the driver's seat and turned the key, giving me a once-over.

Scanning Griffin's face as his intense gaze softened, I noticed a small cut at the base of his jaw. "You're hurt." I lifted my hand and traced the air above the injury.

His brows furrowed, sudden sorrow folding his features, and he snapped his fingers around my wrist. "I'm fine."

"Don't do that." I tugged my arm out of his hold, frustrated. Why was it that I couldn't offer him something in return for his consistent protection that I almost never asked for?

He slowly shook his head, frustration etching deep lines upon his forehead. "Why not? Why are you not scared anymore? They were here—"

"Because you're here," I cut him off. His eyes remained trained forward, staring out into the nothingness that held secrets of his I wished he'd confess to me. He was stained red with the blood of a secret I should've kept to myself. If I had, then we wouldn't be tangled in this mess that we were unintentionally weaving. Still, despite everything that had occurred, it somehow hadn't dawned on him that he was the reason I feared so much less than I had the moment that my father passed. Maybe I should've said something sooner.

"Because you're here," I whispered again, and the tension slipped from his face. Slipping the truck into reverse, we rumbled away from the cliff edge and began putting distance between us and the evidence that violence seemed to follow both of us.

But the thing was, I didn't mind it. If he didn't, then why should I? I mean, yeah, it was disconcerting that we were so frequently bombarded with something that shouldn't be a common occurrence, but who better than Griffin to handle it? Who better than someone equipped with the tools to take care of a situation like this?

"Are you okay?" The words that left his lips were full of things unsaid, worry because he knew. He'd been there for every little trauma-inducing event that had unfolded since moving to this tumultuous little town.

"Right now? Yeah," I answered. And that was the truth. Because at this very moment, I was very much alright because he was here. He made me feel safe.

He was safe.

I wasn't alone at this moment.

"So, does that mean you think Sam won't show up again?" I asked, trying to remind myself of the conversation at hand and swung my eyes to look at Griffin. He clenched his jaw and ran a hand across his stubble, barely flinching when he touched his cut. He didn't answer, leaning against his elbow that rested on the windowsill of his truck.

His eyes drifted through the front windshield as he directed the truck back to the cabin.

I knew the silence meant he didn't believe Sam was done. But I prayed that next time would be the last.

Something was different, again, as we drummed onward, the trees we passed steadily thinning. I watched as he began laying brick after brick on the walls he had already built. The little bit that had broken through, the wrecking ball of mine had only done temporary damage, and he was busy at work once again. There was a part of me that hurt for him, that wished I could take away whatever agony he was battling within himself. There was a war going on in his mind, as if his body came home but he never truly left whatever battlefield he lost himself on.

The cabin loomed ahead as we broke through the forest and pulled back into the driveway. No lights showed, and I felt a sense of relief that we might be able to go to bed without encountering someone else.

Griffin turned off the truck, and I quietly climbed down. My feet sloshed in my wet slippers as we tiptoed into the house; ignoring the pulsing ache from whatever damage my barefoot run had caused. He pressed a finger over his lips, and we crept toward the bedroom barely making a sound. He continued to surprise me with how quietly such a big man could walk.

The bedroom was dark, with Dayton sound asleep in the queen bed beneath Griffin's bunk, and all of the other kids snoring blissfully in their beds. I reached forward and tugged at my fake fiancé's fingers before he was able to climb up onto his mattress. He paused and furrowed his brows.

"Thank you. Again," I whispered as softly as I could, and he gave me a quick smile.

"Nothing to it, smart ass," he answered, though there was something strained in his words. I studied him for a moment longer, but he gave nothing else, and so I tiptoed toward the bathroom.

The moment the shower water was running hot, I slunk naked beneath the stream and plopped to the floor. Steaming liquid slithered down my skin, burning away the chill that had taken hold within my body. I closed my eyes, tucking my knees to my chest, and leaned my head back against the tile.

If it wasn't for Griffin, I would've been what? Dead? Beaten? Kidnapped for sure, but what did Sam want with me? I apparently reminded him of his ex-wife, so was I supposed to be a replacement to fulfill some sick sexual fantasy of his? And what would happen if he showed up somewhere and Griffin wasn't with me?

My stomach churned, nerves prickling within my soul, and the water did nothing to wash it away. Inhaling a shaky breath, a wayward tear escaped down my cheek.

Griffin... I could only imagine what was going on in his head. He desired peace, yet I seemed to only bring him more pain and anguish.

Griffin... My skin tingled, remembering his touch, and I ran a shaky hand over my arm. My lips quivered at the thought of his kiss. Someone so large, so gruff, yet he kissed with a passion that one only found in stories.

Suddenly, I wanted him in here with me. Right at this moment. Something felt like we'd been here before, running in a never-ending circle that continually brought us face to face with death.

Griffin... And every time, he was the only reason I found salvation.

I wanted him in here with me.

Opening my eyes, water trickled over my lashes as I leaned my gaze toward the bathroom door. "Griffin," I whispered. My entire body yearned for him, desperately seeking his comfort and safety. To hell with the fact that I was naked, I could put a swimsuit on. It didn't matter that I was a bundle of confusion. The feelings in me were a whirlpool of sexual desire, fear, excitement, and uncertainty.

"Griffin!" I said a little louder and waited. The water trickled down my body, so much warmer than the lake had been, but I wanted the heat that I got whenever I was wrapped up in his arms.

But he never came.

Long after the water ran rather cold, and my skin was wrinkled raw with blistering heat, he still never joined me.

It shouldn't have disappointed me the way it did, but for whatever reason, it did. It seemed like a rather huge letdown, seeing how he always showed up.

Cleaning myself up quickly, I dressed back in his hoodie. I didn't care that it was dirty, it smelled faintly like him, and I was craving anything from him. Creeping silently out of the bathroom, I paused before climbing my bunk. There he was on his bed, flat on his back, not moving. Barely a sound escaped his lips as his face remained turned toward the ceiling and his eyes closed, his chest rising with slow, rhythmical breaths. Not a drop of dried blood speckled the little bit of his torso that I could see.

A sigh rushed from my lips, and I turned to my bed, climbing to what felt like a lonely retreat from the man that I craved.

Pulling the sheets up to my chin, I turned toward the wall and closed my eyes.

Silence only briefly broken by snoring kids became my tomb. Sleep did not meet me quickly as I would've hoped, and I laid there, waiting for my mind to shut down.

And waited.

And waited.

Faint rustling pierced through the snoring kids, pricking my interest.

Something creaked.

Then my bunk jostled lightly.

Warmth and that familiar citrus scent cascaded over my body as hot breath brushed against my exposed cheek.

Griffin. Everything in me tingled, running hot again as I realized he was next to me, hovering closely. I didn't move for fear that Griffin would leave. My entire body begged for him to stay. He could choose to slip under the sheets next to me and hold me, and I would spin into comfort.

But would he risk stepping across boundaries that weren't there, though he probably didn't know they were non-existent?

Roughened skin gently whispered across my face, pushing some damp hair away from my forehead. My heart jumped, reveling in the rush of desire that crashed through me. He had touched me. However briefly, his skin had danced upon mine. It took everything in me to keep my breathing level, remaining in this state of awakeness but not for fear that I might scare him away.

Then wet lips pressed hot against my cheek, just in front of my ear. Tender and quick, his kiss lingered long after he pulled away. Far after he climbed back down from the bunk, and that single action carried me into dreamworld.

Chapter 23

I groaned, rolling over on my mattress, blinking away the sleep that I hadn't gotten enough of. It had been maybe an hour since I'd dozed off, and I was still struggling to relax. Sitting up, I ran my hand through my messy, tangled hair and gazed around the room in a daze, my tingling sore feet reminding me of the previous night's exploits.

Tilting my head, I rubbed the blurriness from my eyes and stopped, catching sight of a still and slumped figure on the floor near the foot of my bunk. Leaning with his back against the wall and his knees pulled to his chest, Griffin appeared wide awake but stared at nothing. That glassy look I'd seen before back in his eyes.

He'd never actually gone back to bed.

Descending from my bunk, I stepped toward him, seeing his eyes track me, but he didn't move, as if he was aware that I was there, but not processing it. Not even as I sat down in front of him. He was miles away.

"Can't sleep?" I asked, and watched as he blinked slowly but still didn't move. His eyes remained unfocused despite being trained in my direction.

"Griffin. You should get some rest," I whispered, and placed a hand on his thigh. He suddenly jerked away, a snarl lifting on his lips. Balling his hands into fists, he glowered as the film left his beautiful tawny eyes, and he returned to the present

He exhaled in relief and unclenched his hands. "What are you doing down here?" he asked.

"I could ask you the same thing," I muttered and scooted beside him. He shook his head as I reached toward the small cut on his jaw that looked as if he'd cleaned up earlier.

"Why aren't you afraid of me?" he growled, grabbing my hand before I touched him, and he pushed me back.

"What do you mean?" I whispered, but he lurched to his feet.

"You *should* be scared of me. Do you not know the things I've done? What I can do? You worry about Sam?" He raised his hands and waved them toward my face. "But do you not understand what I could do with just these things and nothing else?"

He took a single step toward his bunk, shaking his head.

"I *am* scared of you, Griffin," I whispered, and he jerked to a halt. "But not in that way. Maybe the very reasons that you think I should be afraid of you are the very reasons that I'm not."

His brows tightened, deepening in an expression of confusion and surprise. I'd given him a reason to think differently. Perhaps, it wasn't rational of me, I knew that. But nothing of this here was real anyway, and no matter what, he always brought me some sort of peace and protection. Even at the expense of himself.

"You are unexpected, Jane Barlow," he whispered, moving only his eyes to look at me.

"I was beginning to think you'd forgotten my name, Griffin Marsh."

"I do prefer 'smart ass.'" He grinned reluctantly, and I bit down on my bottom lip feeling instantly better. "Now, go back to bed before we wake the kids and have to babysit at this awful hour."

I rolled my eyes and pointed to his bunk. "You should, too, you know."

Suddenly, his hand shot forward and wrapped around my wrist. I paused, staring at his fingers, wondering what was going on. Slowly, I raised my gaze to meet his. It passed over his plaid pajama pants that hung low on his hips and across his bare torso. Scanning upwards along the dusting of hair running up to his navel and along his chiseled abs, his tatted pecs rose with each breath, and I saw his Adam's apple bob with a slow deliberate swallow in his thick neck. I stopped at his velvet lips. Mine tingled instantly, memory twisting my insides, and melting everything below my waist.

He could kiss me again, and I wouldn't resist.

"You have something of mine," he whispered, and I blinked, confused. Then my cheeks burned as it dawned on me.

"I thought... Your mom wasn't... It was to..." I stuttered, trying to explain why I'd stolen his hoodie. He chuckled, released my wrist, and brushed a finger across my cheek. I shuddered against his touch, surprised and excited.

"I like it on you." He raised his brows and then turned around, quickly ascending his bunk, his sweats outlining his outrageous glutes. I patted my cheeks, trying to understand what I was doing.

This was all fake. Everything he did was for show to make sure that his family never accidentally caught us slacking. Only now I had begun to understand I was caught in this charade, hook, line and sinker.

Quietly, I climbed into my bunk and laid down on the mattress, unable to fall asleep. I stared at the ceiling, raised my left hand, twisting and turning it in front of me, and stared at the ring I'd nearly forgotten about for another hour at least, my heart racing. He intrigued me. I couldn't deny that. Nor could I deny the inevitable feelings that were slowly growing, or the fact that I didn't mind this piece of jewelry on my finger. No matter what, though, I would never act on any of these desires. When this weekend was over and my debt was repaid, these feelings and this beautiful ring would have to go away, and I would make sure that no one found out that I was ever actually interested in Griffin.

Ever.

When I woke in the morning, the sun was barely peeking through the curtains. A soft pink hue lighting the still room. Pushing myself on to my elbows after a restless night's sleep, I glanced around. Every bed was still occupied.

Except Griffin's.

His sheets were tucked in nicely as if it'd never been touched in the first place, and the brown leather decorative pillows were back on his bunk. Everyone else was still snoring, which made me curious as to where he went.

I slipped down the ladder and grabbed my claw clip and glasses from the counter in the bathroom. Wincing, I managed to walk on the sides of my bruised feet, the nylon carpet testing the little nicks and cuts I'd sustained during my flight from the assailants, until I got used to it. Twisting my hair up into a bun as I went, I adjusted the hem of Griffin's hoodie and, with no one around to see, buried my nose in the sleeve that still wafted his citrus cologne.

The kitchen was empty, as was the sitting room. The house was quiet and dark as I crept up the stairs and peeked around the corner. He wasn't up here or outside on the patio. Carefully trudging back down the stairs, I tucked my hands into the sleeves of the sweatshirt and wandered down the only hallway I'd yet to explore. One that the kids and many of the men had left a wet trail to yesterday.

Another cream-hued painting hung along the wall to my left as the corridor split into two. I could either continue straight and follow the bend, or head to my right. The smell of chlorine was faint here, but at the end of that hallway was another door with a sign that said 'swimming pool' beside it. It needed a passcode to enter, but I tried the handle anyway and found it unlocked.

Swinging the door open, I stepped into the stuffy room. Chairs lined the edge of the pool, set up against the outer walls of floor-to-ceiling glass windows and sliding doors. There was a small water slide at the far side of the pool and a diving board beside it.

Water lapped the edge as Griffin stroked methodically from one end to the other, gliding through the water, effortlessly and at ease. I crouched down at the edge and waited as he swam toward me. The rope-like muscles in his back twisted powerfully with each stroke, dancing the large tattoo across his skin with every shift. I shook my head, hypnotized, fighting with the feelings that this simple movement of his evoked. When he reached the end, he paused and stood up. Shaking his head, he blinked and wiped the water from his face. The stubble along his jaw was trimmed nicely as if he'd been up for hours. His skin glistened from the droplets of liquid sliding along the valleys and mountains chiseled upon his steel frame.

"It's early. What are you doing here?" he asked me, leaning back once more in the pool and floating away.

"I could ask you the same thing," I replied, and he rolled his eyes.

"Working out, obviously."

"So, you couldn't sleep is more like it."

"Either way," he muttered and then rocked forward once more. "Go put on a swimsuit and come join me."

I shook my head. "Believe it or not, I'm actually a terrible swimmer. You just happened to pretty much hold me up the entire time last night."

"Speaking of last night, are you alright?" he asked.

Taking a deep breath, I slowly nodded. "A bit bruised, my feet hurt a little, but yeah, I think I'm okay." And honestly, I was. Maybe it was because Griffin was here. Maybe it was because it seemed no matter what was going on between us, he always made sure I was safe. But for whatever the reason, I was okay.

He glided my way and neared the edge of the pool. "Well, good. So, go change, and I'll teach you how to swim."

"Trust me, you don't want to try."

"If you don't want to put a bathing suit on, at least take that sweatshirt off so you don't get chlorine all over my favorite hoodie," he demanded.

"Despite my actions from last night, I don't enjoy the feeling of wet clothes at all."

"Then naked it is." Griffin grinned and gripped the waistband of his shorts. "I haven't been skinny dipping in years."

"STOP!" I shrieked and threw my hands in the air.

"Oh come on. Don't you remember being a teenager and how thrilling it was to go skinny dipping for the first time?" He wiggled his brows.

"No, I do not." I crossed my arms in front of my chest, and he lifted his brows. Releasing his waistband, he waded the last couple steps to the edge of the pool and placed his hands on the concrete in front of me.

"Was it that horrible for you?" he asked, and I shook my head.

"Then it was so exhilarating you know nothing will compare."

I once again shook my head, no. He furrowed his brows confused for a moment and then blinked in surprise. "You've never been skinny dipping before, have you?"

"The first time I let a guy see me naked will *not* be while skinny dipping," I stated firmly, and he pushed off of the edge of the pool, slowly backstroking away.

"So, you've considered the thought of me seeing you naked?" His lips lifted into a grin.

"You're giving me a headache," I muttered, and he chuckled. "No, it's just one of those rules I gave myself when I first started finding boys interesting."

"What other rules do you have?" he mindlessly asked, swirling his arms as I sat down on grating concrete, dipping my legs into the warm water, and easing my aching feet.

"I don't really have more than one."

He stood up straight again, the water sheeting from his body, and looked at me confused. "Your one single rule is no skinny dipping until after a guy has seen you naked somewhere else before?"

"No, dummy. No sex until I know it's love. Everything stems from that, which includes getting naked." I kicked my feet back and forth in the water.

Griffin slowly waded through the water toward me, his gaze fixed upon my eyes with this intensity that almost had me looking away.

Almost.

"That's a pretty old-fashioned way of thinking," he said, and I pulled my lips between my teeth and nodded.

"Quite admirable, too," he added softly.

I sighed as he swam between my legs, easing them gently apart. I didn't fight it, even though I probably should have. "None of my exes thought so."

"How so?" he asked, tipping his head and watching me intently.

"None of my relationships ever lasted long because they either tried to hook up with me within the first week of dating or would cheat on me and say it was my fault because I refused to sleep with them." I mimicked a masculine frown, tucking my head in and deepening my voice. "A man has needs, Jane," I mocked, and he chuckled.

"Anyway, now most of the time when men find out I've never had sex before, they call me a prude." I lifted a shoulder resignedly as his brows twitched in surprise.

"Wait, what?"

I looked away, frustrated. "Of course you'd think that too. Why did I have a small amount of hope that maybe, just maybe, you'd be different."

"Jane," he said, but I still didn't look at him, annoyed that every guy seemed the same. I had been a fool to think any differently about Griffin.

"Smart ass, look at me," he commanded, and for whatever reason, I was unable to refuse. My eyes slowly drifted to his, though I kept the scowl prominent on my face. "I am just surprised to hear that a beautiful woman like yourself is still a virgin. That is all."

I narrowed my gaze suspiciously at him, but he didn't falter in his stare. He'd called me beautiful so casually. Shaking my head, I cleared my thoughts of that distraction and remained steady in my conviction that he was just the same.

"Think about it," he continued. "This world is so deep into hook-up culture that it's extremely rare for any adult woman to at least not have had one partner before. I don't judge what anyone chooses to do with their body; it's their choice. For me, personally, as long as a woman understands how much value she holds and treats her body with that same self-respect that I would show her, I will date her. I've never been into the one-night stand thing, so I would hope that my future partner shares that belief. What I'm trying to say is that your decision is just not often made these days."

I studied his almond eyes, the blue from the water reflecting across his bright irises. "No, I guess it's not," I mumbled and looked down at my legs. At his waist that was tucked between them, so intimately, and yet I wasn't pushing him away, even if this was fake and there was no one else around.

Fingers brushed beneath my chin, and he gently lifted my head. "What I find even more surprising, though, is that you claim to have never been in love."

"I never said that," I quickly countered, and he tipped his head.

"No? You said that you won't have sex unless you're in love. Then you followed that up with the fact that you're a virgin," he explained, and I leaned back on my hands, turning my gaze to the ceiling, and mulling his words

"I was in love once. He's kind of the reason that I have been so stuck on this rule actually," I confessed. I felt his hands grip the sides of my thighs, and he brushed his thumb back and forth across my skin. Electricity rippled through me.

"What happened?" Griffin asked.

"He destroyed me." Closing my eyes, I took a steadying breath. Telling Griffin would mean sharing this story with someone who wasn't my dad. I'd never even told everything to my mom after it all came crashing down. But, it would feel nice to have someone else know what had happened. Even if it wasn't that big of a deal to anyone else, what had happened was a huge deal to me.

"He was my first real boyfriend after high school. I was a brand new college girl, barely eighteen, and feeling like I was on top of the world. He was a couple of years older and in one of my classes. I honestly don't even remember which one. We met and from day one became inseparable. I was head over heels by day two. Naive, I know." I began bowing my head. Griffin was quiet. His expression was solemn, but his fingers were still stroking across my thighs.

"We made it official only a week after meeting, and I followed him around like a puppy. By this point, I'd never done more than make out with a little tongue, so he was giving me all sorts of butterflies as our relationship was on torpedo speed toward disaster. At first, he was kind and caring and asked things about me, but the moment that he managed to convince me to stick my hands down his pants, everything immediately changed. I learned later they call it love-bombing, and it's a form of manipulation." I glanced behind Griffin's shoulder as my cheeks burned red. I was embarrassed, but I had been so young then, and hopefully have grown a bit since then.

"Anyhow, I was obviously inexperienced, so he would bait me into doing things more and more by telling me I just needed more practice to 'get him off,'" I muttered, unable to look Griffin in the face. He was probably laughing at me, and I couldn't bear the thought of seeing him smirk. "From that point on, everything between us was about the physical stuff. He never asked me for permission when he would do things to me, and after his hands had been up my shirt or in my pants, he would tell me I owed him his turn, even if he never was able to get me to you know…"

Tears silently spilled over the edge and crashed down my cheeks. My vision turned blurry as my heart split in my chest. It had been so long since I'd thought about all of this, so much learned since then that I felt sorrow for that girl I'd once been. She had been through so much.

"Anyway, one day he begged me for sex, saying I owed him that after three months of dating, and that he was embarrassed he'd never seen me naked. His friends told him that it was ridiculous. He said they told him I was using him and leading him on. But I hadn't even wanted him to touch me to begin with, because it mostly left me hurting. I don't know how I found the courage to lie to him, but I told him I couldn't see him that night because I had a test the next day."

Fingers brushed the tears away from my cheeks, gently, and I finally looked at Griffin. His face held a strange tension. Rage but also pain. Not at me, but *for* me.

"As I thought over that decision, I came to the conclusion that I must love him, and I was simply scared, so I decided to surprise him. I'm forever grateful and ashamed that I gave in and showed up at his apartment, because I walked in on him screwing my best friend. Of course, he blamed me, saying it was my fault for refusing him. From that moment forward, I set a hard rule, promising myself that *anything* sexual would have to be after love. My parents taught me that sex is supposed to bring a couple closer together, enhance the relationship and not be the sole focus of it. So, while I do think that in some way I loved him, it wasn't the kind of love that I truly desire," I finished, feeling my pulse thud in my ears. Griffin's expression never changed as his eyes stayed glued upon mine. In those seconds of silence, I'd never felt so vulnerable, but I never thought to question why I told him or why I should.

I waited for him to say something as he studied me. The wheels were spinning in his head, I could see they were working overtime by the concentration on his face as he fought with whatever thoughts were riddling his mind. "That was abuse, Jane. You know that right?" he finally stated, and I nodded.

"I told my dad what had happened a couple of years after, and he helped me work through it. You're the only other person who knows now. Or I guess the *only* person who knows since my father isn't around anymore.

I've never even told my mom because I was afraid she'd shame me. Although I know that's ridiculous."

"Knowing you now, I'm surprised you stayed through all of that."

"Again, I was a naive young girl." I managed a small smile.

"You're definitely not anymore," he said, raising one brow and openly running his gaze over me.

"No, I'm a smart ass now, remember?" I said, feeling strangely self-conscious.

"How could I forget? It's my favorite thing." His grin widened and his eyes sparkled.

"You won't tell anyone else, though, will you?" I whispered, and he shook his head.

"That's not a story for me to tell."

"And you don't think I'm a prude?"

"Not at all. Honestly, it's quite refreshing to meet a woman who seems to have more of a long-term mindset about relationships."

"Even if this is all fake," I said without thinking. His grin faltered, but only for a moment before the brightness slapped back on his face.

"Even if," he muttered. Griffin pushed off the ledge and swam away from me. "Go get a swimsuit on and come join. I offered to teach you to swim, and as you've clearly seen, I'm a phenomenal swimmer."

"Yet, I'm a horrible student. Stubborn as an ox."

He snickered. "I'm very aware of that. Now, get a move on before everyone else wakes up and we get kicked out of here."

I inhaled and rolled my eyes.

"Hurry up, smart ass."

Standing up, I saw a subtle, crooked smile splay across his lips before he ducked back into the water and began swimming his laps once more. I placed a hand over my chest as I walked from the pool room. Why was my heart beating so quickly?

Fanning myself, I shook my head. Why was I feeling so hot?

It had to be the humidity in the pool room that was causing me to sweat, nothing else would spark such a visceral reaction from me. Not the idea that he would touch me again. He'd been touching me, holding me last night in the lake, so why was this suddenly different? Or maybe it wasn't. He'd been so intimately standing between my legs just barely, so what had changed? Why was I so calm and excited at the same time around him?

It was the sudden shift of temperature from the pool room compared to the rest of the house. Yes, that was it.

Chapter 24

I stared in the mirror, worrying that I'd chosen the wrong bathing suit. My idiot self had packed only two: a one piece and a bikini. He was going to teach me to swim, so I needed to keep things as distant as possible. Right?

So, I picked my forest green one piece. I loved the way the low crisscross tie design flattered my back. The front was simple with thin straps and high cut-out legs. I really did like the way I looked in it, even though it covered much more skin than a bikini would.

Pulling the claw clip from my hair, I began braiding it down my back as I quietly escaped the bathroom. Creeping through the bedroom past the still slumbering teens, I exited into the hallway and finished wrapping the tie around the bottom of my long braid. It swung against my exposed back as I hustled sore-footed toward the pool room.

Tugging the door open, I saw Griffin was once again swimming a couple laps. He seemed so at peace, so comfortable being alone, I wondered if that would ever change.

Griffin flipped onto his back and swam my way as I waded carefully into the pool. He broke the water, droplets falling from his skin as the most genuine smile filled his face, unlike anything I'd seen from him yet. The water lapped around my waist as I stopped halfway down the stairs.

He walked quietly toward me and then reached forward with one hand. Without hesitation, I placed my palm in his, and his calloused fingers wrapped around mine, practically swallowing my entire hand in his grip.

While it barely seemed like enough time, and he teased me for most of it, he did actually help me improve my terrible swimming skills. I actually enjoyed myself, unlike most trips to the pool.

Poking my tummy as I floated on my back, he jabbed a finger over and over. "Why are you letting your belly sink?"

"Because every time you poke it, it tickles." I choked through some water that splashed onto my face.

He poked my belly again, and I squeezed my abs, giggling. "Stop," I whined as I started to sink.

"You better stick that stomach up, or you'll drown, and I never said I'd save you." He grinned and poked my tummy again.

"Griffin!" I splashed some water toward his face, trying to evade his fingers.

"How dare you splash the teacher!" he cried out with a grin and dove toward me. I quickly ducked under the water and attempted to swim away.

Which was obviously a massive fail as he tossed me over his shoulder, rising from the water.

"Put me down!" I screeched, pounding against his back. He chuckled and dove under the water, holding me tight. I hastily took a breath, and closing my eyes, I waited as he stroked beneath the surface.

It was eerily calm, and I wasn't afraid, despite the lack of control I had.

Eventually, he slowly rose from the water and slid me down from his shoulder. My arms remained tightly wound around his neck in anticipation for another moment where he would dive underneath the surface, his wet skin feeling as slippery smooth as silk.

Except he didn't.

The mischievous grin fell from his face as his lips hovered an inch away from mine. I was stuck in his eyes, captured within a soul that I longed to discover. His hold around my waist tightened, as he pulled me closer into his body. A free hand slid down my legs and lifted them around his hips, pressing me against his entire frame.

And there we remained.

His breath whispered hotly across my face as water cascaded down our skin, pooling between what little space there was. So close. My heart raced in my chest, begging me to remain as still as possible. Wishing this would never end, as he didn't blink and I refused to move. A longing passed through his gaze, locked so strongly upon mine.

Not a sound was uttered as I held tightly to this stranger who was becoming too familiar, too quickly.

His eyes fluttered to my lips. It wouldn't take much to meet them with his own, and I certainly wouldn't fight it.

Kiss me.

It wasn't that hard, and it wasn't like he hadn't done it before.

But this time, there wasn't pressure from anyone else around. There was no obligation to maintain appearances. It was only the two of us, our bodies wound tightly together, that would be witness to this.

Water droplets glistened on his thick, dark lashes that I hadn't had the chance to study before. Sunlight blazing in through the windows cast a deep shadow across his jawline as he instinctively hoisted me even closer against himself. I didn't dare breathe for fear he would let go. I didn't dare blink for fear it would break the spell that had me wrapped in his arms, feeling his heart beat heavily in his chest.

My lips parted ever so slightly as I blinked in anticipation. He leaned closer, hesitating just above my mouth.

A single centimeter would close the gap, so minimal that the ghost of his lips brushed briefly against mine. He lifted a hand from around my waist and tucked a few strands of wet hair behind my ear that had been stuck to my cheek. Letting his touch linger, he pressed his palm against my damp skin, his thumb swiping back and forth in front of my ear.

Ricochets of hazy stars bounced around me, fading everything but him away into darkness. All that was here was him, his kiss, inviting and waiting. Warm and wet, holding that refreshing taste that I longed to have back on my tongue.

My head was swimming, my breathing rapid as I leaned toward him, closing the remaining space between his lips and mine.

In the instant before they met, the door crashed open, boyish chatter echoing through the pool room. Griffin quickly let go of me, and I jerked my legs from around his waist, pushing away. My sheepish gaze flipped to our new companions who had spotted us and stood watching in the doorway.

Dayton was staring directly at the two of us, and an unexpected but familiar face peeked over his shoulder.

"No. Way," Jackson muttered and then slugged Dayton in the shoulder. "You didn't say it was Miss B who was dating your brother when you told me he *actually* brought his girlfriend yesterday." He grinned and wiggled his brows in my direction as Dayton's face fell into a scowl.

"Technically fiancée, and that was on purpose," he muttered, and my thumb felt for the ring I'd briefly forgotten was on my finger.

"Why though?" Jackson asked, still grinning as he pushed past Dayton and nodded toward me in approval. He carried in a couple of pool noodles and stripped his tank over his head.

"It's embarrassing is why," Dayton grumbled, following him in and pulling off his T-shirt. A couple other kids around their age I'd seen since arriving here meandered in, talking amongst themselves.

Jackson rolled his eyes. "Why is it embarrassing? She's hot. So, did you expect your brother to pull any less than someone like Miss B?" he asked, then jumped into the water. It sloshed against my body, and I instinctively waded toward Griffin. I felt like we were overhearing a conversation not meant for our ears.

"That's exactly the problem!" Dayton shouted and then cannonballed in directly after Jackson. "It just seems even more personal and weird because I know her. You know?" Water dripped from his hair after he surfaced, and he shook it off just as Griffin had earlier. They were definitely siblings.

I glanced at Griffin, and he raised his brows but said nothing. Dayton turned and glared in my direction.

"Do you not understand how gross it was to walk in on my brother and my teacher tangled in each other's arms? Knowing I was sleeping in the same room as them?" he cried out, and Jackson snickered.

"Dude, that wasn't that bad," he answered, and shook his head.

"I WASN'T TALKING ABOUT JUST BARELY!" Dayton yelled again, and my cheeks flushed red with embarrassment. "You're lucky you couldn't come until today. It saved you from seeing my brother with a boner caused by our history teacher."

"Dayton," Griffin finally said, and Dayton shook his head.

"Don't. Just go, would you? Take yourself and Miss B and get out of here."

"Come on, man," Griffin tried again.

"I'm not doing this," Dayton snapped. Jackson floated backwards, blending into the group of other kids that had formed at the opposite end of the pool. Dayton slunk this way as Griffin studied him.

Once he was standing in front of us, his eyes narrowed. "You don't get it at all, do you?" he hissed, and Griffin clenched his jaw.

"Then help me understand," he replied, and Dayton shook his head, annoyed.

"You could've said something on Wednesday. Either of you could've." Dayton's eyes snapped to meet mine. "How could you agree to help me knowing that it was you all along?"

I kept my mouth shut as guilt spread through me. Griffin shot me a confused glance, and I shook my head, silently communicating that I'd explain later.

"That's right. You're a coward, and I can't tell if it's because you're ashamed to be with my brother or just arrogant in thinking that this only hurts you if things don't work out," Dayton snarled, and I closed my eyes, thinking *he's so, so wrong.*

"Dayton, I agreed because it is—"

"Don't Miss B. Just don't. I'm still trying to get that image out of my head. My *teacher* and my brother. I understand a little bit why you weren't super open about your personal life, Miss B. Because you are my teacher." Dayton's eyes shot back toward Griffin. "But you're my brother. You could've said something so she didn't have to cross that line."

Griffin clenched his jaw and inhaled deeply. But instead of speaking, he shook his head and turned away. It took two steps for him to reach the side of the pool where he pulled himself up and out. I would've normally ogled, but the situation kept me from doing so. He snatched a pool towel from a chair off to the side, wrapped it around his shoulders and silently stalked back into the house.

"Would you like to at least apologize?" Dayton snapped toward me.

"This isn't as black and white as you're making it out to be Dayton, but I am—"

"Another excuse," he cut me off, and I took a deep breath, reminding myself to stay calm.

"I am sorry it's hurt you, Dayton. That was never my intention," I quickly said, and turned around. I needed to go find Griffin and figure out what was going through his head.

"Coward!" he shouted. "Just walk away like he did!" My heart tore in two. This wasn't the reaction I had hoped for. Maybe it had been a little expected and feared, but I had hoped and prayed that things would go better. Griffin needed to talk to him. He could get through to Dayton in a way I wasn't allowed or able to.

Grabbing another pool towel, I wrapped it around my waist and quickly jogged into the house. My bare feet clapped against the concrete floor, but this time I felt nothing as I rushed toward the bedroom, following a small trail of water, as I attempted to dry myself off.

"Griffin!" I shouted as I burst through the door. He wasn't here, but I could hear the shower running. Shoving into the bathroom, I glanced at the closed door that separated the three sink vanity and the small room that had the toilet and shower.

"Griffin," I called out again, leaning up against the door and pressing my ear close in hope that he would hear me. As I was about to call again, it suddenly swung open. I shrieked and fell into the bathroom, crashing against the cold, tile floor right next to the glass shower door.

"What the—" Griffin shouted as my eyes took in absolutely *everything* my very naked, very fake fiancé had to offer.

Chapter 25

Griffin spun around to face the wall as I clamped my hands over my eyes. That had not just happened. Not to me.

But of course it had. The way my luck had been lately... I managed to bite back a half smile, knowing that at least he had nothing to be ashamed of or hide. Though that was going to hurt if we ever—

Hold on, nope.

"Jane, what in the actual fuck?" he stated flatly, thankfully interrupting my thoughts. I continued to lay flat on the floor with my eyes covered.

"The door opened on its own when I leaned against it," I muttered.

Silence.

An eternity of awkward silence expanded between us, and then I heard a faint snort.

Griffin chuckled, hesitantly at first, and then it slowly swelled into booming laughter. My cheeks flamed red, but I managed to squeak out a few giggles as the awkwardness and silence slithered away.

"Well, how was it?" he asked through fits of bellowing as I turned even more red.

"How was what?"

"Seeing a man naked for the first time in your life."

"You're not the first guy I've seen butt-ass naked." I snorted.

"Excuse me?!" His voice was bouncing with humor. I kept my eyes closed, rolled over, and splayed out flat on my back.

"Did you forget about my ex hooking up with my friend?"

"No."

"And I walked in on Noah humping his pillow when he was like thirteen. When he turned around in shock that I was there, let's just say my twenty-year-old self should've gone to therapy," I choked out through spurts of laughter as Griffin bellowed again.

"Your fault for not knocking."

"That's the thing, I did knock. Twice actually. So loudly my dad yelled at me for disrespecting his door." I breathed through a few coughing fits as Griffin roared harder.

"Oh my hell," he snorted. "Not surprising though."

"Then like a year and a half later, I got really sick and needed to puke. The door wasn't locked to the bathroom, and the light wasn't on, so I went busting up in that joint. I definitely did not make it into the toilet as I walked in on Noah. Again. Having some *alone* time," I said, and Griffin wheezed. I heard him pound a fist against the wall as he attempted to calm his breathing.

"Once I finished puking my guts out on the floor and all over my brother, Noah chased me out of the bathroom still completely naked. I desperately hauled my sick self toward the kitchen where both of my parents were enjoying a glass of wine after dinner," I continued, and heard Griffin fall to the floor of the shower, roaring even louder with laughter.

"I doubt they'd ever seen something quite like that in their entire lives. My brother was kind of chunky at the time, too, so his butt cheeks were just a-slapping as he came sliding into the room. Vomit covered his torso and now shriveled up parts. I will never forget my parents' faces as they stared at my very pale self, collapsed on the kitchen floor, and my brother who hadn't yet realized that he was standing in front of them without a shred of clothing on." I tried to gulp down the recollection of a memory I so wished I could forget.

"Jane, that is the most beautiful and blessed story I've ever been graced with being told." Griffin snorted. My breathing started to slow as I continued to lay on the floor.

I coughed a couple times. "I guess the only question left now is, are you a grower like my brother, or a shower?"

"You know, for someone so innocent, you sure know a lot of dirty things."

"I have a brother, Griffin. Does that not explain it all?"

"Fair enough." He chuckled, and then I heard some movement and the shower turned off. I still didn't move, still stared at the black of my shut eyelids as the door squeaked.

"You can open your eyes now," Griffin said. I carefully peeked through a small slit. He was standing beside me on the right with a towel fully wrapped around his waist, his tawny gaze bright as he watched me.

Pushing myself up, I groaned and rubbed my shoulder that had smashed against the ground first. "You alright?" he asked, and I nodded, standing up. "What did you come here for anyway?"

I blinked and furrowed my brows. Forgetting for a moment why I'd ended up on the floor of the bathroom to begin with. "Oh, I wanted to see if you were okay," I softly whispered, and his brows twitched, bunching together.

"You...what?"

"I wanted to check on you," I hesitantly said, and he took a physical step back.

"You were worried about me?"

I nodded.

"You didn't come here to tell me your opinion on what I should've done?"

"I have an opinion, but no," I replied, and he crossed his arms in front of his delicious bare pecs, the shading of his black tattoos rippling with the movement.

"You're not here to tell me that Dayton is hurting and I should be more concerned about how my actions affect him?"

I shook my head. His eyes widened and brows lifted, looking visibly shocked as if that's who everyone always cared about. Not Griffin.

"Why would you care if I was okay or not?" he whispered, his voice choking on his words. I didn't say anything, unable to trust the sounds that would come from my mouth. He stared at me, bewildered. Water dripped down my back from my damp hair. Goosebumps rose across my skin as I let him study me.

"What's your opinion?" he finally asked, and I narrowed my gaze, questioning if this was a trick or not. He gave me a tender smile. "I genuinely want to know."

I swallowed. "I think you should talk to Dayton."

Griffin's smile fell, and he shook his head. "Of course you do. Everyone thinks I should *talk* to Dayton," he grumbled. "Why is it always about—"

"Not for Dayton, but for you," I quickly cut in.

"What?" he stammered.

"For you, Griffin," I reiterated.

"What do you mean?"

I stood up and stepped closer to him and offered a small smile. "Because. You deserve the kind of love that comes from a sibling. Noah and I may seem like we are always butting heads, but he's been my rock through some of the hardest times of my life. I've never told him what happened with my first boyfriend in college, yet he always knew something was wrong. He was the person I called when Sam hit me. He was the person I called when I thought I'd failed an exam. And then when my dad died..." My voice trailed off as Griffin walked a couple steps closer.

"Nobody should be alone all the time, Griffin," I whispered, and his brows twitched.

"You have no right to be in the middle of this," he quietly said, and I sucked in my bottom lip.

"I know."

He shook his head. "Yet, I'm not angry at you." I barely heard his words as his gaze darkened. "I should be angry with you, but I'm not." My heart raced in my chest as he stared at me. Capturing me in a chokehold as thoughts swam through his mind.

My chest rose faster and faster with each heavy breath. I wasn't afraid that he'd hurt me. I was afraid that I was becoming more attached than I should be. I was afraid of all that I was feeling, everything I couldn't understand as he intensely studied me.

Then he turned and walked steadily out of the bathroom. I closed my eyes and let my body relax into confusion. Confusion over everything. This was fast, so fast. A one-eighty turn from just a couple weeks ago when I'd first met him. I could barely keep up with the anger from his mom, disappointment and sadness from his brother, and the whirlwind of desire for him.

Desire I would forever need to deny.

I quickly turned around and double-checked that I shut the door tightly behind me. Locking it, I let the wet towel fall to the floor and removed my bathing suit before stepping into the shower. The water was already warm as it streamed over my body, my mind swimming with everything.

Yet, only one thing. The one thing I shouldn't ever think about again, but I couldn't help settling on. It was as if someone wrote him in a book and then peeled him from the pages, plopping him into real life with a sprinkle of mystery.

I hadn't mistaken what I'd seen between his legs either; there was no way, even if it was brief. That was not something anyone would forget anytime soon. None of his ex-girlfriends cheated on him for the lack thereof, unless he wasn't that good in bed despite his well blessed—

"What are you doing, Jane?" I gasped out loud. Thinking about such dirty things was absolutely wrong. Especially since it was about someone who would become a stranger the moment this weekend was done.

I should be thinking about how we were going to stage our breakup, not how good or bad he was in bed. Besides, I wouldn't know either way, seeing as I had zero experience in that department. I wasn't curious. Absolutely not.

Shaking my head, I quickly finished rinsing the chlorine from my hair and my body, then turned the water off. Snagging a new towel from the rack above the toilet, I dried myself off and then wrapped it around my torso, tying it tightly near my armpit before unlocking the door. I walked toward the vanity and stared at my reflection.

Time for some makeup. Grabbing my small bag from amongst all of the teenagers' things, I got to work. Humming, I applied some concealer and blush, lightly filled in my brows, and finally got started on a little mascara.

Movement by the door caught my eye, and I turned to see Griffin, fully dressed and leaning against the frame watching me. He was wearing dark green joggers, barely holding together against his tree-trunk legs, paired with a black, long-sleeved sweater. A casual and comfortable look that was very flattering on him and accentuated his sinewy body in all the right areas.

"Hi?" I questioned. He placed his hands against the top of the doorframe and leaned forward.

"Hi." He smiled, and I stared at him through the mirror, holding tightly to my mascara wand. *Ugh,* those biceps. He should *not* be standing like that... "I talked with Dayton," he added, and I took a steadying breath, trying to concentrate on applying the last bit of makeup.

"How'd it go?" I asked, brushing dark liquid over my lashes, using it as the distraction I needed from the lascivious sight Griffin was right now.

"You were right," he said, and I gasped.

"Did you just say I'm right?" I overemphasized my excitement, and he shook his head. Pulling his hands down from that very delicious lean, he walked into the bathroom and stopped beside me.

"I hope you were listening because I'll never say it again, smart ass." He grinned and leaned his butt against the counter. I giggled and finished the last few strokes of mascara.

"So, everything is okay now? With Dayton at least?"

"Yeah, better than okay. Though he says he still needs to talk to you about your 'plan.' Whatever that is." Griffin narrowed his gaze accusingly toward my eyes, before dropping to my lips.

"Mmmmk," I mumbled, brushing some clear lip gloss on.

"That's it? You're not going to tell me what this plan is?" he asked, and I shook my head.

"It's none of your beeswax," I stated, twisting the lid on tightly and facing him. His eyes glanced over me, and he almost forgot to catch the smile that crept across his face.

"You just checked me out," I gasped.

"Did not!" he quickly exclaimed and ran a hand over his jawline. "I was just wondering how much you have left to do before you're ready."

"Right. You totally weren't checking me out. Not at all." I lifted a suspicious brow. He shook his head and turned away. "I just need to finish my hair and get dressed. Why?"

"My family is getting ready to go skiing, so I came to make sure you hurry."

"SKIING?" I shouted. "Like with those two long pieces of wood beneath your feet?"

"Or snowboarding. But yes?" he questioned, and I shook my head.

"Nope. This is not happening," I muttered and ran a brush through my damp hair.

"You don't know how to ski, do you?" Griffin exclaimed with too happy of a grin on his face.

"Don't you dare make fun of me," I coldly stated and threw my hands on my hips.

"I wouldn't dream of it." He grinned wickedly.

"Then what's with that face?"

"What face?"

"That one! The one you get whenever you're about to do something I don't particularly like."

He chuckled. "This is my 'I'll teach you' face."

"I don't really have a choice otherwise, do I?" He grinned widely and shook his head. "Fine. But if I break a bone or die, that's on you. And you don't want to know what will happen after."

"You know I've got you," he answered, unexpectedly solemn, and everything in me relaxed, loosening the tension that held my shoulders up to my ears.

"I want breakfast before we leave though."

"I wouldn't expect anything less." He leaned forward and quickly pressed his lips against my forehead, turned around, and then stopped, stiffening. I froze as a spark fired deep in my chest and sent a warm current creeping from my head to my toes, as though I'd plugged into a light socket. But this wasn't sensual.

Stunned, all I could do was stare at his back.

My heart thumped heavily against my ribs, pounding with the shock rippling through my body and pumping deafening blood into my ears.

And desire. A craving for something as simple as that to happen again. Specifically from him.

He remained frozen in place, each second passing like a drum beating through thick sludge.

His fingers balled into fists, and then relaxed, stretching out.

He'd just kissed my forehead, as if we were two casual lovers in an actual relationship.

Then he strode from the bathroom without another word.

A feeling of numb weakness replaced the warmth as he left, as though my mind and my heart had disappeared with him.

What was that?

Chapter 26

Nervously approaching all the breakfast chatter emanating from the direction of the kitchen, I smoothed my french braids and brushed flecks of lint from the simple black top I'd paired with black joggers. It was probably not the most stylish ensemble, but I was going for comfort and warmth at this point.

Pausing at the corner, I saw glances thrown my way, and the chatter died a little, especially when Cara's icy stare along her patrician nose lifted higher in challenge. Already fully made up, her heavy kohl eyeliner reminded me of a raccoon I'd once seen. It had been rabid too. My father shot it. I wasn't sure what I'd done to make her my enemy, but here we were.

She turned to Nancy, who stood a few feet away and curled her lip up. "Maybe if you hadn't been such a disappointment to your mom and gotten pregnant as a teen, she wouldn't be here," she said loudly enough that I could hear. Loudly enough that much of the chatter dimmed.

Nancy's cheeks lit up pink as the man standing beside Cara stepped in front and gave her the quietest tongue lashing I'd ever witnessed. Her eyes turned dark but she held her tongue from whatever further berating ticked behind her overly-white porcelain veneers. Scanning the crowd, I found Griffin, his back to me, working at the stove on the opposite side of the kitchen island.

Dayton and Jackson flashed me toothy smiles and bumped shoulders, in that knowing manner teenagers had. Whatever Griffin said to his brother seemed to one hundred percent have worked. With a sixth sense, Griffin glanced over his shoulder as I approached and pointed toward the barstools lining the island.

"Sit, I'm almost done." He smiled sweetly, and I nodded. Hoisting myself up on the cold, black leather barstool, I drummed my fingers against the marble countertop as the volume of chatter resumed. Under the pendant lights, the movement made shards of rainbows flare inside my ring, drawing my eyes and causing a small smile to creep across my lips. It really was heart-breakingly exquisite, and he was right. I would've totally picked this one for myself.

Griffin spun around after plating whatever he'd been cooking, and I lifted my eyes to him, watching as he carried two dishes over. "Eggs." He said it as though presenting a five-star main course, smiled, and set it down in front of me. Surprisingly, they looked like the most delicious scrambled eggs to have ever existed. Fluffy and golden, they included all of the bells and whistles that a gourmet chef would add.

"They may be a little smelly but are surprisingly delicious," he said, walking around behind me, and then he paused. Leaning toward my ear, he whispered. "Like your breath before you've brushed your teeth."

"Griffin!" I gasped and slugged him on the shoulder. He laughed softly, rubbing the spot I'd made contact with, and sat down beside me. But I couldn't help but smile. Such a cute and flirtatious comment, even if it was all for show.

It was, right?

As I finished the last bite of egg, two people approached Griffin's back. "Can we ride with you and Miss B?" Dayton asked, and Griffin lifted a brow. His eyes slid to mine for a second before he turned around and rested an arm on the back of my stool.

"You sure you want to? You'll have to deal with all the touching and PDA stuff from us." He grinned mischievously, and Dayton looked ready to puke. "I'm kidding. Mostly. Though, you will have to just accept the music that I play. My truck, my music."

"Sweet!" Dayton grinned. Jackson mumbled a thank you and then they walked away.

Griffin stood and grabbed my empty plate. He carried them to the sink to clean up. I watched him for a moment, realizing how easy things seemed, despite all of the crazy from his family.

"I owe you an apology, I believe," Nancy's voice startled me. I flinched and then turned to my right, away from Griffin. She sat down in his now-vacant spot, wearing a pair of nice leggings and a thick pink sweater.

"For what?" I cautiously asked, and she sighed.

"For how I acted yesterday and the way I treated you."

I watched her for a moment, giving myself a second to decide how to proceed. "If I'm honest, I was a bit shocked. I know the announcement from Griffin and I was out of the blue, but I didn't think you'd react quite like you did."

She nodded, lowering her gaze to the floor. "I was a child myself when I had him, so no matter how old he becomes, I still see that little boy who was forced to grow up too fast. Sometimes, I'm overprotective of him and then overcompensate for everything I failed to do for Griffin with Dayton. Which is no excuse for how I have handled things. But you deserve an explanation."

I glanced toward the back of Griffin as he continued to wash the dirty dishes in the sink. So powerful, so protective. Yet also so burdened.

"I assume you know that we've tried to arrange his marriage and set him up with countless girls before?" she continued, and I nodded, looking back at her. "In all of those years, he would utterly refuse to touch them, barely even acknowledged them, so it shocked me when he announced he was bringing a girlfriend and that it happened to be you. And you're engaged, not just dating. I wanted to protect someone who protects everyone but himself."

She sighed and looked at her son, shame filling her eyes. "He thinks that I don't know he owns the house we rent. Rent that is astronomically too low to even cover a mortgage let alone be profitable. He takes care of everyone else and always has, especially when it comes to me. Did you know he got a job at the age of twelve to help me pay the bills because he overheard me on the phone with my mom, only once, complaining about how expensive things were at the time? He also bought his dad his home, and anonymously gifted his dads' parents money to pay off their mortgage." She paused as my eyes flung to Griffin. I sucked in a breath and pressed my tongue to the roof of my mouth, trying to avoid displaying any look of shock. Griffin was rich, it seemed. Or at least well-to-do.

"Anyway, I was terrified that he had opened himself up to someone who was only using him and going to destroy him in the end. I was worried that he cared more for you than you do for him." She patted my leg, snapping my attention back to her as I slowly exhaled. "But I see the way you look at him. Thank you for getting him to smile again. And laugh. It's been such a long time since I've heard my son laugh. It woke me up this morning, and I couldn't have been happier."

She'd seen the way I look at him? Nancy stood from the stool as my eyes drifted toward Griffin once more. He turned the water off and dried his hands, completely unaware of the conversation that had just occurred between his mom and me. Unaware that so many things were suddenly making sense. I probably should apologize at some point, too, for accusing him of being in his late thirties and still living with his mom, since he apparently owned the house.

Griffin's eyes connected with my unblinking gaze. He furrowed his brows and glanced around me, confused. Yet, I was unable to look away. His lips thinned as he blinked, bewildered. His mom had just supplied me with a key to the walls he surrounded himself with. Walls that he'd spent years building. A big shiny key to his castle that wasn't shared with simply anyone, and I had to be cautious when I used it.

He walked my way shaking water from his hands as his grandma announced that it was time to load. Standing from my seat, I quickly looked away and took a few steps toward the crowd that was wandering out of the house. Fingers wrapped around my arm, gently tugging me to a halt, and I sheepishly looked back at Griffin.

"What was that?" he asked, tossing a thumb toward the stool I'd vacated.

"What was what?"

"The look you were giving me. With those big eyes of yours." He narrowed his gaze, and I blinked, rapidly over exaggerating the movement.

"Oh, my eyes were just a little dry from my contacts," I muttered the lie. He shook his head, not buying it for a second.

"Hurry up, you two!" Nancy shouted. Griffin's attention shifted to his mom who was waving for us to exit the house, saving me from having to explain, then back at me suspiciously. Slipping my fingers into Griffin's hand that was still wrapped gently around my wrist, I smiled brightly in a bid to disarm him.

"Come on." I tugged at him, and he shook his head once more but followed me out of the house without further protest.

I sat feeling stiff and awkward in the passenger seat of Griffin's truck while Dayton and Jackson chatted nonstop behind us. Griffin's attention was on the road and some rock music played softly in the background. Slowly, I began to hum to the early 2000s tune that was playing. Griffin's dimples deepened, and he ran a hand over his stubble.

He quietly joined in and tipped his head toward me. I lifted my brows in shared recognition and then looked back out of the window as we wove through the canyon. The sun was shining brightly and reflecting from the deep snow on the side of the road, making me glad I remembered my sunglasses.

Glancing back toward Griffin, I saw his hand sitting in the middle of the seat between us, waiting. He wiggled his fingers enticingly, noticing that I was staring but didn't turn his head. I could easily place my hand in his. I'd held his hand before, briefly. But it was all for show then, and I hadn't been paying full attention to it.

This felt different.

A *lot* different.

Laughter boomed abruptly from the backseat, snapping me back to reality. This was for show too. I swallowed, and quickly placed my hand in his and entwined my fingers. His were huge, and looking at them, I recalled something I'd read about the length of a man's ring finger in correlation to his...

With a subconscious jerk, I tried to disengage, but he only tightened his grip. Blushing, my widened eyes met his, and his lips twitched upwards with a smile that told me he knew exactly what I'd been thinking, which he quickly hid away.

My heart jumped in my chest as he swiped his thumb back and forth across my hand. It sent shivers down my spine. I liked the solid gruffness to his, the callouses that scratched against my palm. I liked it all too much.

"Hey, Miss B!" Dayton called out from the back seat.

"Yeah?" I replied.

"What's your favorite thing about my brother?" he asked, and Jackson snickered beside him. I narrowed my gaze suspiciously and glanced at Griffin. He shrugged his shoulders but shared my speculation.

"Why do you ask?" I cautiously said.

"Just because," he said, and Jackson snickered again.

"What is going on with you two?" I questioned suspiciously.

"You should scoot into the middle of the seat. Someone might think you two don't really like each other. That you two haven't boinked," Dayton said, and Griffin rolled his eyes.

"So, that's what this is about." Griffin grumbled and let go of my hand. He reached behind him and grabbed at whatever he could. He managed to fist some of Dayton's shirt. Griffin yanked him forward. "Quit acting like a horny teenager and ask something appropriate."

I snorted as Dayton's face went red. Griffin released his little brother and then looked at me. "He's right, though, you should scoot over." He grinned and patted the empty space beside him. It was my turn to have my cheeks burn, but I unbuckled and slid over. Griffin casually slapped his hand high on my leg, those thick fingers sliding deliberately into my inner thigh and squeezing possessively, signaling a right I did not refuse; ignoring his own admonishment to his brother. Luckily, the back of the seat hid his touch from the boys behind us, so he wasn't openly hypocritical to them.

My body sparked like my ring had earlier, with blue fire as his hand remained tormentingly close to a very intimate area. An area that began to throb as he brushed his fingers up and down, back and forth. Apparently mindlessly, and yet I had no doubt he was entirely conscious of what he was doing, especially when he eased my thigh a fraction further open, driving his roaming hand a little deeper.

A sly grin crept upon his face. His eyes were diamond sharp as I swallowed inadvertently, the heat on my face not receding. His jaw worked as he shifted almost imperceptibly on his seat, suddenly glancing through the rearview mirror as a flash of light snapped behind us. I spun in my seat and saw Dayton was smiling sheepishly, his phone pointed in our direction.

"I didn't realize the flash was on." He grimaced and slowly tucked his phone toward his lap.

"Give that." Griffin reached behind me and wiggled his fingers.

Dayton vigorously shook his head. "No."

"Dayton," Griffin demanded again, and his brother quickly scooted as far away as he could.

"No."

"Just leave it be, Griffin," I quietly muttered. My face couldn't be seen at that angle, so if Dayton decided to 'accidentally' upload a photo, that one I was fine with.

"Cara says I should be calling you "Jane," not "Miss B," seeing as you're going to be my sister-in-law." Dayton's innocent words directed at me sent a shaft of pain straight to my heart, and my eyes shot to Griffin's.

"What?" Griffin asked, forgetting all about the picture. He furrowed his brows and glanced toward me.

"What's the harm?" I whispered achingly, my question double-edged, and Griffin watched me curiously. He didn't say anything else as he turned off the main road and drove us up the winding path toward the ski resort.

"My dad could officiate your wedding, by the way!" Dayton quickly added, and this drew a reaction from Griffin. His eyes nearly bugged out of his head.

"I'm sorry, but *what*?!" he hammered home.

"I got Dad to certify to be an ordained minister from some official online website as a joke a couple months back for one of our classes. The assignment was to fulfill three important civilian activities to help contribute to society. Jackson and I convinced the teacher to let it qualify as one of them." Dayton grinned as Jackson wiggled his eyebrows.

I wasn't sure what to think, though I wasn't as surprised as I probably should've been hearing Dayton and Jackson actively choosing to do something like that for an assignment.

Griffin merely shook his head as we rounded a corner. Before us a large cabin rose up contrasting picturesquely with the massive mountain behind that was covered in the whitest snow gleaming beneath the warm sun. Such a beautiful day. I looked at Griffin with delight.

Such a beautiful sight.

Chapter 27

Griffin held tightly to my hands as I attempted to keep my toes from dipping into the snow. As fun as snowboarding was, it was also extremely difficult to get the hang of.

"Don't you dare let go," I said, the snow hissing beneath us as he continued backward drawing me down the hill. He'd made sure that I looked the part with goggles and a helmet, a pair of snow pants, and a coat, but this "fun activity" was turning out to be a lot harder than I'd expected.

"I've got you, smart ass. Trust me." He chuckled and let go of my gloved hands.

"Griffin!" I screeched but didn't fall. Wobbling and bent like a banana, I stole a small amount of control as he smiled but remained close in front of me. Snowy chill bit at my cheeks as we went down the mountain, over and over.

After a couple of practice hours, I was feeling fairly confident and lifted my toes. Twisting to the side, I zoomed past Griffin and cut down the mountain. Obviously at a very slow speed compared to what he was used to, as he barreled by and launched himself off a jump. I shook my head but smiled as he landed nicely and slid to the side, slowing for me to meet up with him.

"Show off," I muttered, and he laughed. Swinging back and forth, he put some distance between us and, in a flurry of snow, turned to wait for me. Just as I was about to pass him, I pointed and laughed and then forgot my positioning.

My toe caught in the snow and with an undignified yelp, I face planted into the powder. Cold, wet, frozen water flew down my shirt and up my nose. Muffled laughter sounded from beside me as I groaned. Pushing myself onto my elbows, spitting out crystals of frozen moisture, I turned and glared at Griffin. He knelt down, holding his chest as he tried not to choke on his own laugh.

"Karma is so beautiful." He grinned.

I rolled my eyes and then flipped my body onto my back. "It's not that funny." I giggled, and he laughed even harder.

"Stop laughing at me," I whined but couldn't stop myself from smiling. Brushing the snow from my face, I pulled up my goggles and squinted through the sun.

His laughter quieted as he leaned on one hand and tilted his head, the smile on his face softened, tender and longing. I blinked, stunned. "You're something else, you know that?" he whispered.

"And you're sometimes a jerk. Now, help me up," I teased. He wiggled his brows. Extending a hand, he helped hoist me out of the cold snow, and I put my goggles on.

I managed to descend the rest of the slope without falling and was super proud of myself as we slowed near the bottom of the lift.

"Let's go to the higher mountain," I exclaimed hopefully. He smiled like an indulgent parent.

"Alright," he replied and helped me out of my bindings on one foot. I followed him farther down toward the larger lift that went higher up the far side of the mountain. It was meant for more advanced skiers and boarders, and I'd been hopeful of trying it at least once before lunch.

Griffin reached for me as we scooted toward the end of the line, his hand wrapped around my waist to help push me ahead. But he didn't let go as we stood in line. Neither of us said anything about it. I worried if I mentioned it, he would stop. No matter how much I worked on convincing myself that all of this was fake, I couldn't shake my feelings that were so real.

We slowly lugged forward, each passing gray chair that swung by toted four people, apparently. Which meant that two strangers would join us and I was still pretty shaky when it came to dismounting.

"Griffin?" I whispered nervously as we inched closer.

He tipped toward my ear. "I'll make sure you're just fine. Trust me." I nodded as he pulled me a little closer, and then a familiar laugh sounded behind us. Sliding away just an inch, we both glanced past a few other skiers and saw Dayton beside Jackson.

Griffin tugged me against his body and waved those that separated us and his brother on. Once Dayton and Jackson were standing directly behind us, Griffin let go of me.

"Yo! Griffin and Miss B!" Jackson said, smiling, and Dayton faced us with a grin.

"I think you can call me Jane, too, *outside* of school, considering things," I said, and they both wiggled their brows. Griffin shook his head but didn't look at me as we inched forward.

"Let's ride the lift together!" Dayton exclaimed, and Griffin bit back a chuckle. I lifted my brows at the smart and sly man who simply winked, his goggles frosted with snow perched above his beanie.

"Great idea," he calmly said, and we slid forward.

Griffin helped position me between him and Dayton, with Jackson on the far side of Dayton. I somehow managed to get on the lift without too much trouble. With how frequently Griffin was holding me lately, it felt almost instinctual on his part. Half the time I don't think he realized he had his hand or his arm around me.

And I didn't fight it or mention it, finding comfort in his touch, despite the conflicting guilt that was steadily rising. I shouldn't let myself feel happy about this, or get too comfortable, I knew that. But it was too late, and I was rather joyful.

We joked and laughed as the lift rose higher and higher, the tips of the trees toylike in the distance. Dayton took another picture I asked to see, but with the goggles and helmets, it was hard to tell if that was even Griffin, let alone who I was. Griffin threw his arm behind me and angled his body so he was leaning against the edge and facing me.

He smiled, his jaw dusted with specks of white. Biting my bottom lip I turned away, unable to stop the racing of my heart. A simple lazy smile from him shouldn't make me that excited, but it did. Fighting it was no use. Not as I found myself replaying that image in my mind over and over again as I looked across the landscape

Wanting another glimpse of that smile set with dimples, I didn't turn my head but shifted my gaze toward him. He lifted his brows and winked, catching my stare, and my cheeks burned red hot as he casually glanced behind me.

The smirk immediately dropped from his face. A stoic mask cascaded over the casual beauty of his features.

"Dayton and Jackson," Griffin barked, his voice demanding immediate obedience.

"Yes?" Dayton quickly responded, not questioning Griffin's change in behavior, and Jackson furrowed his brows. I watched Griffin a little longer and then slowly took a look behind me.

My heart immediately sank. Trembling, I looked back at Griffin, fear turning my stomach into knots. I didn't know the man behind us, but he clearly knew us—his sights locked on us, the deadly twitch of his lips when my gaze connected with his, hidden behind ski goggles, told me that we were his targets. I gaped at Griffin. *Not again!*

"The moment that we get off this lift, you are to help Jane get her bindings on and then go down the mountainside as quickly as possible," he stated, his gaze not leaving the figure on the lift behind us. "Do not stop for anyone. Do not wait for me. Do you understand?"

Dayton and Jackson shared a confused glance but nodded vigorously. "Yes, sir," Dayton said, without hesitation.

"Good. And if anyone you don't know approaches you, you don't let them get near her. Do you copy?"

"Yes, sir," both of them said in unison, no hint of sarcasm in their tone.

"Griffin," I mewled, trying to bite back the curdling in my stomach.

He reached forward and brushed some snow from the side of my helmet. "You need to get off this mountain as quickly as possible, which means I need you to have your best run yet. Can you do that for me?" he asked firmly. I nodded, adrenaline making my nerves prickle beneath my skin like a thousand needles.

"What are you going to do?" I questioned worriedly, and his eyes darkened.

"What I'm good at," he muttered, his gaze returning to the man behind me. I glanced once more over my shoulder and saw a wicked grin now spread upon the stranger's lips, pinching skin beneath the goggles. Dressed in all white, with a few specks of gray and pale green splattered across his snow camouflage ski suit, the man even had the audacity to wave at us. I spun back around, feeling sick.

"Who is that?" I whispered.

Griffin kept his steely gaze trained forward. "I don't know, but I recognize the tattoo on his wrist that he may or may not have accidentally exposed a moment ago. I'm honestly shocked to see it; I thought that they were all wiped out months ago."

"So, he's not after me?" I widened my eyes, nausea roiling within my stomach.

Griffin simply shook his head, whether as a denial or to convey he wasn't sure, I didn't know. But I also knew this was not the time to pry. Now was the time to focus on getting off of this lift without falling. Maybe this man was after Griffin and not me this time. If he recognized that tattoo, then that could mean this assailant tracked Griffin home from whatever mission he'd been on. But the possibility that it wasn't me he was after did nothing to curb the excruciating fear igniting the adrenaline ripping through my veins.

I could see the end where I would need to dismount without falling and quickly do up my board's bindings. Then I would have to make it all the way down the mountain without crashing—and rapidly. All things that were still fairly difficult, and all things I wouldn't be doing with Griffin this time.

My heart raced as we lugged closer and closer to our destination. Dayton and Jackson sat silently beside me, confused but not wanting to question Griffin's orders, looking between themselves and me, no doubt concerned about how I was going to land.

The chair lurched forward and Griffin looked at his brother and his brother's best friend. He was putting all his trust in them. This was no game, and he showed it in his expression. Thankfully, they had picked up on his seriousness, both nodding once in unison, and then he turned to me. My smile was tense as I tried to diffuse the situation for the boys' sake, but it did nothing to help.

Suddenly, my board brushed across the snow and Griffin shoved me forward. I teetered, and Dayton caught me, helping to steer me to the right. Jackson began to do up his bindings before we'd even stopped, and the moment we were no longer moving, Griffin came straight to me.

Griffin, his bindings already secure around his boots, knelt behind me, facing the next approaching lift as my final binding was cinched up tightly. Jackson pushed himself up as Dayton hopped toward us.

The man's board bit into the snow, and his eyes whipped toward us, as black as night. Dayton grabbed my arm and nodded toward the steep run that lay before me. I nodded nervously but began waddling toward the crest.

"GO!" Griffin shouted, propelling himself up from the snow as the man launched toward us. I pushed off the mountain with Jackson right behind me and began sliding down the hillside. Powder sprayed out beneath me, the bitter air roaring in my ears and biting at my cheeks as I threw caution to the wind and pointed the board straight down. No braking, all go. Like my out of control car, hurtling into traffic.

My breath caught in my throat, snapped away by an image of my doom laying ahead, and it almost undid me. Dayton suddenly whipped in front, pulling my attention back, and began leading the way. Tearing a path down the mountain, I slid in ungainly fashion as fast as I could behind him toward the safety of the lodge. My lungs gulped for air and hitched in panic as we carved hard around to the right and I tipped a little too far. Flailing my arms wildly, I managed to correct myself, hearing shouting and grunts echo through the mountainside.

Please let him be okay.

In my peripheral vision, the assailant suddenly snapped out of the tree line on my right, slicing between me and Dayton with Griffin barreling through the trees close behind. He hit a jump and launched himself directly at the hardened enemy who cut across directly on top of my board. Nose-diving, I hardly lost any momentum down the mountain, and my face slammed into the cold, suffocating powder.

Coughing out mouthfuls, snow clouding most of my vision through my goggles, I clawed uselessly with my gloved hands to try and stop myself from gathering momentum and sliding down the hill. As if I was sky-diving through snow, I spun slowly on my stomach seeing Griffin reach down and latch onto his opponent's board. Using their momentum, Griffin hucked him across the nicely dragged snow—pulling his own balance out from under his feet. They tumbled into the treeline, disappearing from sight as my fingers and the lip of my board finally caught in the snow. Fully stopped, I wobbled upright, panting like I'd run a marathon, brushing snow from my face and goggles.

"What is going on?" Dayton asked, climbing up toward me as Jackson skidded to a stop behind me.

"I-I-I don't know," I stammered, my eyes wide as my heart beat erratically. They each took an arm to help me steady. "Let's just get down to the lodge."

Lifting my toes, I shakily began to slowly slide down the mountain once more under the boys' watchful and concerned guidance. Once I felt like I had my bearings, I pointed the front of my board down the hill and, with Dayton leading and Jackson as my wingman, we were off.

Another couple of turns and I caught sight of the green roof of the lodge leering above the top of the forest that still separated us from our destination. For the first time in these long minutes, I had hope that I would actually make it.

Muffled shouting broke through the insulation of snow around us as we cruised faster and faster toward the next bend.

I shot down a small pathway that was a shortcut to our destination, following Dayton's line, and we slid around the curve to the left. Rounding the corner too fast, I nearly fell over as red splotches painted a trail cutting through our path across the snow and disappearing back into the crusty pines surrounding us.

All three of us threw on our brakes. Griffin...

Please let Griffin be okay.

Flipping up my goggles, I stood trembling. My lungs heaved with exertion and panic, not a single one of us daring to move. Everything was deathly quiet.

Too quiet.

Like ice without a single fisherman drilling through to the busy aquatic life below, we remained frozen. We had two options—follow the bloody trail, or ignore it and continue with caution to the lodge.

A gargled shout rang out, impossible to pinpoint in the muted atmosphere, coming from somewhere in the dense forest trees. My heart thumped against my ribs, and I knew there was no way in hell I was about to head to the lodge.

Please let it be the other guy's blood.

Without a word, I cautiously pointed my board toward the split in trees where the trail of crimson led. Snow crunched beneath me, Dayton and Jackson following suit. Blood pumped in my ears as we passed beneath the branches, icicles dangling like daggers from the brown claws reaching toward us, warning us to turn back.

The world around us darkened, the crystal clear, blue sky clouded by the pine needles that spread and stretched toward the sun. Eventually, I had no more forward momentum and sat down with a silent plunk. There was less shouting, less grunting, but the few that pierced the air were louder, closer now.

Griffin...

The blood trail was thicker here. Propping our snowboards against tree trunks, we hiked cautiously through the knee-deep snow among the towering trees.

Sharpened silence cut through the air, not a single note of pain echoed around us as we waded deeper and deeper following the powder. My heart raced, pumping skin-piercing adrenaline through the thick sludge in my veins. And terror. Palpable fear oozed from me. I could smell the stench of my own sweat as it trickled down my spine.

Please tell me that Griffin is okay, that everything is fine.

Lurching forward, I balanced a palm against a tree trunk at the same moment a large hand slapped around the bark. I jumped away, squeaking at the sight of blood splattered upon bare knuckles and freezing in place. Dayton and Jackson slammed against my back just as the sun disappeared, cloaked by a dense veil of pine needles.

Strong fingers dug into the tree trunk.

Huge fingers and a hand with thick veins running across the back that I recognized.

"Griffin?" I gasped, tears of relief welling in my eyes as he dragged himself around the base of the tree.

"Hey, smart ass." His chest rose and fell rapidly, torn fabric clawed by grips of death hung in limp tatters from his torso. The down filling for his black winter coat spilled from the shredded cloth, looking like he'd gone several rounds with a guard dog. Shrugging out of it, the useless jacket dropped from his shoulders.

"You're okay!" I said and crashed against his body, slinging my arms around him. I nearly wanted to cry with the amount of relief at the sight of him.

His chest vibrated with a grunt as he wrapped his other hand around my torso.

"Yeah, I'll live."

"And the other guy?"

"One guy, nothing to it." His answer was vague, but I didn't press for details; I didn't care. He finally let go of the tree trunk and ran his fingers over my helmet, tightening his hold against my waist.

"Jackson, Dayton. Jane and I are going to head back to the Airbnb. That's enough snowboarding for me today, and I'm not-so-politely asking for you two to do the same," he said, resting his chin against the cold plastic protecting my head. They were clearly angling for some answers to the drama, judging by their expressions, but Griffin shut them down with one steely-eyed look.

As his breathing finally began to slow, I glanced under Griffin's arm, which held me tightly, to see grins erupt across both of the boys' faces. It pushed away the confusion in their expressions. In typical teenage fashion, Dayton shrugged his shoulders. "Sweet. We're kind of bored anyway, and I want to hit the pool!" The two boys then spun around, disappearing back along the trail we'd followed.

"If we don't fuss too much about it, they'll probably assume it's some jealous ex-lover of yours," Griffin said with a strained wink.

I sighed in relief as he continued to hold me, fighting the urge to roll my eyes. "Did you get anything out of him?"

"No," Griffin quietly said.

"You recognized the tattoo, so I'm going to assume he was here for you."

"Yeah, that's what I am thinking."

"Then I don't think this is something I need to report, do you? Besides, if I did report him, wouldn't a dead body create an even worse mess?"

Griffin pushed me away from his chest, and cold, ungloved hands gripped my cheeks. "How'd you know?"

I shrugged. This was Griffin we were talking about.

"I'll report him to my CO, since it's my problem to deal with, and leave you out of it," Griffin replied, and he closed his eyes as I plunked my head against him again.

"Let's go back," I whispered.

I felt the relief slump his shoulders.

"Let's go back," he copied, his typically booming voice tender and muffled, vibrating in his chest. Man was I glad he was okay. And I twisted his shirt a little tighter in my fingers.

Chapter 28

I stood in the bathroom, holding my damp swimsuit, trying to decide between that and the bikini that I'd also brought. Distracting myself from everything that had just happened was my primary focus. Only if Griffin mentioned it would I bring it up again. The man had come after him, not me, and he could deal with whatever he needed to on his end with his superiors or whatever.

All I really wanted was to lay on one of the chairs in the sun and nap. To close my eyes and think about nothing. Not men jumping out in the dark or off ski lifts, or Sam, or a meddling Cara. I didn't really care about getting back in the water, and that made the idea of putting on a damp swimsuit daunting.

But the other option was a bikini. I also didn't want Griffin to get the wrong idea, but on the other hand, I didn't want to be wet.

Sighing, I decided on the red gingham bikini. It would also be better for more tan coverage. Though I hoped that it wasn't too inappropriate to wear in front of two of my students, since it showed a little more skin than the one piece.

I also wondered if there was a way to avoid them noticing the small tattoo that ran up my ribcage on the left side of my body. It was a simplistic line design of a small butterfly trail and pretty flowers. Thin and hardly noticeable, but it would definitely spark some teasing if Griffin saw it.

Oh, well. Hopefully the three of them were so occupied lounging in the pool that my presence wouldn't be noticed. Twisting my hair up into its usual claw clip, I walked from the bathroom into the main room. The boys had already disappeared into the pool room, so I quickly grabbed a few towels from the closet just outside the door, just in case they'd forgotten.

As quietly as I could, I slipped inside to find them splashing about. Laughter and shouts echoed as Griffin mercilessly dunked them despite Jackson and Dayton's best efforts to avoid him. Padding across the damp concrete to the far side, I pulled a chair into the bright sun that blazed through the glass windows and laid down flat on my belly.

Untying the top of my swimsuit from the back, I closed my eyes, wriggled into a comfortable position and promptly fell asleep. I briefly woke up an hour or so later, lazily tying the swimsuit back up and rolling from my back to the front before falling back asleep in the steamy warmth to the sound of lapping water.

Cold water drenched me, jolting me awake from the most blissful nap I'd experienced in a long while. Gasping, I sat up as it dripped down between my boobs and slid off my belly and thighs. Griffin grimaced as I turned my narrowed gaze toward the three boys. He immediately pointed at Dayton and Jackson.

"They did it," he stated, and the two boys' mouths fell open in shock.

"Don't you dare pawn that off on them," I snarled, and Griffin gave me a sheepish smile.

"We were kind of hoping you'd join us for a game or two of chicken," he asked, his eyes roaming down my body, and I shook my head, ignoring the shivers that erupted from his obvious desire.

"So, you thought the smartest move was to splash me with water?" I asked, lifting a brow.

"Oooooh, you're in trouble," Dayton sang at Griffin, who shot a glare and slap of water in his direction

"Don't look at him," I said firmly in my best teacher's voice, and Griffin slowly brought his eyes back to mine.

He pulled his lips between his teeth and then gave me another sheepish smile. "Yes, ma'am, but since you are wet now, I would really like to win a game or two of chicken against these two hotheads."

I glanced with a moue at the two teenagers who were grinning from ear to ear, watching the exchange. On the one hand, I could let Griffin lose because he deserved it after splashing me. But on the other hand...

Slowly, I rose from my chair, and Dayton and Jackson both took a step back. "Wow, I didn't know you were that buff, Miss B," Dayton mumbled, and Jackson nodded in agreement. Griffin ran a hand over his mouth, hiding a smile, but his eyes held absolute hunger. For me. My heart jumped into my throat. "We take it back. You return to your nap."

"You scared?" I asked, stalking closer and closer to the edge of the pool.

"Nooooo," Dayton said. I chuckled and pulled the claw clip from my hair. Sitting down on the edge of the pool, I stuck my feet into the water. It was actually quite refreshing after a while in the hot sun.

I looked at Griffin who was watching with a smirk on his face. "I knew you were too competitive to pass this up," he boastfully said.

"Who said I'm going to be on your team?" I quickly replied, and watched as his face faltered for a second. "It was you who splashed the water on me."

"So, you'll let your students win over your fiancé?" he questioned and crossed his arms in front of his bare chest causing the ink to ripple. Dayton and Jackson exchanged high fives and stuck their tongues out at Griffin.

"I never said that either," I replied then slipped into the water. Pushing my hair behind my head, I rose to the surface and awkwardly stroked toward Griffin. He hooked an arm around my waist to keep me floating and tilted his head.

"You're going to be on my team?" he whispered, sounding a question that was really a statement against my earlobe, his hot breath sending a low pulse between my legs.

"Of course, dummy. I can't let those two best me."

Dayton narrowed his eyes and smiled wickedly. "Bring it on, Miss B." He ducked under the water as Griffin slipped below the surface. Swimming between my legs, Griffin set me on his shoulders and then stood up. Jackson balanced on Dayton's and we marched toward the very center of the pool.

Griffin and I crushed the two boys over and over again. No matter who decided who was going to be on whose shoulders, they ended up in the water. After probably an hour of losing, Dayton and Jackson finally put their hands in the air and surrendered.

"Ha!" I exclaimed in triumph as they slowly left the pool. I sat on Griffin's shoulders as he patted my thigh, and we watched the boys leave the poolroom.

Until we were alone. Completely alone.

"You did so good for me," he said, and I giggled.

"We make a good team."

"Yeah, we do," he said and then suddenly dove under the water, dragging me with him. I sputtered, coughing up water that singed my throat and stung my eyes when he finally surfaced. He still clung to my legs, diving back under once more.

I kicked and fought, trying to get out of his grip. Breaking toward the surface, I gasped for air as he tried to pull me under again, but I managed to kick free and swam a few feet away from him. He slipped beneath the water toward me and then bobbed up right in front of me.

I glared at him, genuinely annoyed.

"Your tattoo is pretty," he said, pointing toward my rib. I clamped a hand over it and narrowed my eyes even more.

"Flattery won't work," I harshly stated, and he smiled sweetly.

"No?" he teased, and I shook my head. "Not even if I say that your eyes are the most beautiful shade of gray I've ever seen. They're like the sky right before a storm in the middle of summer."

I made a pouty face. "That might help."

"Or if I told you that I can't help but smile when you smile at me?"

I watched him through a side eye, but his simpering was softening my soul.

"And, despite the fact that you sat on my face at the gym, I've secretly looked forward to seeing you there every day. I knew that whatever sass was coming my way was going to be entertaining."

"I told you not to talk about that again," I quickly said, but I felt that furnace in my belly stoke again in wonder at his words. *He looked forward to seeing me?* He chuckled, swimming a little closer, only his eyes visible above the waterline, not blinking and gleaming with mischief

"I know, but I find it funny."

I sighed as he rose up, watching the water run from his skin. Relaxing, I let my gaze wander over his body. My fingers mindlessly reached forward, and I traced the scar that wrapped around his right arm.

"What's this from?" I quietly asked. His eyes followed my fingers for a moment, then he took a deep breath and gently placed a hand over mine. He didn't stop my movement as I twisted my touch up his arm; he simply followed along.

"Before I was a SEAL, during my first tour, my battle buddy and I were taken hostage. I was strung up by myself in a room with a wire wrapped around my arm," he began, then removed his hand from mine as I began trailing back down his skin. His voice was so quiet, so withdrawn as he continued. "They rigged it up to a machine that sent electricity through it every five minutes. Not enough to kill me, but enough to do some damage as you can see. It took four days before rescue arrived. I made it. He didn't."

I let my hand fall from his arm as he stared at the scar that I no longer touched. "I'm sorry, Griffin," I whispered, and his brows twitched before he brought his eyes back to mine.

"It was a long time ago."

"All the same," I tenderly replied, and he shook his head.

"I don't get you." He launched backwards and swam a couple of back-strokes away.

"How so?"

"You're not afraid to put me in my place yet you express sympathy for me without hesitation."

"So you're confused because I'm not some heartless bitch?"

"Yeah, bluntly put." He stood back upright, and I grinned at the sight; like Zeus, all he was missing was a thunderbolt.

"Do I give off those kinds of vibes?" I feigned being appalled, and he waded toward me, stopping directly in front of me.

"All the time," he teased, then grabbed me around my waist and flipped me over his shoulder. Diving back into the water, I pounded at his back as he once again rose and then dunked me.

Kicking free from his grip, I swam up to the surface and shot through, gasping for air.

Just as I felt the ties come loose from my top.

Chapter 29

Shrieking, I covered my bare breasts as my bikini top floated away, directly toward where Griffin surfaced. He shook his head, still unaware that I was nude from the waist up. Wiping away the water from his eyes, he grinned, and then his eyes glanced down toward my arms crossed in front of my chest.

Immediately, he turned around. "I swear I didn't untie it," he said.

"I know, I did a lazy job when I rolled over from my stomach to my back earlier and forgot about it," I answered. "Now, look down in front of you."

His head dipped down toward the bikini top that floated against his chest. "This is obviously yours." He picked it up and then held it behind him in my direction, without looking.

I quickly waded in his direction and grabbed it from his fingers. Despite knowing that I was tits out, he remained a gentleman, facing the other way.

Even though all he had to do was simply glance over his shoulders and look, not a muscle seemed to twitch. My heart began to race wildly in my chest as I held the bikini top in my hands but stared at his back.

I was not embarrassed by my body, no, it was the opposite. It was simply that the rule I'd given myself all those years ago that continually kept me from indulging caused me to hesitate. Indulging something that two consenting adults could share if they chose to do so, right?

Taking a deep, encouraging breath, I placed the top down on the edge of the pool and gently swam toward Griffin. It was just my top, that was it. It wasn't like I was entirely naked. Plus, he was different from any other guy I'd ever met.

Even if this wasn't love, this was better than anything I'd ever had before.

My fingers trembled as I placed a hand on his forearm and he glanced toward me. At first he simply smiled, meeting my gaze, and then his eyes slid down toward my bare breasts. He quickly looked away as his chest expanded rapidly.

I reached up and placed a hand against his cheek, turning his face toward mine once more. He tipped his head, tension creasing his features as he fought with himself to not look. I stepped against his body.

"Jane," he whispered, cautioning me. I smiled, not saying a word as I reached for his hands and placed them against my waist. "What are you doing?"

"What I want," I quietly replied, and he inhaled sharply.

"Don't," he hissed through his teeth and smashed his eyes closed.

"Why not?"

His Adam's apple bobbed with a stiff swallow. "Don't ask that either."

"Griffin." I placed my hands against his cheeks, and his brows stitched together. "Look at me."

He shook his head, knotting his jaw. "I can't."

"How come?"

"Because, Jane," he paused, and his fingers dug into my back. "Because if I do, I will lose any self-control that I have, shove you against the edge of the pool, and fuck you as hard as I want."

"So, do it." Honey dripped from my words, and his breath caught.

"You told me that you—"

"And I'm telling you what I want now." I placed my hands back against his arms and brushed my fingers up his skin. Goosebumps danced beneath my touch, and his brows flickered. His thick eyelashes fluttered, threatening to open, so I tipped forward onto my toes. "I want you. Right here. Right now. I want you to have me."

His hazel eyes snapped open, darkened, locking onto my gaze for one last brief reassurance. I gave him an encouraging smile as he finally unabashedly examined everything exposed.

And his lips pressed against mine. I enveloped my arms around his neck as he slid his hands around the back of my legs. As he lifted me up, I wrapped them around his waist, and he steadily waded toward the wall of the pool. He shoved his tongue down my throat as his palms slithered back to my waist, dancing electricity beneath his fingers, and braced me against the edge. The rough pool wall grated against my back, but I didn't care.

Everything was focused on him. On where he was touching, on his tongue tasting mine, on his chest rising and falling fast against my bare breasts. Roaring heat pooled low within my stomach. One set of fingers dug into my bare skin while the other one continued to climb the front of my body.

He hesitated just below my breast, and so I took the initiative and pushed his hand up the rest of the way. As he moaned against my mouth, I could tell how much pleasure he took much in feeling everything that was there.

And I liked it. The calloused touch of his hand as he caressed and squeezed something very intimate of mine. Twisting and rubbing in a way that had me nearly drooling, aching with a longing deep within my core.

I leaned my head back as his mouth wandered down my neck and toward my chest. A throbbing between my legs began as his tongue found my rosy peak, and I couldn't help myself. I shoved my hips against his, feeling his hard arousal. He was as excited as I was. As desperate as I was.

With that single movement, I knew there was no stopping. And I didn't want to. Not as he ground himself harder against me, igniting my core to roar with a fire. I dripped as wet as the water that sloshed around us. My skin was hot as his mouth wandered back to mine and he dug his fingers into my ass cheeks, shoving my hips deeper against his.

Sliding my hands down his back, my lips parted as I moaned into his mouth. "Have me."

His chest rumbled with a growl, and he bit down on my mouth. I felt fingers sliding across the waistline of my bikini bottoms as he licked my lips. "But your rule?" he questioned again, and I, in answer, slammed my mouth against his.

His fingers slid against my aching center. He groaned, and I felt him tugging his swim shorts down.

I needed him. Now.

It wasn't a want but a need, and something that I couldn't fulfill any other way. The roaring pulse that was throbbing between my legs would only be satisfied by him being inside me.

"Griffin," I moaned, feeling him ease aside the crotch of my bikini with his thumb and gently probe. I arched against his touch, but he refused and held himself steady, watching me through slitted lids.

I groaned his name again, digging my fingers into the dimples of his hips, trying to haul his touch where I wanted, both of us trembling with desire. He was waiting for something from me, which he must have seen, because with a harsh breath, he grabbed the side of my throat with his lips and teeth and slipped a finger in. Just one finger, but his touch, stroking me, ignited me with more pleasure than I'd known, and I begged for more, grinding against his hand.

He lifted his head, hesitating, but I grabbed the back of his neck and pulled him close, urging him on with a raise of my own hips. Stretching me with another finger, he slipped the next one inside, shooting waves of both pain and pleasure from the pressure. More. I needed more, as he teased me.

His chest rose and fell, pressing against my own body as he added another, preparing me for what was between his legs. Hot breath washed over my neck. I dug my nails into his back, gasping at the dripping sensation, and as he eased his fingers back out, I knew what was coming.

I placed my mouth into his shoulder, muffling my scream of pleasure and turning my lips deliciously slick with his sweat as he finally buried himself entirely inside me.

His body trembled as he held me, my breathing sporadic. His chest rested against my bare breasts, heavy breaths moving his torso up and down as we panted, living in the high that we shared. Every bare part of my skin tingled where he was touching. My arms wrapped around him, and I cursed myself for waiting so long.

Eventually, he slowly slid himself out, with another little groan, as pleasure and peace blanketed his body.

Not a word passed between us. Not a sound besides the lapping of water danced in my ears as I brought myself back to the present.

And then he stumbled backwards, his eyes widening. I grabbed the edge of the pool as he pulled up his swim trunks, and his face immediately paled.

He shook his head, every euphoric blissful moment whisking away in an instance.

"Are-are you okay?" I stammered.

He stared at me blankly for a few moments before closing his eyes. "Shit," he muttered. "This complicates things."

"Excuse me?" I said, suddenly super self-conscious. Feeling cold, I wrapped my arms around my chest and adjusted my bottoms.

He ran a hand over his stubble, saying nothing.

"Did I do something wrong?" I whispered timidly, trying to make myself as small as possible.

"You know how I feel about hookups," he stated. I nodded, confused yet feeling extremely vulnerable. "I don't want you to think I'm some dickhead who hits it and then quits it."

"What are you saying?" I squeaked, tears threatening at the brim. He ran his hands through his hair and turned around. "Are you saying you now feel obligated toward me or something?"

He whipped back around and faced me. "How are we supposed to break up after I take you home tomorrow when that just happened?"

I swallowed as everything crashed and burned. My heart shattered, shame and disgust for myself wrecked my soul. I'd become so wrapped up in the lie, I'd forgotten it was one to begin with. I'd been the fool to think that he cared even half a morsel for me.

Quickly blinking back the tears, I turned to the side and, doing my best to stay covered, I waded toward my bikini top. I put it on as quickly as I could, unable to look at him. I was embarrassed and absolutely destroyed.

Oh, what an idiot I was. Just like that.

The pool room door crashed open, and Dayton walked in, unaware of what had just occurred. "Mom called. They'll be here in an hour, so we need to get ready for the fancy dinner they have planned for your official engagement announcement." He grinned as I faced the wall, my back to Griffin. Dayton's brows furrowed and then he glanced between the two of us.

"Thank you, Dayton. We'll be right out," Griffin said, and Dayton nodded before slowly backing out of the pool room. The moment he was gone, I pulled myself out and traipsed toward the stack of towels I'd brought in.

"Jane, we need to talk about this," Griffin said, and I spun around. His brows stitched together, indecipherable emotions flitting across his face. But for me, all that boiled within my soul was anger and heartbreak.

"None of it was real for you. Was it?" I whispered, and then sprinted from the room as the tears tumbled out.

Chapter 30

I grabbed a random outfit from my suitcase and then locked myself into the bathroom. Everything had changed way too quickly for me to fully comprehend what I was feeling. Rage? Pain? Sadness? Guilt? Embarrassment?

All of the above was most likely the truth. Snatching my phone up that I'd left on the bathroom counter, I swiped through the blurry contacts before tapping Noah's name. I couldn't stay here, not a moment longer.

"Hello? Janey?" Noah's voice pierced through the receiver. I sniffled a few times. "Are you okay?"

"Come get me, now. Please," I cried, tucking my legs tighter against my chest as I leaned against the black cabinet beneath the three sinks.

"Come get you? What's going on? Are you okay?"

"Noah, please. I need you," I whispered again, wiping some of the tears from my cheeks. He deserved to know why, but I was too overwhelmed and unable to say much else.

There was a pause and then Noah spoke again. "Where are you?"

"Bear Lake. Utah side," I choked out.

"Janey, what's going on?" he asked again, and I shook my head, feeling another wave of tears flood my eyes.

"Please, Noah. I just need to come home."

There was silence on the other end and then he sighed. "Send me your location."

Quickly pulling up my maps, I shared it with him and then placed the phone back to my ear. Waiting patiently for confirmation that he'd come get me, I closed my eyes, trying to hide the overwhelming ache that was forming in my heart. I didn't want to leave; I still wanted Griffin, yet I needed to go. I had to.

"Aren't you one lucky sister to have a brother who just so happens to be twenty minutes away at a party that's quite boring?" Noah cheerfully replied, but I couldn't manage to even give him a sympathy laugh. Or sass him in response.

"Thank you," I whispered and hung up the phone as the tears crashed down my cheeks. I jumped into the shower, desperate to get his smell off of me. Desperately hoping to scrub away any place he'd touched me.

My skin was red and raw when I finally exited and pulled on a pair of leggings and a thick, baby-blue turtleneck.

A quick brush of my hair, and I wrapped it up in a new claw clip. The one I left at the pool was just going to have to stay there. I shoved my glasses on my face, placed that way too beautiful engagement ring on top of Griffin's toiletry case, gathered my small makeup bag, and peeked out of the bathroom.

Empty. The room was empty and still, much like my soul. I slipped out and grabbed my suitcase, roughly shoving everything in, and quickly zipped it up. As I walked to the door, I paused, hearing muffled voices outside.

"What did you do?" Dayton asked.

"Butt out, Dayton," Griffin grumbled.

"Just go in and tell her you're sorry," Dayton demanded.

"A simple sorry doesn't fix this. Do you not get that, Dayton?" Griffin shouted. "I need to clear my head." Footsteps receded as my heart plummeted to the floor. A simple sorry and an explanation would go a long way. But I guess for him, he wasn't sorry because this entire time it had all been fake.

Even his words that had spilled so easily from those lips, that he 'didn't like hookups' were insincere, fake—a lie.

With my ear to the door, once I was sure the coast was clear, I snuck out of the room and dashed on tiptoes to the front door. Why couldn't I have simply kept my feelings to myself? Why had I been so bold, and where had I found such a strange sense of confidence? Why hadn't I run like I normally would have? *Why?*

Just why?

No one was around as I quietly shut the door behind me, sat down, and waited, hugging my knees. Expecting Cara to come trumpeting through the door at any minute, I was tense, straining my ears and mentally urging Noah not to dawdle, though I had barely plopped my bum down when a truck came rumbling up the drive. A blue truck that my heart was so happy to see.

Standing up, I waved as Noah loudly tore into the driveway and pulled up in a spray of mud and snow. Leaping up, I raced to the truck and tugged the back door open, tossing my suitcase in as the front door of the house came crashing open.

Slamming the truck door closed, I threw open the front passenger door and climbed in as quickly as I could. Griffin came running out, a pair of sweats around his hips and a wrinkled T-shirt barely pulled over his head.

"JANE!" he shouted as I snapped my door closed.

"Go," I said to Noah, refusing to look at Griffin. "GO!"

Without a word, Noah threw the truck into drive and squealed away from the house in another spray of gravel as Griffin darted out into the frozen snow, barefoot. My eyes slipped to the side mirror, where I watched him collapse to his knees in defeat and become smaller and smaller as we drove away.

I studied him in the mirror until he had completely faded away, and then I continued to stare long after. No crying, I'd done enough of that already.

"Janey," Noah finally said, quietly interrupting the pain that was holding my soul captive. "Was that sweaty hottie I saw?"

I continued to stare out the window.

"You told mom that you were staying with a colleague this weekend." Noah continued to press.

Thoughts littered my brain, as haphazardly scattered as the furniture in the antique store where this whole disaster started. "His mom is the front office manager at school," I numbly replied.

Numb. That was a good word to describe how I was feeling. Too numb to be mad. It was debatable that I should be mad at him, because he was only trying to continue being respectful toward me. Or was he? But our agreement had been to break up after we got back from the reunion, there was no reason that having sex changed that. Except he didn't do hook ups. I had never done hook ups before—I'd never had sex at all—yet here we are, post hook up. If it was even that, since technically we were engaged at the time. Sex hadn't even been on the table. The cold voice of reason that I'd shut down once before piped up, *Stop lying to yourself, Jane. You got exactly what you wanted.*

But not all, I whispered to myself.

It had all been a fake relationship—it was all fake. Everything was fake, and I was the idiot who had thought otherwise. The fool who thought that maybe she'd broken enough walls down to earn his respect and trust. Maybe even be cared about by him.

So, of course he reacted like he had; how was I so blind to have thought otherwise? I was the one who initiated the entire thing anyway. Not him. He hadn't even tried to look. I was the one who had seduced him.

And I was the one running like a coward. Albeit a little too late.

"So," Noah began, piercing through my pitiful thoughts. "Sweaty hottie's mom is your colleague that just happened to invite you to a weekend getaway. Did you know he'd be there?"

"She didn't invite me, Noah," I mumbled, leaning against the window as we continued driving through the darkness. Even the stars tonight seemed fairly dull.

"What?" he gasped. "Then who did? Did sweaty hottie?"

"Will you stop calling him that?" I quietly asked, not wanting a reminder that he had been both hot and sweaty with me. "But yes, he did."

"No way. But why would you lie about it? Mom and I would've both been happy for you, you know that."

I sighed. "It's a long story," I mumbled, closing my eyes. They felt puffy and tired, swollen from all of the crying that I'd already done and knew I would be doing here again in just a few moments.

"I'm sorry for whatever happened," Noah said. "Anything I can do?"

"Just please *don't* tell Mom," I begged in a whisper, and he sighed. He reached over and placed a hand on my shoulder. I flinched, startled by his touch. He shouldn't touch me anyway, I was a dirty whore. Tears slipped out. That's what I was feeling. Finally, I recognized what I was feeling.

I was a whore. Unclean. Trash. Dirty. No wonder Griffin backed off. I'd said so much the opposite and then threw myself at him. All the things we'd done flashed through my mind, and I curled inwardly in shame.

"So, what am I supposed to say when she asks?" Noah questioned.

"Nothing. Nothing at all." I wiped away the tears that were freely flowing.

Noah continued driving in silence. Allowing my bruised soul the space to sit with my thoughts as we cruised through the evening, farther and farther away from Griffin. I needed to simply shut it off. Let it all go and give in to the numbness. Numb was better than feeling dirty. I'd given myself away. Twenty-seven years and I'd simply decided one moment of pleasure was worth it. Decided he was worthy of it. *Decided he was worthy of me*, clarified the voice.

But it had all been one-sided. It would've been worthwhile if he'd shared the same feelings I had, not just the physical, of which there'd been no doubt. But I had convinced myself that he did in that moment, and it had been exactly what I wanted. For that moment, that all-too-brief moment, it had all been worth it.

Then the enormity of it all came crashing in on me. I felt freezing cold despite the heater fan blasting the cabin on high.

I sniffed once more, unable to fight the tears and the truth. Streams of salty tears blocked my nose and throat and dripped down my face. I didn't have the energy to wipe them away, promising myself this one more cry and I would shut it all off. That's what I was allowed. One more really good cry and then I was done. No more.

"Janey, what did he do?" Noah asked, "Do you want me to take care of something? If he hurt you—"

I slowly shook my head. "No, Noah. It's nothing. Really. He did nothing. It was just me," I replied, feeling the last part of my heart that had been holding on shatter in an instant hearing those words out loud—*it was always just me.*

What a fool I'd been.

Chapter 31

I lay on the couch in an oversized sweatshirt Noah had offered to let me borrow. Unable to eat or drink, I simply lay still. Numb to everything, just as I'd promised myself. Mom had tried to press me into telling her what had happened when we'd come home, but I'd merely gone to my room and laid down on my bed. To wait. For what, I wasn't sure.

Sleep never came, so I eventually wandered up the stairs and laid on the couch. Where I'd been since. Noah sat by my feet with a worried look, rubbing them like dad used to do for me when I was sick. Mom was in the kitchen cooking something for dinner that vaguely smelled good but that I wouldn't be able to eat.

Everything should hurt, but I didn't feel anything. Nothing seemed exciting, but nothing seemed sad either. Everything just was.

The doorbell rang, startling both Noah and my mom, but I barely blinked, unable to escape the prison that my mind had become. I was lost but I didn't care. Noah pushed himself from the couch with a look at me and plodded to the door. My eyes tracked him as I tucked my arm tighter under my head and curled into a smaller ball.

I heard it creak as he swung it open. "What do you want?"

"Is Jane home?" Griffin asked, and I should've felt my heart either long for him or break, but I felt nothing. Or pretended to feel nothing. I continued to lay still on the couch, even as my mom ran from the kitchen, oven mitts still on her hands.

"She doesn't want to see you," Noah sharply said, and slammed the door in his face.

"What was that?" My mom gasped, sliding around the corner.

"Nothing important, apparently," Noah said and looked at me. Maybe it did hurt a little. Enough that a single tear slid off my nose.

"That wasn't nothing!" my mom cried out. "That was a man at the door asking for your sister."

"Man? It might have been," Noah replied cryptically as he returned to his spot on the couch by my feet. I closed my eyes and slipped into nothingness.

I was almost late for school the next day. Almost. Numbly, I walked down the busy hall, students greeting each other cheerily after a weekend away. Only seven days of school and it was Thanksgiving break. Seven days of having to put in at least a little bit of effort before I could mindlessly melt into nothingness once more.

Adjusting the hem of another thick, purple turtleneck, I made sure my jeans weren't too wrinkled as I descended the stairs. I think a few students said hello, but I simply continued putting one foot in front of the other.

Once in my classroom, I turned the projector on and pulled up the project they would be beginning. As luck would have it, Dayton would be able to fulfill whatever accidental picture upload plan he'd concocted, and I wouldn't have to deal with a lot of lectures and teaching. They would simply be picking a subject in American history and then doing a presentation on it the Monday and Tuesday before Thanksgiving break.

I settled into my chair as the bell rang for first period. Students quietly filed in and sat in their seats. My mouth moved with instructions once the bell rang, but I felt far removed from this world. Lydia raised her hand at one point, the only student in first period to speak directly to me in class, and asked if I was okay.

Plastering on a fake smile, I nodded and simply said that I was a little tired this morning. I was used to lying by now, found I was pretty good at it in fact, so why should this be any different? The day moved by, monotonously, and I continued to feel nothing.

Until sixth period, when Dayton walked in. He was chatting with Jackson and then both of them quieted as soon as they saw me. I stared at Dayton, trying to figure out why only now he looked so much like Griffin. Not before, just now. Perhaps it was the clench in his jaw?

After I announced the project, I thought it would be a simple final hour as all the other classes had been. Walking back to my desk, I sat down and stared blankly at the computer screen. The class paired up as instructed in groups of four, and of course Dayton and Jackson joined with Marcy and her best friend Lily.

A few minutes later, a notification popped up on my email. Clicking it open, I furrowed my brows. It was an email from Dayton.

> *Hey Miss B. I don't have any other form of contact for you so I figured I'd send these to your teacher email here.*

That was all it said. As I continued to scroll down I couldn't help but cover my mouth with my hand. Picture after picture of Griffin and me. In some of them, it was clear who the photo was of, while others were from an angle where only Griffin was decipherable. How Dayton had managed to take all of these, I would never know, but I couldn't stop looking.

It was the very last picture he'd uploaded that I found myself lingering on. I was sitting on Griffin's shoulders celebrating our win at the end of the chicken wars. His face was so bright as he grinned, dimples pressed deeply into his cheeks. His fingers were holding my thighs, and we both seemed so carefree. I hadn't even noticed that Dayton had taken a picture, being too caught up in the celebration.

But I was oddly grateful he had. Not a single other one showed Griffin in the way this one did. That was the man I'd bared my soul to. Not the one that had destroyed it. Quickly clicking out of the email, I glanced around the room, desperate for the bell to ring. Marcy looked a little annoyed but was once again blatantly flirting with Dayton who seemed very pleased with himself.

Jackson was even putting a little bit of effort into flirting with Lily, though I could only assume it was out of boredom and due to circumstances. It took everything in me to keep my mind from wandering back to that picture, and when that bell finally rang, I sighed in audible relief.

Finally, I could go home, where nothing existed.

Noah went to the gym alone that day.

And the next.

And the next.

Each day he returned to inform me that Griffin asked where I was and if he could see me. Each time Noah shut him down.

Then on Thursday when Noah came home from the gym, he said that Griffin wasn't there.

Nor the next day.

Then it was the weekend. Where once again, I did nothing but lay on the couch.

Monday came and went.

Tuesday was finally here, and I inhaled deeply in excitement. So close to the break. So close to not seeing Dayton and doing everything I could to avoid Nancy in the mornings and evenings, although that was easier as it seemed reciprocal. So close to several days of nothingness.

I liked this nothing. This numbness. It was better than facing what had happened and feeling like I had meant nothing to someone who so quickly had become so much to me. That was the problem, how quickly things had progressed. I'd let myself run away with my feelings instead of staying rational about things.

Watching the third group in my fifth period class present their project, I felt like the empty monotony was beginning to run my life. Finally it was.

Spinning lazily in my chair, my eyes wandered to the open classroom door, and I slammed my feet to the ground.

My heart lurched.

Maybe this was simply my eyes playing a cruel trick on me, as I stared at Griffin. But there he stood. He had on a pair of black joggers and a dark green shirt with a gray jacket unzipped on top. His hands were shoved in his pockets, and he watched me with a pained look on his face.

I glanced away briefly, hoping it was just my imagination, before returning my gaze to the doorway once more. He was still there, completely clean shaven. His hair was trimmed shorter as well, and he looked almost sad.

Quietly standing from my chair, I made my way down the side of the classroom toward the lone figure who stood in the shadows of the hallway. It took everything in me to not cry as I reached the entranceway.

His eyes looked hopeful as I stopped in front of him.

Then I grabbed the handle to the door and pulled it shut without a word.

It was for the best, even if I felt myself twinge with the first ounce of pain I'd felt in a while. My chest heaved as I bit my lip.

Staring at the closed door, I choked back the flood of tears that were so close to the edge. Tears that reminded me of how much hurt and sadness I'd felt that day, but also how much joy. But no matter, I had just made it entirely clear what my intentions were.

Yet, it didn't stop the agony as I slowly drifted back to my desk, begging for that numbness to set back in.

Which it finally did as sixth hour rolled around and Dayton was unusually absent. No reminder of the haunting figure who'd shown up at my classroom door. No reminder of the ache that, for some reason, continued to grip so tightly to my heart.

Chapter 32

There were only two days left until Christmas break, which also marked almost a month since I'd last seen Griffin. A month of numb nothingness. Almost an entire month where Noah had pressed almost daily for details, and yet, I'd barely spoken at all. A month of me being stupid and foolish, thumbing through Dayton's images on my phone. Mom knew something was badly wrong, and though she tried in her way to break through, she was not Dad, and eventually she gave up and left me to wallow. Even most of my students knew something fundamental had changed. Dayton had gradually grown cold toward me, which felt odd at first, until I realized he'd grown cold and distant toward everyone. Yet, another reminder of Griffin.

But that included Marcy and Jackson. The three of them had been inseparable before Thanksgiving, then after, Jackson and Marcy talked to each other more than Dayton spoke in general. He no longer had the spunk I used to find entertaining. Now he just seemed to not care about a thing in the world. His grades were slipping in my class, despite my best efforts, but at the last staff meeting, I'd learned it was that way in every single one.

Obviously feeling the pressure of her family, Nancy tried to approach me at least once a week and would practically beg me to look at the letters that were in the envelopes she gave me. She told me they were from Griffin, but I wanted more than a damn letter apology. Instead, I simply made a point to shove them in the shredder when she was watching me. I was so upset that he couldn't seem to face me. I guess he was as much of a coward as Sam, which was proven when I started returning to the gym, because Griffin was never there.

I hated how much I missed him and how much thoughts of him were beginning to control me once more. After all this time, I'd have imagined that he would be the last thing on my mind. But no matter how hard I tried, I still felt like that vulnerable, dirty whore who had her heart ripped out by someone she should've never given it to.

Adjusting the glasses on my nose, I smoothed out a few curls of my hair that I'd left down and took a deep, reassuring breath. The bell should ring for third period at any moment. Brushing some lint off of my checkered dress that fell to mid-calf, I closed my eyes and waited.

At some point today, that sadness had morphed to a simmering anger, and I was waiting for that to go away too. I wasn't usually an angry person, but after everything, it seemed to be the one emotion I couldn't bottle up and ignore.

The bell rang, and I stood up, beginning my lecture. Just like every day. Just like every other lecture. I rambled through the information, wishing upon everything in me that I could find a way to make the information sound inspiring instead of "teacher burned-out after thirty years" dull and frustrated, which I'd sworn I'd never be. But I managed to stumble through each and every hour.

My knuckles tightened around the wheel as I drove home. Angrier and angrier, fury was boiling unreasonably inside me like molten metal. How dare he speak to me the way he had! What gave him the right to have treated me the way he had, *especially* knowing that I was a virgin before him?

And now? He showed up once in person to try and grovel and then ran away like a coward. That was what he was. A weak, coward who couldn't handle a strong woman with feelings, one who knew her worth. Which made him a coward *and* a liar. Slamming my palm against the wheel, I cursed his name under my breath.

I jerked the car to the right and bounced over the curb and up the driveway. A darkness settled over me as effectively as if the night sky itself had descended and wrapped its arm around me. Not a star shone as clouds covered any silver speckle of light. Snow was threatening to fall, water as cold and solidified as my heart was becoming.

Snatching my purse from the passenger seat, I slammed the car door behind me with every bit of force I could muster.

"You shitty coward, Griffin Marsh!" I screamed into the sky before angrily twisting the front doorknob. Kicking my heels off in the entranceway, my feet slapped against the floor into the kitchen where I found Noah all alone.

His back was to me, and he was pouring himself a glass. My eyes swiveled and locked onto the bottle of whiskey he was holding. *Ahhh!* Just what the doctor ordered, and as I stormed across the floor and snatched it from his hands, I wondered why I hadn't thought of it earlier. I'd placed it to my lips before Noah could even register what was happening.

"What the hell?" Noah whipped to face me, startled. I winced as the liquid burned my throat, but then took another long swig anyway. I swiped the back of my hand across my mouth and glared at Noah.

"Men are fucking cowards," I snarled and whipped around, bottle still in hand. Already determined that he was not getting it back.

The sharp ring of our doorbell pierced the air, pausing me in my tracks. Someone was at the door.

I glared at Noah, who rolled his eyes. "I've got it," he said, as I lifted one shoulder disdainfully and raised the bottle again. My gaze tracked Noah across the floor while gulping down some more whiskey as he swung open the front door. It burned less this time.

I could see him but he said nothing. He disappeared outside for a moment and then he inched his way back inside, looking at his hands holding something. I narrowed my gaze to get a better look at what was resting in his arms as he kicked the door shut.

"Roses. Someone left a dozen roses at the door," Noah muttered and dug through the red flowers, popping the small note off of the plastic holder. My heart jumped in my throat; had Griffin sent me roses? Was he actually starting to man up and reach out to me with something more than a lame ass letter?

Noah's eyes tracked across the note as he read out loud. "*Jane, I know he's gone. So, now it can be just us. Love always 'S'.*" And all hope poured out of me. With a grunt and downing another gulp, I stomped across the floor and ripped the postcard from his fingers. I wasn't going to be a coward and run like Griffin. Not this time.

"Janey, what the hell is that?" Noah asked as I snapped my gaze back and forth across the words.

Shaking my head, annoyed instead of afraid, I tossed the card away like it was a hot coal, but it obstinately fluttered to the ground at my feet. "You've got to be kidding me."

I should've been afraid, but I now had the benefit of Dutch courage supporting my rage.

"Jane, tell me what that is!" Noah sharpened his voice as he bent down to pick up the note.

"That's *Sam*."

"Sam?" His brows stitched together, and then everything on his face seemed to slough away, widening in realization. "Sam from back home, Sam? *The Sam that hit you, Sam?*" His voice sounded angry now too.

I nodded yes, raising the alcohol bottle to my lips.

"We need to call the agents."

Sighing, I downed another generous swig. "Then call the agents Noah! What the fuck do I care?" I turned away and stumbled toward the stairs.

"Janey, you can't just walk away!" he called after me, but I didn't listen, didn't stop.

I locked my door, hearing knocking now and then and sometimes my name, time passing in a drunken blur until the whiskey and exhaustion knocked me out cold. The delicious bliss of black when it came was a welcome relief to the emptiness and anger I'd felt for far too long. No irrational thoughts lingered in my head, keeping me awake. There was nothing but a different hollowness. I'd long since blown past any self-control and while it didn't make me feel anything else, at least it made the pain less.

My head pounded as I tried opening my eyes in the gray morning light, punished by the worst hangover I'd ever felt, one I couldn't blame on anyone but myself. Groaning into my pillow, I felt nausea roll through my stomach before throwing back the bedding, sending two empty vodka bottles clattering to the floor.

Rubbing the sleep from my eyes, I squinted through the dull but nonetheless blinding light and groggily sat up. Vague memories of last night flashed through my mind, and I clamped a hand around my mouth.

Snatching my phone off my bedside table, I stabbed in the passcode and stared in wide-eyed horror. No, no. Surely I hadn't been *that* drunk. I couldn't have been!

There was message after message, saying the most horrendous and blunt things about how I felt. Messages I'd sent to none other than Griffin himself. In my drunken stupor, I hadn't held back. I'd let him have it, telling him exactly how upset he had made me.

Explicit words were used, calling him everything under the sun and moon. There was no rectifying the situation either, seeing as there was no unsend button.

Quickly locking my phone, I flipped around and buried my face in my pillow. What in the world had I done? I never lost control; that wasn't me. That wasn't the woman my father had taught me to be. I wasn't one to get drunk either. I'd never been that drunk before. Now I was one of *those* people in addition to being a whore.

Kicking my feet, I screamed into my pillow as a sharp rap sounded on the door.

I shot my head up and stared at my bedroom door. My eyes slipped to my clock ticking on the wall, and I shrieked in horror. I was late. It was the last day of school before winter break, and I was going to be late.

Scrambling off the bed, I tore the door open in fury and was met by my mom's wide eyes. "Jane, dear," she muttered in shock. Then she waved a hand in front of her face. "Phew. You need a shower and change of clothes."

"Right," I muttered. Turning around in a daze, my shoulders fell. Despite the alcohol and texts I'd sent in anger, I didn't feel any better. In fact, I felt worse today than I had this entire time. Now, I'd added embarrassment to everything else.

"Jane, why didn't you tell us about Sam?" my mom asked, stopping me in my tracks. I spun around with bloodshot eyes and simply looked at her.

"And make you worry even more? No, thanks. Besides, it's not that big of a deal."

"Well, the agents think it is. They are double checking to make sure that none of our data has been leaked, and—"

"Okay. Awesome. Like I said, we are just fine. The FBI didn't even technically move us." I spun around and marched toward my mom, the world around me ringing in my ears. "You chose to move, asked Noah and I to uproot our lives based on a *recommendation* from them. Whatever they're doing to rectify this situation with Sam is probably just a courtesy because of Dad's sacrifice. We've been here long enough, if anything were to happen, it would've already!"

She pursed her lips and shook her head. "Well, they're going to send Sam back home, and they'll monitor him closely to make sure he never shows up here again."

I tossed my hands into the air, because it all sounded too easy. But maybe, this entire time, it had been that easy concerning Sam. But I was overcome with anger. "Great. If they're so good at protecting people, then why is Dad still dead?!" I snapped, and my mom's face paled. Too far. I'd taken that too far.

"I'm sorry," I quickly muttered, my eyes widening as she plopped onto the edge of my mattress.

Her face turned cold. "It's fine. Just rub more salt in the wound. It's not like I didn't lose my husband at all."

My shoulders sagged, and I took a hesitant step in her direction. "Mom, I didn't mean it like that. I'm just upset, okay?" Upset about Griffin. Upset about my dad. Upset about whatever I'd done to deserve the cruelty this world was showing me.

She whipped her head toward me, narrowing her eyes. "Is that why you got so drunk last night?"

I pulled my bottom lip into my teeth but said nothing. *Let her think whatever she needed to.*

She sighed and slapped her thighs, knowing that was as far as I was about to let her in, and stood up. "Go, you stink." She nodded toward the door.

My feet somehow took me across my room, and I managed to grab a clean dress, any dress, from the closet. I showered, pulled my hair back into its usual bun, and put my makeup on in enough time to make it to school just as the first bell rang.

All I registered about the entire day was that Nancy made no attempt to give me another letter.

The next day, my time was spent staring at my phone in horrified fascination, biting my nails with anxiousness and waiting for his reply to the most awful words I'd ever said or sent. Words I hadn't even said to Sam.

Truthful, but awful, and embellished with a lot of swearing.

Yet, Christmas came and passed, and when I still hadn't heard from him my anger had shifted. In the next stage of grief, I was no longer angry at him, but angry at his silence. Any reply would've done. That's all. Even a texted *k* would have sufficed. I was ready and would've taken one of his letters now, too, but no, he was proving as much of a coward as I'd thought him to be.

My eyes read my accusing and unanswered texts over and over. Each time it became clearer and clearer to me how true my words rang. He had shattered my very heart and soul and deserved whatever rebuttal came from me. He said he didn't do hookups, but he did. Said I could trust him—but I couldn't.

But he also did say from the get go that it was a fake arrangement, and I hadn't included any of that part.

I leaned back against the couch alone again, despite Noah's constant pestering that I should join him for his New Years Eve party. Even my mom had happily dressed a little fancy, for a party she'd been invited to with her new book club friends.

A tear of self-pity rolled down my cheek, and I used the sleeve of Griffin's sweatshirt I was wearing to wipe it away, still holding a hint of what could only be imaginary citrus. Despite it all, I craved his smell. Still craved some sentiment of feeling close to him.

I was turning into that crazy ex who wouldn't let someone go. Even if I wasn't technically his ex.

Raising my knees to my chest, I stared at the television, playing countdowns across the world. Not inspired by the fireworks, none of which could ever match what I'd experienced with Griffin for the first time in my life, I padded into the kitchen and opened my mom's special cupboard. I hadn't touched a drop of liquor since I'd drank myself into oblivion, but tonight was New Year's Eve, a night one should celebrate even if on their own. One night couldn't hurt. Besides, maybe attempt number two at drowning my sorrows would work.

Without bothering about labels, I took whatever was in the front and carried it back to the couch, popped the cap, and took a long swig. It didn't matter what it tasted like; as long as it helped pass the time, it would do. I knew I was unraveling, and yet, I didn't care to stop it.

The room spun as I let more brown liquid slide down my throat, while I stared at the image of Griffin and me in the pool, his mouth wide, both of us laughing.

I think there was another bottle on the floor at some point, but everything was hazy. All the colors were blurring together. Nothing was solid anymore, and I felt like I was floating on clouds.

My phone was in my hand as I sent yet again another text to Griffin, reminding him of how much of a coward he was. Even though the relationship had been fake, he should've been man enough to own what had happened.

I giggled and hiccupped, as I mischievously smiled. Pressing send on the text, I rocked backwards on the couch.

And then bubbles appeared.

The world around me paused. Was he actually reading my texts? Had he seen them? What had I done?

And then two words came through.

> Jane I

There was no punctuation, no emoji attached, not even a full sentence, nothing, and my stomach twisted with embarrassed rage.

"Next time I see you," I slurred. "I'm going to punch you in the fucking face." Swinging a lazy fist, I giggled and then fell to the side. Right into a solid wall of something hard.

"What is going on with you? Sam is gone, and has been for a while, so what's up?" Noah's voice pierced through the haze in my mind, and I rolled my head awkwardly to the side to see him. He was what I'd fallen against. Pushing my head upright, he settled me against the seat.

"I don't know what you're talking about." I grinned stupidly and swayed, threatening to topple over. He pressed a finger into my shoulder and barely had to apply any force before I plopped sideways on the couch. Another giggle left my lips.

Noah sat down beside me and inspected the alcohol bottles I'd already finished. "Yes, you do. Because this is the second time you've gotten drunk, and you've never been drunk before. You're worrying me, and you're worrying mom."

The idiotic grin slipped from my face as a tear tumbled uncontrollably out of my eye.

"Janey, what happened?" he softly whispered. I blinked, choking back pain that I hadn't let myself be consumed by. Exhaustion felt by this unexplainable burning. I was stuck in a cage in my head with nowhere to go.

"He's the worst of them all," I muttered. "And he can't even be bothered to answer a single text with anything coherent."

"Who? What are you going on about?" Noah asked again, sitting beside me as I let the tears silently slip down my cheeks. Anger, rage, hate, embarrassment all cascading down with the liquid that stained my skin.

I hugged the cushion to my chest and shook my head. "It was all fake, yet for whatever reason, I thought what was growing between us wasn't."

"Jane, you're not making any sense," Noah pressed.

I plopped my head to the side in his lap and told him everything. Every little thing that happened between Griffin and me—including Sam's involvement. It was such a relief, every word out of my mouth lifted some of the lead from my chest. So nice that finally, someone else knew about it all.

"So, he fucked you and then said that it wasn't worth shit?" Noah angrily clarified, and I nodded, pulling the pillow closer to my chest.

"Pretty much. He was my first, too." I snuffled into Griffin's sleeve, and Noah stiffened.

"Wait, you're telling me that I had sex before you?"

"Obviously. Even Mom knows you're a manwhore," I answered with a little hiccup and a little smile.

"Rude." He chuckled and then sighed. "And he hasn't said a thing to you since?"

"Other than 'Jane I'. His mom hasn't even tried to offer me a letter in a while. I would accept that at this point." I lifted my phone, opening the messages to show him proof. Noah took it from my hands and scrolled through the embarrassing length of texts that I'd sent. I watched through a teary haze as he furrowed his brows and then pulled out his own phone. His thumb tapped on his screen a few times before dropping my phone back in my hand. His eyes were intense, staring at his screen as he ferociously typed something himself.

"Noah, what are you doing?" I asked.

"Blocking his number from your phone, telling Griffin exactly how I feel about this entire thing, and then blocking his number from mine," he angrily answered. I shook my head but smiled as the world spun faster and faster around me. Telling Noah hadn't gone as horribly as predicted, and it wasn't like it would ruin anything now. There was nothing left between Griffin and I to ruin anyway. But it didn't mean that I wasn't hurting.

Being honest, it hurt like hell.

Chapter 33

Today was easier. Or at least it seemed to feel easier. Perhaps it was, knowing that Noah had spam-texted Griffin a couple of times before cutting all ties with him helped. Or maybe it was the fact that time was passing, healing the wounds, and Griffin's complete absence made things feel less raw. Though the feelings of desire for him seemed to not have dwindled much. I hated that every once in a while, I swear I caught a whiff of him, or heard his stupid chuckle. I'd turn whenever I heard someone say smart ass. I hated that every so often, one of the songs we'd sung to came on, and I would find myself lost in those memories.

I hated that stupid picture that I continually pulled up on my phone.

I tucked some of my straightened hair behind my ear, pushed my glasses back up my nose, and returned my attention to the sea of papers covering the desk. There were too many pages to grade before the weekend, yet I needed to get them done to stay on schedule. Tapping my pen against the desk, I scanned the next test. Ticking red marks at each wrong answer, when the door flew open, banging against the bookshelf.

Glancing up from the blurring words that I'd read too many times, I forced a small smile to my lips. "Hello, Dayton." I placed my pen down as he approached my desk with a determined look on his face, gripping tightly to the top of his backpack. He set it down on the edge of my desk and unzipped it without looking at me.

"What are you doing this weekend?" he asked in an adult tone that made me furrow my brows. I'd noticed the downward shift in his voice, the deepening, the similarity to Griffin's.

"Why?" I hesitantly replied as he dug through the papers stuffed in his book bag.

"Because I can't do this alone. Look, I know that you and Griffin fought that day at the cabin. I'm not stupid, despite the fact that everyone else believed his lie that you were feeling sick and needed to go home early, I saw the ring you'd left, and you haven't worn it since," he continued, finally finding whatever it was in his backpack that he'd been searching for. Turning around to face me, he clutched a small white envelope in his hands.

I clenched my jaw but didn't say anything.

A letter. Finally, after two months of nothing, a letter. This one I wouldn't shred.

Dayton sighed. "No matter how mad you are at him, I know you care about him. Or at least you did, which is why I am asking if you have plans this weekend."

"What does that have to do with me caring about your brother or not?" I questioned, suspiciously.

"Because Griffin asked me to do this, and you can't leave me to do it alone."

"Griffin asked you to give that to me? To do what?" I raised my brows.

He gripped the envelope tighter. "Look, I'm not supposed to know, but I know you know about the contract. That explains why you would agree to marry him so fast after meeting him. So, I need you to come."

I swiveled in my chair, facing him directly. "Contract? What are you talking about? What does being engaged to Griffin have to do with a contract?"

"You don't know?" he asked, visibly taken aback, and stepping away.

"I know that your mom tried to arrange his marriage a few times before and that your family is very...involved in his personal life."

"Yes, but that's all because the deadline is creeping up. Fast. In fact, it was supposed to be when my mom turned forty, but Griffin managed to get an extension to the end of his..." Dayton's voice trailed off and mouth fell open as he saw my shocked silence. "You really don't know."

I shook my head and sighed. Of course I didn't know. It wasn't like Griffin shared anything too personal about himself. It had all been fake to him. Anger resurfaced.

"Explain," I demanded.

"I'm not supposed to know this, but I'm nosy. Apparently, if Griffin isn't retired from the military, running the family business, and married by the end of this year, Grandma won't give out a dime of inheritance. And it's *a lot*. Grandma and Grandpa are like old-money rich."

"What?!" I gasped, his words confirming my thoughts about his grandma.

Dayton nodded. "There's a contract and everything. Griffin had until Mom turned forty to be married, retired, and running the family company, or zilch, no money. But, apparently when Griffin was twenty-one, he got lawyers involved and renegotiated things so he had until his twentieth year in the military. He wanted a full twenty-year career."

I stared at Dayton, unsure if I believed what he was saying. Things like that only happened in fiction. "Are you messing with me?" I hissed, and Dayton shook his head.

"If I hadn't heard Mom and Dad arguing about it at one point, I wouldn't believe it either." My heart fell to the floor. The engagement, the fake relationship, seducing me, was all so Griffin could get even more money than he already had. Didn't he have enough to buy a house for his parents and his dad?

I swiveled to face my blank computer screen. "That greedy, gold-digging bastard," I muttered, and Dayton sighed.

"Look, I shouldn't know this either, but Cara gets the inheritance if Griffin doesn't end up fulfilling the contract in time. And I do not want to see her with it because of how she treats my mom, Griffin, because of how she treated you over that weekend." He lifted the envelope toward me and set it gently on the edge of the desk, like it was fragile and might crumble. I stared at it, wondering what he was getting at.

"The least he could've done is be honest about things," I angrily retorted, mainly to myself. Reaching forward, I picked up the envelope and flipped it over. It was sealed with a fancy wax stamp that rich people in the movies always used. So, not an apology letter despite Dayton saying Griffin asked him to give it to me?

"What's this?"

Dayton took a deep breath. "An invitation for my family's annual Valentine's dinner."

I chuckled humorlessly, popping open the seal with my nail and sliding out the invite. It was on expensive parchment with gold trim, detailing the event. "This looks really fancy," I muttered, impressed despite myself, and annoyed that Griffin was too cowardly to bring it to me himself. Apart from the fact his number was blocked in my phone, and the last time he had shown up, I'd slammed the door in his face.

"Yes, it's always black tie, and I know it's short notice but..."

I flipped the envelope back and forth between my fingers but said nothing.

He added resolutely, "I don't think Grandma will accept that you two are engaged if you're not there tomorrow night, meaning—"

"All of that money will go to Cara." I set the invite down on my keyboard and looked up at Dayton. He tugged at the hem of his white, long-sleeved shirt, and lifted a knowing brow. "So, your entire argument is banking on the idea that I hate Cara more than I'm pissed at Griffin."

His gaze lowered to the floor, and he squeaked a toe back and forth against the tile. "Yes. I guess it is." He sighed, sounding reasonable and more adult than ever. "You can be mad at Griffin all you want, but please."

I shook my head. "Griffin should ask me himself," I argued.

"Right, cause that's possible." Dayton lifted a brow, and I sighed. He wasn't wrong. It's not like I let Griffin talk to me when he was at least still trying. Which meant that the only way I'd end up at this dinner would be through someone else's invite. Dayton's invite. Which Griffin knew.

But, now knowing that he'd literally used me for money, to gain wealth, that small sentient moment of longing snapped away with the anger that filled my soul. "Isn't owning two houses enough?" I questioned, and Dayton furrowed his brows.

"Did you and Griffin ever actually talk?" He stared at me, wide-eyed and confused.

"What does that mean, Dayton?" I grumbled.

"You didn't know about the contract, and now you're acting like you don't know about his money situation." He chuckled to himself. "Technically, I'm not supposed to know either, but like I said, I'm nosy."

"Spit it out, Dayton. Or I'll say no to the invite." I lifted my brows and folded my arms in front of my white blouse.

"Griffin's rich as balls, Miss B. A self-made man without this inheritance. He owns *more* than two houses and several apartment complexes. I even think he has some ownership in a couple hotel chains, but yeah," Dayton explained, and my mouth fell open. An image of the engagement ring I thought could never be real inexplicably came to my mind. Apparently, we didn't talk, not really, even if he did say he owned his parents' home that they "rented" from him.

I wasn't sure if I really wanted to go to this dinner tomorrow evening. It wasn't like Griffin actually cared a whit for me. Speaking of Griffin, he would be there tomorrow, and I wasn't sure if I was ready to see him again. Especially now knowing that it had always been about riches and power. A small fact he'd conveniently left out. Wait, that didn't really add up if he was as rich as Dayton said. So, if not money, was all of this for control? To simply make sure that Cara didn't end up with the inheritance?

Honestly, no matter how much of a gold digging, greedy bastard Griffin seemed, Dayton wasn't wrong in assuming I hated Cara more. Letting her have the money irked me more than playing this game a little longer for Griffin.

My shoulders sagged, and I let my hands fall in my lap. One thing I knew was true, was that he didn't deserve the pressure that came from this stupid contract. Regardless of the fact that it was for greed, it was something that had lingered over his head for twenty years, maybe longer.

I leaned forward and bumped my head against my desk. Curse my stupid, empathetic, pathetic self for still wanting to help someone who had hurt me so intensely. Curse my stupid self for falling for him in the first place, for giving him a piece of me that still clung to him. And curse my competitiveness for simply wanting to shove it in Cara's face, even if that meant more pain for myself. At least tomorrow, I could yell at Griffin. Get it off my chest for good and tell him how much of a horrible human being he was to his face.

"Alright, I'll see you there tomorrow," I said, and Dayton grinned.

"Yes! Thank you Miss B!" He smiled and quickly left the room.

My eyes swiveled back to the fancy formal invite. I would need to buy a new dress for this occasion, and once Noah found out, how would he feel? He knew everything up to a point, and now I knew it all, yet I still agreed to help Griffin.

Or maybe I was mostly curious as to what would happen. Cara couldn't win. My mind swam, drowning in confusion at everything that I'd just learned. Though things that hadn't made sense before, did now. Like why his grandma and mom wanted him to retire—they wanted him to receive his inheritance. Or the attempts at arranging his marriage. It seemed despite their grandma's doting behavior toward Cara, she didn't want her taking control. Which was interesting.

Whatever happened tomorrow, as long as I screwed up Cara's plans, I could handle everything else. Including coming face to face with Griffin himself.

When I would punch him.

Hard.

Chapter 34

I adjusted the pale purple, off-the-shoulder sleeve of my dress, which was floor-length made from absolutely exquisite silk. Its simple design could have been bespoken—hugging my hard-earned curves, and daringly backless with a small pearl chain that clasped at the top and dangled down my spine. The sleeves tightened against my wrists and the neckline displayed my collarbone. My hair softly draped to the nape of my neck, and I'd applied heavier than usual makeup with a darker red lipstick.

The courage that I had felt yesterday when I'd agreed to this "date" was long gone. Now, I simply felt like an idiot who was clinging moronically to some hope to a thing that no longer existed. Never existed. It was increasingly clear as I reflected that if Griffin really wanted me there, he would've asked me himself. It was becoming more like Dayton simply wanted to stick it to someone which was the only reason why he asked me to be his non-official plus one. I grasped the pearl chain at the back of my neck. Maybe I shouldn't go.

A soft knock sounded at my door, and it creaked open. I watched in the mirror as Noah poked his head in.

"Don't say anything rude," I muttered as he entered, wearing a pair of shorts and a T-shirt.

"You look very pretty, Janey," he quietly said.

"Am I doing the right thing?" I asked, watching him through the reflection in front of me. He inhaled deeply and shoved his hands into his shorts pockets.

"I think you deserve some sort of closure, if that's what you're asking. And I'm very curious to know how this inheritance stuff is going to play out, so I selfishly want you to go so you can spill the tea after," he answered with a sly grin. I rolled my eyes but chuckled softly.

"Me too," I sheepishly said, and he pulled his hands out of his pockets and grabbed my white, pointy toe heels beside the door.

"Well, then get going. Besides, I'd also like to know exactly how rich this dude and his family are. Sweaty hottie may be a coward and jerk, but he's apparently a rich coward with a rather mysterious contract for us to unfold." He grinned as I ripped the heels from his hands.

"You need a new nickname for him," I muttered, strapping them on as he wiggled his brows.

"Look, I know he hurt you, but at least you lost your virginity to someone as... well, gorgeous and complicated as him."

"Ugh! I'd have preferred him to be simple so I wasn't in this situation months later, going to a stupid Valentine's dinner, with his brother no less, simply because we're curious." I pointed to my chest and thrust my finger into his before sliding past.

Noah followed me up the stairs, loudly inhaling the cloud of perfume following me. "It smells like it's not just curiosity that got you to agree."

"Shut up, asshole," I argued and stomped toward the front door. "Where's Mom?"

"Working late. Her book club met earlier today, so she took the evening shift," he answered, leaning against the kitchen counter as I turned the knob.

"Tell her not to worry if she gets home before I do," I said, and Noah nodded, pulling a wry face.

"Go punch sweaty hottie for me. Though maybe not in the face. I like his face."

"Sure you're not gay?"

"For him, I'd consider it," Noah answered with a grin as I shut the door behind me. I quickly pulled myself into my car and plugged in the address I read from the invite that perched in my open clutch beside me. The drive was estimated to be longer than I expected, but I'd left enough time to make it there fashionably late if I didn't lose my brakes or have a flat.

My heart pounded the entire drive. Taking me closer and closer to someone I hadn't seen in far too long. Closer and closer to someone who clearly didn't want me around. What if he showed up with some other girl? Maybe I'd be able to sneak away before too much attention landed on me. I felt the first twinge of a tension headache in the back of my skull.

Turning off of the highway, the road curved through some trees and then burst out into a beautiful city. Life was buzzing here. Bright lights flashed as I slowly made my way in traffic toward the spectacular stone building indicated as my destination by the blue pin creeping closer on my map. I turned my music down as the GPS alerted me in monotone that I was almost at my final stop.

The large building rose off to my right, bedecked with twinkling, pink lights reflecting from paintwork as vehicles pulled beneath the overhang. It looked like a grand old hotel, set with a red carpet and bollards as if to keep away the throng of non-existent paparazzi. Pedestrians stopped and pointed, trying to get a look in the double-doors above the steps. Feeling increasingly nervous, I signaled and followed the slowly moving line toward the carpeted stairs that led toward two double, golden doors being held open by butlers.

This wasn't the place. Was it? I confirmed the address and slowly continued to creep forward. There was a uniformed valet waiting to take and park the few cars that people had driven, while most guests seemed to have arrived in limos. Astounded, I assumed there had to be more than one party occurring with the sheer amount of people entering the building.

I stared in awe as I slowly pulled forward and put my car in park. Stepping out, a gloved hand extended and helped me exit. Holding my clutch to my chest, the valet slipped inside and waited as I walked around the front of my vehicle. My heels seemed to echo extraordinarily loudly along the pavement as I approached the stairs.

Griffin was somewhere in there. Whether he would be happy to see me or not, seemed to be the other question. If I turned around now, no harm would be done. If I went inside, however, the feeling in my gut told me something would occur, because there were two or more well-fed bears looking for more, and I was the stick about to poke them. All I could hope for was that I'd escape with my skin intact and, at the very least, I would get closure. I could see his face and speak with him, and once and for all, give him a piece of my mind.

Taking a deep breath, I lifted my chin and walked up the stairs, right through the gleaming double-doors. There were signs in front of me, three different ones with hands pointing in three directions, guiding guests through the massive lobby toward their respective parties. The shades of gold and ivory colors in the marble rising around me reflected the same sense of wealth as the soft classical music that played behind the cacophony of whispered voices echoed from the vaulted ceiling.

A grand staircase rose opposite me, spiraling upwards with a flourish and a gold railing beneath the crystal chandelier that lit up this room. A mural was painted upon the ceiling, small pictures of things I could barely make out at this distance. One more thing that seemed to be from the movies.

I spun in a slow circle, staring at the grandeur around me. Marble pillars rose to each side, with secretive looking doors tucked away farther along. It was exquisite. I felt underdressed despite the new gown I'd bought. There were women with more jewels and glitter than I'd ever seen before with their hands tucked in true gentlemen's elbows.

A throat cleared to my left, and I stopped spinning like some awestruck ballerina. Dayton stood beside me in a very nice tux. "Hi, Miss B." He grinned.

"This is very pretty." I smiled painfully, knowing that he was about to lead me to Griffin. Though the lighting was warm and dim, I was sure the anxious blush blooming upward from my chest would soon be visible to everyone.

"We are this way." He tossed a thumb behind him, and I slowly followed, weaving around other groups making their way toward their dinners. We passed between two marble pillars and then he tugged at a heavy door, which swung open with surprising ease.

Inside the packed ballroom, the atmosphere was far livelier than I expected. The conversation was loud above the music played by an elegant string quartet and punctuated by even louder laughter, assaulting my ears. There were many people I didn't recognize, and some I did, mingling about. Some danced at the base of the musicians to my right. Some, mostly sharply dressed men, simply stood conversing elegantly with a glass in their hands around the refreshment table at the far side. Others mingled in front of another set of double doors, while the rest stood around glass doors that let in a soft, cool breeze from the sparkling night air outside.

My eyes were on a swivel, desperately searching for someone I wasn't sure I was ready to confront. And I had yet to see him. However, my eyes did land unexpectedly on a grinning Jackson who came jogging my way.

"Hey, Miss B!" He waved.

"Jackson! Why does it not surprise me that you're here," I answered, and he shrugged his shoulders.

"Pretty sure that Dayton's mom just thinks I'm part of the family now. I got my own invite this year even, and Marcy's here, somewhere."

"I thought Marcy was with you?" I looked at Dayton, and he grinned.

"She is. Lily is here with Jackson. Though, we figured if you turned down the first invite, I'd use my plus one to drag you here cause you wouldn't be able to leave me hanging." He and Jackson bumped fists.

"You two need to stop meddling in other people's lives," I chastised, realizing that the invite I'd been given was not as a plus one, but for me specifically. At least one person expected me to be here, wanted me here. Both boys gave me a cheeky grin.

"But it's too fun!" Jackson said, and I shook my head.

"Anyway, mingle. Enjoy food. They'll announce when it's time for dinner," Dayton continued, and then he and Jackson were gone, leaving me before I had a chance to stop them.

Slowly, I wandered through the party, accepting a long-stemmed champagne glass from a waiter before putting it back on the tray of another. The last thing I needed was to fuel myself with alcohol. People stared. Others whispered. I gritted my teeth inside, though I didn't slow enough to listen. I had one goal, and that was to find Griffin and tell him exactly how he'd made me feel and then leave. Plus, if I lingered too long, there was a chance that someone like Cara would find me.

Above the music and chattering were gentle tinkles from the crystals in the chandeliers that floated on the ceiling. There was a beautiful serenity about this place. The soft, warm shades of ivory and gold, pale browns and even some whites turned what could be a cold ballroom into an inviting abyss. One that beckoned to drown out my sorrows and the increasingly frustrating anxiety that was zapping through my veins. There was still no sight of Griffin yet, though I caught sight of Cara, her hair twisted high on top of her head in a beehive.

A soft *tink* of glass silenced the crowd around me, and eventually the musicians stopped playing. Turning to face the direction of that universally commanding sound, I had a chance to study the older gentleman standing with a glass in hand. Beside him was Griffin's grandma, her weathered face beaming brightly and cunningly. The man had snowy, white hair and was quite thin. Large, old-fashioned glasses sat on his nose as he adjusted the lapel of his black tuxedo.

"Before we begin tonight's feast, as you all know, we are missing one of our beloved guests. He has asked that the following people join me in a private room for a moment before dinner begins." The gentleman paused, and my brows furrowed. I saw Cara straighten up, her bony shoulders shifted backwards in her red dress as if she knew something. She brushed her hands across the fabric, trying to smooth out a few wrinkles in her full volume princess-style ball gown. It was pretty, but seemed a little too young for her.

The gentleman cleared his throat and held up a small paper. "Nancy and Brent Pitts," he said first, and Cara continued to smile haughtily as Griffin's mom and his stepdad, whom I recognized but never officially met, walked toward the man I assumed to be Griffin's grandfather. He kissed Nancy on her cheek briefly as they passed through the door behind him.

"Dayton Pitts. You can bring Jackson, Lily, and Marcy if you want," the gentleman continued, and I watched in even more confusion as the three of them grinned and whispered amongst each other before disappearing into the room.

"Obviously myself and you, my dear," he said next, and chuckles sounded around the room. There was the confirmation that he was Griffin's grandpa.

"Mr. James Marsh," he continued, and I watched as a frail, yet tall man timidly walked forward. His face was hollow and weathered, but you knew he had once been handsome. And he looked so much like Griffin. Older, yes, but his bone structure was so similar.

Then, once he'd disappeared into the room, silence fell again. Griffin's grandpa furrowed his brows and tilted his head. Whispering something to his wife, she nodded, and then he lifted his gaze.

"And last, Jane Barlow," he announced.

My mouth fell open as I froze in disbelief. Griffin's grandma lifted her chin beside her husband and slid her gaze across the crowd. *He'd just said my name, right?* From the corner of my eye, I watched as Cara blinked in utter shock. She swung her head around, searching, and eventually her eyes locked onto me. But I still couldn't move. Why me? Why was my name called?

"Jane? There is a Jane Barlow here?" Griffin's grandpa bellowed again.

"No. You must have it wrong. Griffin gave you the wrong list!" Cara called out. Her shrill voice sent a jolt through me as murmuring began to spread around the group. I was so confused, yet somehow my feet slowly shuffled forward. My heels echoed loudly, pounding back against the deafening stares that were turning to face me.

So many eyes in a room where I knew almost no one. Why was I on this list? Why was there a list? Why had Griffin made a list? What was going on? It had just been Griffin's immediate family called back, so what was my name doing on this list? And where was Griffin in all of this?

The crowd parted as I found myself emerging in front of Griffin's grandparents. His grandma raised a brow, her gaze slipping to my bare left hand that I quickly tucked against my leg. His grandpa gave me a gentle, encouraging smile, glancing at his wife, but the moment he did so, the smile fell. A stiff, cold mask shuttered his face as I passed by. Numb, walking in a haze, I drifted around them and gripped the handle that blocked the path everyone else had disappeared through.

As the door creaked open, the groan echoed throughout the entire ballroom, stares still drilling into my back. Quickly, I scurried into the room and shut the door behind me, closing my eyes in relief.

Taking a deep breath, I turned and found myself being watched by everyone who had just been asked to enter this room as well. And of course, Dayton was grinning like he knew something he shouldn't.

Chapter 35

They were all seated around a small, circular table nearest to the entrance. Covered in beautiful white linen cloths, many more stretched behind this one. At the far side was another small, raised platform for instruments to be played upon. Lights were twinkling above the set tables, each placed with golden utensils and plates trimmed in delicate shining gold.

Servers stood quiet and still off to the right beside two small doors that swung both ways—waiting to serve us our dinner. There were beautiful roses for centerpieces and a hue of pale pink dancing amongst the whites and creams.

I hesitantly made my way to one of the empty chairs near the family. Dayton wiggled his brows along with Jackson as Marcy and Lily's brows furrowed. Nancy's face was unreadable as was her husband, Brent's. James looked confused as he watched me approach the table. I slid my chair back, and it squeaked along the marble floor making me wince before quickly sitting down.

The door I'd just come through swung open again with a thud, and in walked the last two people we were waiting for. As they approached the table, one waiter carried a serving tray with envelopes stacked on top toward us while the rest of the serving staff disappeared through the swinging doors.

I stared at the platter as it was set down, and then he disappeared as well, leaving this room quiet and still. Nobody moved. Not even Dayton who had a tendency to fidget. He simply waited. Waited for whatever was going to happen. I was waiting for Griffin to make his appearance.

"I know you wish he could be here with us tonight, but hopefully this will be the last holiday that you'll spend without your son, without our grandson, if he's really serious about things," Griffin's grandma began, looking intently at her daughter. Nancy offered a stiff smile in return as I watched becoming more confused.

"You know Griffin writes a letter every holiday he's deployed for a few people. So, Nancy, if you'll do the honors since it's, again, hopefully going to be the last one," his grandpa continued as my heart stopped.

Deployed? Did he say deployed? As in gone for the military?

I shot my gaze toward Dayton, but he was staring intently at the letters on the silver platter sitting between us. How long? Is this what he meant when he said Griffin wouldn't ask me? More like he *couldn't* ask me to come. So that text, was he out of cell service for much of the time, and the single moment he had any, only 'Jane I' came through? And the letters that Nancy tried to give me weren't because it was a romantic gesture but his only form of communication? Which only can mean that the lack of them lately was because he was unable to write any at the time. I wanted to melt into the floor with every realization that held the ring of truth.

I watched with bated breath as Nancy reached forward and grabbed the first envelope. Slowly, she read the names on each of them and began passing them around. Mine was at the very bottom. Last, once again.

Her fingers trembled as she lifted it from the platter and stretched it toward me. As my hand clamped around the envelope, she tightened her grip. I felt disoriented, and simply reacted to the world around me. Somehow, I think she realized I was utterly lost because her brows abruptly softened and she released the letter.

The moment the letter was in my hands, everyone tore open their envelopes. Nothing but the sound of shuffling paper could be heard along with the faint music drifting in from the other room. I stared at the scribbled name on the front of the envelope, written in slightly messy handwriting.

Griffin's.

Slowly, I ripped open the sealed envelope and pulled out a few sheets of paper. Folded into thirds, there was a letter for me. Glancing up from the stack, I met the grinning eyes of Dayton. He winked and then quickly returned to his own letter. He'd known. Somehow, Griffin must have known that I shredded all of his previous letters and knew Dayton would convince me to come. Which meant Griffin had something to say that he couldn't risk me ignoring any longer.

I quickly flipped open the pages and couldn't help but smile at the first three words written across the top.

> Dear smart ass,
>
> I don't even know where to start. My mom says you shredded my other letters, which I can't blame you for. And I know there is a break between the last time she tried to give you one and when you'll receive this note. We headed out on a mission and communications were cut off for a while. I tried to text, but service has pretty much sucked this entire deployment so I hardly turn my phone on anymore. Anyway, I've written this a hundred times only to end up rambling on about shit that doesn't really matter. Everything I should've said, everything I shouldn't have said.... You don't have to read this if you don't want to, but I'm hoping that somehow you give me the chance.
>
> I'm sorry.
>
> Dayton told me that day to simply say sorry, but I was too stubborn and confused at the time to get past my ego and do it. What I said to you that day did not come out the right way. I never meant for you to think I suddenly felt obligated to you in any way or that everything we shared was for show. If I'm being honest, I was scared and I don't really handle being scared well. I was scared that if I told you how I truly felt, you'd feel trapped with me. I have a whole lot of baggage that I've not told you about that's stuck with me. So, I stumbled over trying to tell you that if you still wanted out after our fake relationship ended that Sunday,

you could have it. Regardless of what we did and how I felt about it.

My feelings didn't matter, don't matter, not even now. All of that is up to you.

I was also mad that day. At myself. I'd let myself fulfill a fantasy that had been running on repeat in my mind for days with complete disregard for any self control I should've shown you. You deserved to have your first time feel absolutely breathtaking. To have your body worshiped in a way I failed to do that day in the pool. In a way I wished from that moment forward I could have done.

Now here I am, rambling again. I'm not good at these feelings and I doubt any of this makes much sense. It barely makes sense in my own head, let alone figuring out how to voice the thoughts. What I'm trying to say is that I don't really know what love feels like, but what I felt, and still feel for you, sure seems a lot like what I imagine it to be.

Yet my actions told you differently. I'm not mad that you refused to see me after and I hope and pray that you aren't feeling guilty for any of it. I would've done the same if I'd been in your shoes.

Jane, I wish every day that passes here that I had been more of a man and simply told you what I'd felt before orders came in.

I miss you.

This probably sounds possessive now, after all of this time, or even if this much time hadn't passed, it would still feel the same. We'd barely begun to get to know each other. I hope that when I *come home, you can find it in your heart to forgive me and grant me another chance.*

I know I don't deserve that... I shouldn't even ask for one, but I promise when I return, especially because of things I need to tell you about that weekend, I'll explain everything. Answer any questions you have honestly. I'll tell you exactly what I should've said that day. What I wanted to say. I'll give you the world if you'll let me.

And one more thing. If Sam shows up again, tell Noah and don't be afraid to throw a punch or two like your dad taught you. Sometimes a little violence is needed. I also hope you'll start smiling again, it sure is my favorite thing to see. The guys will give me a load of shit if they ever find out it's you who I've been thinking of when things get rough out here.

Anyway, I think that's it. I miss you, smart ass.

Yours, Griffin

I stared at the paper, my hands trembling. Confused and maybe a little happy? Yet I wasn't sure how much I truly believed the words he'd written down. All of this was a lot. Everything I'd learned over the past couple days and now this, it was all so much. Still, if Griffin was serious with what he said, when he makes it home, I'll ask him about this contract for his inheritance. The one thing that's fueled every event in his life lately and now mine.

But that all seemed such a fleeting thought as my eyes whipped back toward a singular sentence he'd written. *What I'm trying to say is that I don't really know what love feels like, but what I felt, and still feel for you, sure seems a lot like what I imagine it to be.* Those were his words, not mine. Or were they something he simply wanted to share to try and manipulate me once more. But my heart leapt as I clung to that sentence. Things had progressed fast for me, but it seemed the same for him. Which only terrified me even more.

If he truly does care for me and wants me, then still, why did he have to say what he did? It hurt regardless of what he was saying now. There were muffled voices echoing around me as I continued to remain lost in a world that was suddenly so befuddled.

His beautiful hazel eyes drifted in front of me. Those tawny eyes that had watched me ever so intensely. I closed my own eyes and felt myself fall once more for the very face who was passing through my mind. So perfect. His hands, rough and calloused brushing across my skin sent shivers through me once more.

Even his voice. Deep, touched briefly by smoke that caused a grittiness to it. I could hear him so clearly, as if he was in this very room.

My eyes shot open in shock.

That's because he *was* in this room.

There on the table beside Griffin's grandpa was a laptop with the very man I'd just been thinking of grinning back from it. Nancy squealed in glee as he waved at the family seated in a circle.

"Griffin!" Dayton shouted, his eyes sparkling so brightly at the sight of his older brother.

I stared at the computer screen, studying the still effortlessly handsome features that watched me in return. His hair wasn't as neatly trimmed, and he had a full, thick beard growing on his face. The skin exposed upon his cheeks was a little dirty and quite tanned. The green, short-sleeve shirt he was wearing hugged shoulders that I couldn't believe looked even broader.

His eyes, though, still as intense as before, refused to look away from me. Even as he reminded Dayton to work hard at wrestling so when he came home, he'd be able to beat his big brother. Even as he spoke such kind and encouraging words to his father, whom I learned was apparently in recovery from a heavy drug addiction that nearly took his life a few times. Even as Griffin listened to his grandparents give him life updates, and his mom tell him he needed to shave, he stared at me.

Eyes that held me captured and entranced. I was so confused. Desperately, I wanted to trust him, but after all this time he hadn't even spoken my name yet. After all this time, there was still so much anger and uncertainty.

I was scared.

Despite the excited chatter going on around me, I couldn't hold it in anymore and blurted out, "I hate you."

The entire room fell silent. Angry and shocked gazes flung my way. I wasn't even sure why that's what I said, but I did. Griffin knotted his jaw, and the hopefulness in his gaze faltered. Here he was on this screen, hearing me speak, speaking to his family for probably the first time in a while, and those were the first three words I'd said.

His grandma hissed at me. "How dare you say that to my grandson." Steam flared from her ears as she watched me intently from across the table.

I shook my head again as tears slipped over, crashing silently down my cheeks. Pushing back from the table, I inhaled sharply, absolutely shattered. It wasn't that I really hated him, I simply hated that I felt so much anger for him. So much disdain and yet also this overwhelming craving for him.

Wiping the tears quickly from my face, I spun away from the table and dashed toward the door.

"JANE!" Griffin shouted, but I didn't stop. Didn't pause as I pulled at the door handle and rushed out into the ballroom. Eyes flew to me, breaking their blissful unawareness of what had just happened. I wasn't even sure why I'd run away. After all this time apart, there was my chance to say something to him. To listen. To apologize for shutting the door in his face that day at the school.

But all I'd done is run away.

Muffled footsteps followed me as I gripped the letter tightly to my chest, unable to move. Unable to breathe as my head swam with everything that had just happened. Turning around and walking back into that room would afford me another opportunity to speak with him. To let him talk and explain himself. But it would also destroy my already shattered heart once more.

"Miss B?" Dayton's hesitant voice sounded behind me. I slowly turned around, wiping away the new tears swirling with mascara that smudged my cheeks. His eyes were soft as he gave me a tight smile.

"How long?" I choked out.

He furrowed his brows. "How long for what?"

"How long has he been deployed?"

Dayton shrugged his shoulders. "He left before Thanksgiving break, that Tuesday. So it's been about three months."

I covered my mouth with my hand realizing what that meant. The day that I'd shut my classroom door in his face was the day that he'd been deployed. No wonder he'd disappeared. And all I'd done since was call him a coward and whatever other horrible things I'd thought of.

"Are you alright, Miss B?" Dayton asked, and my eyes widened as I slowly shook my head. I wasn't. I was entirely confused. And the last thing I'd said is that I hated him. I didn't hate him. I was angry and hurt. He'd written a letter that I wished he'd said to me in person, but he hadn't been able to say those things in person. Did he actually mean them? How many of those words were a lie to save face, to make sure he got his money or was it all the truth?

Spinning around, I pushed past Dayton and shoved open the doors once more. Standing up from the table was Griffin's mom and Brent. They waved at the screen where Griffin was smiling, though his eyes seemed so hollow.

"Be safe, son. We love you!" Nancy said, and Griffin clenched his jaw. Leaning forward on the screen, his hand reached forward.

"I lied!" I shouted. My heart raced in my chest as the screen froze.

Chapter 36

Griffin's figure was completely still, frozen in time. His arm was stretched forward, blurry on the screen from turning the video off right before I had a chance to stop him. I was the coward, not him. He'd tried in every way he could to get me to simply give him a chance to explain, and I'd refused.

"I lied..." I whispered again, collapsing to the ground. Nancy's arms draped around my shoulders as I shuddered, trying to stop the tears from falling to the ground. But it was no use, they fell anyway.

"I don't hate you. I don't hate you," I continued to cry out, realizing how wrong I had been this entire time. He'd hurt me, yes, and he needed to grovel for that. But I was tired of feeling so empty.

Nancy ran her hand over my hair and sighed. "It will all work out," she whispered, and I shook my head.

How? How was it all going to work out after what I'd just said? The last thing he heard from me was that I hated him, which was untrue. Our relationship wasn't built on anything solid, it was a rocky foundation at best, but there was something there. There always had been. The moments of truth were real and raw. It was a matter of deciding to trust him fully or not, and I'd been a coward.

She let me sob for as long as needed before I finally sniffed and looked up. Nancy gave me a tight-lipped smile and then extended her hands. Slowly, I rose from the floor and felt a rush of anger piled in amongst the dread. Anger at myself and everything going on. It wasn't like I could simply call him right away and fix what I said.

"Oh my gosh," I whispered as it dawned on me. I just did the same thing he had—said something entirely stupid out of shock and confusion. Ignoring the contract, ignoring the entire reason that he asked me to be his fake fiancée, ignoring all of that, what we shared in the pool was real. His words in the letter were real. And I reacted in fear, just as he had. It was my turn to suffer. My turn to have to simply wait and hope. Hope that maybe we could have another chance.

The contract didn't matter to me at all.

Brushing myself off, I looked at Nancy who fixed a bit of my hair, dabbed at my makeup with a lace handkerchief, and then smiled once more as I put Griffin's letter into my clutch. "It'll all work out. I obviously didn't believe it right away, but he cares about you."

I inhaled deeply and shook my head. "I'm not sure anymore," I whispered, and she hooked my hand in her elbow.

"I am, and if anyone knows, it's his mother," she stated and guided me back out into the ballroom.

Nancy walked with me a bit through the crowd before slipping away with Brent. I was left alone, but not for too long as Dayton skipped his way over to me. He looked quite a bit more grown up in a suit with his hair nicely combed and gelled to precision. A little more like Griffin.

"The Commander wanted me to give you something," he said, and stretched forward his hand.

"Commander?" I questioned, slowly taking the things from Dayton's hand.

"Griffin. Commander Griffin James Marsh," Dayton replied as I looked down at the two items I'd been handed. First was a picture. A simple, very handsome looking picture of a slightly dirty and bearded Griffin in his gear. He was holding a rifle in his hands and had a cigarette hanging from his lips, his face encircled in a small cloud of smoke. Stern and powerful, it seemed almost unreal and extremely attractive.

Written on the back was a single sentence:

Even this was real to me.

The second thing had me staring in bewilderment. "What's this?" I asked, lifting the velvet box I recognized toward Dayton.

"A ring box, obviously," he said, clasping his hands behind his back.

"I know that. Why do I have it?"

"Because it's yours, obviously, and we have to make the official announcement tonight because time is ticking."

"I don't want this if he doesn't mean it," I stated and tried to push it back into Dayton's hands.

Dayton rolled his eyes. "Miss B, did you not read the back of the picture? He wants the girl he loves to have his engagement ring, no matter how things started." He winked.

Bewildered, I tipped my head closer to him. "And what do you know about how this started?"

"Griffin wrote me a letter too, Miss B." He glanced over his shoulder as Jackson and Marcy appeared through the crowd, stopping beside Dayton and smiling.

"Which said what, exactly?" I asked, spinning the box between my fingers. I knew what was in here. And I knew how gorgeous I thought it was. But I was trying to figure out if this part was all for show for the contract still, or a promise of something in the future. That if those words on the back of the picture meant exactly what Dayton said they did.

"Things about the contract, about you two." He lifted a brow.

"You're not going to tell me anything, are you?" I questioned in return.

"Nope." A sly grin spread across his face. "You'll have to ask Griffin when he gets back himself. Though, I do want to say that this inheritance contract isn't just about Griffin. In fact, he couldn't care less about the money. He's already a self-made man anyway—"

"So now everyone will think *I'm* a gold digger," I muttered. "I come from a not super wealthy family. I am a teacher. That's not a huge income either."

"Wait a second," Marcy stated, looking between Dayton and I. "Miss B, are you and Griffin engaged?" She gasped and slapped a hand over her mouth.

"That's the lie they're trying to convince everyone of." A shrill voice pierced through our intimate conversation, and I turned to see Cara stalking our way. Her hands clutching the skirt of the bright red dress that brought out the red undertones of her skin, darkening the circles that formed beneath her eyes. She looked like a hawk with wings outspread, creeping toward its prey.

"Excuse me?" I questioned.

She clicked her tongue. "I can't believe the audacity that you have. Showing up here like you have some sort of claim to Griffin. That ring is *not* yours."

"You're exactly right, Cara. It belongs to Riley." Griffin's grandma clicked gracefully over to us, joining the conversation.

"Who is Riley?" I asked, furrowing my brows.

"She's his last option for an appropriate match. I picked her out myself." She gave me a dainty smile, gently smoothing out her curls, and slipped a picture out from her purse.

"He loves Jane. Not Riley. So he definitely won't agree to any arranged marriage to a random girl when he's got his actual fiancée right here!" Dayton's expression was fierce, as he spoke, stepping up as Griffin's proxy, and I looked between Dayton and Cara.

"Stay out of this boy, you are not involved!" Cara snarled.

"Cara, dear. Quiet." His grandma waved a hand toward her and stretched forward the picture. My eyes scanned the beautiful, blonde woman poised in the picture. The girl was stunning to say the least. Baby-blue eyes with golden hair that curled softly around her dainty body. A thin waist and skin that was lightly kissed by the sun. Her smile was delicate and feminine, lips full yet not to the point that they drew your attention away from her exquisite, turquoise eyes. Thick, dark lashes batted beneath her soft brow ridge, and her button nose was as delicate as her small hands clasped in front of her.

She wore a soft blue dress that fell in stunning waves to her feet. Cinched tightly around her waist, with a swooping neckline that a sparkling silver necklace sat around, shone against the light. Dainty flowers were stitched into the material, her sleeves were the same sheer tulle that sat gently around the pleated skirt portion. She looked like Cinderella herself. It was quite uncanny how similarly she looked to Cinderella, and I wondered if that was the point.

"Why would you even try to push Riley on Griffin? Wouldn't that screw you over?" Dayton cried out, pulling my attention from the picture, and Cara whipped her eyes toward Dayton.

"I'm not, I want him to remain single and—" She cut herself off, snapping her brows together, and stepped closer to Dayton. "What do you know, boy?"

"Everything. I know everything." He glared at her. Her eyes flickered with panic before she recoiled, trying to regain whatever upper hand she held. I realized that I was still missing something. Whatever Griffin had shared with Dayton shifted things. But that wasn't pressing, not at this moment anyway. Griffin wasn't Riley's or anyone else's. He also wasn't someone his grandma could use and manipulate all for the sake of money. He was mine. Regardless of the uncertainty between us, I had his ring. I had some claim to him. And I was angry. I'd been angry for months.

Cara cleared her throat, returning her steely gaze to me as I calculated my next move. "So, if you know everything, you know that Griffin and Jane were faking the entire time at the Airbnb," she said, letting a devilish smile fill her face.

"Cara, we have no proof of that. But it's no matter, I won't let my grandson marry someone as unsuitable as you." His grandma butted in, snatching the picture back from me. Her lips raised in a conniving smile. "It is my money after all, and I can't imagine him desiring someone who looks, well, like *you* dear."

"What's wrong with how I look? Do I have a stain on my dress that I didn't notice?" I replied, quickly scanning myself and seeing nothing.

She clicked her tongue. "No, I'm talking about you in general. How could you, with your masculine muscles, even turn his head?" Griffin's grandma dangled the picture of the girl in front of me. Her perfect cheekbones and unblemished skin glowed. "Compared to this young lady, you're so...unfeminine. So uncouth, and dare I say, dirty."

I inhaled deeply, trying to remain calm. The anger that was sifting through me was barely held at bay by the small amount of self-control I had left. I simply stared at her, praying I kept my mouth shut so as to not make a fool of myself more than I already had today.

Cara huffed, and waved a hand at me. "You know Griffin only cared about the show he put on with you, anyway. Touching you would've made him sick; he just wants the money." Cara gagged in my direction.

I took another deep, sustaining breath, but it was barely enough to contain the beast pounding with an ax at the lock in my head. Not today. My smart ass self needed to bite her tongue. But these two women were berating me in front of impressionable teenagers and dragging me through the mud, all so Cara could possibly get her hands on some money that wasn't hers in the first place. And his grandma simply wanted to have control over someone else's life.

"You four," I started, looking between Marcy, Lily, Jackson, and Dayton. "Either cover your ears or leave the room, because my self-control is dwindling at an alarming rate, and what I want to say is very inappropriate for you guys to hear."

Cara threw her head back and cackled, the entire room falling silent at the sound. "They don't need to leave. It's not like you're actually going to say something. It was always Griffin who came to your defense because you're too much of a coward to stand up for yourself."

I clenched my jaw but remained silent.

She continued. "Just another reason why the only logical conclusion is that your relationship was fake. That he was *disgusted* by you," she spat. "He simply knew how to put on a good show. Kissing you in front of his mom or when his brother walked in. He had to make sure that no one suspected he wasn't going to fulfill the contract. I mean, we all know how desperately Nancy needs the inheritance."

I furrowed my brows. Nancy needs the money? I thought this was money for Griffin.

"Cara, dear. We don't need to involve a stranger in this." Griffin's grandma quickly stated, and then turned her attention to me. "Now, be a dear, and give me that ring back. I'd like to take it with me when we introduce this young woman to her future husband." She stepped forward, her heel clacking on the surface and she raised her palm toward me.

"This isn't yours." I placed it against my chest defensively.

"It's also not yours. My grandson had certain terms to meet, and one of those was getting married before the end of the year. Just because you have a ring for a fake—"

"Darling." A weathered hand rested on his grandma's shoulder, cutting her off. Griffin's grandpa stepped forward, stopping beside her. "Are you entirely certain that Griffin doesn't love this woman? He did give her that ring."

"They got in a fight! She gave it back!" Cara butted in and lifted her nose, grabbing the front of her dress. "And I also bet, when no one was around, he was nauseated by you."

Her lip curled up in a sickening horror. She stepped toward me as rage seeped through every pore of my skin. Steam crashed out of my ears. The damage those words could've done if she'd spoken them to younger me was astronomical; now they only fueled the anger that Griffin had always helped keep at bay. No one spoke of another person as if they were a curse to touch.

She giggled again, unrestrained by her in-laws, and flicked a finger along my jaw. "So unfeminine, so gross. I bet that's what the fight was about. You wanted him to touch you and he refused. You should be ashamed of yourself thinking that Griffin would ever want to actually touch you. To feel your body. I can't believe you think he'd actually be turned on by it. Again, that's why he only ever touched you when someone else was around."

"I'm pretty sure the pool was completely empty when he fucked me while you were twiddling your fingers by the fire," I snapped, and the entire ballroom gasped, then filled with a dead silence. Even the music stopped playing, strings came to a grinding halt. His grandma touched her pearl necklace, blinking wide-eyed with shock, but it was the slight smirk that spread briefly across Griffin's grandpa's face that fueled me to continue.

My self-control was gone, and I was seeking blood. "He couldn't keep his hands or mouth off of me. Wherever he wanted to touch he did, with pleasure. All over my body. If he really thought I was disgusting, why did he constantly like to bring up the time I sat on his face."

Cara's mouth dangled open in shock.

"You know what else?" I continued, snapping my gaze to Griffin's grandma. "Isn't it interesting that Griffin had *years* to find a wife, yet he never did, and it only took a few weeks of us knowing each other before he willingly bought me a ring. Willingly took his pants off for me."

The entire room was frozen, caught in the midst of my heated and unfiltered thoughts. Thoughts that I couldn't stop no matter how much I had wished to keep them a secret. Precious memories and moments that I wanted to keep between only Griffin and me. But I also wouldn't allow someone to speak to me the way that she was. Not ever. Not again.

I sighed as the anger slowly began to roll away. "But you want to know what's truly sad?" I asked the two women who had turned so white, it looked as if I'd drained every drop of blood from their scrawny bodies. "I'm disappointed."

Cara shakenly scoffed and crossed her arms, trying to regain control of the situation. "Why should we care—"

"Cara, hush." His grandma silenced her again, firmly back in control as the color rose in her cheeks, flickering her dark gaze toward me. "Why should we care if you're disappointed in us?"

"No, I'm not disappointed in you two. I'm disappointed in myself." I looked down at my clutch and slipped the ring box and picture inside.

"What?" His grandma furrowed her brows, baffled. As baffled as the ballroom was as whispered questions filtered around me.

"I'm disappointed that I feel this need to give you proof from my private, personal relationship in order to justify why my body is as deserving of love as anyone else's; why I deserve to be engaged to him and eventually marry him." I lifted my chin, spun around, and walked proudly toward the double doors—catching a glimpse of pride flickering behind Griffin's grandpa's gaze.

Nobody dared to move as I made my exit, praying that I hadn't made things worse. For myself or for Griffin.

But damn, I was proud of myself for sticking up to her. For every girl who ever felt anything less than. For the girl I once was and the woman I had become.

Chapter 37

I threw my heels to the side, holding onto the door for some stability. What had just happened? Jealousy? Was I jealous over someone who wasn't technically mine? Either way, what a stupid, childish reaction I'd had. Sort of. The outburst at the beginning was certainly foolish, but the ending, that controlled jab, that was kind of nice. I closed the front door carefully, hoping not to wake my mother.

Stepping quietly, I walked into the living room, flipped on the light, and then shrieked, and covered my eyes with my hands.

"JANE!" Noah cried out in shock.

I heard blankets and pillows scuffling across the couch fabric, and somebody smacked into something. Slowly, I began to laugh, not realizing I'd completely ignored the grunts and moans. I bellowed harder and harder as my mind replayed the scene I walked into. At least this time, Noah was enjoying himself with a girl.

"You aren't supposed to be home yet," he grumbled.

"Are you two decent now?" I managed to say between my fits of laughter.

"Yes," Noah sheepishly answered, and I uncovered my eyes to see the once-naked Noah covered waist down by a pillow and his female partner wrapped up in a blanket. Her cheeks were pink, flashing bright against the dark complexion of her skin. Her tight curls were all over the place, frizzy from the very intimate event I accidentally interrupted. Her eyes were wide, dark brown and unable to look at me directly. She had the most beautiful heart-shaped face and an ass that I was still dreaming of getting, even after years of squats.

"Hi. I'm Jane. Noah's older sister," I said, grinning widely at the two of them.

"Jada," she muttered her introduction, tugging the blanket farther up to her chin.

"What are you doing home already?" Noah hissed once more, glaring at me.

I sighed, picking up the clutch that I'd dropped. "Let's just say things didn't go as planned." I brushed some crumbs off of it and looked back at Noah who tilted his head.

"Was Griffin there?" he asked.

"Sort of?" I replied.

"What kind of answer is that?"

"The only one I can give you," I muttered and picked up some of my dress, turning toward the stairs.

"How was he sort of there?"

"He's deployed, Noah. Out of the fucking country," I grumbled, taking a couple steps forward.

"What?" he shouted, and I lifted a brow. "For how long?"

"Oh, you know. Since the day I slammed my classroom door in his face. That explains pretty much everything. Then when he video called in, I told him I hated him. So, yeah, that happened." I walked toward the stairs, gripping the railing, and paused.

"Janey, are you alright?" he quietly asked, and a tear slid hotly down my cheek. I swiped it viciously away, but I didn't turn around to look at him, unsure of what to say.

"You have company over, Noah. Don't worry about me," I finally said, and quickly ran down the stairs. I shut my bedroom door behind me and laid down on my bed. Holding the clutch tightly to my chest, I stared at the unmoving ceiling fan above my head.

I was tired. So tired of feeling lost and confused. So tired of being left in the dark. I staked some claim today that I didn't even know if I had because who knows if that ring still mattered. Especially since I told Griffin that I hated him. I didn't. It was the opposite.

A soft knock sounded on my door. Groaning, I rolled off of my bed and walked over. Pulling it ajar, Noah stood outside, waiting in a pair of shorts with his brow raised.

"Where's Jada?" I asked.

"The bathroom." He pushed open the door and walked inside.

"She's pretty." I followed after him as he plopped down on my bed.

"Don't tell mom what you saw."

"She already knows that you're not a virgin."

"Yeah, but she doesn't need to know that things happened on her couch."

I chuckled. "How'd you meet her?"

"She's in one of my classes."

"How long have things been going on?"

"For a month now, actually."

I gasped. "Is my baby brother settling down?"

He slugged me in my shoulder. "Shut up. I'm not here to talk about myself."

"You should be with your girlfriend. It's Valentine's Day, and I ruined your sexy time."

Noah rolled his eyes and bumped into my shoulder as I gripped the clutch tighter. "I have a minute. Now spill. What happened?"

So I ran over the details in a shortened form and told him everything. How it wasn't just unexpected, arranged marriages that Griffin had enlisted me to help him run from, but an actual contract because of some stupid inheritance that I was suspicious about. I showed him the letter Griffin had written and what I'd said. How I was too late returning back into that room to tell him I'd lied. Then the confrontation afterwards with his grandma and Cara and what she got out of the deal if Griffin didn't fulfill his end of the bargain.

Noah simply listened, and when I was finally done, I pulled the picture and ring box out of my clutch. "This is Griffin's," I said, showing him the velvet container. "Who fucking cares about the stupid inheritance and it being the reason he asked me to fake being his fiancée for a weekend. I don't want a fake engagement, Noah."

"What *do* you want?" Noah simply asked, and I closed my eyes.

"A chance to tell him what I should've said," I whispered. "A chance to start over, to find out if he really meant everything he wrote."

Noah didn't say anything as I held the picture and letter in one hand, while clutching the still unopened box in the other. He simply let me sit there in silence, considering my words.

"So, why don't you tell him exactly that?" he finally said.

"How?"

"Write him a letter, obviously."

"This isn't a conversation that should happen over a letter," I muttered, and Noah chuckled, standing up from my bedside. He placed a quick kiss against my forehead and left my bedroom without another word.

I'm not sure how long I sat there in the still darkness, but I couldn't find the energy to move. Not at this moment. Yet, I had to remain hopeful. Maybe, like Nancy said, things would work out. Once Griffin returned home, at least I would know if I still had a chance with him or not. Until then, I would cling to the hope that there was.

Placing my clutch, the picture, engagement ring box, and letter on my nightstand I laid down on my side, makeup and dress still on. Tomorrow, I will figure out what to do about the ring. Tomorrow, I will make a couple of copies of his picture to have in my wallet and by my bedside. Tomorrow, I will deal with everything. But tonight, I was going to sleep before my mom came home and asked me questions I wasn't ready to answer.

Questions I didn't want to face just yet.

WHAT I SHOULD HAVE SAID

Monday morning was as dreary as the rest of the weekend had been. Even with the opportunity to tease Noah about his new girl, I hadn't found the usual satisfaction in doing so that I was searching for.

Slowly, I made my way to my classroom. The new semester had started a bit ago, so I no longer had the same students as before. Which also made me wonder how I was going to snag a chance to speak with Dayton.

There was a small matter of what I'd said at that fancy dinner. If word got out around the school, who knows what would happen.

Pushing some papers to the side on my desk, I dug into the salad I'd brought for lunch. Placing a napkin on my lap, I crossed my legs and took another bite. Maybe if I asked Nancy to have Dayton, Jackson, Lily, and Marcy come to the office I could talk to them then.

No, that wouldn't work. I shook my head and readjusted the claw clip I was using to pull all my hair back. Shoving my glasses back up my nose, I brushed a few crumbs from my black turtleneck bodysuit I'd paired with some dark green trousers. I needed a new tactic, but what?

As I took another bite of my salad, my classroom door swung open and in walked the very four students I'd just been thinking about. "Miss B!" Dayton said, waving. Jackson, Lily, and Marcy grinned as they all approached my desk.

"What's up?" I casually said, leaning back in my chair.

"We just wanted to come see how you were doing. You know, after Saturday," Jackson quietly said.

"You four aren't going to tell anyone, right? If anyone else learns what I said, it could cause problems with my job and everything," I quickly stated, and they all shook their heads.

"Our lips are sealed." Dayton mimed zipping his mouth shut and throwing the key away. I sighed in relief.

"Thank you," I muttered, turning back to my salad and pushing some lettuce around with my fork. "Sorry for not staying for dinner."

"I can't believe you stood up to Cara and my grandma like that!" Dayton blurted out, and I lifted my eyes to meet his.

"What?"

"No one talks back to her. Ever. Not even my mom. I never understood why, but yeah. You seriously put her in her place." He grinned, and I shook my head.

"Little good it did, other than make me seem like a slut," I muttered, and then whipped my eyes up to the four of them again. "You did not hear me say that."

All of them nodded in agreement, and then Marcy spoke. "Miss B, why'd you tell Dayton's brother that you hate him?" I clenched my jaw and looked away, my eyes finding the picture that Dayton had taken moments before the most wonderful and horrible moments of my life. Griffin looked so happy, so at peace. Next to that picture, I had tucked a copy of the most recent one the man himself sent.

Her gaze followed mine and she furrowed her brows. "Wait a second!" she exclaimed, and clamped a hand over her mouth. Pointing at the pictures, she shook her head. "I can't believe I didn't place this until now, but you're the girl in the pictures! The ones that I saw on Dayton's computer.

The ones he 'accidentally' uploaded. They are of you. I guess I should've recognized that look of love on his face even then!"

I didn't answer. Couldn't answer. I only prayed it was true. Wishing upon every wish possible that he really did still care for me.

She turned her head toward me once more. "So, really, why did you say that you hate him? Why aren't you wearing the ring he gave you? I want to see it." Marcy gestured toward the picture at the pool again. "Besides, you clearly love him, too, so why would you say that?"

Love? Yeah, no. Absolutely not. But feelings, those were there.

I sighed. "Because I was afraid, Marcy. I was scared, so I lied. And ruined everything."

"Can't you just tell him you're sorry?" She lifted her brows, and Dayton rolled his eyes.

"I thought adults were supposed to be smarter than us, yet you're giving Miss B the exact same advice I gave Griffin. Seriously. Just tell him you're sorry; he will say he's sorry too and voila!" He clapped his hands together. "All will be right again."

I laughed. An actual laugh. "If it was that simple, don't you think I would've already said that? I have to wait until he gets home because this isn't something that can be fixed over a letter. There's also the fact that he may not want to have a conversation with me. Which, he has every right to be as petty as I was, so yeah. I wish it was as simple as that."

Dayton pulled his lips in a thin line and narrowed his gaze as Jackson rolled his eyes. "Adults," he muttered in annoyance. The four of them pushed off of the desks and turned to leave.

"Seriously, why is it so hard to just say sorry?" he muttered before following his friends out of my classroom.

It annoyed me even more that he was right. If I had simply accepted Griffin's apology, or given him one myself, we wouldn't be in this mess to begin with. I shouldn't have agreed to a fake relationship to begin with because now it was this massive mess of real feelings that I wasn't sure could be salvaged even with a simple "I'm sorry."

Chapter 38

Another Monday came and went, signifying an entire week of nothing again. The agents were slowly backing off as the threat seemed to be non-existent to our family. Everything seemed to be backing off. I saw less of Dayton and his friends, less of Nancy at the front desk, even less of Noah as he spent more time with his new girl.

I was jealous. Jealous of the simplicity of their relationship. All of this turmoil over someone who was never technically mine in the first place. Even the gym seemed emptier, less.

Oh, well.

Determined to make the best of this random Tuesday, I pulled my little car into the school's parking lot and leaned back against the headrest. Time would help. The more time that passed, the less this wound would hurt. Just another thing that would be less. Twisting the ring around the chain that hung from my neck, I tucked it back into the collar of my vintage dress. I constantly felt torn wearing it, but he'd given it back to me for a reason, right?

I snatched my bag from the passenger seat and stepped out of my car.

Walking toward the school, I pulled open the front door to find it a bit livelier than usual. I smiled to myself, pushing some hair behind my shoulder. I'd left it down today, letting the waves cascade over my back as I stepped inside the school.

Making my way toward the stairs that led to my classroom, I felt a shiver run down my spine. Glancing around me, I pulled my lips tight. It seemed as if everyone was watching me. Hushed conversations and whispers behind my back floated toward me. I quickened my pace, wondering what was going on.

I was simply reading into things.

That had to be it.

Residual fear from what happened with my father was creeping up.

Yeah, that had to be it.

Shaking my head, I skipped down the stairs hoping to escape that odd sensation. Only to be met by more stares as I made my way to my classroom. It wasn't enough to simply disappear inside my room this time. As the day passed, it seemed that all of my students were staring.

Watching me. Looking at me differently. Those that normally participated seemed less inclined to do so, and those that slept most of the time were wide awake. Every conversation naturally dimmed as I would pass by.

Even the teachers in the lounge seemed to not want to be near me today. Nobody sat near me or spoke to me. Even Brooklyn, my next door teacher, whom I had recently become close to, avoided me. The next day was just as bad, if not worse. The students were now less inclined to hide that they were whispering things about me.

Third period couldn't end quickly enough so I could eat lunch in peace by myself today. Alone, in my classroom, without anyone around. I finished my lecture and faced the class, smoothing out my dress.

"Any questions?" I asked, watching as a couple students snickered.

Mason raised his hand, winking at his buddy a few seats away. I gestured for him to continue. "Soooo, been to any pools recently, Miss B?" he snarkily asked.

My stomach dropped.

"What'd you say?" I questioned, my heart jumping in my chest.

He leaned back haughtily in his chair and sunk deeper in his seat. Tugging at the strings of his sweatshirt, he waited as a couple kids chuckled before speaking again. "I'm simply asking so I know what ones to avoid until they've been cleaned after your use."

I furrowed my brows. "What are you talking about?" I asked again, and the entire class burst out in laughter.

"You never struck me as someone who would bang someone like that," his buddy called out, and a couple girls snickered.

I shook my head, praying that this wasn't happening. I was even more confused than before. Marcy, Jackson, Lily, and Dayton had promised they wouldn't say anything.

"Mason, I don't know what you mean?" I quietly said, and the entire class laughed again.

"Is that a fetish of yours, Miss B? Getting dicked down somewhere public," one kid called out.

"I heard that you sit on people's faces too," another student shouted, and my hand slapped over my mouth. My lip trembled as I bit back the tears of fear that were building.

My eyes darted around the classroom as they continued to giggle and snicker, shouting derogatory things toward me. Slowly, Penelope stood up from the front. She was quieter than most of the kids in the class and always kept to herself. She walked over to my computer and pointed, pushing the braid behind her back.

"Can I?" she softly asked, and I nodded in shock. Penelope opened up an internet tab and typed something in as I watched in utter horror as my face showed up on the screen. Standing across from me, wearing my dress from that night, was Cara in her bright red ballgown and Griffin's grandma.

"What's that?" I pointed at the video that had over 400,000 views, captioned *Teacher Talks Dirty*.

Penelope stepped away from my desk. "It's what everyone's talking about." She tugged at her jeans and twisted the hem of her oversized T-shirt. She quickly walked back to her desk and sat down as everyone burst out laughing.

"Go ahead, Miss B. Watch it!" Mason taunted. He snickered along with a couple of his friends. Quickly, I shut the projector off and sat down at my computer. "Oh come on. It's not like we haven't seen it already," he whined as I pressed play.

This wasn't happening.

Somebody recorded the entire conversation and edited it. I watched in horror as the video had me repeating what I'd said over and over in that stupid parody form. Sometimes the cuss words were edited out, other times, they weren't. I stopped the video before even half of it was done.

And just in time.

There was a knock at my door just as I hit pause, and then it swung open. I fought back the tears as none other than Principal Adams walked in. I hadn't seen his face in ages, and he gave me a tight smile. Running his hand over his thinning, gray hair, the wiry man with deep smile lines seemed pained today.

"Sorry for the intrusion, Miss Barlow," he said, adjusting the tie around his plaid button-down shirt. Behind him, Nancy came walking in. She refused to make eye contact with me.

I watched as they both wandered to the front of my classroom and faced my students. "Mrs. Pitts will finish out your instruction for today. I need to borrow Miss Barlow for a bit," he sharply said, all lightheartedness vacant. I quickly exited out of the browser and took a deep breath.

"Be good for her," I instructed, knowing what was about to happen, and followed behind Principal Adams. The walk down the hallway and up the stairs was completely silent. I felt as if I was a child being sent to the principal's office. In trouble for something that wasn't exactly my fault yet at the same time was. It had all gone wrong. Someone had videoed my entire conversation with Cara, then posted it online. Somehow, the entire school saw it, and now I was in trouble.

But I couldn't be entirely angry. I had said those rather crude, blunt words, though most of the context was missing.

We walked through the empty front office and rounded the corner, heading toward the principal's office.

He turned the handle and opened the door. I stepped into the room that felt hollow and ominous. Principal Adams walked behind the black desk straight across from me and sat down in his pleated leather chair. He gestured to the two black chairs in front of his desk before facing his computer screen and clicking a few buttons.

I scanned the small office, my eyes gliding past the plaques and posters, and the bookcase to the left. My heart stopped as I padded softly forward, feeling shrouded in darkness despite the bright reds that offset the onyx color. Sitting down gently in the chair, I waited, but he didn't speak.

Not a word for several moments as he continued to click away on his computer. The blinds covering the windows to my left were pulled closed, making the room feel even darker than it should. Finally, he stopped typing and swiveled to face me.

"I assume you know what's going on."

I nodded and swallowed. "I just learned about it. Though, I would like to say, in my defense, there is a lot of context missing around the video, and I'm not at school when it happened," I quietly muttered, and he sighed, leaning back in his chair. Clasping his hands together, he rocked back and forth.

"Regardless, I've had parents emailing and calling 24/7 these past two days. Upset. You can't blame them," he softly said, and I shook my head.

"No, sir. You can't."

"You're a phenomenal teacher, Miss Barlow. The kids love you. I also know that they simply find the video entertaining, and it will die down in a week or so."

I looked up, feeling a small glimmer of hope. Which immediately died again as he sighed and continued. "But until it does fade away, I don't think it's appropriate for you to be teaching here."

"But-But-But it has nothing to do with the students. I wasn't teaching when it happened and—"

"But there were students around, were there not?" He turned his computer screen toward me. I stared at the still video. Clear as day, Dayton, Marcy, Lily, and Jackson were standing in shock beside me during a part of the video I hadn't seen yet.

He sighed and ran his hand over his hair again. "I don't want to do this, but parents are threatening to pull their students and remove funding if some action isn't taken. You know how important parent donations are for our small town school."

"Am I being fired?" I asked, fighting back another wave of tears and pain.

"I'm putting you on unpaid leave effective immediately until I deem the situation to no longer be of pressing matters. Then we will reevaluate if you're still a good fit here at Redwater School," he bluntly answered.

"You'll reevaluate," I muttered and clenched my jaw.

"I'd watch what you say next, Miss Barlow. It was your mouth that got you here in the first place," Principal Adams stiffly stated, and I sighed.

"Outside of school hours, off school grounds."

"Yes, but we've already gone over that."

"It was concerning my personal life, too, which shouldn't be something that the students know about." I pushed back from his desk.

"Yet your personal life apparently involves four of our students and our wonderful front office manager."

I stood up and shook my head. "Right. My apologies. Am I free to go?"

He nodded. "Jane?" he quietly said, and I blinked, sighing heavily. "I truly am sorry. You've raised the grades in such a short time of being here. You're an incredible teacher."

Turning around, I walked toward the door.

"You can head back to your classroom and gather any personal belongings you'll need while on leave before you go home," he added as I turned the doorknob and exited the office.

Chapter 39

Noah found me on my bed, my mom had already come and gone with questions that I didn't answer. I got fired. The simplest way to explain things, while the more complicated was the truth. I was on unpaid leave *until* I was fired.

Life was crashing down around me, and we hadn't even been here for a year yet.

"So, you're just not going to talk to anyone?" he pressed. I buried my face deeper into my pillow, my makeup smearing in the process. "No explanation as to why there's a small box of your things sitting on the floor beside your bed, or why Mom says you came home before lunch?"

"It doesn't matter," I muttered into the pillow.

"Obviously it does, shithead." Noah lightly pushed me in the shoulder. I groaned, rolling around to glare at him. "Good, now spill."

"No." I slammed my face back into my pillow but grabbed my phone. Peeking out with one eye, I found the very video that had circulated at school and showed it to him. Noah's mouth fell open wider and wider. I clamped my hands over my burning earlobes and turned away, not wanting to watch the entire thing.

"Did you seriously say all of that?" he finally asked, prying my fingers away from my head when the video was done playing.

"Cara and Griffin's grandma deserved it, okay?" I gruffly stated, and he threw his head back, laughing.

"So, what are you going to do now?" he asked, and I shrugged my shoulders, sitting up.

"I'm on unpaid leave until this blows over at school, and then it'll be reviewed by the district, and most likely I'll be fired," I explained, and he lifted his brows.

"A hell of a way to go out though. I'm kind of proud of you." He grinned, and I rolled my eyes.

"Yeah, well, now I don't have an income or anything to do," I muttered in defeat.

Noah furrowed his brows. "What are you talking about? For one, you don't really have any bills, seeing as your car is already paid off and you live at home again. Two, I say you see how jacked you can get. Show them how strong you can become in the face of adversity. Piss that Cara lady off even more." He grinned wickedly. "She made rude comments about your buffness, so I say throw it in her face even more."

I furrowed my brows, fired up a little but also nervous. "What if Griffin doesn't like it?" I whispered, and he rolled his eyes.

"Dummy. Obviously he will. He knew you lifted before having sex with you. You sat on his face in the gym, too, so get over this desire to be dainty and embrace your buff bitch phase. You can be all girly around him if you want, but let's see how far you can go until he gets home. Obviously without the scary drugs, 'cause your face is too pretty to mess with."

I smiled, happy to have some sort of purpose. "Itty bitty waist?"

"Big ole' ass." He wiggled his brows in response and then left my room.

It was the distraction I needed and about damn time. Every minute of my day was spent either in the gym or making sure that everything I did aligned with nutrition and recovery. I knew it was obsessive, but honestly, I couldn't stop. I didn't want to stop. Now I knew what was meant by the 'post-break up glow,' and me being me, I doubled it. I was post-breakup fake fiancée and post-breakup job.

I became stronger, faster, more powerful than ever before. There wasn't a moment where I had time to think about all of the crazy that had occurred as I merely trained to become the most athletic version of myself. I wasn't just lifting either, I picked up some MMA as well, honing the skills that my dad had taught me, fueling the courage Griffin had fed me.

The school year was nearing the end of April, only a month or so away from summer, and there was still no message from the principal that my case would be reviewed. But I didn't care anymore. Noah had been right.

The amount of money I saved since living at home had carried me through any of the unusual purchases that came outside of what my mom bought, plus some.

Dayton and his mom did stop by at some point to apologize for the video. Apparently, Cara had been secretly recording the entire thing and then posted it. Besides that, Nancy hadn't said much else and quickly left with Dayton in tow. He gave me a pained smile as I knew that time was only making things feel more final.

The sun was shining brightly overhead, warm and hot as I lay in the front yard reading a book. As my obsession slowly settled, and I accepted the excess free time that I'd never had the luxury to experience before, I was finding my mental health becoming vastly better. I could genuinely smile and enjoy the simple things these days.

Though, my heart still ached for Griffin. Still longed to simply tell him how sorry I was.

Most of the time I managed to keep myself distracted enough to not think about it. Today however, as I stared at the page of my book, I was unable to keep him off my mind. I lay on my belly, running a thumb back and forth across his picture. Mom was at work and Noah was at school, which left me by myself to whittle my time idly away.

Time that I should be spending reading, but instead, as the music in my headphones played, my mind as usual turned to thoughts of Griffin. Wondering where he was and if he was safe. I wondered if he ever thought of me, and if maybe I should write to him about what had happened. Except too much time had passed.

Writing him now would only leave more to say. It would bring up more that I should've said on Valentine's Day. No, I simply had to be patient and wait. Someday he would hopefully return, and even if all that I was afforded was a second to tell him that I was sorry, that would be enough. Because there was also a part of me that still wanted him to tell me he was sorry as well.

He had promised in his letter that he would answer anything I wanted to ask, which fed me with hope. A measly amount of hope, but enough that despite the overwhelming finality of everything I'd been feeling lately, there might be enough of a burning ember left to reignite something.

Sighing, I closed my book and rolled over onto my back, adjusting my black tank top.

My eyes widened in shock as a strong hand closed violently over my throat.

A small pinch from a needle pierced the side of my neck as I brought my knee up to nail the man holding me down in the balls, but my world turned black before it connected.

I hadn't even been able to scream.

I woke groaning, my head pounding as I felt my body sway back and forth. I tried to open my eyes but was met with darkness. Some sort of material, which smelled dry and dusty with more than a hint of old vomit, was fitted over my head, letting in very little air. Every suck of breath drew it to my face, and for a moment, I thrashed with panic, realizing that my hands were bound by the wrists excruciatingly tight behind my back.

With little to no choices available, there was only one thing I could think of. So, I took as deep of a breath as I dared, braced my abs, and screamed as long and as ear-piercingly loud as I could. I wasn't going to go down without a fight. Not this time. I would fight just as Griffin had.

The sharp tones of the yells followed by jabbering I couldn't understand told me that my abductors weren't impressed by that sound in such a confined metal space. I felt a small sense of achievement before someone hissed "Shut her up!" with a thick accent that I didn't recognize.

With a jostling metal wall to my left and a sense of vacant space to my right, I took the gamble and threw myself to that side, away from the voice and kicked my legs under me, standing up. Instantly, there was a jolt beneath my feet, and I lost my balance. Going down, and unable to catch myself, a fist landed sickeningly against the side of my head, and I fell to the rattling, moving floor, stars swirling in my vision. Rhythmical humming met my ears as I lay there, my world spinning. I was on the floor of some sort of vehicle going somewhere fast, but where, I didn't know.

I knew that I would look absolutely ridiculous, but I flailed my legs, kicking as hard as I could at whatever I could reach. Several grunts snapped to my ears as my feet connected with something, and then I heard the same voice speak.

"Make her stop," the man hissed. That's when I realized I hadn't stopped screaming.

Pressure clamped around my throat again, and then that same pinch bit through my neck, and the world went black once more.

Cold.

Everything around me felt cold as my blistered eyes peeled open. It smelled musty and dank, and I could hear a small drip of water methodically plunking every couple seconds in a far corner.

Groaning, my hands now unbound, I gripped my head as my eyes adjusted to my surroundings. Shock coursed through me as several other girls, all quite small and much younger than me, crowded in a corner. I pushed myself up, in spite of being dizzy, and sat on the edge of a nasty mattress that had yellowing and brown stains and smelled like the sewers.

I gagged as the pungent odor of feces and urine invaded my nose. The four other girls I saw weren't entirely unclean, but I could tell from the greasy, uncombed hair that they hadn't had a shower in at least a few days. The smallest girl clung tightly to the thinnest of the four, all of whom had dark circles beneath their eyes.

My eyes scanned the rest of the room. There was a singular bucket in one corner where the smell seemed to be coming from. No windows lined this room, and the only light came from the cracks around the door opposite the bed I didn't want to be laying on.

Standing up, I swayed, still dizzy from whatever drug they'd given me, and sat abruptly back down on the edge of the mattress, snapping my hand to my necklace that the ring no longer hung from. But there was no time to panic, no time to wonder where it went as the door swung open. Light blazed like the end of times through the dirty room, and a couple rats squeaked, disappearing back into the cracks of the walls.

The girls huddled even tighter in the corner as I shaded my eyes, squinting. I could barely make out the silhouettes of two rather burly figures before a bag was shoved over my head once more and that all too familiar pinch was felt in my neck.

"Assholes," I managed to mutter before everything faded away once more.

Chapter 40

My arms were numb as I came to, hoisted above my head. My knees pressed into cold stone and the sterile stench was overwhelming, as if strong cleaners frequented this room. Slowly, I forced my eyes open, my head splitting at the seams, and immediately wished I wasn't awake.

A chain attached me to the ceiling directly above a drain. Across the small, square room was a long table with sharp and pointy tools I'd never seen before resting upon it. All of them looked very dangerous. Four extremely burly men with guns stood beside the single door that was to my left.

One of them knocked on the wooden frame when my head swung to look at them. Faint light streamed into the room behind me through a small window that told me it was somewhere around midday, wherever I was, and that I was in a basement with the window well surrounding the glass.

The door tossed open, and in walked two more men, one of them seeming a little familiar, as if I'd seen a hazy picture of him somewhere, only once, forever ago. I furrowed my brows, trying to recall where I'd seen him before as my head continued to pound and I swung slowly in place, understanding only that I needed to keep him in sight.

"I'm assuming you know who I am," the man spoke, his dark beady eyes raking over the tools shining on the white table. He adjusted the lapels to his gray, pinstripe suit, and then pushed back his jet black hair. His nose was unusually long and hooked at the end, haughty and much like a beak. Much like someone else's I'd once seen. He had gaunt cheekbones, but not like he was starving, but because he could afford it. This strange man exuded wealth, and a dark haunting shadow seemed to follow him around the room as he circled me.

"The dickhead who kidnapped me," I finally responded, and he tossed his head back, cackling. His hair shone from the gel but hardly moved as he snatched what looked like a metal rod from the table.

"Where is it?" he snarled and rushed toward me. A maddened bull to a matador.

I flinched but lifted my chin. "Where is what?" I asked.

He turned away and put his arms behind his back, strolling in a small circle to my right. "We couldn't find it on your father's body, so he must have given it to someone." He swiveled back to face me. "My guess is to you. His beloved and precious daughter."

"I have no idea what you're talking about," I said, and he waved a hand toward the second man that had entered the room with him. This guy was short and stubby, missing an eye, and had a long scar running down the side of his face. He tugged a leather apron around his waist and opened up some strange hole in the wall off to the side of the table.

I heard a roar and caught sight of a fire blazing inside. It was a kiln of some sort. My bowels cramped, knowing something the rest of me did not.

"I know it's not anywhere on you, I already stripped you and searched," the man behind me continued, strutting toward the stumpy dude in a white tank top that had some nasty grease stain on it. My eyes widened in fright as my heart began to race, catching up with my stomach.

"I have no idea what you're talking about," I quickly said, as the stumpy man grabbed the rod from his companion's hand and then shoved one end into the fire. "I don't even know who you are."

"Well." The man in the suit began to unbutton his jacket. "Let me introduce myself personally. My name is Alberich Riku Schnur, and I—"

"Killed my father," I finished, recognizing the name from the reports that I wasn't supposed to have seen but had looked at. All of my father's old files flashed through my mind. He was the very man that led the massive cartel my dad had been after all of those years.

"Yes," he hissed. "So, you do know me."

Turning around, Alberich marched toward me, rolling up the sleeves of his black shirt. "Now, you will tell me where it is, or I will make sure you never forget me again."

I shouldn't have, but I did. I hocked a huge wad of snot in his face that was too close to mine. "Where what is?" I snarled, and he wiped the snot from his face as the stumpy man pulled the pulsing red-tipped rod from the fire.

"The files your father collected," he spoke again, the accent in his words becoming thicker by the second. Suddenly, hot searing metal slammed against my exposed lower back. Nothing like I'd ever felt before could describe the sensation that exploded from that touch through my body.

I screamed so high I thought my throat would split, then bellowed with a primal, guttural sound, the pain bubbling through every inch of my body. The smell was horrendous as my flesh began to melt away. Then the rod was ripped off, pulling skin with it, and I cried out once more, falling forward so much that all of my body weight rested against my already straining wrists.

"Where is it?!" he screamed in my face, ripping my head up with a single hand.

"What," I coughed. "What does it look like?" I asked, falling forward as he shot up and stalked toward the table. Grabbing what looked like a long whip with spiked, metal ends, he turned around.

"I really hate disrespectful bitches," he calmly stated and walked toward me. "Your father had everything about us recorded somewhere, but we found nothing on his body. So, where is it?" The whip slammed against my back, and I cried out in a voice I did not recognize from the white hot excruciating agony. The world spun. The stench of iron mixed with burning flesh filled my nostrils, and I dry heaved.

"WHERE. DID. YOU. HIDE. IT?" he screamed again, pulling back his arm and sending the whip cracking against my back. I collapsed like a burst balloon. My eyes closed, and I slammed headlong into that blissful space of black nothing.

WHAT I SHOULD HAVE SAID

The stench of iron wasn't nearly as strong when I came to again. This time the entire right side of my body was numb as I pried open my crusty eyes and pushed to my feet off the cold stone ground, still in the same room except there was a slight red tinge to the damp gray stone beneath me. Manspreading in front of me were Alberich and the short dude, patiently waiting.

As soon as my eyes met Alberich's, he nodded, and my arms were wrenched above my head, pulling me onto my knees once more. I winced, groaning in pain, and the world spun as he stood up, holding the same miserable looking whip that had slashed across my back the last time. A spray of small blood spots had fanned out on his suit shirt and pants in evidence of what he'd already inflicted.

"Let's continue, shall we?" he said, stalking forward. The stumpy man walked to the kiln and again pulled out the hot, metal rod.

"I'm not saying shit," I hoarsely said, wriggling, then wailing that banshee scream, whose last notes were just a squeaking exhalation, as the whip struck me in my back once more. He managed to ask me twice, each time with another lashing, before he let stumpy press the rod against my open wounds and I passed out again. The pain was all too much. All of this was too much.

Sweat dripped from my brows, the salt burning my eyes as I groaned, the recognition of where I was rushing back into my head. This time it wasn't cold stone or that sterile smell blended with iron that hit my nose. It was that pungent odor of human waste. I leaned over the side of the nasty bed and vomited, unable to contain what was left in my stomach. The pain in my back caused me to screech as it speared through my entire body from the movement.

Tears dripped down my cheeks. "I DON'T HAVE WHAT YOU WANT!" I shouted, frustrated and scared.

"Shh. Too loud they come back," a hesitant voice said beside me, and I wiped some sweat from my eyes as a cold towel pressed featherlight against my back. I winced and laid back down on the nasty bed, too tired to sit up.

"Sorry," I whispered, turning my head slightly to face the young woman who was helping me. She was the slender girl with thinning dark brown hair who seemed to be the oldest out of the four. Her clothes were a few sizes too small, the tank top barely covering her waning stomach. The white color long turned cream. Her shorts were tiny and a pale shade of pink, too small for her. I could see her hip bones protruding from them.

"How long have you been here?" I asked as she pressed another damp cloth against my back. I hissed as it stung but didn't protest.

"Long time."

"What do they want with us?" I asked, and she shook her head.

"They want something different for you than for us," she said, and I furrowed my brows.

"What do they want from you?" I hesitantly asked. I already knew the answer and almost didn't want to hear what she had to say, but I asked anyway. The youngest girl here had to be barely thirteen, if that.

"I stay and men come. The other girls may leave with men forever for the right money or may stay like me. I am too old to leave now," she answered as if it wasn't a big deal, and my heart shattered. She had been here long enough that to her, getting sold to nasty men was normal.

"Why do you say they want something different for me?" I asked, as she pressed another wet cloth to my back.

"They hurt you. Make skin not beautiful. You make no money. You old," she answered, and I leaned my head back just as the rickety wooden door thundered open again.

The stumpy man strolled in with two armed guards in mismatched army fatigues, one of which was dangling a black bag. I didn't need to guess who it was for. All the girls scrambled into the dark corner, leaving me alone on the bed. He sneered at me and smiled coldly. "Good. You're awake. Time for another round."

"Fuck...you," I snarled with the last bit of energy I had left as the bag was roughly yanked over my head again and, as the guards took one arm each hauling me back to the chamber of horrors with my knees dragging on the stones, the world went black.

Time became incomprehensible as I passed out again.

And again.

And again.

The nasty bed that I woke up on was becoming less and less gross to me simply because it meant no torture. That same girl helped clean me up before stumpy showed up with his goons again.

I could barely lift my head, unable to look and see if there was any sun coming through that small window as I screamed from the literal salt that Alberich shoved into the open wounds on my back.

"FUCK YOU!" I shouted again with the only ounce of energy I had left, as the hot rod pressed against what had to be the last open spot of skin upon my back, before passing out with the smell of searing live flesh assaulting my nose.

Chapter 41

With no idea how, I was back in that small room with the same girl tending to my wounds again. They must have only been surface deep, or I would've surely been dead by now. For that small blessing, I deduced Alberich Schnur wasn't trying to kill me. He wanted whatever information he thought I had but certainly didn't.

"You need to hold your tongue," the girl chastised me as I lay on my chest with my head to the side and my arms folded beneath while she worked with feather touches that felt like branding irons.

I chuckled in spite of the pain. "What's your name?"

"Ishani," she quietly whispered.

"That's beautiful. I'm Jane," I replied as she applied some sort of ointment to my wounds. "Why are you helping me?"

"They tell me that I don't see men if help make sure your wounds heal," she answered.

"Just like I thought. They're not trying to kill me. Yet," I murmured to myself.

"I don't understand. They make beautiful woman worth no money yet don't kill?"

"I have something they need," I answered and tucked my chin against my arms, wincing at her touch. "Do you know how long I've been here?"

She shook her head. "Schedule changed. Before you came, two times of water and one food. Now, only water when bring ointment, and food seems to be forgotten."

"How many times have they brought water and ointment?"

"Each time you here. So, three now," she replied, and I banged my forehead against the bed.

"I'd like to kill him," I muttered, with another wince.

"Why not just give him what he wants?" she asked, but all I could do was sigh, knowing I didn't actually have anything of value and unable to tell Ishani in case they were listening. After that first round of beatings, I knew letting him think I had what he wanted was my only leverage keeping me alive.

Suddenly, something unusual pricked my ears and made me turn my head toward the small, locked door. I held my breath, concentrating hard, hearing the faint sounds of a commotion. The dim yellow light that typically shone through the cracks of the door flickered. Stiffly, I sat up, all of us focused on the doorway, as sounds of violence rapidly neared but just as quickly stopped. Inside the room was as deathly still as the outside corridor had become.

I shivered as Ishani grabbed my hand, pulled my black tank out from under the mattress, and dragged me into the same corner that the other three girls huddled in. Waiting with every nerve stretched thin, several girls gasped when the weak light snapped out, leaving us in pitch darkness. Then I caught a faint click, and Ishani's hand dug into mine. It sounded as if the lock had been carefully disengaged. The sound sent adrenaline bursting freely into my veins, pushing aside the pain and exhaustion that had been making me sluggish only a moment ago.

I felt her hand slip the tank into mine, and I tugged it over my head with difficulty as a muffled groan echoed in this hollow room, and I realized it was mine.

My eyes widened, adjusting to the darkness as the door swung open with a soft creak. My brows furrowed, and I tipped my head, both terrified and curious as a hulking figure slipped with deathly silent footsteps into the room at a crouch.

Silhouetted against the vague grayness and clad all in black, a balaclava was tucked around his throat, hiding his mouth and nose from sight. Night vision goggles masked the rest of his face, his black helmet protecting him the way the bulletproof vest that clung to his chest did. Weapons were strapped around his thighs, and with his rifle tucked neatly into his shoulder, he did a quick sweep of the room and then lowered his gun as the girls shrank back tighter into the corner.

Raising a gloved finger to his lips, he placed it over his mouth, motioning for us to be silent. My blood ran numb, both unafraid, but not relieved as I heard a muffled yet unmistakable pop beyond the doorway.

I stalked the man with my gaze as he swept along the room's perimeter, placing small devices at what seemed deliberate points. As he crept closer, not a sound echoing from his black boots, the girls backed themselves ever tighter into the corner.

Without thinking, I threw my arms out in front of them, offering some comfort and protection.

Then he straightened, pointed at me, and wagged a single finger, motioning for us to follow him.

I stayed put and kept the girls in place.

He paused at the doorway and spun back around. Tipping his head, he used his entire hand to wave us to follow.

Still, I stayed put, narrowing my gaze.

Several more pops sounded closer, and then a soft rumble shook the ground. The devices the man placed in the room beeped once, and a red light began blinking busily. He motioned again this time with a lot more urgency.

As one, the girls and I quickly crept after him. Ishani's fingers found my wrist, clutching tightly to me while guiding the youngest girl forward. We were not nearly as quiet as the lumbering man leading us down the hall who should've made quite a ruckus.

My fingers slipped across the musty stone wall, damp from moisture collecting against the rock. Pale moonlight streamed in through the barred window opposite the room we'd been held captive in. Rather than a hallway, shadows danced amidst the darkness in the long tunnel stretching in either direction before us.

Following the man to the right, my stomach churned, nausea rising into my throat as I nearly gagged at the overwhelming smell. Rich iron invaded my senses, and I glanced down at my fingers, rubbing them together. Red. The moisture along the wall had been blood. Scanning my surroundings, it took everything in me to swallow down the rising vomit. Crimson streaks dripped down the walls pointing like macabre arrows to the stone floor where we stepped over and around sprawled, mangled bodies.

The sight was indescribable, and I involuntarily stopped walking a few steps later. Ishani bumped into my back, but my body refused to move. Laying before me was the worst I'd seen. A body that my mind found impossible to conceive was without a head. Doubling over, I puked violently, the burning, yellow liquid mixing with the pool of blood no longer pumping from the ragged meat of the man's neck.

Ishani shrieked, shoving the youngest girl's face into her torso before she could see the gore as a couple of the other girls retched.

"We have to keep moving," the man said, low and urgent, appearing in front of me and strategically placing himself to hide the decapitated body.

"I... That... He's..." I tried to form words, but nothing came out.

"We're in a time crunch to keep you safe. Commander and I have already cleared this area, but it won't stay that way for long if we don't haul ass," the man said again, nodding down the hallway.

Commander? That one word broke through the fog holding me in place.

Another low rumble reverberated beneath my feet, wiggling some rocks loose.

"Breathe through your mouth, it won't smell as bad," he quickly added and turned on his heel. Parting my lips, I wasn't sure if the taste in the air was any better than the smell, but he'd said a word that had me feeling a little hopeful.

Commander. It couldn't be... Could it?

Stumbling forward, tripping over a body part I refused to look down at, we rounded a corner and emerged at the base of narrow stone stairs. I locked my gaze onto the man who signaled us with a closed fist and stopped walking. Keeping my eyes steady on someone who was alive, who looked mostly normal, I resisted the urge to drop them to the warmth I felt pressed against my ankle.

It was a freshly dead body, I instinctively knew that, but I didn't want to *see* it.

Popping noises erupted rapidly and erratically above us, echoing down to our chamber—noise I was familiar with.

Gunshots.

"Shit just got a bit messier than expected," the man said, glancing over his shoulder at us after murmuring into his radio. Packing the rifle against him, he added, "Timeline changed. The rival cartel showed up sooner than anticipated. We've got two convoys waiting near the gate across the courtyard—four APC's total. I'll provide the necessary cover, but if I tell you to run, you run like fucking hell to that gate. We've got men waiting near the vehicles. Don't stop running. Don't look around. Don't wait for me or anyone else. Do you copy?"

Another wave of adrenaline bit beneath my skin as I nodded fervently, and he crept a few sideways steps up the stairs. Shuffling around a body, draped upside down, he stooped and tugged out a knife protruding from one gore-filled eye socket. The metal squelched upon removal, and all of the blood drained from my face.

Wh-wh-why would he do that?

Ishani's fingers dug into my wrist, gently urging me forward as she dry-heaved, but still climbed toward the silver light that flooded the top of the stairs.

Bathed in moonlight, the man rescuing us peeked around the corner at the top and I pressed as close to him as I could without touching. There was a colonnade with several open doors to the left, and large, shattered glass windows to the right—neither areas would provide cover from the chaos unfolding before us. The sound of explosions was deafening, the flashes of gunfire even more so. In the courtyard were dozens of men, running and shouting and I couldn't tell who was who. Bodies were everywhere, strewn in the wine-colored stains that oozed thickly across the ground.

Ishani finally puked as the man flipped a switch on the goggles covering his eyes.

"There," he whispered, nodding toward the tree line beyond an iron gate that rose in front of a forest. Toward freedom from the violence and death surrounding us. Adrenaline pulsed, urging me to run, pulling rational thought from my mind.

Freedom.

Escape.

Safety.

He glanced at his wrist as we huddled next to him, hidden from the murderers, the chaos, and bullets whirring through the air.

Tremendous vibrations erupted around us, rock crashing from the buildings in tune with debris sprayed violently from the gates. The metal groaned and buckled as they were torn apart. A wave of new men, dressed in random garb immediately dashed through the opening, shouting words in a language I didn't understand.

"To the fountain!" our rescuer shouted, seeing an opening for us.

He peppered his gun around us and raced forward. My ears rang with blood, adrenaline, fear, and the roaring traces of bullets. I grabbed Ishani's hand, sprinting out of the shroud of darkness behind the man, and barreled toward the geyser bleeding a red river over stacked stone halfway between us and freedom.

A bullet grazed past me, flying by so close that the air ripped my ponytail sideways.

Barely able to breathe, my bare feet slapped over slick stone, all my pains forgotten.

"Faster!" the man shouted, barely audible. He whipped sideways, squeezing the trigger again, dropping someone to the ground.

Focusing my blurry vision on the only thing in this expanse of open space that would provide some cover, I raced faster, Ishani flying beside me, and the others strung out behind.

He swung sideways, squeezing the trigger again, dropping someone I never saw but heard thud to the ground.

But then my feet slipped out from under me, and I tumbled, slamming to the blood-soaked stone on my shoulder. Ishani screamed as my wrist tore free from her grasp. My back woke up, and feeling the fire trying to consume me, I could only grimace as I shouted, "GO!" Waving her on as the man protecting us, skidded to a halt and aimed above my head.

A shot rang out as I pushed myself up, and then someone tackled him to the ground. Stumbling a few times, I managed to rise and take a step forward when an arm wrapped around my shoulders and jerked me to a stop.

"Hello, creature. Planning on playing hero today?" Stumpy snarled and jerked me backward. I kicked out behind me uselessly as his arm snaked around my neck and he squeezed my throat with his bicep. Coughing, I scratched and tugged at the pressure that was slowly cutting off oxygen to my body. Black began to cloud the sides of my peripheral vision. Darting my gaze around, I saw our rescuer caught in hand-to-hand combat with three others. I knew he was going to be no help.

Gasping for air as the hold tightened, my blurry eyesight connected with Ishani, watching me with her hands over her mouth, and the girls crouched beside the fountain.

I couldn't be the only one stuck here.

I couldn't die here.

I stopped thrashing. As I dropped into the pressure around my throat, he lowered his arm enough for me to brace my legs and rocket backward, slamming the back of my skull into the short man's nose. His grip slackened with a gurgle just enough that I managed to gulp a little bit of air down my throat and rammed my elbow into his gut. He released me completely, the wind knocked from his diaphragm, and I spun around as a shrill whistle pierced the air.

Metal grated across stone.

Stumpy was bent and gasping, as I caught sight of the fighting knife sliding toward me, the one that had recently resided in a dead guy's eyeball.

He had only enough time for his single eye to widen as I lunged forward, and snatched it off of the stone, then drove it into his throat. Stumpy's body crumpled to the ground as he coughed and choked, black blood curdling between his teeth and pouring out of his mouth.

My heart raced as I stared at the man dying by my hands, unsure of what should be going through my head.

The bullets that whizzed past became faint, non-existent.

He wasn't actually going to die, right?

Stumpy coughed, blood gargling with his reflex.

The strain in his face loosened.

He's dying.

It was my fault. I stabbed him in the throat.

But he was going to kill me. He had already tortured me and found joy in it.

Stumpy's body went limp, a last garbled breath leaving his lips before he lay still.

In the moonlight, his pupil dilated and then turned a glassy kind of dull like a gutted fish

He's dead.

Fingers wrapped around my wrist, rough fabric gloves scratching against my skin.

"I-I-I—"

"Come *on*!" A man's voice. The man who was trying to get us to safety.

Right, safety.

Snapping out of the haze, I spun around, too fast. The world twisted around me, dizzying me and pain shot up my back.

I stumbled over my own toes.

"Hey!" he shouted. "HEY!" His hand shook my arm, and I blinked rapidly. And he suddenly threw me forward. Whipping around, he popped a couple of shots off as I blundered forward.

Come on, stupid body! Wake the fuck up.

A thunderous boom exploded in front of me, splitting the top of the fountain and sending a spray of sharp stone shards down around Ishani and the other girls. They screamed, covering their heads with their arms. That familiar surge of adrenaline-forced energy raced through my veins, and I dashed the final feet forward, throwing myself next to her.

"You okay?" I gasped.

She nodded, her eyes bulging out of her head in fright. I brushed some debris from her shoulders and glanced around me. Our only mode of protection was once again locked in battle with more assailants. And it hit me—we couldn't stay here. We were sitting ducks for the turf war that had apparently started too soon.

Scanning the courtyard, my eyes rested on the broken gate. There were convoys out there, right? That's what he'd said. I raised a finger, pointing at our freedom. Ishani followed my gaze, flinching as more dust and rocks cascaded around us.

She nodded once, and then we darted upright, spinning toward the gate, and took off sprinting just as Alberich stepped into our path. I didn't have time to wonder where he came from as I leaped back, my arms swinging out to balance me.

Shoving the youngest girls forward, Ishani commanded that they run and not stop. Alberich didn't appear to care as they raced around him because he lifted his handgun and aimed it squarely at my chest.

"Normally, I like to play with my pets first, but this...this will be just as satisfying," he snarled. My breath hitched as I stared at the barrel of the gun that was about to be my demise.

"Run, Ishani," I mumbled, my eyes fixated on the muzzle. I had a gut-wrenching memory of one just like it waved in front of me only months ago before it was pressed between my eyes. But, of course, Alberich knew none of that, as he laughed.

"Yes, Ishani. Run," he taunted, "I only want her." She took a hesitant step forward.

I slowly lifted my hands in supplication, my heart pounding in my chest. "Let me go. I don't have what you want."

"Exactly," he snarled and squeezed the trigger. I closed my eyes, flinching as two shots rang out simultaneously.

Death barreled my way.

Yet I didn't feel the impact from a bullet like I should've.

Cracking my eyes open, I blinked fervently.

Alive.

I was still alive. Slapping a hand over my chest, feeling my heart trying to escape out of my ribcage. I exhaled and tears rumbled down my face. Never before had I welcomed relief so openly. Glancing at the man whose bullet was supposed to have hit me, I sucked my bottom lip between my teeth.

Alberich had a gaping black hole in his head. He still stood, but then his body veered sideways and he plopped at an odd angle to the ground.

Dead.

Good. That's what he deserved. A soft grunt escaped the lips of my companion, and I slid my gaze to Ishani.

No!

She slowly collapsed toward the ground, holding her chest as crimson seeped between her fingers.

"Ishani!" I gasped, catching her before she hit the stone, and I crumpled to my knees. "No, no, no. You'll be fine, you'll see." I brushed some hair from her gaunt face, cradling her to my body. This wasn't happening. She had not jumped in front of the bullet meant for me.

She gave me a pained smile as I shook my head, tears streaming down my face. "No, you have to make it. You're almost free." I pressed a hand over her wound, the rapidly oozing blood streaming around my fingers.

She coughed. "I'm already free. I feel so peaceful," she whispered.

No, no. Alberich was supposed to have shot me, I'd accepted that fate. Why'd she have to sacrifice herself like that?

"Ishani, the girls. They need you," I said, rocking her back and forth, and she shook her head.

"They have you now." She coughed up a dribble of darkness that collected at the corner of her mouth, and I cradled her head tighter into my lap. Pressing harder against the wound, I felt her shudder beneath my palm and then a drawn-out breath escaped her lips.

She stopped moving, her head lolling with my gasps.

Nothing.

"No. No," I whispered, shaking her head. "Ishani?" I pounded on her chest, thinking this could not be real. A young girl just took a bullet that was meant for me and died.

"Ishani!" I cried, shaking her harder. I just had to close my eyes and then wake up from this nightmare. Squeezing them shut tightly, tears streaming wet and warm down my cheeks, I counted to three before cracking them open in hope.

Chapter 42

Bullets blazed over my head as I collapsed onto Ishani's body. Screaming in horror, I held her as return fire zapped above me. She was gone, and it was my fault. She was dead because of me.

Lifting my eyes, I caught sight of two men dressed totally in black gear, covered head to toe just as our first rescuer had been. They grabbed the three girls beside the gate and guided them into the forest.

A heavy hand clamped down on my shoulder, ripping me backward. I screamed again as I was dragged away from Ishani's body by another of Alberich's men. His suit coat was torn to shreds, and his eyes were hollow.

"LET GO!" I shrieked, his hand gripping a handful of my hair and jerking me backward, snapping my gaze skyward. He lifted his gun and balanced it over my shoulder, using me as cover as I clawed wildly at his grip. Then a dull thud sounded, a spray of wetness cascading over the side of my face.

I coughed as his hold slackened, dropping my gaze to be level with his face. He grunted, a hole seared between his eyes, as hollow as he was.

A drop of blood slithered from the wound.

Tearing my head free from his grip, he fell to his knees, his empty eyes glazing over before slumping against the ground. I gasped in horror, staring for half a second before spinning around.

Scrambling back to Ishani's body, I pulled her into my lap and scanned my surroundings, looking for our—or my—rescuer. A fire erupted in a building, sending black smoke curling toward the sky as the ground trembled and stone crumbled. Where was the man that had freed us from that cell? Surrounded by violence and terror, I found him with an assailant's arm wrapped around his neck.

It wasn't him that shot the man nor Alberich. There was no way that was possible. So, who had?

And then my focus slid to a tall man dressed all in black striding like the angel of death, only a few feet from us. His lower face was covered with a balaclava, his goggles were upturned on his helmet, and a bullet proof vest covered his chest. Weapons were strapped to his body and wound around his powerful thighs. Gloved hands held a rifle to his shoulder. The sights were narrowed in on the man that had dragged me away a moment before.

He swung his barrel toward the other comrade and squeezed the trigger. My shoulders flinched, snapping upwards as a hole seared between the eyes of the assailant with his arm wrapped around the first rescuer's neck. And with a single nod from this new man, my original rescuer took off toward the gate.

Slipping my gaze back to the figure oozing death, he slowly lowered his gun and lifted his sights from the dead assailant. My eyes met his, and I squinted in disbelief.

My heart stopped.

I was certain those were hazel eyes that looked back at me, dancing with the flames that I could never forget.

"Griffin?" I gasped, overwhelmed with absolute and total yearning.

And knowledge that I was going to be okay. Gasps of air escaped my lungs, biting back the waves of exhaustive tears of solace.

And the man began to run the last few steps straight to me.

Raising his gun, he peppered someone behind me before pulling a knife from its sheath on his chest and slashing it across an oncoming assailant's throat. I flinched and clutched Ishani even tighter, bending my head to hers as he finally reached me.

"Hey, smart ass," Griffin quietly said, squatting down beside me. I wanted to believe it was him but struggled to trust my eyes. Time froze, as I started to thaw in his gaze but not for long enough. "We have to go." He placed a hand on my shoulder as I began to violently shake my head.

"Come on," he gently prompted again.

"NO!" I shouted, shoving him away. "I won't leave Ishani." I pulled her tighter into my lap as tears streamed down my cheeks. He was here. I couldn't believe he was here.

"Jane, we *really* have to go." His voice deepened, a commanding "don't mess around" tone filtering through. I shook my head again. Griffin quickly glanced at his watch and sighed.

Stooping down, he hoisted Ishani's dead body over his shoulders. "Let's go," he commanded again, and took off running. I followed as he bled into the darkness, as quiet as a mouse, but never moving faster than I could go. Brush tickled my bare legs as I dashed behind him toward four armored military vehicles, making more noise than he did despite the obvious size difference.

He raced toward the third vehicle and a door swung open wide. Gently placing Ishani's body into outstretched hands, he sprinted back to my little legs that could now barely keep up.

He swept me into his arms and ran, carrying me the last bit of the distance toward the second vehicle. Black as night, we shot into the metal tomb, landing semi-gracefully onto the floor as the doors swung shut. Splayed out on top of Griffin and overdosed on adrenaline, my various pains, for the time being at least, were distant twinges.

"Go," Griffin said, and the entire convoy immediately whipped around, barreling away from the compound. Gently, he released me from his arms and pulled down his rag from his face. I waited for half a second as he climbed into a seat just as the ground rumbled. Pushing myself off of the floor, I hesitantly scanned my surroundings. Sitting directly against the back were three other men, clad head to toe in black fatigues, just as Griffin was.

He found a seat facing the back beside another man with bright green eyes and helped me off of the floor. Up front, I saw two more men, one of whom adjusted the rear view mirror to watch.

Another vibration sent the vehicle shaking, metal clamoring as we rattled heavily away from the mansion. Through the fortified window, I saw the entire compound was up in flames before another massive explosion went off, shattering the very place I'd just escaped from.

Rubble cascaded high into the sky before spreading wide and crumbling to the ground, with debris hailing down on our vehicle.

"What the fuck?" I blurted out, running high on adrenaline and disbelief and the entire group in the vehicle snorted, bursting out in laughter.

"Sit down and hold on," Griffin demanded.

I glanced to my left, realizing that I had climbed halfway across his lap to see out the window. I rolled my eyes and pulled myself down beside him, silently grateful that he was here. But I still had a bone to pick with him.

"Report," Griffin said, and the man sitting on my right shifted in his seat.

"Last one will explode in three, two, one." A final rumbling occurred, and I watched as one more ball of fire shot into the air. "Everyone is accounted for."

"Good. Radio command, tell them we are on our way home," Griffin responded.

"Yes, Commander." The man beside me answered briskly, speaking into his shoulder mic as the driver accelerated our getaway. Apart from the roar of the engine and the squeaks of the cabin, there was silence and the awkward tension was palpable as several sets of eyes within balaclavas flickered back and forth between Griffin and me.

I tossed a glance at the man beside me, his face completely blank as he stared without seeing the man sitting opposite as we rattled over bumps and rocked around corners. I winced from the jostling, a smidge of fleeting pain snapping up my back, but my focus was on him. A lot had just happened, but I didn't really care so much about that anymore. I'd waited way too long to see Griffin again.

"I lied," I blurted out, grabbing for a handhold after bouncing almost a foot off the seat.

Griffin's face twitched. "What?" he muttered, shoulders back and hands braced on his spread thighs.

"I said I lied," I repeated, white-knuckled and holding on for grim death, catching him as he looked at me from his periphery, and he bit back a grin.

"I heard you the first time," he answered without looking at me, and I furrowed my brows.

"The first time? Then why'd you say what?" I muttered, annoyed, finding absolutely nothing amusing about any of this.

"Because I just saved your ass and you're giving me attitude," he fired back to which I immediately rolled my eyes.

"How long was I there for?" I asked, my body thumping hard against his tree-like arm as we zoomed around yet another corner, this time almost on two wheels, making me start to wonder if the driver wasn't deliberately shaking things up back here.

"Three days," said the thick-set man sitting directly across from me who never budged and seemed to be planted in concrete. Pulling away his balaclava, he gave me a boyish grin as my mouth opened, and I slowly turned to Griffin.

"It took you *three* fucking days to come find me?" I snapped, hearing some of the men's suppressed laughter.

Griffin's mouth fell open in disbelief. "Three days? You're pissed about three days? I was halfway across the world, in the middle of an op, when

I learned about what happened. Exactly how fast is appropriate in your worldly opinion?"

"The day of," I stated matter-of-factly. My heart raced with excitement at his closeness and his sweat-tinged scent, belying my words.

"Yeah, Commander. The day of." The man sitting beside me grinned openly at both of us, his green eyes sparkling as he, too, pulled down his balaclava, exposing a round face etched with an unexpected hardness.

"You better shut your fucking mouth before I shut it for you, Bernie," Griffin grumbled. He turned his gaze toward me. "As for you, smart ass, I'm pretty sure three days to take down an *entire* cartel is a new record."

"Ohhhh, so that's what you care about." I folded my arms, still facing him, then flung them wide and grabbed Griffin's bicep as we jolted over a pothole.

"Excuse me?"

My words jounced up and down in time with the wheels, strange, sharp pinching snapping through my body. "You...care about the fact that you...took down a cartel...not that I was taken hostage...and was...nearly...beaten...to death ...several times. No, that...didn't matter at all."

The men around snickered as Griffin glared at me, effortlessly riding the bumps. "No, not at all. It didn't matter that I cashed in six different favors to change orders and fly from another country in three fucking days to save your ass. All I cared about was the cartel."

The road smoothed, and I released his arm reluctantly. "I should have known. This is why girls always fall for the villains in books, at least those guys are willing to burn down the world for them."

Griffin shook his head. "I burned down an entire cartel for you, but I guess that shit doesn't matter," he grumbled, and I giggled.

Clamping my hand over my mouth, I swallowed the rest of the semi-hysterical laugh before he lifted a brow.

"Why didn't you write?" he asked, and I sighed, the pain starting to edge back after the adrenaline rush.

"Yeah, why *didn't* you write?" Bernie added.

"Seriously, though, he would wait every time mail came in just hoping that there was a letter from this one girl." The guy to the far right spoke, and he pulled down his mask, a thin red mustache peppering the top of his lip.

"Then we'd have a very awful day of training because the Commander only received a letter from his mom." The man across from me said, pulling his balaclava down next. He was as blond as they came, his jaw square, and smile widening as he shot a glance at Griffin, who was glowering at the men.

The last guy pulled his mask down, freckles covering his features. "Will you just kiss her already? We all know you want to." He grinned as Griffin's cheeks, what little I could see of them beneath his beard, flushed red.

"Go on," Bernie prompted.

"Kiss her. Kiss her," they all chanted, and Griffin closed his eyes, shaking his head. I remained frozen in my seat, facing Griffin's profile, unsure what to do.

My answer came when he suddenly reached over and grabbed my cheeks with one hand, then planted his lips against mine. I closed my eyes, sinking into the sweetness of his taste. Lips I wished had pressed against mine for so long. His week-old beard scratched, and his mustache tickled, but I didn't care as the velvet softness deepened.

I couldn't help myself. There was already too much time spent waiting, and I wanted nothing more than to lose the rest while kissing him, touching him, being held by him. So, I jumped forward, crashing harder against his mouth.

His chest vibrated against mine as he chuckled, but his lips held mine with all the fervency he possessed. One hand snaked around to the base of my hair, gripping tightly as I threw my arms around his neck.

We broke apart for half a second, panting, our hot breath mixing between our barely parted lips.

"I missed you," he whispered.

"I missed you too," I replied.

And his hot kiss met my swollen lips again. His other arm slipped beneath the hem of my tank at my waist, brushing across my skin, and then up past my shoulder blades, pressing deeply against my back to bring me closer to him. Against the slashes and burns crisscrossing almost every inch of my skin, which also came alive under his touch.

I immediately writhed and cried out in pain, breaking what had been such a perfect moment.

"Jane?" he said in shock as I crumpled forward in agony. I closed my eyes, my breaths coming in shallow spurts.

My vision became hazy as I blinked, trying to fight away the woozy excruciating dizziness. Griffin stared at the blood dripping from his palm and plonking onto his thigh.

"What the?" he muttered, and then quickly grabbed my shoulder, spinning me around and making me yelp. Raising my blood-soaked tank slowly up, I heard his sharp intake. I cried out in silence, pain ripping through me again as the fabric tore from my skin, and I groaned.

"Pull over," he commanded loudly.

"Sorry, Commander. But we can't," Dom said from up front.

"I *said* pull the fuck over," he growled. "We need the medic from the APC behind us."

"Commander, we are in a dangerous area. Only two more clicks before we meet up with base command," Dom reiterated.

"I don't give a—" Griffin said as I leaned over to the side and vomited from the agony.

"Commander?" Bernie asked, everyone's attention returning to me.

"Hey, smart ass, I need you to focus on me," Griffin said, cupping my face as my head bobbed back and forth. Fighting between the darkness that was trying to swallow me whole, and his handsome face was grueling and exhausting. I wasn't sure how long I'd last.

"They gave me," I started and coughed as another wave of pain shot across my back. All the adrenaline that had kept the anguish at bay was gone. I could feel everything now because I knew I was safe. Curse him for making me feel safe.

My words, slurring, I mumbled, "They gave me a lot of drugs to knock me out."

Griffin gently lifted me into his lap, cradling me against his chest like I was a newborn without touching my back. "Faster," he commanded. "We've got to go faster." Dom radioed to increase speed before the entire caravan raced forward more rapidly.

"I can feel it happening again," I muttered as my vision darkened. "Not from drugs this time."

"Jane, I need you to look at me." He gripped my chin tightly.

I reached up with a shaky hand and ran my fingers across his beard. "I don't mind this," I mumbled.

"Too bad I'm going to shave it all off as soon as we get home," he murmured.

"Why? Getting used to it." I sounded as lightheaded as I felt.

He glanced at his companions and then back to me. "That's exactly why," he teased, and I chuckled, coughing.

"Good thing I have that sexy ass picture of you."

"I'm always a sexy ass." He grinned, and I tried to shake my head. I closed my eyes as the world spun. I knew what was coming, the fuzzy stars dancing across my vision warned me of the upcoming, uncontrollable event.

"Hey, hey. Open your eyes. Look at me. Open them for me."

I tried to pry them open, but I was so tired. And cold. I shivered for a moment before finding those blurry hazel eyes watching me intently.

"I don't want a pity engagement ring, by the way," I said, trying to rally.

"That's what you want to talk about right now?" he answered, brushing his fingers across my eyelids.

"Yes. Why would you give me that if you don't mean it?" My voice faded as I struggled with consciousness. "You just want your money." The world was becoming so gray, so dark. I squinted my eyes, taking a pained breath in. His eyes, I needed to just focus on his beautiful, hazel gaze.

"I did mean it," he replied, and I tried to roll my eyes, not having the strength to hold up my own head, letting it rest in his hand.

"Nothing more romantic." My voice was nearly inaudible, so far away, and I couldn't keep my eyes open any longer.

"Jane."

I could hear his voice somewhere at the end of the rapidly darkening tunnel I raced down.

"Jane. Smart ass!" He sounded desperate and worried.

Not my Griffin. That was something he never was.

"Baby, I need to see those eyes of yours. We're almost there."

It was strangely soothing, and his steady heartbeat next to my ear drummed a rhythm that was lulling me into that darkness that was just an inch away.

"Jane... please," Griffin quietly begged once more, and I took a deep breath.

The darkness left as I faded into a peaceful abyss, to feel pain no more.

Chapter 43

I heard a faint beep and my mouth was drowning in cotton.

Coughing lightly, I groaned.

What happened to the bliss I'd slipped into?

Blinking, my eyelids drooped heavily as I pried them open and managed to mutter a single word. "Griffin?"

"Hey, Janey," a different man said. Another voice I recognized. My vision slowly adjusted to the bright light. A figure drifted into view in front of me, sitting beside the rather stiff bed I was laying on. Everything smelled clean and sterile—dry. Even the mattress had a fresh scent to it.

"Noah," I mumbled and blinked again, prying my eyes open wide. The faint rhythmic beeping sounded louder as I inhaled that familiar hospital smell. The curtains were drawn closed over the window I was facing. Noah was sitting in a brown chair he'd dragged beside my bed, his hand holding mine. My entire body felt heavy and numb, and the side I was laying on ached. The walls were an off shade of white, with crinkly paper covering the plaster. A tray sat at the foot of the bed, and a clipboard rested on top.

"How you feeling, Janey?" he quietly asked, and I closed my eyes, trying to roll to my back.

"Don't." He grabbed my shoulder, keeping me on my side.

"Where am I? Where's Griffin?" I asked, focusing on the monitor that was above Noah. I knew where I was as I watched the monitor beat along with my heart, but it felt like a logical question to ask.

"The hospital. He's outside having a smoke," Noah replied.

"And Mom?"

"Bathroom." He smiled softly. "You gave us quite a fright there."

I chuckled and winced in pain. "Ow," I muttered.

"I'll take Mom to get some food and send Griffin up," Noah quietly said, standing up. I shot my hand out and grabbed his. He smiled again. "I'm not offended you asked for him, don't worry. And I haven't said anything to Mom, though you should probably tell her soon. I'm running out of excuses as to why this strange dude's been lingering around." He suddenly dug into his pocket and then pulled out something. Opening his palm, a silver chain unfurled between his two pinched fingers. "I found the ring in the grass the day you were kidnapped." Stretching forward, he wrapped it around my neck, locking it in place, and the ring bumped against my chest. "I also don't know what I'll say when she sees that engagement ring hanging around your neck. Plus, apparently she doesn't trust or like Griffin. At all. She used the excuse of his tattoos, but we both know that's just a cover for all of her fear and anxiety concerning what you went through."

"Thank you, Noah," I said hoarsely, and he leaned forward, kissing my forehead.

"Hurry up and make things official with sweaty hottie. It's not like he ran into fire for you or anything." Noah turned around and walked by the end of my feet.

"Fart face," I called out after him, glancing over my shoulder the best I could.

"Love you too, sis!" he replied as the bathroom door swung open. Noah gestured for me to lay down and close my eyes, pretending to be asleep. Quickly, I plopped my head back down on the white pillow and draped my eyelids down over my gray eyes.

"Let's go get some food, Mom," Noah said as the beige door clicked shut behind my mom.

"But what if she wakes up?" my mom asked, her voice a little strained.

"Then she will be here waiting for us. You need to take care of yourself, too," Noah replied, and I heard feet scuffle across the tile floor.

"And if that boy with those tattoos shows up again?" my mom protested.

"Man, mom, he's a man. Then he shows up. You've gotta get over the fact he's got tattoos mom. They look sick. Plus, he saved her life, so he's gotta ask questions for the report or whatever. When she does finally wake up," Noah responded with an inflection that only I understood, and another door handle clicked.

"Fine," my mom muttered. I heard more feet shuffling around and a few muffled conversations from outside my hospital room, and then it was silent once more. All except for the beep that continually sounded from the monitor.

I opened my eyes and stared at the blue curtain hanging over the window. Waiting.

The wallpaper was peeling a little in the upper corner.

Then I heard the door creak open, and I glanced over my shoulder to see the very man I'd been waiting for. I smiled, my heart jumping in elation as he closed the door and faced me. His shoulders fell in relief as he quickly walked to the bedside and took Noah's vacated spot.

"Hey, smart ass," he quietly whispered and placed a gentle kiss against my forehead. My skin danced warm beneath the brief touch of his lips. I attempted to scoot closer to the edge and grunted in pain. "Hold still. You'll hurt yourself worse."

"What happened?" I asked.

"I should've seen it, baby girl, and I didn't. I'm sorry," he muttered, and I closed my eyes, inhaling deeply as he brushed his fingers across my cheek.

"It was dark, and I had on a black tank. Don't you dare apologize for something that wasn't your fault," I mumbled against his chest, soaking in his comforting presence.

He sighed and pressed his face into my hair. "Are you okay?" he whispered, and I glanced up to see his brows knitted, pained. "Your skin was lacerated pretty badly. Doc said the wounds were oozing some pus from an infection you developed." Deep creases marred his forehead. "Those bastards really did a number on you..." His voice hitched. "Shit, I'm seriously sorry."

"Stop. I thought about having you grovel after what you said at the pool, but I don't like it." I grabbed his dark blue T-shirt and tugged him closer to me.

"If you pull me any harder, I'll end up on that bed with you, and I don't think your doctor will appreciate that."

"How long was I out?" I asked.

"A couple days. They sedated you to clean out the infected and dead skin and then stitched you up good as new." He pressed his lips against the top of my head. I took another deep breath. He smelled sweetly of citrus with a faint hint of smoke. "Your mom gave you a bath. I was bummed that the nurses didn't ask me first."

I lightly slugged his arm, grunting from the small amount of pain that shot through me from the movement. He chuckled and slid away, bending down so his face was level with mine. I smiled, his tawny eyes studying me deeply.

"You shaved a little," I whispered, running my fingers over his whiskers.

"Just cleaned it up." He lifted his chin, and I giggled.

"Kiss me, Griffin," I whispered.

And he didn't hesitate, planting his lips against my mouth roughly.

His velvet kiss had only barely connected when the door came bursting open and loud chattering shifted immediately to men whooping and hollering, cheering in taunting satisfaction as Griffin pulled away. He shook his head, and my gaze slipped toward the door at five men whose faces were familiar. Griffin gave me another quick peck before letting me go and turning back around to face the window.

"I let the guys know you were awake after Noah came to get me," he muttered.

The guys?

"Are you embarrassed?" I asked, teasing him as each one stalked into the room with wide grins on their faces.

"No."

"You totally are." I giggled.

Pointing at the closest approaching guy with a very thin mustache, he spoke. "That's Duncan. The one with blond hair is Mikey, who also brought you from that nasty ass room by the way." His finger slid to the thick-set man who looked like he was built like a rock. "That's Ford. Bernie's got the green eyes and baby face, and last but not least." He paused as an olive-skinned man with dark amber eyes sidled up. "That's Dom."

"Your SEAL team or however it works?" I asked, and he nodded.

"Glad to see you're awake and safe," Ford said kindly.

"Nice to meet y'all. Thanks for saving me. I'm Jane." I smiled as they nodded acknowledgement one by one. All of them surrounded my bed, and Bernie leaned against the edge of the mattress with a mischievous grin lighting up his face.

"Oh, we know who you are," Bernie teased.

"You better shut the hell up, Bernie," Griffin grumbled, obviously recognizing his tone.

"Why? Embarrassed that your lady might find out all your dirty little secrets?" he bantered.

"I don't have any dirty secrets," Griffin countered.

"Pretty sure the port-a-potty ain't that clean, Commander," Duncan spat, and I furrowed my brows.

"Oh, shit." Mikey snorted. "Which picture was it last time, Commander? Oh, wait, you only have one." I glanced between Griffin and the rest of the guys as he gave them the silent treatment.

Bernie laughed along with Duncan. Ford tipped his head toward Mikey. "Lonely! Oh, so lonely!" He began to sing, and Mikey leaned back laughing.

"Not when he disappeared to that port-a-potty instead of joining us for poker night. He didn't feel lonely then." Duncan wiggled his brows.

"A man's got needs, we all know that," Bernie added.

"I'm confused," I muttered, both mine and Griffin's cheeks burning red as he turned away from me and the guys.

"Ya'll better shut the hell up before I fucking break your legs and cut your dicks off," Griffin grumbled.

"Ah, man, that means no fun times alone with a picture of a beautiful woman for us either," Bernie whined.

"At least we had more than one picture of our women to indulge in, unlike the Commander there," Mikey added, and it suddenly clicked. I spun my gaze toward Griffin. I knew exactly what they were getting at, and I couldn't help but find myself a little... excited? Or was it just the pain medication? Whatever, that didn't really matter. As long as the picture they were referring to was of me, of course I was excited.

"The girl in person is better than that picture anyway!" Bernie responded, and Griffin glared at him.

"Watch what shit you say next," he snarled, and the guys laughed.

"She was still in a fucking bikini, and while that's nice and all, come on. She wasn't even partially nude. Plus you're in the picture too. But I guess a guy does what he has to with what he's got," Bernie answered

"You'd think that you shitheads don't listen to me by the way you're talking now," Griffin rumbled and rolled his eyes.

He glanced toward me so I pretended to be confused and innocent to the conversation that was going on because I was very much fascinated. "How the hell did you guys know, anyway?" Griffin asked, sending death glares toward his buddies.

They chuckled and looked at Ford who gave Griffin a boyish grin. "We noticed a pattern where you'd randomly be extra nice to us in training. So I may or may not have followed you one night."

"You're fucking serious right now, aren't you?" Griffin grumbled and shot his hand forward, grabbing Ford by the collar.

"I'm sorry. Uncle! Uncle!" Ford called out, gasping for breath. Griffin released him and leaned back.

"Just ignore them, Jane," Griffin said, and I grinned.

"You should've told me, I would've sent you something better than a bikini pic." I batted my eyelashes at him as every mouth in the room fell open.

Silence.

Griffin stared at me, unable to speak. Bernie coughed, choking, unable to form words as I once more smiled innocently at Griffin.

He opened and closed his mouth, furrowed his brows, and then tried to speak again.

I shrugged my shoulders and faced the rest of the men. "Anyway, how'd you find me in the first place?" I nonchalantly asked, finally coherent enough to ask the questions that I desperately wanted, no *needed*, answers to.

"No, we aren't glazing past what you just said," Griffin finally muttered, and I lifted my brows, widening my eyes once more. "And don't give me that all innocent look. You knew *exactly* what we were talking about, didn't you?"

"I thought you said she was innocent, Commander?" Bernie muttered, still in shock.

"She's not weirded out by that at all," Mikey mumbled, watching me in awe.

"Where the hell do I find a girl like her?" Ford smacked his lips together.

I stared at Griffin. "What did you tell them?"

"It's not like I have a lot of people to talk to out there." He grimaced.

"What did you tell them?"

"Everything," he muttered under his breath.

"What?"

"Everything," he mumbled again.

"Speak up," I demanded.

"Everything, okay?" He looked at me as my mouth fell open.

"So, you talked to them before you even muttered the word 'sorry' toward me?" I glared at him.

"You refused to talk to me, and it wasn't like I had a choice on when I was deployed."

"But you could've tried harder!"

"Tried harder? You shut your door in my face, smart ass, and shredded all my letters without even looking at them!"

I knew that we should have this conversation in private, but apparently they already knew everything anyway. And I'd waited too long, nearly died, for this conversation to not happen.

And I blurted out, "Well, you're the one that fucked me and then told me that you wouldn't hold me to it!"

"I wasn't exactly thinking straight!" he snapped in response. "Plus, you said you hated me, so isn't that the same thing?"

I blinked in shock. "How in the hell is that even remotely the same thing?"

"You lied too!" He threw his hands in the air and leaned his head back. "We should not be having this conversation right now."

"Well, when would you like to have it?"

He shook his head. "What did you want me to say, Jane?"

"The truth. I wanted you to tell me the truth!"

He snapped his gaze to me, his eyes darkened beneath his brows. "So, me telling you that I was in love with you that day wouldn't have freaked you out? Because I'm pretty sure—"

"You what?" I cut him off.

"You heard me," he said.

"Obviously she did," Bernie interjected, grinning.

"She just wants you to tell her again," Mikey said, smiling. My eyes drifted around the blaring bright hospital room. Every single one of the guys was smiling, excited by this show. Slowly, my gaze landed back on Griffin. He ran a hand over his stubble and shook his head.

"Ya'll fuckers are just going to make this weird," he muttered, and I giggled.

"Exactly." Bernie grinned, and Griffin sighed. He rolled his head toward me and chuckled to himself, a smile slowly creeping across his face.

"I love you, Jane. I have since you sat on my face," he bluntly stated.

"Wait, what?" Bernie blurted out.

"When did she sit on your face?" Ford whined.

"Why doesn't a girl want to sit on my face?" Duncan muttered.

"I thought you told them everything?" I raised a brow, and Griffin rolled his eyes.

"Not like that, idiots." Griffin ignored my comment and shook his head.

"You barely knew me then."

"Doesn't matter." He shrugged his shoulders.

"That explains why you constantly went from one mood to the opposite and would be frustrated with me." I gasped in recognition.

"I wasn't frustrated with you, I was pissed at myself. What type of shallow, low-life falls for another dude's girl?" He sighed and ran his hands over his jaw. "Jane, I really am sorry for everything that hurt you." He gave me a small smile and then looked away, shame embellishing his typically stoic features.

"I'm sorry I told you I hated you," I whispered, and he chuckled.

"Good thing I heard you say you lied before the video feed cut out entirely." He grinned, and I watched him for a moment, shocked to say the least.

Then his gaze narrowed, and he looked at me. "That still doesn't explain why you didn't write to me?"

My cheeks flushed red, embarrassed. "I wasn't exactly sure how to begin. There was a lot to say, and I didn't think a single letter was worthy of this kind of conversation," I muttered. Griffin's gaze softened, and he shook his head. "Oh, by the way. About those texts, I'd appreciate it if you just deleted—"

"Oh, I already read them." He cut me off, and my mouth fell open.

"What?"

"Yeah." He nodded slowly and lifted his brows. "I tried to respond once, but service was shitty out there. Then, your brother told the FBI agents the moment he got home and found you missing. He kept pestering them until they decided a joint operation was a good idea, which meant that we were contacted. Specifically my team because, again, your brother can be annoying as hell."

I chuckled; he wasn't wrong.

Griffin continued. "Anyway, we were relocated so service with my phone was reliable to help us determine your location. And I read them all, including the ones from your brother."

"My bad." I grimaced, and he chuckled. "How'd you end up finding me anyway?"

"Well, the cartel obviously thought that your dad gave you vital information, or they wouldn't have ever taken you," Griffin said.

"I know that, dummy."

"Will you let me talk, smart ass?" he grumbled.

"I like her. I like her a lot," Bernie interjected, grinning.

"*Anyway*," Griffin emphasized, pausing before continuing. "I realized something. What did your dad give you, the very last thing he gave you, before he was killed?"

I furrowed my brows, watching this handsome man. "Uh, that picture," I said.

"Right, a picture. A picture of Noah and you," he said and then paused.

"What's so weird about that?"

"It's a picture from your dad of your brother and you. Not of your dad and you. Why would a father give his daughter a picture like that and not his spouse?" Griffin asked.

"What are you getting at?" I pressed, and he faced me.

"It should've been a picture of you and him. But it wasn't. Plus, when Cara tried to burn it, I saw something odd along the charred edges that wasn't there before. And your dad was clearly smart, so I had them scan that picture and upload it, following a hunch. I was right. Overlaying each pixel of that picture was coded data. A massive amount of coded data about the cartel. Everything about Alberich Schnur. After adding in the smidge of missing data that was burned off in the fire, everything else was easy." He leaned his head back, smiling triumphantly.

"Don't let this go to your head anytime soon. It still took you three days," I grumbled, and the team laughed. But Griffin's face fell as he stared at the monitor beeping beside my head.

"I know," he muttered.

Silence blanketed the entire room as my heart began to finally slow. No longer was I in danger. No longer was I aching for someone who seemed a lifetime away. He was here, right beside me yet his mind was somewhere else.

I reached forward and rested a hand on his hip, gently bringing his attention back to the present. "I was just teasing," I whispered, and he gave me a tight smile. But he didn't say a word. So I licked my lips and smiled. "You missed it though. I totally took out a dude as we were leaving that place. Mikey tossed me a knife that had been in some dude's eyeball, and I stabbed Stumpy in his throat."

His eyes slid toward me. "Stumpy?"

"Long story," I muttered.

A smile caressed his lips. "You did so good for me," he muttered.

"And what about the other girls that were rescued with me?" I quietly asked, wondering if I wanted an answer or not.

Griffin gazed at me tenderly. "Safe. Starting brand new lives." Relief swirled warm in my belly and a gentle exhale left my lungs.

"Hate to break up this riveting reunion, but we gotta bounce," Bernie interrupted. Griffin winked and rose from beside me. It was intriguing watching these men bid their farewells. Words exchanged that I purposefully chose not to listen to, hugs, and a strange sense of finality sifted into the air.

But I remained aloof, confined to my bed to provide them with whatever privacy they needed. Eventually, each of them came and offered me a simple goodbye, promising to stay in touch through Griffin, and then my rescuers were gone.

Leaving me alone with a man who still owed me answers.

Chapter 44

"Griffin, you said I could ask you anything and you would answer it honestly," I began, and he sat down in the chair beside my bed.

"Yes, I did," he answered.

"Were you ever going to tell me about the inheritance?"

He looked a little surprised for a moment. "Dayton told you, I assume?"

"Oh, I got fired because of what I learned from Dayton," I replied, and he blinked, shocked.

"What the fuck?"

"Yeah. Dayton told me that Cara gets your inheritance if you're not married and retired and working for the family business or whatever by the end of this year. Anyway, I argued with Cara and your grandma because they both called us out for a fake relationship and said that my body was disgusting. That you wouldn't ever find me attractive or worthy to touch."

Griffin raised his brows and let his eyes slide up and down my body. "Cara's bat shit crazy. If you weren't all injured and hooked up to these machines, I'd already be balls deep in you so—"

"Griffin," I quickly slammed my hand over his mouth, feeling my figure beginning to heat up. He wiggled his brows as I lowered my palm. "Anyway, I may or may not have used some very choice words because I was upset, and Cara recorded it. She posted it online, and since your brother and a few of his friends were standing beside me, it made some parents really upset."

"I want to see this video." Griffin grinned and I rolled my eyes.

"Focus."

"I'm very focused." He narrowed his eyes directly at my chest. I followed his gaze and shook my head, folding my arms over my breasts.

"Griffin, don't make me laugh, it hurts too much," I scolded, and he gave me another sheepish grin. "Technically, the principal put me on unpaid leave until things settle down and my case can be reviewed, but once that happens, I'll just end up getting fired."

"Which does explain how you were snatched from your lawn in the middle of the day when you should've been at school teaching," he muttered, and I nodded.

"We are so off track. Anyway, that brings me back to my question. Were you ever going to tell me?"

Griffin exhaled slowly. "I wanted to, but I had no idea how to even begin."

"I couldn't care less that it was all fake to begin with, you had your reasons and owed me nothing at the time. But now I need to know, do you actually find me attractive? Your grandma showed me a picture of her match for you, and she looked like a real-life Cinderella."

He chuckled. "Good thing I fancied Belle and Mulan growing up." He brushed some hair from my face and smiled. "Though, I really am preferring this extra buff smart ass right beside me."

"I had a lot of extra free time." I blushed, and he cupped my cheek.

"I like you, Jane Barlow. No one else," he softly said. "I don't care if it started out fake or not, those are real memories, real moments with you."

"I have no job, no money anymore, Griffin. I still live with my mom and little brother, and I'm pretty sure my rundown car has more miles on it than the last hooker Bernie slept with."

His grin widened. "Good thing I have way too much money and couldn't care less about any of that. Inheritance or not, I just want you." He leaned forward, and my heart kicked in my chest. His tawny eyes pierced into mine before flickering to my lips and then gently drifting toward them.

"You need to end this shit with your family, Griffin," I blurted out, closing my eyes, interrupting him before he could kiss me again, no matter how much I wanted him to.

"What?" he softly said, stroking my cheek once more.

"I don't care that you initially used me for money. I get you not wanting Cara to have it, but come on, is it really that big of a deal? Don't you have enough?" I coughed slightly, and he stood up. Walking around the mattress, I heard him turn the sink on across from the foot of my bed and then he returned.

"Here." He lifted a cup to my chin and helped me awkwardly drink some water. "Baby girl, I wish I could, but it's not that simple."

"How is it not? You're the one who has to be married by the end of the year and quit your job. Not anyone else. Your grandma is literally forcing your hand for who knows what reason." I lifted my fingers and brushed them along Griffin's lips.

"She punished my mom for getting pregnant with me as a teen. This is her solution to get my mom and I to prove we're worthy of the family." He closed his eyes, leaning into my palm and kissing it. "Jane, this isn't just about me."

"Griffin, you've spent your entire life protecting everyone else. Taking care of everyone around you. But what about yourself? Don't you deserve that same kind of love?" I whispered, and he sighed.

"You're annoying sometimes, you know that right?" He opened his eyes and lifted his brow. I grinned with as much energy as I could.

"Tell me again how much you love me?" I said, closing my eyes.

"So, this means we are dating now, right?" he asked, his breath washing over my face, so close to my mouth. I peeked through my lashes and bit back my smile.

"I don't know if I can date someone, seeing as I'm technically already engaged."

"That's just a formality." He shrugged his shoulders, inching even closer to my lips.

"And I have this little brother who might just try to steal you away," I teased.

"I thought he was straight?"

"He is. Except for when it comes to you," I muttered and felt his lips brush across mine like a feather dancing with the wind.

"Don't worry. I only have eyes for one girl."

"Good, cause my mom apparently doesn't like you either."

"What?" He gasped. "Why not? I'm amazing."

"Noah thinks it's because of what happened," I muttered and leaned forward. "But she used the excuse of your tattoos and probably thinks that you influenced me to get mine. Which in her head, equates you to a horrible person and the reason I got kidnapped." My lips touched his as he smiled.

"Damn it, 'cause I was thinking of getting another tattoo soon. Maybe a few more," he quietly said. "And I'm the reason you're not *still* kidnapped."

"I've always wanted another one on my back. Like right down my spine. So now would probably not be the best time to get it, right?"

"Mmmm." He closed his eyes, and I followed suit. "That sounds like a perfect place. Reminder of just how badass you are."

"You won't find it gross?" I hesitantly asked, and he shook his head, his mouth swiping back and forth across my lips.

"Scars are hot." He rose up a little, causing my head to tip backwards, and then pressed his lips against mine. I sighed as he parted his mouth and slipped his tongue between my teeth. It was quick and he pulled away again. A whine escaped my lips.

"Later, smart ass," he muttered, and I opened my eyes, pushing my bottom lip out to pout.

"Wait," he suddenly said and sat down in the chair. "Are you saying your mom doesn't know about us or what I am to you?" I shook my head. "Why not?"

"What was I supposed to say? One, she thinks I'm still a virgin, Griffin. So how was I supposed to explain to her the situation when a pivotal part of it was a result of what occurred in that pool? If I even mention that you've stuck your dick in me, she's going to be twice as pissed that you 'soiled' her precious daughter." I grinned as Griffin narrowed his gaze.

He folded his arms in a gruff. "You asked me to," he muttered, and I giggled. "It's not like I used you to merely get my rocks off."

"No, just my picture while halfway across the world," I teased, and he shook his head.

"I went years being completely abstinent after my ex and I broke up. Not even a quick something by my own hand. Then you came along and screwed all that up," he mumbled sheepishly.

"In a port-a-potty of all places."

"It wasn't always in a port-a-potty, and it wasn't that often, okay? Just a few times."

I giggled and then coughed, the jolt in my body causing my back to pinch. "Ow," I muttered, and he shifted forward in his chair, concern filling his face. "I'm fine." I quickly reassured him, and he leaned back.

"Why aren't you creeped out by that?" he cautiously asked, and I shrugged.

"It would be weird if I didn't reciprocate your feelings, but I do."

"Oh?" He lifted his brows. "So, you love me?"

I pulled my lips between my teeth, wondering how far to take the joke. "I am...fond of you," I replied, and he rolled his eyes.

"Smart ass."

I grinned.

"So, what do I have to do to get you to date me?" he pressed again, and I shook my head.

"I don't know. Why do you want to date me?"

"Well, for one, I want to have sex with you again." He gave me a goofy grin.

"Griffin," I grumbled, and he threw his head back, laughing.

"You make me laugh. You're absolutely beautiful and have an attitude that not only annoys me sometimes but keeps me on my toes. But most importantly, I might just want to marry you for real someday, and I can't do that if we're only fake engaged," he replied.

My stomach turned, butterfly wings creating a hurricane of excitement inside my soul. *He what?*

"Hmmmm." I paused and squinted, narrowing my gaze toward him. "There's only one problem with that."

"Which is?" He tilted his head.

"That would mean the only guy I've ever slept with would be you."

"What's wrong with that?"

"What if someone else is better?"

"Bitch, please!" He flicked his wrist, and I laughed, which caused me to wince and cough. He leaned forward and brushed his lips across my ear. "I guess I'll just have to make sure you never feel the need to wonder about that."

I smiled and closed my eyes. Griffin pressed his lips against my hair once more and then stood up. "I need to tell your doc you're awake. And I should probably let my mom know I'm home."

"Wait." My eyes shot open, and I looked up at Griffin, who shoved his hands into his jean pockets. "You're home? Like for good?" He nodded. "But don't you still have some time left?"

He shook his head and smiled. "Only a week, so they let us all leave early due to special circumstances. And I am officially retired." He glanced at his watch. "Well, in a few hours I will be, but eh."

"*Retired* retired?" I asked, and he nodded. "Are you going to take over the family business like your grandma wants?"

His brows twitched, the brightness in his eyes dimmed a little. "I'm working on that with my grandpa."

"If you're not, then what are you going to do with all that free time?"

He shrugged his shoulders. "Maybe take you to Paris or some beach far away. Who knows?" Griffin smiled once more and pulled his phone from his pocket.

My heart began to race. Was he leaving me alone? When would he come back? *Would* he come back? I stared at him as he began to walk around the foot of my bed, and then he paused.

Slowly his eyes slid to mine. "I'm not leaving the hospital, okay? Just making a few calls and sending the doctor in." I hesitantly nodded. "You're safe, baby girl. I've always got you."

Griffin waited for another moment and then his feet disappeared through the door. It clicked shut and I was left alone, lying on my side in silence once more. I should've just told him that I loved him. I should've simply said yes to dating him. But I really did want all this nonsense with his family to be resolved. Things were complicated enough since my mom clearly did not like the man that I was absolutely, irrevocably smitten by.

Chapter 45

Listening to the constant beep chasing away time, I lay on my side playing all the scenarios in my mind of how my mom was going to react when I told her that I was into this guy that she apparently did not approve of. Every single one involved some degree of verbal fireworks despite the fact Griffin was the reason I made it home safely. Getting past that, I was also supposed to somehow explain to her that I'd known this guy since we moved here, catching Noah in the net of lies that he'd been telling to cover for me.

I tried to think from her perspective of how traumatized she would feel knowing her daughter had been kidnapped. Part of the problem was that, to her, I was still her little girl who'd barely had her first kiss, let alone been with a man, rather than a capable grown woman of twenty-seven. I argued to myself that was really a double standard seeing as she didn't particularly care about Noah's sexual escapades, almost hearing her voice saying *But he's always been that way*. Every which way I turned it, she wasn't going to be happy Griffin wasn't a clean cut, white collar businessman regardless of how rich he was.

I cocked my head to the side. He had come in and rescued me like a superhero. That had to give him some bonus points toward my mom. Right? Several, even.

Ugh. Shouldn't things be simple now that I was home alive?

More lies were piling on top of each other. I hated lies. I needed some time and space to sort through my thoughts. Maybe more so, I needed time to process what I went through those three days with someone who understood it on a personal level.

Griffin had been kidnapped before. And lost someone he'd been kidnapped with.

I heard the door click open again and tried to look over my shoulder. Several people walked into the room. Two nurses went straight for the clipboard and monitor while an older, bald gentleman with thin glasses stopped in front of me.

"Hi, Jane. I'm Doctor Smith. How are you feeling?" he asked, his forehead wrinkling as he lifted his brows, offering me a smile with his thin lips that seemed a little odd on quite a round face.

"A little crummy, but I'm alright," I muttered, and he lifted his own clipboard, scanning through his charts. One nurse started to fidget with the catheter, and I winced as she removed it.

"You have several sets of sutures and some staples in your back that will need to come out in a week and a half at your follow-up appointment. As long as you don't experience too much discomfort, you should be right as rain after that." He smiled and then glanced around the room.

The two nurses walked back over and whispered a few things, and then he wrote something down before returning his attention toward me. "I'll have the nurses bring you some ointment for your burns, pain medication and some antibiotics, as well as a packet for post op care when they come in to check your vitals again. Until then, do you need anything else?"

"When can I be discharged?" I asked.

"In the morning."

"How about sooner?"

He furrowed his brows, a frown creasing his features as the door swung open once more and footsteps entered the room. "I mean, if you really insist, this evening, but you'll need someone to take care of you for a few days while your body heals."

"We'll do it," my mom quickly said and stopped by my side. The doctor offered a tight smile. He patted my leg and then nodded to the nurses.

"They'll be back in two hours, and if nothing has changed, you're good to go." He nodded, pushed the glasses back up his nose, and then turned around. The two nurses in purple scrubs followed the doctor out. I barely paid them any attention. It wasn't my mom or Noah who I wanted to take care of me, it was Griffin. But I still hadn't resolved how to approach that subject.

"How are you sweetheart? When'd you wake up?" my mom asked. Noah shot me a glare, and I smiled stiffly.

"Not too long ago." I brushed it off as she sat down in the chair, and Noah nodded his approval. My mom's hair seemed a little untidy, and the bags under her eyes were quite evident. She ran a hand over the frays that were coming loose at the hem of her simple red T-shirt. Even her jeans looked a little crumpled.

"As soon as they allow it, you're coming home with us. Then once you're healed, we are moving back to Washington," my mom stated determinedly, and my mouth fell open.

"What?" I gasped and looked between Noah and my mom. He subtly shook his head, shoving his hands into his sweatpants and leaning back against the wall. "Why?"

"How about there's nothing here for us? You lost your job and were kidnapped. Noah can transfer back to his college. And besides, we moved here because of the threat from the cartel. There's no cartel left." She brushed some hair back toward her ponytail, speaking under her breath with disdain. "Apparently thanks to some brute, who keeps hanging around for some reason."

"No." I shook my head, desperately trying to sit up. "No, I don't want to go back."

"Oh, don't be ridiculous. You can contact all your friends again, and your old school has already agreed to take you back. I called them yesterday." My mom placed a hand over mine, looking pleased with her plans.

"Mom, you're not listening. I don't want to go back. I like it here," I stated again, a little firmer. Noah wiggled his eyebrows and settled against the wall waiting for the showdown. I glared at him to shut him up.

"It's not up to you. The FBI has already offered to help move us back. We'll have a bigger house and everything can go back to normal," she said.

"I'm an adult, Mom. You can't make me." I coughed, and she patted my hand.

"Oh, sweetheart. Where would you live?"

"I'll find a place."

"With what money? Both of my kids may refuse to tell me why you lost your job, but I still know that means you've been living off of savings and *my* money. So, when the savings run out and I'm gone, how will you afford a place? Plus, Susie has already called twice now that the FBI filled her in on your sudden departure. She's excited to have her best friend back."

I pushed myself up as far as I could, groaning and clutching my side. My gaze shifted to Noah, pleading with him to say something. To stop this nonsense. "Susie and I can visit. Call, text, facetime," I choked out in desperation. "Noah?"

He sighed. "Mom, I do have a girl I'm kind of dating. I've been wanting—"

"Noah, you'll find another girl. You always do." She waved her hand, brushing him off.

"But Mom, he's talking about an actual girlfriend," I pleaded with her.

"I've made my decision. Now rest, I'm going to bring you some food," she said and quickly stood up from the chair. She grabbed Noah's arm and tugged him forward, but he slowly shook his head.

"I'll wait here with Jane," he muttered quietly, and she shrugged her shoulders.

"Suit yourself." Leaning forward, she kissed my forehead quickly and then was gone. She was acting so strangely. Though I couldn't blame her. I knew the emotional roller coaster my kidnapping must have caused.

Between that and dad getting killed, there was the viable explanation for how she was acting.

"Sit me up," I demanded from Noah. He walked toward me and helped me move off my side. "I don't want to leave. I'll figure this out." I stared at him, and he chuckled. "What's so funny?"

"You have a mega-rich boyfriend who I guarantee would want you to move in with him. You don't have to leave if you don't want to." He grinned, daring me to argue.

"That's not the point, Noah. Besides, we haven't really established anything since there's still some shit with his family to deal with that concerns money."

"Okay. So figure that shit out and then you can stay."

"And what about you?" I gestured toward him as he sat down in front of me, and the door behind me opened once more. Turning my head, I glanced over my shoulder to see a slightly confused Griffin take a few steps inside.

"You know, if I didn't know that you two were siblings, this would be a very awkward thing to walk into." He lifted his brows accusingly. Glancing back at Noah, I chuckled to myself. The chair he was sitting in was nestled between my legs.

"I brought food," Griffin added. He walked toward us, holding a couple of bags of what smelled like the most heavenly morsels I'd eaten in my life. As he rounded the foot of the bed, I grinned.

"You brought *chicken nuggets*?" I squealed in glee, recognizing the bags.

"Why is every girl the same?" he asked Noah, who shrugged his shoulders as Griffin tossed him a bag of Chick-Fil-A. He wheeled the tray around and set the food and drinks on top of it.

Chapter 46

Within five minutes, my belly was swimming with nuggets and fries that were about half gone. The current dilemma about my mom wanting us to move back to Washington was completely out of my mind. Noah and Griffin were both sitting in chairs, joking about who knows what.

Humming to myself, I lightly bobbed my head back and forth, and their laughter died down. "What?" I asked with a mouthful of chicken nuggets, realizing both guys were silently watching me.

"Happy?" Griffin questioned, raising a brow, and I nodded giddily. Then I realized what was going on, and I narrowed my gaze.

"Stop mocking me. I haven't eaten anything in forever." I glared at him as his grin widened, and he shared a knowing glance with Noah. "I am also the one in the hospital gown, so cut it out."

"Smart ass." Griffin winked slyly as Noah's mouth fell open.

"Excuse me? What'd you call my sister?" he snarled.

"Noah!" I called out as he lunged toward Griffin, who threw his hands in the air. "It's not like that!"

Noah paused, his hand around Griffin's collar, gripping his T-shirt tightly. "What?" Noah asked, quickly glancing from me to Griffin.

"It's kind of become a term of endearment of sorts," I explained.

Noah looked bewildered. "Him calling you a 'smart ass' is a nickname?"

"Yes?" I unconfidently replied. Noah snapped his head back and forth between Griffin and me.

"You're being serious." He slowly released Griffin's collar as we both nodded. Chuckling, he smoothed out Griffin's shirt, his cheeks turning red as he recognized his overreaction. "Sorry, man, but only I, as her brother, get to talk shit to her."

"All good," Griffin muttered and then shoved another fry in his mouth. With everything that happened, I could easily give my brother a pass. Heightened emotions were an understanding result, for not just me but for all of us which would probably lead to a few more instances like this.

"So, when Mom returns from the cafeteria, how are you explaining this?" Noah asked, tossing a thumb toward Griffin. Griffin remained silent, stuffing more food between his teeth.

"I'm telling her the truth," I said between mouthfuls. Both Griffin and Noah stared at me in shock.

"What?" they said, simultaneously.

I shrugged my shoulders. "I don't want to move, so she might as well know the real reason why."

"Move?" Griffin asked, swinging his confused expression to my brother, then back to me.

Noah sighed, wiping ketchup from his gray T-shirt. "Mom just announced she is moving back to Washington. Seeing as we live with her..." His voice trailed off as he looked down at his shoes.

"Jane?" Griffin turned toward me.

"Don't get upset at her. Mom literally *just* announced it, and Janey's fought it from the beginning," Noah defended. Griffin clenched his jaw. "So, are you going to tell her to move in with you or what?" he finished, and Griffin chuckled.

"Technically I still live with my mom, too," he muttered.

"What? I thought you were rich, with giving Janey such a fancy engagement ring and everything." Noah spewed a few fry crumbs.

"He owns the house. And several others," I said, washing down the last nugget with some water.

"How many others?" Noah skeptically asked.

"Seven. Though I'm probably going to sell two or three of them. It's becoming a bit of a hassle managing them all if I'm being honest. I have enough apartment complexes to worry about. Speaking of, I probably have one vacant you can rent if you want to stay," Griffin replied to Noah and lifted a casual brow as my brother's mouth fell open.

"Eight houses total? And it's becoming annoying? The fuck?" Noah gasped, and I giggled, which hurt.

"Ow," I muttered, wincing, and both of their heads shot up, concerned. I waved a hand at them. "I'm fine."

Griffin watched me for a moment before speaking again. "Move in with me," he bluntly stated. I should've felt my heart leap, should've been excited by the offer, but it tore me in two. I'd never blatantly gone against my parents' wishes, and saying yes would do just that.

I stared at him as he continued to chew, and then he furrowed his brows. "You don't want to," he muttered.

My shoulders sagged. "It's not that simple, Griffin," I said quietly.

He looked at me, his face contorted with confusion and pain. "How the hell is it not?"

I sighed. "Look, my dad just died, and if my mom moves back to Washington, she would be alone. Plus, I don't want you to ask me to move in because you're forced by the situation. My best friend is also back there, and the school I used to teach at would take me back. And this is all moving—"

Griffin stood up, cutting me off, his face pulled tight, but his voice remained calm. "Is that the life you want? Your old job back? Your best friend close to you again?"

"Griffin," I said, coughing a little as he shook his head.

"Well, let me know when you figure your shit out. If that's the life you want, then go. If not, give me a call, 'cause I'll be here waiting," he grunted and walked toward the door. I couldn't turn around as I felt my heart shatter. He wasn't listening. Again.

"Griffin!" I shouted. "That's not it!" I coughed again as his footsteps paused.

"How is it not? You're the one that said this is moving too fast." He sounded so cold, so unfeeling as a glimpse of pain crept through his voice.

"You're not listening," I hoarsely cried out and leaned forward, attempting to stand from the bed. My body plummeted to the ground, my legs still weak.

"Jane!" Noah shouted, and before I knew what was going on, four arms were gently lifting me back into bed.

"What the hell were you thinking?" Griffin asked, his brows knitted together tightly upon his face. Noah backed off to the side, shaking his head.

"I was thinking you weren't listening to me. You were leaving again." I coughed a few times and winced, leaning back on my side.

"I didn't leave last time, smart ass. I was deployed," he softly said, the pain still in his voice.

"You left. I was all alone. Confused. Hurt. Pissed off," I stated, staring at his hazel eyes. His chest expanded, and he knelt down, lowering himself to my eye level. "And now you're leaving again, and you won't listen to what I'm saying."

He watched me, his face pulled into a stoic mask I hadn't seen in months. "Griffin, my dad died. Nine months ago, my world was turned upside down. I had to leave everything I knew and found myself flying through a whirlwind that I am still trying to process. You can't blame my mom for thinking that the best next step is to go back to our old life. The world where her husband existed and her daughter had a job. Where her family was whole." I paused as Griffin's jaw clenched but his eyes softened.

Reaching forward with a trembling hand, I cupped his cheek. "At one point, that's what I was waiting for too. Confirmation that the cartel was neutralized, and that I could go back to my life. But somewhere along the way, this became my life. *You* did. But I don't want you asking me to make another big change because you're forced to by the circumstances."

Griffin's lips twitched upwards. "When have you ever seen me forced to do anything?"

I raised an accusing brow.

"Okay, dumb question 'cause you're right. But technically, no one forced me to do any of that. I just wanted to take care of my mom," he muttered.

"Take care of your mom? What do you mean?" But at this point in time, I didn't care as much about getting an answer to that as I did something else. "You know what? We can talk about that later. What I want to know is what do you want now?" I asked, dropping my hand from his cheek, and he leaned forward.

"Now, I'd like you to agree to date me for real so I'm not asking you to simply be my roommate. I already feel like I have three of those," he whispered, and pressed his forehead gently against mine.

"I'm not living with your mom, or Dayton, or your stepdad," I stated, and he chuckled.

"You also said things felt like they were moving fast," he replied.

"We've known each other for a while, but technically you've only asked me to be your girlfriend starting today, and I haven't even said yes. Plus, you were deployed for a lot of that, and I was mad for the other part," I explained, and he closed his eyes but smiled.

"Then how about this? I'll find you a vacant spot in one of my apartment complexes, then we can look for a house together. That way a little bit of time can pass while we date before we move in together and we won't be living with my family," Griffin offered, and I felt my own mouth creep upwards.

"Okay," I whispered, and he sighed in relief. "You promise you're not asking because I'd move away if not?"

Griffin shook his head. "I kinda like having you around." He gently placed his lips against my forehead as a small cough sounded behind Griffin.

I glanced around him to find Noah standing there with a sheepish grin on his face.

"You can have a vacant room, too, Noah," Griffin waved his hand. "Though you will owe rent."

"Oh come on. I'm practically family!" Noah whined, and I snorted.

"I'll give you the family deal then." Griffin rolled his eyes as Noah pumped his fist in glee. "You pay double."

"What?" my little brother gasped in shock, nearly falling over. I laughed, coughing a little again as Griffin winked.

"I still want to try and convince Mom to stay first," I quietly said, and Griffin nodded.

"Done." He grinned and quickly pecked my lips, stepping away.

"Yuck!" Noah shouted, and I rolled my eyes. "Just because I'm okay with you two being together doesn't mean I want to see any of that PDA stuff," he added, and Griffin chuckled as I felt my stomach cramp. Great.

I knew what that meant, as I grunted in pain.

Chapter 47

Griffin furrowed his brows, cautiously assessing if I was okay. "Sit me up, please," I muttered, and he reached forward, carefully slipping his hand beneath my shoulders and tilting me upright.

The moment I was sitting, I felt that all too familiar gush of blood drip out between my legs.

Of course I had to start my period.

Of course it had to be now.

Of course it was when I had nothing but a stupid pale blue checkered hospital gown on. But, it may have been a small blessing in disguise, because I also recognized how full my bladder was. The nurses had already removed the catheter before I ate my meal, which replenished my body with plenty of fluids.

"Alright, don't be grossed out, but I need to pee and I started my period," I muttered, and Griffin shared a glance with Noah.

"Which means what?" Noah asked.

"Which means I need one of you idiots to find a pad and some underwear or some shit while the other one helps me get to the bathroom before I piss myself," I stated, and Griffin snorted as Noah's cheeks turned bright red.

"I'll start looking for a pad or whatever." Noah quickly volunteered, and scrambled toward the cupboards that sat beneath the sink. Griffin leaned forward and tucked his hands beneath my armpits.

"Lean forward without bending your back so you don't hurt yourself, and I'll pull you upright," he said.

Nodding, I swung my hands forward, gripping his shoulders and rocked my body into his arms. My bare feet plopped against the cold tile as Griffin steadied me.

I shuddered as even more bloody liquid slid down my legs. Unusually large clots, too—probably a result of everything that I went through.

Clenching my jaw, I stared at Griffin, wide-eyed and embarrassed. Behind me on the bed was a red stain, left where I'd once been sitting and more was oozing toward the floor as we stood still.

"Griffin," I whispered, unsure of what he was going to think.

"What, baby girl?" he replied with a tender smile.

"I need to ask you something really gross," I sheepishly said, and he tilted his head, standing up straight and stepping back.

"Not much grosses me out anymore," he nonchalantly answered, leaving his hands around my waist to hold me gently upright.

"Including blood?"

"Your period doesn't get to be an excuse to turn me down in the future." He winked, and I rolled my eyes. "Bad timing?"

"Yes, dummy." It did pull a small giggle from me before I took a deep breath and swallowed my pride. "I have blood running down my legs and really don't want to make more of a mess than I already have…"

"Roger." He saluted me with a major grin and then jogged toward the bathroom. I sighed, slipping the monitor off of my finger, knowing what I'd just gotten myself into. Noah continued to panic, flipping through cupboards like a madman and muttering to himself. His eyes lifted to mine, and he spotted the blood on the bed and his face paled.

"It's a normal bodily function, Noah." I glared at him, and he shook his head.

"I know. I can't find anything. There's nothing here," he said, panicked, and I chuckled to myself as Griffin returned from the bathroom holding some toilet paper.

"Go look in there, dipshit." Griffin tossed a thumb to the bathroom, and Noah fervently nodded.

"Right. Right. Right," he muttered and quickly disappeared through the door Griffin had emerged from. Shaking his head, Griffin made his way back over to me and knelt down in front of me. He placed his empty hand against my hip and slowly began wiping the blood off of my leg, from ankle to thigh.

"A warning if you decide to take advantage of your situation and look up my gown," I began, and Griffin glanced away from my legs to look at my eyes. He grinned wickedly and wiggled his brows.

"You're a little late on that, smart ass," he teasingly said.

I rolled my eyes but smiled. "Well, don't judge me. I happened to miss my wax appointment while kidnapped... So, yeah."

He grinned even wider and rocked back on his heels. "Good thing my favorite part of Boy Scouts was all things involving wilderness exploration." Looking back at my legs, he continued to gently blot at the blood as I bopped him on the back of the head.

"Ow," he said, rubbing it with his free hand. "What was that for?"

"You know what that was for."

"You're the one that asked me to get between your legs, smart ass."

"You didn't have to seem so enthusiastic about it."

"Any opportunity to be near my favorite dessert will be met with much enthusiasm." He grinned as my mouth fell open in shock. My cheeks turned bright red as he chuckled in absolute glee.

"I hate to push you, but I really have to pee. Hurry up please!" I desperately begged, all of my dignity absolutely gone by now. I felt a little more blood slide down my leg again, and he simply wiped it away.

"Griffin..." I pressed again, tapping my toe to keep myself from peeing right here.

"Noah's still in there," Griffin said, finishing cleaning me up the best he could, just as I heard that familiar sound of a door opening. Thinking it was Noah, Griffin and I both whipped our heads toward the loud noise as not just one person entered the room, but five.

I froze.

Griffin froze.

My mom standing in the doorway froze, her mouth wide open.

You could hear a pin drop miles away with how absolutely still it was. Full of tension and shock. I knew it looked bad. Of course this was the moment that my mom would return and with Griffin's mom. Another head popped around the doorway, and I groaned internally. Dayton also had to see this.

"WHAT THE HELL?" my mom shrieked, as her eyes connected with the scene displayed before her. Dayton seemed unfazed right before his mom slapped her hands over his eyes. Nancy heavily sighed, and two nurses walked into the room.

"You filthy piece of shit!" my mom shouted at Griffin. "Stop him." She directed toward the nurses—even though playing bodyguard wasn't technically part of their job.

"Ignore her please and just take me to the bathroom right now," I snapped at Griffin.

"Yes, ma'am," he said, standing up. He threw an arm around my hips and then gently helped me take a few steps around the bed, dragging the bags that dripped steadily through the IVs into my arms. One hand of his was full of bloody toilet paper, hiding it away as respectfully as he could while he kept me steady to the best of his ability with the closed fist. My legs were stiff, my back rather tight, and I was grateful he was next to me.

My mom came barreling into the room right behind the two nurses who immediately stepped in front of us, blocking my path.

"Move," I snarled, staring at all three of them. I didn't care what they'd seen or were thinking. My bladder was ready to explode, and the longer it took me to get to the bathroom, the more mess I would make being on my period.

"Let go of my daughter this instant. How dare you touch her like that when she's—"

"Stop! It's not what you think. Now, please move," I reiterated, closing my legs a little to try and cut off the clot of blood that slithered down the inside of my thigh. She folded her arms, standing between the two nurses that blocked us from going around her. My entire stomach hurt from clenching so hard.

Turning to Griffin, I pleaded with my eyes. "Move them or something. Please," I sobbed.

"If you touch us we will call security and have you kicked out," one of the nurses said before Griffin was able to move.

My stomach lurched as I tried to squeeze my bladder tighter. Frustrated and annoyed, time was running out.

"Fuck it," I muttered under my breath and closed my eyes. To hell with being bashful and trying to stay somewhat decent. "I started my period and Griffin was cleaning up the blood. I have no underwear on and don't know how long I can keep holding my pee. So, will you get out of the fucking way so I can get to the toilet?" I demanded, silencing the commotion. In a daze, all three women parted the way, stepping back toward the wall.

My mom blinked, watching me as Griffin guided me forward once again. Noah of course only now made his entrance, shoving his head around the bathroom door, and held up a really thick pad—much like the ones given to a mom directly after birth.

"Found one!" He grinned, and then his mouth flew wide open.

Without looking away from Griffin and I, my mom dug through a new bag she was holding as we neared the bathroom door. Griffin grabbed the frame and nodded for Noah to get out of the way. He handed me the pad while simultaneously skirting toward the opposite wall.

"I have your underwear here, Jane," my mom muttered and quickly jogged toward us, stretching forward her hand which held a fresh pair of underwear. Griffin lifted his brows, giving her a steely gaze as he snatched it from her hand and then shut the door behind us.

Rushing to my left as quickly as I could, Griffin helped me sit down awkwardly and not a moment too soon as everything came rushing from my bladder. I gripped his shoulders as he knelt down in front of me and simply waited.

"I'm sorry for how crass that sounded," I muttered, and Griffin snorted. He began pulling open the pad and attempted to attach it to the underwear.

"It's backwards," I said quietly. "And you have to pull the tabs off the wings to make them sticky."

"Oh," he mumbled, narrowing his gaze. "Damn, it's like I'm trying to solve a Rubik's Cube." His massive fingers stuck the wings to each other by accident, and he peeled them apart before finally getting it to work.

I giggled. "Thank you."

Griffin gently lifted one of my legs and slipped my feet into the panties. "Planning a mission is easier than figuring out how one of those works." Pausing, he handed me some fresh toilet paper and gave me a second to wipe and clean myself up. He gently lifted me from the toilet and finished pulling my underwear on.

"Let's get out of here," I said without thinking, and his entire frame melted, softening.

"What?" he asked, furrowing his brows, trying to hide the excitement that rolled hot off of his shoulders.

"Take me away from here, explain to me what's really going on, because I just have a really hard time believing the idea that you're simply a greedy bastard. Take me away from here so it's just the two of us. So I can process everything that just happened away from everyone else. With you, and only you," I restated, and Griffin reached around me, flushing the toilet before guiding me to the small porcelain sink above a set of brown cupboards.

"Your mom spent three days not knowing where you were or what was going and you just want to leave again?" he asked while I washed my hands.

"I need some peace, Griffin. And an explanation from you. But I don't have the energy to fight my mom about us moving right now. Plus, she's also not going to give up on what she saw just barely, and I'm exhausted. I hurt, I was kidnapped and tortured, a friend died in my arms, I killed someone, and I just need to feel calm and safe for a bit. Please," I begged him, word vomiting everything, as he gently handed me a few paper towels from the dispenser to my right. Once my hands were dry, he threw the mess in the garbage beneath the sink and turned to face me.

"Okay," he whispered, and I smiled, my heart finally calming for the first time since I'd woken up.

"Okay," I repeated, and he smiled too. His hands slowly gripped my waist and gently tugged me forward.

"You need to say something to your mom, though, so she doesn't worry," he whispered, dipping his head, and I nodded.

"I'll send her a text after we escape." I grinned, and he chuckled.

I took a deep breath, not ready to return, as my eyes locked onto his gaze. It had been so long since we'd had a moment to ourselves, some time alone, and here we were, locked away in this little bathroom.

All by ourselves.

Griffin's gaze flickered to my lips, and that was all the invitation needed. Gripping his shirt around his stomach, I pulled as hard as I could, and he crashed his mouth against mine. I didn't hesitate to part my lips, and he shoved his tongue down my throat.

Desperation and a neediness filled my body as I pressed deeper into his kiss. He tasted absolutely incredible as his tongue ran across mine. It hurt a little as I arched my back, but I barely noticed with my chest pressing against his entire body.

His heart was racing as one hand slid behind my neck and he intertwined his fingers in the base of my hair. Tilting my head back a little more, he quickly nipped at my lips and then dove in again. My breath hitched as I felt his excitement physically grow.

So, I shoved my hand into his pants and gripped his raging hard-on. Shocked, he broke the kiss and whimpered from my touch. My entire core heated up, and a throbbing ached between my legs until his fingers wrapped around my wrist, and he slowly pulled my hand from his waistband.

I stepped back from the kiss, confused. His eyes remained closed, his chest heaving before he slowly shook his head.

"Why not?" I whined, and he clenched his jaw.

"Because your mom and my mom are both sitting out in that room, waiting for us."

"It won't take very long," I continued, and he chuckled.

"No, it probably wouldn't," he muttered, and I grinned, trying to push my hand back toward his pants, but he shook his head again. "Stop, smart ass. Do you not remember what I said in my letter concerning the next time anything like this happens?"

I furrowed my brows for a moment and then tilted my head. "That's what this is really about," I mumbled, a little surprised, and he nodded.

"Jane. I made you a promise I intend to keep. The next time you and I become intimate won't be rash like last time." He let go of my wrist and brushed some hair away from my face. "I intend to love you the way you deserve."

I smiled, my cheeks turning a soft rosy pink. "Okay," I whispered in reply, and he leaned forward, kissing me on the forehead and then slid down to hover above my mouth.

"But don't think for one moment that I did not enjoy your hand in my pants." He placed a tender kiss against my lips. I nodded as he slowly pulled away. Taking a deep breath, I leaned forward, collapsing against his chest.

"I should probably write that text," I said, and he placed a kiss against the top of my head.

"What are you going to say?" he asked, and dug through his pocket. Pulling his hand out, he handed me my cell phone.

"How do you have this?" I gasped, unlocking it, and he chuckled.

"Noah gave it to me when he met me at the hospital. You'd left it on the lawn when they took you, and apparently they didn't find anything in it that they thought was valuable," he answered, and I pulled up my mom's contact. Quickly, I wrote out a message and showed it to Griffin.

"Mom, please don't be worried. After everything that happened, I needed some quiet to process it. A lot happened that Griffin understands in a way that no one else does. I'm safe and will come home when I'm ready. I love you. I will be okay. Ask Noah if you are worried." He read aloud and then handed it back.

"Sounds good to me."

"By the way, since when do you smoke?" I asked as he gripped my hips again and helped me meander to the door. Walking wasn't terribly hard; it was mostly the fact that at any point, if I twisted my back wrong or even bent too far, pain shot through me.

"I always have. But we were around kids and my family or the gym most of the time before I was deployed."

"That makes sense," I replied. Taking a deep breath, we shared one last glance before he turned the doorknob and we left the bathroom. Ready to escape.

Chapter 48

I bit my lip as we walked back into the room. Nancy was sitting on a chair by the window, next to my mom. Noah and Dayton were arm wrestling on the floor beside them, as the nurses were finishing up with a change of sheets on my bed.

Once I made it back to the mattress and sat down, Griffin walked to my left and leaned up against the wall. He dug through his pockets while one of the nurses walked around to the other side of my bed and opened a tube of ointment. He pulled a cigarette from his pocket and slipped it between his lips, leaving it unlit and hanging from his mouth. And I really liked the view as his piercing tawny eyes tracked me slowly across the room.

"You'll need to keep the skin soft and moisturized to make sure the elasticity remains. Otherwise you'll always feel uncomfortable," the nurse behind me explained, and she pulled apart my gown in the back. Slowly, she adjusted the bandages and applied the ointment. I watched as Griffin studied her movements carefully, and the other nurse began to slide the needles out of my arm.

"With how everything looks, and like the doctor said, you can go home. Here is the packet with post-op instructions, and don't forget the medications," the one behind me added when she finished up. She handed me the bottle of ointment, along with a stapled stack of papers and two pill bottles, and then walked back to the other side of the bed. She faced my mom. "You'll need to bring her back in to get those stitches and staples removed for her follow up appointment in about ten days."

My mom slowly rose from her seat and walked toward me, holding the bag of clothes that my underwear had come from. "Thank you," she said, smiling kindly, and then the nurses left.

Immediately, her gaze narrowed. "You are a grown woman, Jane. I can't believe the indecency displayed. That was very crude, just announcing something so personal in front of men."

"Mom," I muttered. Griffin rocked the cigarette to the other side of his mouth, his eyes tracking around the room, calculating.

"And what's your excuse about the guy between your legs when we walked in?" she hissed through her teeth.

"He was cleaning up the blood from my period so it didn't get on the floor," I stated, and Dayton snorted.

My mom glanced at him, confused. "What's so funny?" she asked, and he shrugged his shoulders.

"I just find it ironic that you're shocked by any of that. This is Miss B and Griffin we're talking about," Dayton said, and it was my turn to be shocked.

"What's that supposed to mean?" I asked, and he chuckled again.

Griffin grinned to himself. "Why are you like this?" he asked Dayton, who simply gave us a cheeky smile.

"You know them?" my mom asked, tossing a thumb toward Dayton, and I nodded.

"Dayton was in one of my classes, and his mom is the front office manager. Wait, how do you know them?"

She glanced between Nancy and me. "Book club," she answered. I could see the confusion in her eyes as she slowly began to pull out the clothes from the bag. "I brought the baggiest shirt in your room that I could find. Which was this hoodie." She placed a black sweatshirt into my lap, and I picked it up, smiling to myself as my eyes slid across the gym logo on the back. Griffin raised a subtle brow, remaining silent in the corner, recognizing it as well.

"Turn around, please, and close your eyes," I demanded. Everyone except for my mom was respectful of my wishes, facing the opposite direction as she helped me out of the gown. Once it was off, she slipped the massive hoodie on, drowning me in comfort and that ever faint smell of Griffin that still lingered.

Gently pulling me forward, she bent down and tugged out a short pair of biker shorts that weren't too high waisted. I slid off of the bed, standing up straight as she helped wiggle them on and then guided me into a pair of sandals.

"Mom," I quietly said. She stood up and looked at me. Tired. "You know I love you. Right?"

She nodded, her smile relaxing. "Of course. Though, we are going to have a discussion about that tattoo of yours and that ring around your neck."

"I'm safe now," I continued, and she let out a heavy sigh. "But I'm also really tired. I need some peace and time to process everything. I can't do that if you're constantly pressuring me about moving. Or upset and yelling because I'm making my own decisions." Her brows furrowed and she took a step back.

Taking a deep breath, I gave her a comforting smile. "This has nothing to do with you. This is for me, and *only* me," I said, subtly grabbing the medications, ointment and packet, and then looked at Griffin. "Now."

He shot off the wall, swooped me up in his arms, and took off out of the room.

I wrapped my hands and legs around his body, cradling as tightly as I could to his chest.

"JANE!" my mom yelled.

Footsteps crashed after us as Griffin rammed his finger into the elevator button. I buried my face into his neck, closing my eyes, and trusting that he had this. One arm supported me beneath my thighs as I heard the familiar ding of the elevator opening, and then the doors closed just in time.

Griffin's chest heaved as the floor lurched beneath him.

The moment it stopped, he was sprinting again. I could hear shouting and commotion chasing us out of the hospital as he ran faster than I could've on my own two legs while uninjured—and he was carrying me.

A blast of warm sunshine plastering into my cheek caused me to open my eyes.

I found Griffin smiling to himself as he ran across the parking lot and wove in and out through a whole bunch of vehicles. Rounding a corner, he stopped at his pickup truck and ripped open the backseat door.

"JANE BARLOW!" my mom's shrill voice pierced through the open air. Griffin glanced around and then chuckled to himself as he helped me slide inside.

"She's still at the entrance." He winked and then shut the door behind him. Rushing quickly around the front, he climbed inside and roared the vehicle to life. The tires were squealing across the pavement before she took another step. I quickly pressed send on my text message and then laid down on my left side.

"I hate that you put me in the backseat," I grumbled as Griffin drove.

He chuckled. "You can't sit up like normal, so it's the safest place for you. Besides, now you can rest."

I sighed. He was right. This was the most comfortable spot for me, and the safest. It sucked that I had to stare at the seats, but I was pretty tired. Getting some sleep sounded quite nice.

I yawned and tucked my arm under my head. "Where are we going anyway?"

"You'll see," he tenderly said as my eyes drooped. So calm. So peaceful. No one telling me what was happening next. No one to take me somewhere I didn't want to go. No one was mad at me or hurting me.

"By the way," he started. "I like that hoodie of yours."

"Yeah, it's pretty nice and comfortable," I responded.

"Where'd you get it? Because I've been trying to find mine for a while that looks *exactly* like that," he asked, and I giggled.

"I went to a cabin once with this guy that I really like. This was his, and it somehow accidentally ended up in my suitcase," I groggily answered.

"So, can I have it back?"

"Can I have my virginity back?"

His eyes snapped to the rearview mirror, nearly bugging out of his head. Sucking my lips between my teeth, I giggled. Again. And closed my eyes. "Besides, it fits me better and smells like you." I smiled to myself, imagining what his handsome face looked like at that moment.

I heard a faint chuckle. "I definitely like you better in it."

"I bet you'd like me better without it," I said without thinking, and heard him laugh again.

"You're damn right," he said, and I smiled.

"You weren't supposed to agree with me. That's a very lustful thing to say."

"Well, do you want me to lie instead?"

"In this situation, absolutely."

"The last time I did that, you got mad at me," he answered.

"That was different."

"Obviously, smart ass. I love you in that sweatshirt, and I'd love you without it. Better?"

I giggled, smiling to myself. Nobody had ever flirted with me like this. He was sweet and yet also had a very dirty mouth. I liked it a lot. "Much," I quietly replied. Silence drifted between us, but not the kind that felt awkward. It was comfortable. I was finally able to think for a moment. Somehow, we still had to deal with the entire situation of his stupid inheritance. I wanted a full explanation and the truth.

Then there was this new dilemma that we faced concerning the fact that my mom wanted us to move. I didn't want her to end up alone in Washington, but I also didn't want to move away from Griffin. Maybe I could somehow convince her to stay even though her first impression of Griffin wasn't the greatest. But this little town in Idaho had become home.

Griffin had become home.

No matter how hard I tried to ignore it, I was absolutely in love with him.

"Griffin?" I lazily asked.

"Hmmm?" he said, turning the radio on quietly.

"I think maybe we can date," I muttered, and he laughed.

"That's good to hear," he cheerfully replied before I finally fell into the most restful slumber I'd experienced in months.

Chapter 49

I stretched, yawned, and flinched at the tightness in my back. Slowly, my hands brushed against the silkiness of the sheets that I was laying on. Something warm was wrapped around the front of my body, steadily rising and falling. Soft and deep. I wiggled my way closer, the right side of my body sliding across the bedding.

Blinking, I cracked open my eyes a little confused. Griffin lay in front of me, shirtless. We were in a bed, and I was tucked up against his chest. White sheets were pulled up around his hips, one arm draped lazily over my waist. He snored softly, and I smiled to myself.

I could ask him how I got in here later. Or how I was in a mostly fresh pad. Or where we were. Right now, I felt home. Safe. I didn't want to lose that feeling, so I inhaled deeply and then closed my eyes, listening to the calm rhythm of his breathing. Sunlight gently brushed against his ivory skin, tanned from a lot of time spent outside.

Waiting was easy. I pretended to be asleep, not wanting to disturb the absolute perfection of this moment. Eventually, I felt him stir a little, and then his arm slid quietly off of my waist. The warmth of his body left the bed, and I barely heard his feet whisper across the floor. A door clicked shut and, within another moment, the shower turned on.

Opening my eyes, I looked around the room. It was fresh and clean, and smelled as such. A fake bamboo design etched along the flooring, light brown matching the cream shade of the walls. I was facing the bathroom door that sat beside the alcove of the entrance. There was a low table off to the side with an aloe plant sitting on it. Beside that was a TV mounted above a nice rattan dresser.

Grunting, I managed to briefly look behind me. A small sofa sat in the corner beside large, white curtains hanging over sliding glass doors. There was an end table on my side of the bed with a hanging lamp above it, matching the one on Griffin's side. We were in a hotel, I assumed.

I sighed, burying my face into the pillow, and waited for Griffin to finish. Eventually the shower turned off, but he didn't come out of the bathroom, and I was getting antsy. I wanted out of this bed.

Slowly, I managed to slide myself backwards toward the edge of the bed. My feet dangled off the edge, and I dipped them to the floor before using my arms to push my body upright. It was uncomfortable but not unbearable.

Padding quietly across the floor, I tugged the curtains open and stared in shock at the scenery. How long was I asleep for?

WHAT I SHOULD HAVE SAID

Unlocking the glass door, I slid it open and stepped out onto the beautiful deck overlooking the ocean. Waves crashed against the sandy shores, people hanging out along the beach or in the water itself.

Taking careful, steady steps, I walked toward the railing and leaned up against it, smelling the salty air. It filled my lungs, and I closed my eyes, letting my skin soak in the moisture. I should be scared not knowing where I was, but I felt nothing except freedom and peace.

"Good morning, smart ass," Griffin's voice drawled behind me. I opened my eyes, happy, and turned around to face him.

"Where are we?" I asked and blinked, a little shocked. He'd shaved his face, leaving only a hint of stubble. Long enough to not be scratchy, but short enough I could now see his jawline. He left his hair tousled just right, an effortlessly messy look.

He winked, noticing my surprise and walked toward me. "California."

"I was asleep that long?" I gasped, and he chuckled, pulling me gently against his body.

"You were tired, smart ass," he whispered, kissing my head. I wrapped my arms around his torso, fisting his fresh gray T-shirt. He had on a pair of shorts that showed off his muscular legs and the tattoo on his thigh. I smiled against his chest as he made sure to not touch my back too roughly.

"So, what now?" I asked, and he chuckled.

"We rest. I turned our phones off completely, and we can stay for as long as you want. We don't have to do anything or we can do whatever you want. Whatever you need," he answered, and I breathed out, feeling my entire body collapse into his.

Griffin helped me into the cutest backless jumpsuit I'd ever owned. Pastel blue, lightweight fabric, and it had a deep V-neck which also snatched in my waist nicely. He'd ordered a whole bunch of outfits that were backless simply to make sure I was comfortable, and we'd spent the past nine days doing absolutely nothing.

Which was everything.

We talked, more than I'd ever talked to him or anyone before. Taking walks hand-in-hand along the beach and eating delicious food at the pier.

His fingers slid along the nape of my neck as he buttoned the back of my dress. His lips pressed against my bare skin as I held my hair out of his way. I giggled and closed my eyes. Things seemed too perfect, too absolutely like I wanted them to be. Probably because we hadn't broached the topic of his inheritance or the weighted ring dangling against my chest.

"You know," Griffin started. "There's one thing about this that I've *really* been enjoying."

"What's that?" I asked, letting the hair fall along my shoulders and back.

"The fact that you haven't worn a bra this entire time," he replied, and I turned around as quickly as I could. He was grinning from ear to ear as I shook my head.

"Except you've not once tried to grab my boobs." I wiggled my brows as his mouth fell open.

"I've been trying to be respectful since you were injured," he muttered in defeat.

"Then how have you been enjoying it?"

"Because it's the simple fact that I know you're not wearing one and they still look like that." His eyes greedily raked across my breasts. I shook my head but smiled.

We eventually made our way down to the beach, finding a small spot to sit down and watch the waves together. He stretched out behind me, carefully supporting my body without putting too much pressure against my back, which was healing quite nicely and didn't bother me much anymore—other than the sutures sometimes caught on things and pulled at the skin.

A family splashed in the water, and I watched as the mom laughed, picking up her littlest while the dad tackled the older kid. They giggled and hollered, reminding me of my own brother and parents.

"Do you want kids?" I quietly asked.

Griffin leaned forward and placed one hand on his leg beside my body. The other one trailed along my arm. "Yeah. I've always wanted a few since I didn't really get a sibling," he answered, his eyes gently tracking the family. I smiled and glanced at his face over my shoulder.

"How many is a few?" I asked, and he lifted his brows, thinking for a moment.

"Six," he answered, and my mouth fell open in shock.

"Four sounds better," I replied, and he chuckled, placing his chin against my shoulder.

"With you?"

"If you still want six, you'll have to find someone else because there is no way I want to be pregnant six times. Four pregnancies are still pushing it," I replied.

"Then four is the perfect amount 'cause I don't want to have kids with anyone else." He placed a kiss against my neck, and I closed my eyes. All these plans for a future I hadn't thought about in so long. A future that was beginning to sound so nice.

"I got an appointment scheduled at a hospital here for you to have your stitches and staples removed tomorrow. I got your doctor to send over your history so we didn't have to return home," Griffin said, interrupting my peaceful moment I'd fallen into. Though that was good news as well.

"When do you want to go home?" I asked, and he shook his head.

"Not right now."

"That's not really an answer."

"I like this right now. Slow, simple. Just you and me," he quietly mumbled against my neck again, and I bumped my head lightly against his.

"But it can't last forever," I whispered, and he sighed.

"I know."

Slowly, he pulled away from my back and then stood up, brushing the sand from his shorts and offered me a hand. Tenderly, he helped me to my feet and then took it upon himself to brush the grains from my bottom. I giggled, then he interlocked his fingers in mine, and we slowly began walking back to the sidewalk running between the beach and our hotel.

"Griffin?" I hesitantly began.

"Hmm?" He glanced my way and lifted a brow.

"What are you waiting for?" I asked.

"Waiting for? Huh?"

"You said the next time we are intimate, it will be different. Well, we've had nine days of being absolutely alone, and you haven't even attempted to get me in bed."

He stopped walking, holding me steady as I turned to face him. Griffin stared over my shoulder, lost in his head for a moment. Then he let a small smile creep across his face. "It has been different, baby girl. Why does being intimate have to mean getting naked and having sex?"

I blinked, a little confused. "Because that's what you constantly tease me about."

His gaze slid back to my eyes. "True. And it's not that I don't think about it or haven't wanted to. I guess I'm just waiting for the right moment where I can enjoy every inch of your body without fear that I might hurt you."

"Oh," I muttered, embarrassed for asking—because that made sense—and looked at my feet.

Griffin's fingers gently pressed beneath my chin, lifting my eyes back to his. "Don't do that," he said.

"Do what?" I mumbled.

"That. Where you become embarrassed. You're Jane Barlow. The badass bitch who was unafraid to ask me to wipe blood from her legs. The girl who wasn't afraid to put me in my place when I overreacted to the thought she was dating her brother. The girl who sat on my face at the gym yet still approached me after. The same girl who wasn't afraid to have an entire make-out session in a grocery store with a practical stranger to avoid having a conversation with a stalker." He grinned as my lips slowly lifted at the corners.

"And tomorrow, when the doctor gives us an update on how you're healing, I'll know just how much longer I have to wait before I get to see my girlfriend completely naked," he added, and I stepped into his embrace.

"You know, why is it the inexperienced one who is aware there are more positions than the one that puts me on my back?" I asked against his chest, and he burst out laughing.

"I don't want to be limited in my options," he replied and kissed me on my forehead.

"Then take me to get some food because it's either you satisfy me in bed or satisfy my hunger, boy," I whined, and pulled away. Narrowing my gaze, I glared at him. Griffin shook his head, smiling.

"Man, I love you." He took a deep breath and grabbed my hand, resuming our walk.

"I love you, too," I casually said, and Griffin's eyes immediately widened. His fingers tightened around my hand, and I could feel the sweat pooling on his palm. I'd never said it out loud to him before, and I saw him fighting his urge to make this a big deal.

Bumping my shoulder against his arm, I smiled. "You can freak out. It's okay," I quietly said, and he immediately let go of my hand. Placing his palms against his own face, he spun in a circle and muffled a shout of joy. My smile widened as I watched him do a couple fist pumps in the air and have a mini moment of celebration.

Then he took a deep breath and immediately resumed his typically calm demeanor. But the grin on his face didn't disappear as we meandered farther along the beach.

Chapter 50

Griffin sat on the deck as I walked out with two cups of coffee. Mornings here were nice, and I wondered if this would be what it was like when we lived together. This morning in particular was the best. We'd been to the doctor's office, my sutures were removed, and I'd received an all clear. I offered him a cup and sat down in the patio chair beside him, the sun barely breaking the horizon. It was bright orange this morning with a faint hint of pink. As pretty as this was, I was beginning to miss the mountains.

Turning sideways I looked at Griffin. He sipped the coffee, leaning back in his chair, shirtless. Wanting to be close to him, I stood up from mine and padded over. Setting my cup on the small table between the two chairs, I plopped down in his lap and curled up against his chest. He kissed the top of my head and ran a hand up and down my arm.

I had taken to wearing one of his big T-shirts at night since they drowned me and didn't rub my back. He'd taken a liking to that apparently, and I'd noticed over the past ten days as several more mysteriously showed up in the suitcase he'd bought me. Once we'd returned to the hotel, I jumped right back into what had become my unofficial PJs.

"Mornings are becoming my favorite," I casually said.

"Mine too," he nonchalantly replied, taking another sip of coffee. Mindlessly, I began to run my fingers across his well-muscled abdomen, tracing across each defined mountain and then up to his chest. My eyes lazily tracked across his pecs, following my fingers that were outlining the ink tattooed upon his skin. Slowly, I meandered over to the piece that trailed down his ribcage.

"If you don't stop that, I might not be in control of my actions for much longer," he suddenly growled, and I paused, only then realizing that my fingers had dipped lower. Low enough that they were sliding across the waistband of his shorts.

"I need to know," I whispered, letting them linger.

"Need to know what?" he asked, and I took a small, shaky breath in.

"What it feels like to be loved by you," I answered, and Griffin's chest rose sharply. He didn't move, nor did I, not for a moment as I knew he wrestled with himself.

"I made you a promise, baby girl," he hesitantly said.

"My sutures are gone. So keep it."

His eyes slid to my hopeful gaze. Waiting another half a second before giving me a tender smile and then sitting up. Gently, he lifted me from the chair. I wrapped my legs around his waist as he easily carried me into the room and sat me down on the bed.

I waited a little longer as he simply looked at me, the breeze dancing across the room. Slowly, he descended and placed a kiss against my lips. Gentle and calm. His arm snaked around my waist as he crawled on top of me, almost too gentle. Too calm.

"Griffin," I whispered as his mouth trailed down my neck and across my collarbone, one hand traveling down my side to push my shirt up.

"Hmmm?" His lips vibrated against my skin, his calloused fingers touching way too softly.

"I know you. I know you're trying to love me the way you think I want to be loved, but I want you to love me the way *you* want to."

He paused everything, his shirt just below my breasts, and lifted his face to meet my gaze. "What are you saying, smart ass?"

"Stop being so polite. I like the aggressive side of you. Every time you've kissed me, and I mean really kissed me, it's never been this...nice. I'm not fragile, you know," I breathlessly explained, my heart pounding in my chest. A single brow of his twitched, and he tipped his head.

"Shut the fuck up, and let me worship you," he growled and rammed his lips against mine. Hot and wet, no longer quite as hesitant as before.

There it was.

I knew this was going to be worth every ounce of frustrating, pent up patience. And I closed my eyes, my world turning black as every color imaginable began dancing beneath the feel of his body against mine.

Every touch, every kiss of his lips. Every brush of his breath across each exposed inch of skin felt breathtaking as I became naked within a matter of seconds.

He was gentle and kind, sort of. Mostly very controlling in every way I wanted. Needed. Each word that slipped from my lips, each sound that escaped my tongue begging for him to not stop, increased his hungry need for more. For the more that I'd been craving for far too long.

I never thought a moan, his moaning, could elicit such a primal response from me as he slowly did exactly as he said he would. Not a single second was wasted or taken for granted. He took his time, as if memorizing every curve, every bump, every flaw and perfection across my skin. His fingers dug into my hips, tightening his demanding hold on me, commanding more from me. The smell of him, the feel of his calloused fingers and hardened frame would be forever imprinted upon my soul.

Each new touch shared drew us closer and closer to each other. It wasn't lustful or selfish, but it wasn't entirely selfless either. As our sweat intermingled, skin on skin with his mouth on some place very intimate, I'd never felt so close to someone as I felt to him. And I wanted it to be him. I couldn't be more grateful it was him that took me to that almost painful place of euphoric bliss.

He raised himself up and pushed hair away from my face, flipping us around. I gazed down at him, and his hunter eyes darkened, wrapping a hand around my throat and pulling me into his kiss once more. I didn't care where his lips had just been. It was as if he wanted me to have a taste of the one thing he'd been fantasizing about for far too long. And my world became his in that moment as my fingers threaded through his hair. Every vulnerability laid out to see. His world became mine, nothing separating us as I opened my legs. Not a single thread of fabric was in the way as he fulfilled his promise and took me as gently and roughly as before.

Fingertips traced tenderly down my side, digging into my skin. Lips pressed against my lips as I gasped, feeling lightheaded and excited. A rush of painful bliss coursed hot through my body as he whimpered, growing toward our shared peaks of arousal. That sound became burned into my memory, and I found that release he'd been edging me toward for a second time.

His quickly followed, his fingers digging into my hips as he collapsed beneath me, moaning, still caught in the high. I didn't want it to go away. I didn't want to lose this moment that would forever be only ours, but I had no choice, and as he breathed hard, panting with me, it slowly slipped away.

After a moment, I opened my eyes not really looking at anything, floating in a daze. He laid me against his chest that was rising and falling quickly, the hair tickling my ear, but I relished in the closeness. He kept his eyelids closed, his expression so peaceful as he faced the ceiling fan that was whirring above. The curtains danced against the wind that gently tossed through the cracked glass door.

He had kept his promise.

It had been different than last time and in all the right ways. Soul binding. My heart was his forever and his was mine. Something he knew as a smile slowly crept across his lips. Not one of satisfaction like he'd just won a trophy, but one that showed absolute joy.

Eventually, Griffin shuddered and then opened his eyes. He glanced toward me and gently kissed my forehead. "You should go pee," he said, and I looked at him, taken aback.

"That's what you want to say?" I asked, and he chuckled, pecking my lips really quickly.

"I don't want you to get an infection. If you do, you won't be so eager for round two." He grinned, and I rolled my eyes.

"Always the smooth talker," I teased, and he chuckled.

"Smart ass." He spanked my bottom lightly.

I awkwardly rolled off of him, but he stopped me and grabbed my face. Pulling me forward, he pressed his lips against my mouth once more. Lingering.

"I am very much in love with you," he whispered against my mouth, and then suddenly jolted out of bed.

"You're not going to help me?" I whined as he danced away. He rolled his eyes but returned and then helped me waddle into the bathroom. We took care of business, then found ourselves back in the bed. I draped a leg over his side while he ran a hand up and down my back, careful to avoid any of the still tender skin.

"We should go back," I finally said, and Griffin inhaled deeply.

"Yeah," he quietly answered. I think both of us had been thinking about it for a bit now. Ten days was quite some time to be completely checked out of reality.

"After we go into town one more time."

Griffin lifted his head slightly and furrowed his brows. "Why?"

"Because I..." *I want to stay for as long as possible.* "I want to buy something to take back for my mom and Noah."

He chuckled and gently sat up. "I'm hungry, and you should probably eat something before we go home anyway."

"So, that's a yes?" I asked, crawling toward him. His eyes flickered down my naked body, and he shook his head with a grin.

"Fine," he answered, and I did a little happy dance. "Now, get up," he said, swinging his legs over the edge of the mattress and standing up. I quickly crawled after him, jumped off the bed and grabbed his hand.

"What?" he asked, lightheartedly, but also annoyed I'd stopped him. I wiggled my brows and then pressed his hand against my bare breast. He gave me a boyish grin and then grabbed both, squeezing.

"Titties!" he exclaimed with glee as a small raucous started outside of our room's door. I couldn't quite understand the words being said, but it piqued even Griffin's attention. We froze, locked in place and glanced toward the entranceway, simply watching.

Then something disengaged, and a beep sounded before the door came crashing open.

"THANK YOU!" my mom's shrill voice sounded, and she stumbled in the room. Along with Nancy and Noah, plus two hotel security guards. "How dare you kidn—" she began as everyone's eyes connected to the scene that was *exactly* what it looked like.

Nobody moved.

Except for Griffin. He immediately removed his hands from my boobs and snatched the sheet that had been shoved to the end of the bed. He draped it over my body before anyone really had a chance to see me.

Griffin, on the other hand...

My mom's eyes moved down to everything that he was blessed with. I watched the anger shift in her face to awe as Noah's mouth fell open.

"Damn," Noah bluntly stated as Griffin glanced around the room and quickly grabbed a pillow to cover himself with.

The two hotel security guards glanced between each other, confused and embarrassed. They both opened and closed their mouths, unsure of how to proceed. Nancy shook her head but said nothing.

Griffin awkwardly shuffled to the side to make sure he was standing in front of me. Protecting me even more, regardless of his own dignity, and then I watched his entire back tense up. His muscles danced as anger seeped off of his skin.

"What the fuck do you think you're doing?" he snarled, and the two hotel guards visibly took a step back. Even my mom flinched. Noah grinned wider and leaned against the doorframe.

"Told you she was fine," he muttered, wiggling his brows, and my mom waved a hand at him. My cheeks burned hot.

"Melissa, we really didn't need to come," Nancy interjected.

"Exactly. So leave," Griffin growled.

"You took my daughter away, and this is what I find?" My mom glared at him, but he didn't budge.

"Tell me, Mrs. Barlow. Exactly what is it that you found? A happy daughter? Who's safe?" he began.

"A daughter who was obviously, clearly, um…pressured into…uh…" my mom mumbled and then glanced at Noah, who was still grinning.

"I'm assuming you don't need us?" one of the guards interjected, and Griffin shook his head.

"Sorry, sir. Ma'am." He nodded at Griffin and me. "We were told that they accidentally left the key in the room and there was a baby locked in here," he muttered as the two of them slowly backed out of the room and disappeared.

Griffin returned his intense gaze toward my mom despite the fact that he was standing butt naked with nothing but a pillow to cover him. "You were saying? Because escaping for a while was her idea, which she texted to you. And she completely consented to everything that happened here," Griffin firmly stated.

My mom's cheeks turned red. "I would've consented, too," she mindlessly muttered, and then slapped a hand over her mouth.

I snorted and then coughed as Noah nearly keeled over from the door frame. "What'd you just say?" Noah asked.

"Nothing," my mom muttered, her eyes continually flickering down to the pillow and then back up to Griffin's face. Eventually her gaze slipped around his figure and met mine.

"I understand you being concerned, but did you not get my text? Or talk to Noah at all?" I asked, and she sighed. "How'd you find us anyway?"

"Your doctor's appointment. I went to the hospital back home looking for you, and he told me that your records had been transferred here," my mom sheepishly answered.

"Speaking of the doctor's appointment, since that's already happened and it's nearing one in the afternoon, she needs food, so do y'all mind? I'd like to put on pants, at least, before we finish this very well-timed conversation." Griffin stared aggressively toward them. Noah grabbed my mom's arm and gently tugged her out into the hallway. Nancy mouthed "sorry" before following them out, and the door clicked shut.

"You're kidding me right?" I muttered, as Griffin dropped the pillow and plopped flat on his back on the bed.

"I mean, at least it was after everything," he replied with a stiff chuckle.

"You were literally grabbing my boobs, Griffin. And this time, it was exactly what it looked like." I closed my eyes as his chuckle relaxed.

"It was totally what it looked like," he mumbled, his chuckle turning into a laugh, and I couldn't help but join in.

"Well, if she had any doubt before, it's been entirely confirmed," I said between coughs.

"So, we can fuck in your bed now too?" Griffin questioned, and I slapped his thigh.

"Inappropriate."

"My bad. I mean make love?"

"Just because you call it something different doesn't make the answer different."

"Which is a yes because she totally knows."

"You're too loud for that to ever be a comfortable possibility." I grinned, and he sat up.

"I'm pretty sure that was you." He kissed my cheek before I pushed him off of the bed.

"Go put your pants on before we get into any more trouble," I replied, and followed him to get dressed as well. Another cute, white backless dress was in store for today.

Chapter 51

It was silent as we stared awkwardly between one another. The booth at this restaurant felt all too small. Griffin's left hand snaked to my leg, squeezing it lightly to try and calm me down. My mom refused to make eye contact with Griffin, sitting across from me all while Noah grinned like an idiot to my left on the rounded portion of the booth. Nancy sipped on some water straight across from Griffin, the chatter and music dancing around us.

Griffin leaned over and whispered in my ear, "Can I get drunk?" he asked, and I shook my head.

"No," I muttered.

"But it's after your appointment. All your stitches and staples are gone, so I don't have to be as cautious. Plus, I would really like to forget the fact that my girlfriend's mom has seen my cock."

"Are you ashamed of it?" I asked, and he pursed his lips.

"Obviously not. It's just weird."

"Well, it's not like your junk has been inside my mother, so it's not that weird."

"When you say it like that, it is."

"So, care to share with the rest of the group what you're saying?" Noah butted in, grinning wickedly.

"Shut your mouth, ass face," I quickly said, and he wiggled his brows.

"You're talking about sweaty hottie's dick aren't you?" Noah said, and my mom literally slapped Noah. Then she shrieked in fright and patted his cheek, apologizing over and over again. Griffin closed his eyes to keep his cool as Nancy finally set down her water.

Griffin leaned toward me. "Sweaty hottie?" he whispered in my ear. I shook my head, silently telling him not right now.

Noah wiggled his brows and grinned again. Using his fingers, he formed a large circle. "Thick dick. Impressive dick." Then he slid his hands apart from each other. "Long dick. Enormous dick," he said just as the waitress walked over and plunked some chips aggressively in the middle of the table.

"Sorry to burst your bubble," she started, tucking some short, black hair behind her ear. "But usually men are very incorrect when describing their own junk." She grinned maliciously as Nancy and my mom both went bright red.

Noah simply chuckled and leaned back, stretching. "Oh, I wasn't talking about my own." He lifted a single brow directly at Griffin. The waitress stood up, looking between my brother and the man sitting next to me. Griffin's face was completely blank, his eyes watching the front door across from us. But I could see the corners of his mouth creep up in a subtle smile.

Her face paled as she made the connection, and her eyes widened.

"Um, okay. Uh, your food will be out soon," she quickly stammered and then rapidly disappeared. Noah snorted as Griffin closed his eyes but didn't say anything.

Nancy sighed. "Melissa. Your daughter and my son have been together for months, like eight months I believe, so I think it's time to move past things," she said, changing the subject, and my mom whipped her head to Nancy.

"I'm sorry, what?" she gasped.

"Yeah. He brought her to the cabin during our family reunion, where they announced the relationship and engagement."

Griffin clenched his jaw as Noah lifted an accusing brow.

I glared at him, telling him silently to not say a word.

Without words, he asked how much I would pay him.

Psychically, I simply made sure he knew that Griffin could kill him and never be caught.

"They were faking it," Noah blurted out defiantly, and I groaned as Griffin shot a death glare toward Noah. Who actually flinched.

"What?" Nancy and my mom both said at the same time. It was time to come clean; there was no backing out of this now.

We told them everything, from the antique store, to Sam. To the deal we made, to the fake engagement, and finally finishing with today. With this moment. Somewhere along the way, I learned that it was the video posted online that triggered the cartel's movement to capture me, and Griffin had been trying to shift some things around about his inheritance.

"Mom, I need you to trust me. I get that when Brent fell sick, you burned through your retirement savings, and refused any financial help from me, choosing to go back to work instead," Griffin said, as Nancy slowly shook her head in denial. And my ear pricked, intrigued. *What did any of that have to do with the inheritance?* "I get that when I was born, Grandma refused to give you your inheritance because you were a teen. I know she wasn't happy with what happened, so her way of teaching you a lesson was to hold me to something when I became an adult and then give it to me instead. But it's rightfully—"

"Hold on," my mom said, interrupting. "So you two don't have feelings for each other, but have now slept together? More than once? And Griffin traveled across the world to save you, but all of this is fake for some inheritance contract?"

I shook my head, annoyed that she cut off my boyfriend. "Not exactly. The engagement was fake at first, but the relationship is not fake now."

"The feelings were always real, but the boyfriend/girlfriend/engagement status was fake at the beginning," Griffin explained, tipping his head sideways, a little confused himself.

"If Cara learns of that, regardless of the fact that you two are actually together now, she will use that to get to the money," Nancy said in warning.

Griffin sighed. "Which is why I've been working with Grandpa for a while now."

"Griffin, what is going on? Why are you so willing to suddenly retire? Why did you convince Jane to be your fake girlfriend, fiancée or whatever in the first place? Why do you care about the inheritance now? None of that is like you," Nancy hissed, leaning forward across the table. Griffin squeezed my thigh a little tighter.

"Because it's all for you! All of it, Mom! This money isn't *my* inheritance, but yours. I made an agreement with Grandpa that I would be willing to run the company. I'd get married before the end of the year without complaint if *all* of the money goes to you and Dayton. I don't get a dime of it; I've never wanted it. I just needed time to get Grandpa's assurance that he would convince Grandma to pay it out to you," he paused, and everything clicked in my head. The desperation, the exchanged looks between his grandma and him, the surprise from his grandpa when I actually showed up to the dinner. All along, his grandpa knew that this was in the works, what he didn't know was that our relationship became real for Griffin.

And I had no idea until now that all along, he had never used me for personal gain.

His shoulders slumped forward. "I got a text thirty minutes ago, saying that I need to get home to sign the revised documents because Grandma finally agreed."

"But Griff, honey, you could still lose it all. If Cara can stop you before you sign those documents, convince Grandma of any doubt, you'll lose it all," she whispered, and Griffin slowly shook his head.

"I won't let that happen. Mom, you'll be able to retire and solely take care of Brent. Dayton will be set for life. Everything will be worth it."

"But I know you don't want to run the family company. You never have."

"I'll figure that out too. Let me do this for you."

"I just want you to be happy, son," she pleaded. Griffin glanced at me and gave me a tight lipped smile.

"I am. I don't think I've ever been happier, because of Jane. I know it's crazy, I know it sounds irrational because of how it all started, but I need you to understand that for me, it was never fake. That the moment she waltzed into my life, I knew that I could do this. That I could see myself married. Which meant you would be able to take care of Brent at home, for however long he has left."

She sighed and closed her eyes, reaching across the table. Griffin grabbed his mom's hand with his free one and squeezed. They watched each other silently, lost in a world that only a mother and son could share.

My gaze slid to my own mom who was watching a little confused. Eventually her eyes flickered to mine, her shoulders softly falling.

I gave her a tight-lipped smile and lifted both of my hands onto the table. Clasping them together, I leaned a little forward. "I think you know why I don't want to leave Idaho now," I quietly said, and she slowly nodded.

"All for some guy," she grumbled.

"Mom, it's not—"

"You have your best friend and a job waiting for you back in Washington. Is he really worth it?" she cut me off.

"Yes, Mom. He is. I can call Susie or go visit, and I'll figure something out job-wise," I bluntly stated.

"I get that I'm not your father, but why won't you listen to me? You're going to give your life up for a guy?" She waved a hand up and down at Griffin. "For him?"

"I'm not giving up my life, Mom. Why can't you see that?" I couldn't believe what she was saying as Griffin's hand began sliding up and down my leg, offering me support and comfort despite being engaged in his own conversation.

"You have nothing here *but* him," my mom said, his hand suddenly drifting a little higher than expected. I kept my focus on the conversation at hand.

"He's enough. Don't you see that?" I sighed and then clenched my jaw as Griffin's hand slipped under my dress. I shot him a sideways glance, but he didn't even look at me, still engaged in a conversation with his mom.

"He has done nothing but take care of her, Mom," Noah hesitantly added. "Even if things were fake for a while."

She scoffed as Griffin's fingertips reached the crease between my hip and thigh. He slid them back away, and I exhaled lightly.

"I can't believe you've been sleeping with him despite it being fake," my mom said.

"We've only had sex twice, so I don't know if that counts as consistently sleeping together," I muttered, slowly becoming distracted as Griffin's hand reached that crease again. Except this time it crept a little higher.

"Twice? That's it?" Noah gasped, and I rolled my eyes. "And you knew what he was packing?"

"Noah," I hissed through my teeth as Griffin subtly lifted the edge of my panties and then immediately paused.

My mom sighed once more and took a swig of water. "You're not going to change your mind, are you?"

I shook my head as Griffin's fingers shot away from me, landing in his lap like he'd just touched a hot coal. I wasn't sure what to do, dripping from the idea that he had been touching me rather intimately but also a little confused that he had removed his hand so quickly as if I'd been something dirty to feel.

Though, we were in the middle of a restaurant and with family.

"I don't want to move, either, Mom," Noah interjected, and she waved her hand.

"Thank you, Noah. But I'm still trying to process that my daughter is willing to change her entire life for one guy," she grunted, and Griffin stretched his fingers as if to shake off the lingering ghost of my skin beneath his palm.

Turning to me with an innocent look, Noah asked, "Do *you* want to move, Jane?" I could only shake my head as I clenched my jaw, watching Griffin through my periphery as he balled his hand into a fist. My heart felt like it was going to pound out of my ears as my skin prickled with goosebumps, catching sight of him subtly shifting his legs a little wider.

"I'm going to be a dad," Noah suddenly blurted out. My mom and I both looked at him. Shocked. I slapped both hands over my mouth, my attention torn away at the revelation of such unexpected, jolting news.

"What?" my mom gasped.

"I figured since everyone is airing out all their secrets, I'd share mine as well." Noah gave us an awkward smile.

"You got Jada pregnant?" I breathlessly exclaimed, bewildered to say the least.

"Jada? You couldn't find a girl a little more different than Jane?" My mom glared at Noah.

"Her name may be similar, but she's nothing like Jane, Mom." Noah said. I inhaled sharply, covering a snort as Griffin tugged at his jeans, trying to stretch the fabric away from his crotch.

Both my mom and Noah looked at me, so I quickly opened my mouth and spoke through the rising humor bubbling in my throat at the sight of Griffin's fidgeting. "He's right, Mom. She's got the most beautiful, curly, black hair and dewy skin. Dark as can be."

My voice cracked, a laugh begging to be released as Griffin sank a bit deeper into the booth, and juggled one knee anxiously.

My mom furrowed her brows and looked at Noah. "With how active you are, I thought you'd at least be smart enough to use a condom," she muttered.

"I did. It broke," Noah grumbled in response. I sat as still as possible; any remnants of me being confused as to why he pulled his hand away so quickly were long gone at the realization as to what was causing him to now shift so uncomfortably.

"I'm going to be an aunt before I'm a mom." I blinked, letting things sink in.

"What are you going to do?" my mom asked as Griffin lifted his hand from his lap. He reached forward, grabbing a chip while his leg still bounced wildly.

Shoving the salty snack into his mouth, he chewed and leaned back in the booth, tossing an arm across the back of my shoulders. And then almost as quickly as he rested it against the plastic booth, he slipped it away and sat forward. Leaning against an elbow, he snatched up another chip.

"She's keeping it. So, obviously I'm going to take care of the baby. And Jada. I really care about her, Mom," Noah said, narrowing his gaze suspiciously at me and Griffin.

My mom sighed. "Such a strange turn of events. My son is having a baby, and my daughter finally opened up her heart again."

Griffin swung an arm around my shoulders again. Removing himself from the conversation with his mom that he'd been engaged in this entire time, he turned toward me and said, "I need to take a piss. I'll be back." He kissed my forehead and then scooted out of the booth.

My eyes tracked him toward the back of the restaurant, past the light browns and reds. Past the fun surf design and aesthetic of the bar in the center of the room. Then he disappeared inside an alcove.

My mom and Noah slipped into a conversation between each other as I returned my gaze to the table. Nancy happily munched on some chips, and then inserted herself in the conversation.

She helped get my mom a little excited about the baby. They even chuckled a few times and made some comments about the cute baby clothes that my mom would buy.

I didn't say anything, waiting for Griffin to return, wondering how my mom actually felt about him, because it seemed she still didn't like him. Noah had simply diverted her attention.

Which I was a bit grateful for, but it left my stomach turning. Glancing over my shoulder, I watched for Griffin, who still hadn't returned.

"I'm going to go check on Griffin," I blurted out and slid across the red plastic covering the booth seat. Nobody even acknowledged me as I stood up and walked toward the back of the restaurant.

Chapter 52

The alcove was a little dark, two separate bathrooms, though they were both individual use and for either gender. One was wide open, so I assumed the locked door was the one Griffin was in.

"Griffin?" I asked, knocking on the door. Silence was my answer, and then the lock disengaged. Turning the silver handle, I cracked open the door, and a hand clamped around my arm. It snatched me quickly into the bathroom. I yelped, startled as Griffin locked the door behind me.

"What's taking you so—" I started, and then my eyes connected with Griffin's unzipped pants and his very erect dick.

"I have been waiting for it to go down so I can finally pee, and nothing's working," he muttered, annoyed and frustrated. I clamped a hand over my mouth, giggling—evidence to what I'd known had been causing all the fuss back at the booth, now stared back at me.

"It's not funny," he grunted again, leaning his back against the cold bathroom wall and closing his eyes. "I haven't touched it either."

"Did you take something, old man?" I hesitantly asked between giggles.

"It functions just fine on its own, smart ass. This is your fault." He gestured to the problem but didn't move.

"My fault? How is it my fault?" I asked, shocked.

He squeezed his eyes shut even tighter. "Because you are the only thing on my mind. And you clothed makes me hard. So, you see my dilemma." Griffin opened his eyes and stared accusingly at me.

"Have you always been this horny, or is this a new thing?" I questioned, taking a deep breath as my heart began to race. I made a decision to do something about his issue, something I'd never done before, and I was a little nervous.

"I'm a dude and have a hot girlfriend. I've always been this way. I can just voice it now," he grunted as I walked toward the paper towel dispenser to my left. Grabbing two, I turned to my right and tapped back toward Griffin, who eyed me suspiciously.

"I get it. You're not filtering your thoughts anymore." I looked down at his feet and placed the paper towels side by side on the dark brown tile.

"It's such a relief, too," he replied, and then furrowed his brows as I knelt down on them, making his cock eye level. "What the hell are you doing?"

"You said it's my fault, so let me fix it," I replied, took a deep breath, leaned forward, and ran my tongue over the tip. His eyes went wide, and then he let out that small whimper I loved.

"This won't take long," he moaned as I stuck it into my mouth.

WHAT I SHOULD HAVE SAID

He gripped my hair as I did everything possible to not gag on his size. Hot, thick, liquid shot against the back of my throat. I pulled away and swallowed, my skin feeling hot and warm from such an act I'd never willingly performed for anyone before—until now.

Griffin stood there, stunned for a moment as I rose from the floor. Grabbing the paper towels, I casually walked toward the garbage can and tossed them.

"I'm not sure if you heard, but Noah got his girl pregnant," I said to break the silence, attempting to not cough and choke on the remaining liquid that seemed to stick to the back of my throat.

Griffin still stared at me for another few seconds before slowly nodding. "Well, shit," he muttered, only halfway aware of what I said.

"Okay, I believe your problem is solved, so I'll head back out." I pushed a few stray strands of hair behind my ear as he slowly nodded, stuck in a daze. My cheeks flamed red as I turned around and quickly dashed out of the bathroom.

Walking as rapidly as I could without drawing attention, I rushed to the bar in the center of the room and slid onto a stool.

The bartender turned his head, his narrow blue eyes paired well with the shaggy blond surfer hair he was sporting. His floral-patterned shirt pulled the aesthetic together.

"A shot. Please." I desperately begged, needing to calm myself down after such an act that filled me with an exciting rush.

"Of what?" he asked.

"Anything," I mumbled half-coherently, as thoughts of Griffin's blazing hazel eyes boring into mine, with his fingers threaded through my hair, created another wave of slick arousal between my legs.

The bartender watched me suspiciously but filled a tiny shot glass and slid it my way. I snatched it from the countertop and downed it as quickly as I could—the tequila burning my throat and fanning the flame hot in my stomach.

"Everything alright?" he cautiously asked. I nodded, placing the cup down in relief.

"Uh-huh," I muttered, knowing I would one hundred percent do that again. Just the thought of Griffin...

The bartender furrowed his brows. "I should've asked before I gave that to you, but just to cover my bases, how old are you?"

I looked up with shameful eyes. "My brother reminded me I'll be twenty-eight next week. I don't know how to feel about that because, well, it's almost thirty." I leaned forward, placing my hands on my legs and sighing. His eyes raked over my body, and he lifted an impressed brow. I followed his gaze to my breasts and quickly moved my arms up to the bar, covering my cleavage.

Chuckling, the bartender turned around and began fixing a glass. Eventually, he slid across the cutest umbrella drink I'd ever seen. Granted, other than the past two most recent times of getting drunk, I never actually drank so, I had no idea what this was.

"I didn't order this."

"It's on the house. Call it an early birthday celebration." He smiled and picked up a glass to dry from behind the bar. Slowly, I brought the straw to my lips and took a swig. It was surprisingly fruity, and the alcohol taste was mostly masked by whatever it was.

"Oh, that's good," I moaned and took another drink. He chuckled as a shadow fell over me.

"What are you doing?" Griffin's voice pierced the happy state I was in. Opening my eyes a crack, I sheepishly grinned.

"She's having a drink, on the house. Who are you?" the bartender asked, defensively.

I tossed a thumb Griffin's way while finishing the last bit of my drink. "That's my boyfriend."

Griffin sat down as the bartender's brows lifted. Surprised. He got to work on another drink, sliding a beer toward Griffin halfway through.

"Damn," the bartender said.

"What?" I asked as Griffin looked from the beer to me then back to the beer.

"Just surprised. Your boyfriend is actually in your league." He grinned, and Griffin lifted the drink to his lips, unfazed.

"She is fucking hot, isn't she," he said after lowering the beer, and the bartender nodded, sliding another glass toward me.

I giggled, taking a sip of my drink. "Griffin, the bartender also just insinuated that you're hot too." Griffin simply took another swig of his drink while the bartender lifted his brows with a sly grin.

"I know how to appreciate a man when it's deserved," he said, cleaning a glass again.

"It's definitely well deserved." I happily sipped on my drink that was turning my entire body a little warm.

"By the way, you said no drinking. So, what are you doing over here?" Griffin interjected.

"Do you really want to go back over to that table right now?" I asked.

"What's at the table?" The bartender lifted his brows curiously.

Griffin threw a thumb my way. "Her little brother just announced he got his girlfriend pregnant. Oh, and her mom wants them to move back to Washington instead of staying in Idaho."

I pointed toward Griffin, surprised he even remembered the news about Noah. "His aunt wants his mom's inheritance even though it'll take care of his stepdad who is quite sick."

Griffin lifted his brows again. "And her mom and my mom broke into our hotel room. Her mom thought I'd kidnapped her."

The bartender blinked, slammed two shot glasses onto the countertop, and poured us each one. Griffin downed it without hesitation, and the bartender quickly refilled it. I took my time, knowing I was already buzzed.

"My mom didn't know about us either." I swung a finger between Griffin and I.

Griffin looked toward the bartender who was watching us intrigued. "We were also butt-ass naked, and I was holding her tits when her mom and my mom broke into our room."

"That's gotta be the best timing in the world." The bartender chuckled. He tossed his head toward me, eyeing me up and down really quickly, then grinned at Griffin. "I would've been grabbing those..." The bartender's voice faded rapidly and my gaze slipped to my boyfriend.

The steely, warning glare Griffin was shooting at him was all that was needed.

The bartender cleared his throat, turning away. "So, um... Do you have a sister?" he asked.

I shook my head, stealing a second glance toward Griffin who remained rather poised with his hunter's cautionary stare. "Just that dumb ass little brother sitting over there who is only twenty-one and got his—" I paused. "Griffin, he turned twenty-one and I missed it."

Jumping down from the barstool, I quickly walked toward my brother.

Slapping a hand around Noah's wrist the moment I got to the table, I dragged him out of the booth. "Do you have your ID?"

"Yes? What the hell, Janey?" he asked, stopping me. I glared at him silently telling him to come with me. Then he wouldn't have to sit alone at this table.

He stopped protesting immediately as I dragged him toward the bar. Throwing him toward the stool next to me, I sat back down and smiled at the bartender.

"My little brother needs a drink." I grinned, then widened my eyes at Noah. "It's legal now dumbshit. You're twenty-one. Happy late birthday. Sorry I was literally kidnapped during that time!"

Noah's face brightened, and he snatched his ID from his wallet. The bartender's mouth formed a perfect "O" staring at me. Griffin inhaled deeply, smiled to himself, and took a swig of his beer. Right, I'd blurted out that I was actually kidnapped. Eventually, the man shook his head, chuckling and poured Noah a shot.

"Why are you guys over here?" Noah asked.

"Really?" I questioned, dumbfounded.

"Avoiding Mom and Nancy." he grumbled, downing the drink.

"Obviously."

"You left me alone to listen to Mom scold me about getting Jada pregnant," he muttered.

Griffin chuckled. "Should've used a condom."

"I didn't see one on your dick after fucking my sister," Noah grumbled, and Griffin rolled his eyes.

"She just finished her period three days ago. Women don't ovulate the day after they finish their period. It takes two weeks, dummy," Griffin replied, and Noah groaned, bumping his head on the bar.

"Do you still have an apartment I could possibly rent? For three, now?" Noah asked with his head against the table.

Griffin chuckled. "Yeah, I should have something. So that means you're not leaving?"

"Why would he leave? You should see the ass on his girlfriend," I muttered without thinking.

Noah whipped his head off the table. "Excuse me? That's not what this is about. Though it is nice."

"Nice? Noah, it was the first and only thing I saw when I walked in on you two naked, on the couch, and with her on top." I giggled lightly and took another sip before frowning. "Do you not understand how jealous I am? I can squat a shitload of weight, hip thrust even more, and my ass doesn't look nearly as big as hers."

The bartender chuckled. "I don't think your boyfriend is an ass guy, sweetie."

Griffin smiled to himself. "Correct. Though it is nice despite your reservations."

I flipped my head to the side and Griffin shrugged his shoulders.

"What?" he said.

"You really think my butt is nice?" I widened my eyes, tears forming in them.

"Yes." A crease formed between his brows. "Are you crying?"

I sniffled, quickly wiping them away. "No. But that's so sweet of you to say," I quietly said, pouting a little and finished my third fruity drink.

"I think you're drunk," Noah added, and I slugged him in the arm. "Ow. That actually hurt."

"You deserved it." I returned to the new, nice, fruity drink that made my insides all warm. Griffin leaned back a little and watched me.

"You really love my sister don't you?" Noah suddenly said, taking another shot that the bartender offered. I smiled at Noah and then looked toward Griffin.

Griffin's face seemed more relaxed, his eyes full of everything I knew he'd never be able to say.

"So, how do we convince your mom that I'm not some disgusting dick?" Griffin muttered.

Chapter 53

I crashed into the booth, Griffin and Noah dashing after me. Pointing a drunken finger toward the man I loved, I giggled and hiccupped then spoke to my mom. "Griffin's got a dick!" I exclaimed with every fervency in my voice.

My mom's mouth fell open in shock. "What?" she gasped. Noah chuckled to himself as Griffin rolled his eyes, gently grabbing my wrist and pulling me back upright. Shaking my head, I cleared my mind and tried to speak what I'd actually meant to say first.

I giggled. "Griffin's *not* a dick, Mom," I said, slurring once more, and then collapsed against Griffin who stood beside the booth.

My mom sighed and shook her head. "Tattoos, a potty mouth, and he smokes. What's to make me think otherwise?" She gestured toward Griffin and then glared at Noah. "And you. What do Jada's parents think?"

Noah grimaced. "Technically, they don't know yet. We were planning on telling you guys and them at the same time. Over something like a nice dinner." He ran a hand across the back of his neck.

"Mom, why do you have to be so mad about superficial things like tattoos? Or the fact that he says bad words sometimes. I say bad words." Griffin pulled his lips between his teeth and kept me from falling over.

"It's because they are on the guy that my daughter is dating," she grumbled, crossing her arms. I narrowed my eyes, glaring at her.

"That's such a dumb reason. It's not like you've cared this much before." Even though it'd been years since I'd had a serious boyfriend, it was still a valid argument.

Finally, after the silence had overwhelmed the entire group, my mom sighed and looked directly at Griffin. "If you hurt even a single hair on her head, I still know people who know how to dispose of a body without getting caught." She lifted her brows, and a small smile spread across Griffin's face.

"Yes, ma'am." He gave her a subtle nod and then gently helped me sit upright on the booth.

"So," my mom continued, looking at me. "What are you going to do for work since we're staying?"

I gasped. "We aren't moving?" I grinned, and she shook her head.

"My family wants to stay, so why would I go anywhere else?"

"Then why did you push so hard to move?"

She gave me a soft smile. "Your dad isn't here anymore to play hard ball, so I had to vet things out first."

I giggled as Noah slid into the booth beside me. Griffin was staring intently at his phone. All along my mom had simply wanted to make sure that we would be okay, that everything would be okay.

"Though," my mom continued. "Have you heard back from the school?" I shook my head, no. "Then what are you going to do? You can't just sit around doing nothing forever."

"Why not?" Noah interjected, and my mom glared at him. "*What?* It's not like they'll need the money." My mom narrowed her gaze suspiciously as Noah glanced at Griffin. "Speaking of, why don't you just hire fancy lawyers for her or threaten a lawsuit against the school district or something?"

Griffin lifted his brows and glanced up from his phone, shoving it in his pocket.

"I don't want that. I want my job back on my own, not 'cause my boyfriend threatened something like that," I slurred, and Noah rolled his eyes.

"You're the only person I know who wouldn't take advantage of the fact that you have a super rich boyfriend," Noah muttered, and I giggled, swaying sideways as my mom's brows furrowed in confusion.

"What are you talking about?" She glanced between Griffin and Nancy, whom I'd almost forgotten was here.

"Speaking of doing things, what's your plan when Grandma inevitably finds out this was fake? You know she will, regardless of the agreement made between you and Grandpa," Nancy asked Griffin as I folded sideways on the booth.

"I haven't quite figured that one out yet." He pulled out a pack of cigarettes.

"And here I was, thinking you weren't scared of a single thing. But you are. You're scared of your grandma." I gasped and he tipped his head in my direction, raising a single brow.

"Let's get you some water to sober up." He got up and walked toward the entrance of the restaurant, ignoring my question as I dropped my head back down on the booth seat.

"How dumb," I muttered.

"Will someone please tell me what you meant by 'rich'?" my mom asked again. I waved a hand as Noah chuckled to himself. The waitress from earlier brought some water to the table and poured me a tall glass as my mom stared between the three of us waiting for an answer.

Nancy smiled flatly at the eavesdropping waitress. "Can we get the check please?" she asked.

"It's been taken care of already." The waitress smiled sweetly as I sat up, groaning and gulping down some water.

"All of it? And the drinks that I know were had at the bar?" my mom asked, glaring at me.

"All of it. You have a wonderful day." She smiled once more and left as my head spun.

Nancy smiled and patted my mom's arm as her head whipped back and forth between the empty space the waitress had left and Nancy. Slowly, they slid out of the booth as Noah dragged me with him.

Pushing open the front door, I gazed around through the bright sunshine. Griffin stood off to the left, leaning against a palm tree and facing the ocean. Smoke curled around his head as everyone approached him, except for me. A sudden wave of nausea washed over me, and I clutched my stomach.

"I'm not feeling well," I groaned, and spun around rushing back into the restaurant. Everything passed in a blur as I sprinted into the bathroom, shoved open a stall, and hurled up most of my stomach contents. Sweat slithered down my back, dripping from my face as I vomited again, heaving up every last thing that had entered my system.

Driving the porcelain bus between my knees, between groans, I made a promise that I would definitely *not* be getting drunk again anytime soon.

Once the last of the nausea had passed, and there was nothing more curdling within my stomach, I wiped the back of my hand across my lips and exited the stall. Running my hands under warm water, I washed them up, ready to exit and return to Griffin.

I tossed the wet paper towels into the trash and bumped open the door with my hip. Everything just felt so light, so free, so…peaceful. Something that was beginning to be a constant. And maybe still a little discombobulated from the alcohol that was running, albeit a bit thinner now, through my warm veins.

Ducking around the alcove, my eyes latched onto the restaurant entrance as a hand clamped down around my wrist. I didn't have a chance to glance to see who it was as I was dragged to the side, through a back door, and out into the warm sunshine.

"What—" I gasped, gaining my bearings as my heels bumped across the ground, the hold on my wrist tightening, deep enough to bruise. Shaking out of the daze, it hit me—I was being kidnapped.

Again.

Adrenaline and fear tore through me like an over-sharpened razor blade.

Snapping my gaze to the hulking figure dragging me down the side alley, farther from my companions, the fear turned to annoyance.

"Let go of me, Sam!" I snarled, jerking my arm away from him and trying to go dead weight.

"No, I told you I'd get you," he hissed in response, tugging me against him. My shoulder twinged, stretched to its limits.

I rolled my eyes. "You're an idiot. Psychopath, but an idiot, too," I grumbled, too surprised and lightheaded to be thinking straight. He sneered down at me, his eyes dark and hooded, but I wasn't afraid, as I gave him a wide grin in reply, then opened my mouth wider and gave him both barrels.

Wailing a blood curdling scream, I dropped all of my weight toward the cement below my body. He stumbled, startled by my abrupt change in position as I forced him to literally haul my entire weight on his own. I didn't stop screaming either, even as he clamped a hand over my mouth.

I could fight him, but I was still drunk and knew my coordination was not at its finest. Besides, there was someone here with me who could do a hell of a lot more damage than I could. So, I bit down, hard. The taste of iron tinged my tongue, coating my mouth as he ripped his hand away from my teeth and hissed, "Ow! What the fuck, you bitch!" Sam stopped, his blond hair in major disarray as he inspected his bleeding palm.

Now was my time.

"GRIFF—" I only managed to shout half of his name as a massive, steel-cut frame barreled into Sam from the side. My would-be captor immediately released my wrist, and I sat down hard on the cement.

But I didn't move. I should've called the cops. Or should've made some effort to stop him, but I didn't. Instead, I watched as my boyfriend stood up and waited for Sam, writhing with the wind knocked out of him, to rise.

Griffin's gaze was dark, but there was no mask of death covering his features this time. Instead, I smelled the blood in the water, watching the excitement of battle that danced behind the hazel eyes—which I absolutely loved.

"What the fuck are you doing here?" he snarled as Sam pushed himself to his feet, wavering uncertainly.

Sam balled his fists in front of him and stepped toward Griffin, who stood there casually. "I waited, biding my time until the agents were gone," Sam said, and then he lunged at Griffin.

Griffin swerved to the side gracefully and planted an open palm against the back of Sam's head, shoving him face first to the ground. He landed with a thud. I snorted approval, and slid back, giving room for the two men. Sam placed his hands against the cement and shoved himself up, blood dripping from his nose.

"And what? You thought, 'hey, now's a good time to pounce'?" Griffin taunted as he simply waited for Sam to get steady on his feet and face him.

"All that is standing in my way is you, and one on one is a lot easier than one versus a whole bunch of agents," Sam answered, wiping some blood on the back of his hand.

Griffin rolled his eyes as Sam lunged a couple times close toward Griffin but remained out of range. My boyfriend's lips twitched upwards, and he winked at me as Sam cocked back a fist and threw it toward Griffin.

He parried, slapping it out of the way, and then shoved his palm against Sam's forehead, knocking him backwards, and Sam landed on his back.

"You think I'm easier to handle than multiple agents?" Griffin asked, stalking forward so he towered over Sam, who was gasping for air on the ground. "You should've taken your chances with the agents, because I'm the fucking devil."

Sam spat out some blood and pushed himself up on his elbows. "You're not overseas anymore, soldier. You can't just kill me and get away with it. The cops will come."

A wicked welcoming grin slid across Griffin's face, like he'd just received an invitation to unleash the hounds of hell, sending a chill down my spine. I sensed Sam had unwittingly taken things down another notch or two to a level not meant for regular people. He clearly had no idea who or what he was really dealing with.

Griffin stooped down and grabbed Sam by the collar of his sweat-soaked and blood-spattered T-shirt. The veins in Griffin's arm rippled, pulsing with his too calm heartbeat. The muscles flexed, tensing as he lifted Sam from the pavement with one hand.

"You should *hope* the cops get here. They're the only ones who can save you from me," Griffin growled between his teeth and plunked him back down on his feet. Sam's eyes widened, recognition coming too late laced with regret as Griffin released his fingers from around the fabric, tipped his head, and pummeled a sledgehammer fist into Sam's face.

His head snapped back as bones crunched, and he collapsed as limply as a doll tossed to the ground. Unconscious, not a sound left his lips as his eyes rolled into the back of his head.

Griffin squatted down, placing his elbows against his thighs, and tipped his head, a crazed look on his face. One that should have filled me with fear for the man that I absolutely owed my life to. "Should have" was the key word during this entire crazy ordeal. But instead, my body roared with fire as I stared at this man capable of so much violence, protecting me no matter the costs, holding restraint as he coolly reached forward, lifted one of Sam's limp arms, and checked his wrist for a pulse.

"He's alive?" I asked, watching Griffin uncaringly drop Sam's arm back to the cement.

Griffin nodded. "He'll live."

"So, do we…report this?"

Griffin's brows twitched, and he swung his gaze to me. "I think your mom has that covered," he answered and flicked a chin toward the front of the alley where he'd come running from.

Noah, my mom, and his mom all stood there, watching. How much they'd seen, I had no idea, but I didn't care to ask either. All I knew was that my mom was on the phone with someone, Noah was grinning from ear to ear, and Nancy looked unperturbed.

Swinging my gaze back to Griffin, heat rushed into my cheeks as I met his intense eyes. "Should I be concerned by how unfazed you are by this?" he asked.

"Probably," I answered. His eyes dipped to my lips as I stood up, and he ran his gaze lazily over my figure.

He swallowed stiffly, his Adam's apple bobbing with the movement, and his breath hitched in his chest. "I fucking love you," he stated lowly as sirens pierced the air around us.

I giggled. "I love you too."

He inhaled deeply and pushed himself upright. "That wasn't much of a fight. Kind of boring if I'm being honest." He stalked hungrily my way.

"You made him look like a complete fool though."

Calloused hands grabbed my cheeks, and he pushed my back up against the brick restaurant building. "I wanted to beat his skull in so his brains were a pile of mush on the pavement."

"But you didn't," I whispered as his body heat engulfed mine, his chest pressing against mine.

"No, I didn't."

And his lips rammed against mine. The kiss was aggressive, and it tasted like smoke and alcohol with a hint of sweat. Then it was over too soon.

He pulled away but left his mouth hovering over mine. "If we were alone right now..."

Keeping my eyes closed, I smiled against his lips. "You'd have to catch me first," I teased, and felt his heart jump in his chest.

"What are you saying?" he lowly replied, his voice sensual.

"That we should go back to that Airbnb and have a do-over since Sam won't be around."

I cracked my eyelids open, meeting Griffin's dark, lustful gaze. "And what do I get this time if I do catch you again?"

"I think you know." I swallowed stiffly, excited, and his chest vibrated with a low growl.

"Well, then I hope you've improved in your ability to run away, because otherwise, I will find you and fuck you within a matter of minutes," he said, nipping at my lips. Everything in me churned with a blazing fire, heating my core up rather quickly.

"You should bring that mask you were wearing when you rescued me from the cartel," I blurted out, unable to control my thoughts, as a rush of arousal dripped between my legs.

His hands plunked against the wall on each side of my head, and he pressed tighter into me, flush against my body. "When I catch you, I won't be taking it off. That would be a waste of time."

A soft moan left my lips at the thought. "Fuck, Griffin," I whispered, my body on fire.

And the sound of footsteps against pavement neared us, interrupting our moment of delicious tension that had me desperately wishing we were already alone.

He cleared his throat and stepped an inch away. "I'm glad you're safe," Griffin quickly said quite loudly, shifting the conversation to something appropriate.

"Thank you, again." I whispered, tipping my head up and brushing my lips against his mouth.

He chuckled, his hot breath mixing with mine. "Think you can avoid getting kidnapped for a couple months this time? I would like a little break from beating people up on your behalf."

"So, what you're saying is it's your turn to be kidnapped next?" I teased.

"No, my CO says that guy on the ski lift was a fluke. He apparently was here visiting someone on vacation, so he was alone," Griffin answered, swiping his thumbs back and forth over my cheeks.

"Okay, so how about neither of us get kidnapped for a while?"

His lips lifted in a grin, brushing lightly over mine. "About fucking time."

Chapter 54

An hour later and we were finally watching Sam be driven away in handcuffs, arrested and going to jail for who knows how long. The police were satisfied, plus there was plenty of evidence and witnesses to what happened today as well as past actions. It felt relieving to know that Sam was not going to be a problem again. For a long, long time.

Griffin slipped his arm around my shoulders and pulled me into his chest, gently pressing a kiss against my forehead. "Ready to go home?" he whispered against my skin, his lips warm and wet.

I nodded, wrapping my arms around his waist. "You have no idea," I answered as my mom, Noah, and Nancy walked our way, leaving the last officer.

"I was wrong," my mom immediately said, looking directly at Griffin. His brows twitched. "I know I told my daughter that we were staying, that I accept you, but I owe you an apology said directly to you. I was wrong for judging you simply because I was afraid."

Griffin didn't say anything, he simply nodded once in acknowledgement.

Nancy sighed, a soft smile smoothing her tired features. "Look, we should get going. Dayton has his championship wrestling match in two days, and you two are clearly more than just fine, so I say we go catch the next flight out of here. What do you say, Melissa?"

"Did you already buy tickets?" Griffin asked, and Nancy shook her head. He pulled out his wallet and grabbed a wad of cash from it.

"I don't want your money, son," she said, placing a hand on his arm.

"Well, I'm not going to let you fly home on the cheapest flight either. I want you safe and comfortable so—"

"Stop," she said sharply, and he paused. "It's not your place to take care of me, Griffin. You're my son. I should be the one taking care of you. I should've been the one to take care of you all this time, all these years."

Griffin watched his mom for a moment before slowly putting his wallet back in his pocket. My mom leaned toward me and whispered in my ear, "So, is he like *rich* rich?" she asked, and I slowly nodded.

Noah suddenly grinned and slapped a hand on Griffin's back. "You and Jane drove here, right?" he asked, and Griffin narrowed his gaze.

"Don't even think about it," Griffin grumbled as Noah's grin widened wickedly.

WHAT I SHOULD HAVE SAID

I leaned against Griffin's shoulder as he drove us along the freeway. Noah sat on the right of me while both my mom and Griffin's mom happily gossiped in the backseat of the truck. My eyes slid up toward Griffin's face as he watched the road in front of us, one hand resting on my thigh.

How handsome he looked and how safe I felt. So calm, so much relief. My dad would be proud, and somehow it made sense that he knew I was okay. That Mom was okay. That at some point, Noah would be okay too. Though I honestly didn't get the vibe that he was upset that Jada was pregnant. He was grinning at whatever text message he just received.

Griffin cracked the window beside him and hummed to the music softly playing. This I could get used to. This was exactly the life that I wanted. Something with adventure that still excited me, but also made me feel right at home. Right at peace with life.

That was something I wanted for Griffin too; though I could see the tension still held in his face as we drove along. Drove toward home, where I knew that everything concerning the inheritance was going to have to come to a head.

His eyes slid to the rearview mirror for a moment, locking with Nancy's. She had the same stressed look on her face, but neither of them voiced anything. I snuggled in a little tighter against Griffin and he inhaled deeply, letting his broad shoulders finally relax.

My eyes felt groggy as the day wore on and the sun eventually began to set. Slowly, I slid away from his shoulder and then laid my head in his lap.

He placed a hand on my arm, cradling me in and continued to drive in silence.

Safe. I felt so safe. Everything was okay. The cartel was gone, Sam was arrested, and Griffin and I were together. So much relief flooded my body it was like an euphoric drug, and I finally fell asleep.

The rumbling stopped, slowly rousing me from my slumber. Not quite ready to move, I remained still in Griffin's lap with my eyes closed as he put the truck into park.

"I'll be right back. Mom, if you want to jump up to the front," Griffin quietly said.

"Don't you dare move," my mom replied, and Griffin stiffened. "You think waking Jane up is the smart thing to do?"

"I was going to carry her in without waking—"

"You think letting her wake up *alone* is smart?" my mom interrupted Griffin, and I could feel his confusion.

"What?" he hesitantly asked. I kept my eyes closed, pretending to not listen to this conversation.

"Either you have to sleep here or she goes with you. You're her safe place, and it's my job to make sure she stays safe." My mom seemed to be chewing him out. Griffin remained silent as the door opened, and I felt Noah leave the truck. "Jane should be with you, where you are."

Another door opened and the truck shook once more as my mom and Nancy climbed out of the backseat. Before it slammed closed, I heard my mom speak once more.

"Thank you for being exactly who she needed. Joseph would be proud if he were still here, I just know he would. He and Jane were always close, so it was the hardest on her when he was killed. She's herself again, and I have you to thank," my mom said, and a wayward tear slid down my cheek. Griffin ran a hand back and forth across my arm, remaining quiet, and then the door shut and the truck was silent.

We didn't move, not for quite some time, as I imagined Griffin waiting for my mom and Noah to enter the house. Then he turned the key over and we were pulling out of my mom's driveway.

I stayed still in his lap as we rumbled slowly down the dark road. My heart felt so full, so at peace and rested. Everything about this was coming together just as Nancy had said it would. My dad would be proud like mom said, and that was something that I couldn't deny myself. He was my hero, had been my hero. Now, Griffin was one just as much.

My chest rose as I took a deep breath in. Fingers whispered across my skin. His fingers. Touching me so tenderly that I scooched a little closer onto his lap.

Everything was okay. Well, almost everything.

There was the small matter of the large inheritance still looming over our heads and I wasn't sure what was going to happen. Would it count if Griffin and I continued to date seeing as technically it did start out as fake?

And my job status did concern me a little. I never wanted to be viewed as a gold digger, yet here I was, jobless and with a man who was wealthy beyond imagination. Though there was a small part of me that wouldn't protest the idea of being a pampered housewife. Maybe five kids instead of four would happen.

That would mean a lot of sex with Griffin, at which thought a delicious shiver raced through me, and that was also something I wouldn't ever complain about. I bit back a smile as my mind danced over every recent, naked moment that we had shared. Fitting it in my mouth had not been an easy task, nor that comfortable. But it surprised me with how much I'd enjoyed it.

Everything had my heart pattering quickly in my chest. My mind wandered to the moment in the hotel we'd shared. Raw, vulnerable, true lovemaking, and I wanted it all over again.

I just wanted him close to me, sharing everything I could with him. Even as his hand drummed against my arm, my body began to heat up. Something as simple as a loving touch and I could feel that dull ache starting to develop between my legs. All he needed to do was pull over and we—

My eyes shot open as I realized that I'd been having very dirty thoughts about Griffin with his mom still sitting feet away in this truck.

His gaze quickly glanced down at me and he furrowed his brows. Opening his mouth, he went to say something and then slammed on the brakes.

"What is that?" Nancy gasped, adjusting in her seat beside me.

"Not what, Mom. But who," Griffin quietly muttered, and then sighed as he began inching the truck forward.

"What's she doing here this late?" Nancy replied, as the tires crunched over tar, turning off of the main road.

"Did she get to Grandma first?" Griffin asked, rolling to a stop.

"She wouldn't be able to convince her to forgo the contract amendment, would she?" Nancy suddenly shoved open the door and barreled outside. Griffin remained seated in the idling truck as I slowly lifted myself upright.

"What's going on?" I whispered. But Griffin didn't need to answer as my gaze connected with the front porch of this white brick home. We were parked in the round-a-bout driveway, both staring at the arched alcove where Cara, Griffin's step-dad, and now Nancy were aggressively speaking.

"I can have Noah—"

"I should tell you," Griffin cut me off, watching the arguing trio on the steps. Behind Brent, the front door cracked open and Dayton's face appeared around the corner. "No, not Dayton," he whispered.

"Dayton knows about the inheritance, Griffin. He's known for a while," I reassured him, and Griffin whipped his gaze toward me.

"Did he seem upset?"

"No."

"Mad? Hurt? Frustrated?"

"No? He seemed to understand, I think. Though I guess I'm not sure if he knows that technically some of the money will be his," I muttered. Griffin shot out of the truck. I watched as he jogged toward the front porch and finally slipped out of the truck myself. I could hear raised voices, Cara's mostly, piercing through the cool, evening air.

As I hesitantly crept forward, I could finally make out more of the conversation that was occurring.

"Call her here now," Cara hissed. "Or I'll call her for you."

"Is that why you came here?" Nancy glared at her, shoving her hands on her hips.

"I came to stop Griffin. To stop Eleanor from making such a rash decision. The money will be mine. It's rightfully mine! She promised it to me because of your foolish decision to be a slut and get pregnant while in high school. The money had to go to her daughter, and she decided her chosen daughter was better."

"You don't know shit," Griffin interjected, and Cara rolled her eyes.

"I know more than you think. I know that your relationship was faked. But did you know that there is a clause where you have to actually be in love with the woman you marry to receive the inheritance if she's not one of Eleanor or Winston's choosing?"

Griffin clenched his jaw but made no move to speak.

He knew. His silent answer told me that he knew, and my stomach dropped. My fingers snapped to the ring around my neck. No wonder he wanted an engagement, not just a fake girlfriend. He had to make sure we sold this charade no matter what. And I wasn't sure how to feel about that.

"See? Another obvious clue that she *wants* me to have it. Not your mom. Besides, you don't actually love that bitch," Cara added, a smirk caressing her face.

"Don't you fucking call her that," he snarled, and Cara's upper lip curled in disgusted annoyance.

"Does that not just prove to you that he does?" Nancy shot in as Brent lifted his tired gaze to meet mine. He looked rather confused as Dayton sighed heavily and leaned against the doorframe.

"Cara, the documents were signed over seven hours ago. so give it up. There's nothing you can do." Griffin shoved his hands in his pockets, and my brows stitched together as Nancy swung her wide, shocked gaze to her son.

"Wh-wh-what do you mean they were signed seven hours ago?" she asked.

"My lawyers sent them to me electronically while we were at the restaurant. Mom, you and Dayton get the first installment starting January first of next year. I will begin working under Grandpa in a week and then become President by the beginning of next year as well," Griffin answered. I felt like a fly on the wall of a conversation that I should not be involved in.

"Bu-bu-but you're not married!" Cara screeched, trying to gain any leverage back.

"Good thing that's about to change." Dayton stepped forward and grinned. "Right here, right now. Thank you all for coming to this marriage ceremony to witness the beautiful union of two people very much in love. Dad will be officiating."

My eyes widened first in shock, and then in recognition. *That's right. He mentioned his dad is ordained or whatever it's called.*

Every mouth fell open, except for mine, as I bit back a chuckle full of both nerves and...excitement? And Brent thinned his lips, shooting a warning glare at Dayton.

"Officiating? What the hell?" Cara gasped.

"Yes. Officiating. The ordained minister, my dad, shall make this ceremony official. Griffin, do you have the ring?" Dayton answered with wicked speed. *That ever devious boy.*

Griffin slid his gaze toward me. Every pair of eyes followed, and my skin prickled. His stare held me steady, processing through the confusion and abrupt announcement that Dayton made. Slowly, he nodded, coming to terms with whatever was in his mind. He had one more thing he had to do to fulfill his end, which involved me.

Silence swept across the darkened night sky. The crickets that had been steadily chirping ceased. Even the leaves that rustled in the breeze fell quiet, submitting to the tension that swirled between Griffin's hot gaze and my stunned figure.

"Don't do it, son. Not for me or your mom or even Dayton," Brent cut the stillness, clamping a hand on Griffin's shoulder. "You deserve to be in love, not just settle for someone because you're once again taking care of everyone else but yourself."

That hurt. But I understood—he was protecting Griffin.

He glanced at his stepdad. "Son?" His voice quivered as the older gentleman gave him a silent nod.

"Good thing I'm not settling." Griffin smiled, returning his hazel eyes to me. "Jane, come here please," he called out softly.

I hesitated. If I went to him, answered his beckoning call, that was already an answer before I spoke. But I couldn't resist his tender smile, and the longing in my heart pushed me quietly forward. My tired feet carried me steadily across the darkened lawn and slowly up the steps. My heart was pounding, racing with the tension that slithered thick around us like a fog that hadn't quite dissipated.

The man I loved shoved himself around Cara and slipped his fingers into mine. "It's fast, I know," he quietly said into my ear, his eyes searching my soul. "If it's too fast, then okay, I'll figure out a different way to help my parents." I listened, not to what he was saying, but what he wasn't saying. The unspoken words from his lips, silently asking me something I wasn't even sure I was ready for. I still didn't have a job, was still simply trying to find my footing in this world.

But maybe it wouldn't be so terrible to do it with Griffin. All of the unknown that swirled around me, curling its fingers tighter around my figure, suddenly felt lighter. I nodded briefly, and he raised his brows in disbelief.

"You want to do this? For you, Jane. Not for anyone else," he muttered.

"For me." I paused as his hand slipped to the back of my neck, fiddling with the silver chain. "And for you, Griffin Marsh."

The edges of his lips twitched upward as he snapped the chain apart. "I can get you a different ring if you want," he replied, and the engagement ring plunked into his palm, free of the necklace.

"I just want you to ask me for real this time," I answered, lifting my left hand.

Warm breath washed over my face as he leaned forward, calloused skin brushing over my finger and he pushed the ring on. "I would've bought a fake ring if I hadn't meant it the first time I asked."

And his lips captured mine.

"I'm pretty sure you're supposed to kiss *after* you say 'I do'," Dayton muttered annoyed, and Griffin smiled against my mouth.

Epilogue

Three years later

"Hurry up or we'll be late for Dayton's graduation!" Griffin shouted from downstairs.

I ran a final coat of mascara over my lashes and waddled away from the counter.

"Where's Joe's diaper bag?" I called back, racing out of our master bedroom and into the hallway.

"I have it," he replied, and I peered over the banister. Griffin was tugging on our eighteen-month-old's shoes while our twins twirled around him.

I smoothed out a few wrinkles in my dress, hoping that I hadn't missed a spot when shaving my legs this morning. "Where's Lily's bow? I had one in both her and Dot's hair earlier."

"Lily, where's your bow?" Griffin asked one of the twins, as I carefully began to descend the stairs. I could barely see my toes at this point, and I heard our almost three year old daughter giggle.

"What? Why is it there?" he muttered, and I managed to find my footing on the landing as Griffin slipped the bow from Dot's hair and put it back into Lily's. Both curly haired girls now had matching checkered dresses and bows.

Griffin lifted his eyes toward me and smiled. "Mmmm. I don't think you've ever looked more beautiful in your life." He leaned forward and gently kissed my lips then placed a hand on my very swollen belly.

"Or fat," I muttered, and he chuckled.

"No, smart ass," he whispered in my ear. "Just beautiful."

"And very pregnant. I have to pee again."

"Can it wait until we make it to the school?"

"Let's hope." I waddled toward the door, grabbing the two girls' hands. "I am so grateful this is the last time I will be pregnant," I muttered, tugging on the handle.

"Oh, you have one more to go," my husband said behind me, and I whipped around to meet his grinning face. He winked.

"Excuse me?" I shoved my hands on my hips but struggled to keep a stern look on my face at the sight of his amusing smirk. "We agreed on four kids."

"No, you agreed to be pregnant four times. We had twins during your first pregnancy," he explained, and I playfully swatted at him. I knew it was crazy, already being on my third pregnancy in three years, but honestly, I didn't mind. Carrying another child of ours didn't sound too terrible.

"It's the perfect compromise," he continued. "Five kids, four pregnancies. Besides, with the recent changes at the company, I've been able to be home more." He grinned even wider, and I shook my head.

"We will discuss this later when the kids aren't around," I replied. My cheeks were beginning to hurt from the smile that had crept upon my face.

"I like those discussions. All alone with my amazing and sexy wife." He whisked by, carrying Joe and the diaper bag.

"Griffin, not that kind of discussion," I called out, quickly shutting the door and following him to our SUV. "But go on," I added with a wink.

"If you weren't so damn good looking, it wouldn't end up being 'that kind of discussion.'" He wiggled his brows, opening the back door.

"And that is why I'm pregnant all the time," I muttered, and he laughed.

"First off, if you don't want another baby, I'm totally okay with that. But second and more importantly, I won't apologize for enjoying sex with my wife," he replied, as I helped the twins into their car seats on the opposite side of the black vehicle.

"Jada and Noah are coming tonight to the graduation dinner, too, right?" I asked, changing the subject.

"Obviously. My mom already texted to say that your mom is there with Ella." He shut the door and jogged around to my side of the vehicle. I waddled toward the front passenger door and paused in front of him to gaze up into his eyes.

He was simply watching me, happy.

That glazed over look he used to carry so often had been vacant for a few years. And I loved it. It made me so happy to see him so relaxed. Even when

I'd been worried he'd end up lost after taking over his grandpa's company, he'd found it rather nice to have so much free time compared to life in the military.

Though that was also why I ended up pregnant so quickly after we were married. He had way too much free time on his hands, which he filled with being with me. I didn't mind. In fact, I enjoyed it. He even did a couple bodybuilding shows and also picked up teaching firearm safety as a volunteer for those interested in the community. He went out with his Navy SEAL buddies and Noah all the time.

But what made me the happiest was seeing him and Dayton. Not only did Griffin have the family he'd always dreamt of but never thought possible, he also had a brother. His brother. A wife, children, a brother, parents—including Brent who was doing better with the treatments that Nancy could afford now. All of it. Everything had worked out for him.

There was a small part of me, though, that felt like I was living someone else's fantasy.

"Is everything okay?" Griffin whispered, furrowing his brows.

I gave him a tight lipped smile. "Yeah, totally."

"You're a horrible liar." He chuckled and reached forward, wrapping his arms around my waist. "Tell me, my love, what is it?"

I sighed and closed my eyes. "I love you. I love our life. But once in a while…" My voice trailed off.

"Once in a while you… What?" He brushed some hair from my face.

"Once in a while I feel like I'm merely fulfilling what everyone else wants for me," I whispered my confession, and Griffin slipped his fingers through my hair around the base of my neck.

"And what is it that you want? Just for you?" he asked, his eyes twinkling in mischievous delight.

I lifted my gaze to his, searching his curious soul. He was my safe space, the one person who never judged me for wanting something that wasn't his idea. I grinned and tipped onto my toes. "I want to feel like a rebellious teenager for a moment. Take a break from adulthood."

Griffin lifted a brow. "Keep talking."

I pressed my lips against his and then whispered in his ear exactly what I wanted to do. He listened intently, stepping against my body, and when I was finished, he nipped at my neck. "I think your mom is available for a few days to watch the kids. And I know the perfect getaway spot."

"I'm not going to magically be unpregnant, though, you know that," I replied, and he chuckled.

"So, instead of calling it skinny dipping, we can call it 'we probably shouldn't be doing this' dipping," he replied with a wink.

I rolled my eyes as he opened the car door. "Ha. Ha. You're so funny."

"My wife just admitted that she finds me funny!" he exclaimed as he helped me buckle myself in.

"Don't sound so excited because that'll never happen again," I taunted in response, and he chuckled, shutting the door in the process. But I smiled to myself because I was excited. Just because I was a mom—and a very spoiled housewife—didn't mean that I couldn't still have some of the adventures of my dreams. We'd traveled to so many cool places over the past three years, also revealing that he knew several languages.

And he'd held up to every promise he'd ever made me. Every. One.

The vehicle rattled as the hunky man of mine climbed into the driver's seat and turned the engine over. The grin on his face was as wide as when I'd told him what I wanted to do.

"Don't look so giddy," I chastised again, and he simply swung his head toward me and wiggled his brows.

"Do you not realize how long I've been waiting to do this with you?"

"What?"

"When we were at the cabin years ago, you remember I made a passing comment about skinny dipping and you told me you were a virgin?" he asked, and I furrowed my brows and then a light bulb went off.

"Since then?"

He nodded. "It's something I should've said but never have."

"Why not?"

"It's been three years and you still haven't figured it out?" He furrowed his brows, and I shook my head.

"Because, smart ass, no matter how it seems, all of the sexy time stuff is always in your control. Always your decision. I didn't want to push you."

"So instead, you just kept your mouth shut," I confirmed, and he nodded.

I pursed my lips. "Well, stop it. Next time, just say what you want to say before it becomes something you should have said."

He chuckled and placed his hand on my leg. "Yes, ma'am."

I smiled. I was ready for our next adventure. We were ready for our next adventure. I slipped my fingers between his and squeezed. My best friend, my lover, my protector, and my biggest supporter all wrapped into one.

Everything was set right in life. No matter where things took us, everything would always be right with him. I settled back against my seat, content and at peace. Everything I once needed to say had been said. Now there was nothing but the future full of possibilities ahead of us.

A future shared with those I loved. With the man that I loved more than anything in this world. My life was his; my world was his.

A brief, tender kiss pressed against my cheek. "I love life with you," he whispered.

And I closed my eyes. Me too.

Me too, Griffin Marsh.

Acknowledgements

To my amazing beta readers who definitely made this book come together in a way that I couldn't have done alone!

To my Beta Reader turned proofreader, Dyan Howden. Thank you for helping tip my book onto a whole new level! I'm so blessed to have connected with you, and not just for my novel's sake, but on a personal, friendship level as well! Makes the world feel a little smaller.

To my spicy sensitivity reader, Daleina. You're absolutely amazing, and thank you for helping me flush out the spicy scenes so that it remains in my element!

To my beta reader turned cover artist, YOU ARE AMAZING!

About the Author

R.L. Atkinson

Born and raised in Utah, R.L. Atkinson enjoys a busy life as a mom and wife, taking care of all kinds of animals. She uses her personal life experiences to help bring reality to all of her novels. Writing has always been a passion of hers, and publishing is a dream come true.

All of her novels can be found on Amazon!

Follow her on Social Media:
TikTok: @romanceauthormom
Instagram: @romanceauthormom

Made in the USA
Columbia, SC
01 October 2024